NEW HEAVEN, NEW EARTH

Books by Arthémise Goertz

Give Us Our Dream
The Moon Is Mine
New Heaven, New Earth

New Heaven, New Earth

Arthemise Goertz

SEARS READERS CLUB · CHICAGO

NEW HEAVEN, NEW EARTH

Library of Congress Catalog Card Number: 52–13464

Printed in the United States of America

This is a special edition published exclusively for the members of SEARS READERS CLUB, P. O. Box 6570A, Chicago 80, Illinois. It was originally published by McGraw-Hill Book Co., Inc.

To the memory of my grandmother
and the summer home in Mandeville

CHARACTERS

The Beach People

Dr. Victor duRocher
Dr. Michel duRocher (Papa), his father
Nanaine duRocher, his aunt
Uncle Ulysse, Victor's uncle
Colette Roussel, Victor's cousin and fiancée
Olympe, Colette's mother
Julien, Colette's father
Leon, her brother
Marcel Lavalle, Leon's friend
Harry Lockwood, son of a Chicago engineer
Palmyre Delamare, lately from Paris
Miriam, her daughter
Madame Vigée, a friend of Nanaine's
Madame Larouche, her daughter
Dr. Alcide Larouche, Victor's cousin,
                              a wealthy New Orleans doctor
Féfé Larouche, daughter of Dr. and Madame Larouche
Madame de Gerbeau, another friend of Nanaine's
Minerve Vignaud, Madame de Gerbeau's married daughter
Celeste, Madame de Gerbeau's spinster daughter
Fauvette d'Eaubonne, an impoverished blueblood
Mr. Néron Paviot, her boarder
Madame Morel, wife of the town banker

The Townspeople

Dr. Cyprien Jolivet, the local physician
Aurélie Blanque-Coulon, the widow he marries
M'sieur Bidault, the mayor
Aristide Préjean, the marshal

Father Guichard, the priest
Madame Naquin, wife of the postmaster
Hippolyte, her son
Colin Menard, publisher of the newspaper
Ovide Clouzat, the undertaker
Guy Chauvin, the druggist
Alceste Moreau, the fisherman
Télémaque } eldest and youngest of
Hercule   } Alceste Moreau's sons
Alex Gravois, the barber
Emile Dufour, the baker
Justin Dufour, the baker's son
Homère, the lamplighter

The Woods People

Philo Fanchon, a charcoal maker
Felix, his son
Alphonse Gaspard, a moss picker
Madame Gaspard, his wife
Numa, their son
Masoom, an Indian girl
Choctaw Joe, her husband

The Servants

Zeph
Glad, his wife
Bazile, his father   } with the duRochers
Cumba, the grandmother
Zulime, the great-grandmother

Noonoon, with Uncle Ulysse

Bibi, Palmyre's housegirl, later with Madame Vigée
Narcisse, Palmyre's carriage boy

Doudouce }
Coco   } with the Roussels

Zabette, Coco's mother, at the hotel

One

The lake was smooth. A white cloud dropped its shadow at some distance from the boat. The five-o'clock sun was bright, the sky already summer blue in May.

This was the way he remembered it. He remembered, too, that in less than fifteen minutes Lake Pontchartrain could change from complete calm to frothing fury. New Orleans was out of sight now. In a little while, the misty-green line of the Mandeville shore would appear. As the *Camelia* left the city farther behind, the green would grow clearer, and the white patches on it would become houses. Then he would see the silvery curve of beach . . . and finally the roof and galleries of "Clair de Lune." . . .

He could scarcely wait. The happiest days of his life had been spent in the resort across the lake. There he had hunted chicken frogs and 'coons—there he had gone fishing with Zeph. He remembered their pirogue. He had given Zeph—or had Zeph given him?—half-share in the boat the morning Zeph fell out of the persimmon tree and lay all but dead beside the carriage house. They were both nine then. "Pas mouri—Zeph, don't die!" He had spoken Zeph's kind of French, but Zeph had not opened his eyes. "I will give you my pirogue if you do not die!" Zeph's eyes reappeared in his black face. "I accept—if you will do me the honor to accept half in return." Then his eyes had closed again. Afterward, it was found that he had fractured a hip.

The white boy had gone away to his Jesuit teachers. He came home in the summer and was free once more in the town by the lake. When he was sixteen, he started the study of medicine. At twenty-two, he began his internship at Charity, and for the last five years he had been at the Ancon Hospital in Panama. Now the prospect of recapturing the old freedom excited him oddly, though he would not keep it long. Unless his father were seriously ill, he intended to return to the Isthmus in a fortnight.

The *Camelia* was carrying a Saturday crowd. The passengers showed a preference for the front deck, and the doctor found himself somewhat in the way of young ladies and chaperones. He took a place standing against the rail, beside two ladies who seemed as impatient as he to see land. The older of the two was looking through binoculars.

He heard a chorus of laughter. It came from a group of girls circled about a brunet who was reclining in a steamer chair. A green veil tied her hat on and was knotted in a bow under her chin. She wore a fashionable serge suit, and her crossed ankles, as she lounged back in the chair, showed from under her skirt enough to reveal fine lace stockings.

The doctor felt that the ladies were laughing at him. Immediately he became conscious of his soiled white-duck suit. The train that met the *Camelia* was notorious for its ten miles an hour achieved amidst prodigious belching of smoke. The wise passenger always carried a whisk broom to brush off cinders and an extra handkerchief to wipe the soot out of his ears and nose. The doctor had been unprepared. With a flick of a finger, he dislodged the grime that had settled in the crown of his Panama.

It developed, however, that the young ladies were laughing at his beard. He had grown a shaggy Vandyke as protection against mosquitoes and tropical insects; it had proved helpful on his trips through Chiriquí and Divala. On returning the last time to Ancon, he had found his aunt's cable, ending on a note of alarm. "*Come at once. . . .*" There was the governor to see and arrangements for leave to be made. Learning that a ship was ready to sail, he had taken the first train to the Atlantic side. There had been no time to go to a barber in Colón. In New Orleans, during the hours between docking and boarding the *Camelia*, he had bought new suits and shoes and some linen, but had not given his personal appearance enough thought to look for a barbershop.

"I would feel like a hunted animal, if I lived peering out from a bush like that!"

She laughed again, holding an end of the veil against her lips. All the girls laughed with her, like ladies in waiting around a queen.

"I don't know. . . ." The youngest wore the blue uniform of a convent school. "De Maupassant has written a story called 'The Mustache.' In it, a woman says it is delightful to *kiss* a man with a mustache."

The chaperone looked up from her book. She had red hair and freckles. I know her, the doctor thought.

"You shouldn't read such stories. And you shouldn't think about kissing men." She added, "Where does one buy the works of de Maupassant?"

The girls laughed loudly. The one in uniform pretended shock. "Mamzelle *Fauvette!*"

Of course. Fauvette d'Eaubonne. Always thin, she had grown gaunt since he last saw her, and the shabby dress she wore had the air of having been a gift from the wardrobe of somebody's grandmother.

The queen spoke again.

"I would not mind kissing *one* mustache. But one at a time, I tell you. Not so many bunched together on the same face. But *no!*"

They had been speaking French, and when she said "But *no!*" she threw a hand out as if she were tossing away something distasteful. Her ivory skin, flashing dark eyes, and black hair waving up from her forehead in a pompadour made her vividly beautiful.

"*Colette!*" Fauvette d'Eaubonne objected.

Colette Roussel. . . .

The doctor looked again. Now he could see her full face and the dimple in her chin. My cousin. Yes, my cousin has become beautiful.

In 1904, when he had left, she was only fourteen. He remembered her as a clumsy young person who disconcerted him by staring. He was ten years older than Colette, and their interests had been worlds apart. She was still going to the Ursuline Convent when he was interning at Charity Hospital. He recalled how she had drawn away when he went to tell her parents good-by; she had stepped back and put her hands behind her, and said in a tremble, "Papa says you pickle babies in bottles." They had laughed. Julien had been referring to an embryo he had been shown. . . . Colette was no longer the shrinking, silent adolescent. And though she still stared, she did it with sparkle and vivacity. What a difference five years could make.

He wondered if he had changed so much himself. Perhaps so, for obviously no one recognized him. He had been to the bar and taken his Sazerac near a poker game enlivened by Judge Chambert and the cotton broker Auguste Romain. Both the old men had known him since he was a boy; but Auguste had his back turned, and perhaps the Judge was too busy winning to notice anybody. Besides, the Judge was drinking. The blood seemed ready to burst from his face. He must be nearly eighty, an age at which an apoplectic type should not be drinking recklessly. His jowls hung over his high collar, and his hand shook as he reached again and again for his glass.

The doctor finished his Sazerac, thinking, Everything here is the same. . . .

Only his cousin had changed, very much indeed. He thought of making himself known to Fauvette d'Eaubonne. "I am Victor duRocher. . . ." Then he remembered what the train had done to his white suit, and decided to stay where he was.

The young ladies tired of him and turned their attention to his neighbor at the rail.

"Nature is so unjust," babbled the girl in uniform. "Now there next to Bluebeard is somebody who could use what he does not need. On her head."

"It would not match," observed another.

"Contrasting colors are fashionable this season."

Noisy appreciation rose from all around the circle, with the exception, this time, of Colette. She regarded the target of the remarks pensively. Fauvette d'Eaubonne recalled that she was here to keep the young ladies ladylike, and glanced up from her romance to frown.

The doctor looked at the girl beside him. She was slight and pale, hardly more than sixteen. She had taken the binoculars from the older woman, and was looking through them with an intensity that showed in the set of her lips. Her nose was small and straight and her oval cheeks too thin. She wore a long gray cape over a blue dress, and under the net yoke of the dress her bosom rose and fell with excitement. The hood of the cape had fallen back, leaving her head bare. It was a very light brown head, almost blond, and the close waves were cropped so short that from the back she might have been taken for a boy. The short hair curled softly on her forehead and above her ears, blowing in the breeze. Victor concluded she had been sick. Scarlet fever, perhaps.

The woman with her could have been an older sister. Her hair was auburn; tiny spirals the color of red gold had escaped her barrette and hung on the nape of her neck. She wore a traveling suit that molded a magnificent figure. With one hand she held on to her hat. The other rested on the girl's shoulder. They were speaking in English.

"I see a patch of water lilies," the girl said. Her voice was brisk. It was not of the South.

"When you see lilies, land is near." This was the languid speech of Louisiana.

The wind had changed, and the lake had broken into a riot of whitecaps. Several ladies, who had helped themselves too generously from their picnic baskets, disappeared. The strains of "Over the Waves" from the string band on the deck below came up less clearly now, having to compete with the swish of water. The sun was slipping down the sky and the wind had moved the white clouds to the west. They were becoming pink and orange tinted. The green mist along the shore line assumed the reality of trees. At length, the bathing pavilions built over the water all along the lake front came in sight, and skiffs and pirogues and sailboats bobbed up and down like corks tethered to sticks.

13

The white mirage looming out of the green mass on the left was "Clair de Lune."

"Would you care for the glasses?"

"If you please." He took them from her gratefully.

Somebody was in the belvedere, looking out over the lake. That would be Nanaine—his father's sister. Even from here he recognized the straight, haughty bearing.

"Merci bien, Mamzelle." He returned the glasses. In his excitement, he thanked her in French.

She smiled. "Il n'y a pas de quoi, M'sieur."

A while passed before he realized that she had answered him in French—the French of Paris, not of New Orleans. Then she must certainly have understood the girls' unpleasant remarks about her cropped hair.

With a hiss of water from her big side wheel, the *Camelia* moved crabwise to her landing apron on the Cape Charles wharf. The pier was packed with people waiting to welcome relatives and friends; parasols, veils, and handkerchiefs waved. The ropes whipped through the hawser holes; Negroes on the wharf threw the nooses over the pilings and moored the boat. Her walking beam grew still. The gangplank went out with a clatter.

The band started a march, and the passengers who had been enjoying the breezes on the upper decks crowded to the red-carpeted staircase.

The doctor was at the back, near the top step, and could see the faces mirrored in the pier glass at the foot. He did not know why he chose to concentrate on Judge Chambert, except that the Judge's face, dark red before, had assumed a pathologic purplish tint. The old gentleman looked more like a bear than ever, his grizzled hair hanging loose on his forehead, his eyes bulging under shaggy brows. He was staring into the glass below as if he saw a ghost. The doctor thought he was looking at the beautiful woman with the girl who had lent him the binoculars, but he could not be sure. The woman was laughing and talking like a person happy to be home.

14

The close column in the corridor below began to move and the phalanx on the staircase broke up. The girl and the woman disappeared with others in the direction of the gangplank. The doctor himself was about to start down, when he felt a flutter of confusion behind him and heard a groan.

The Judge had slumped to the floor and would have rolled down the staircase if it had been clear. In the ensuing confusion, the captain appeared. The doctor was already at Judge Chambert's side, unbuttoning his collar, untying his cravat. The more curious lingered and had to be told to move on. The Judge could not speak. His eyes still glared as if at a vision. The cyanosis in his face deepened. The doctor felt his pulse, listened at his chest. The Judge was past the help of amyl nitrate or morphine. His huge bulk lay grotesquely crumpled at the top of the staircase, one hand tearing at his shirt, the other closed around a rung of the balustrade.

The doctor flicked a fingernail against the glazed eyeball. There was no reaction.

Two

The gate was open to receive them. As the barouche rolled in, two little Negroes who had been sitting under a pecan tree came running.

"Miché Vic a pé vini!" The boy ran alongside the carriage, his calico kilt flying. The little girl in her long guinea-blue skirt trailed behind him.

Zeph stopped the carriage at the foot of the stairs. He climbed down from the driver's box and stood with his arm crooked for Nanaine to steady herself as she got out.

"Miché Vic—"

"M'sieur the doctor," Nanaine corrected. "Yes, he has come home. Now, allez, allez!" She shooed them off with fluttering motions of her gloved hands.

"Who are they?" Victor asked.

"Doze lil bebbies mine," Zeph grinned.

"Get the baggage down and bring it to the house," Nanaine said. "Then put the carriage up for the night." She turned to Victor. "What Mass do you wish to attend?"

"Pardon?" The doctor had been looking after the children as they went off in the direction of the servants' quarters. Zeph with a family was a big change. And there would be others. . . .

"I said, what Mass do you wish to attend? Father Guichard says Mass at six, eight, and ten."

"What one do *you* attend?"

"At six."

"Very well."

"No, tomorrow I think it had better be ten. You will need to rest."

His aunt had invited him to make his choice and then, the conventions of courtesy observed, had chosen for him, as always. No, he assured himself, everything will be the same.

"Clair de Lune" had been built by the doctor's grandfather in 1845. The second story stood some ten feet from the ground, on columns of whitewashed brick. Latticework all around enclosed a large and airy basement. Wide galleries stretched upstairs along the front and sides, graced by square colonnettes of solid cypress supporting the roof. The house was planned to escape flood when, as sometimes happened, the waters of the lake piled up beyond the beach. At the same time, it ensured catching the summer breezes, whether they came from north or south, east or west, for all the rooms opened on the galleries, and when the French doors were thrown open, the apartments were constantly swept with flower-fragrant air from the garden.

Live oaks, magnolias, and pecan trees shaded the level lawns. A hedge of Cherokee roses partitioned the duRocher property from the Roussel place next door where Colette lived. Cape jasmine and gardenia bushes clustered at the foot of the broad stairs, and roses lined the central walk and climbed the brick columns and bloomed against the white lattices. The fruit trees were in the rear—fig and pomegranate, pear and plum and peach and persimmon. So were the cress beds, watered by the overflow from an artesian well that gushed night and day into its broad brick basin.

The Michel Victor Pierre Jean-Marie duRocher who had built the house called it "Clair de Lune." It was true that its white grace against the green of trees held something of the sorcery of moonlight, even by day. The name, written on a cypress board in this Michel Victor duRocher's own hand, was affixed to the gate in a brass frame. Every year, Nanaine had the flourishing script gone over by an expert engraver.

To Victor's amazement, his father, attended by Bazile, was waiting for them on the front gallery.

Victor embraced the old man, who looked exceptionally well. He did not say, "I expected to find you in bed," though the words pushed at his lips. He thought, I must be a monster, since I am irritated to see my father up and about. It was true that the old gentleman was using a cane, but at eighty he could be expected to need one. Victor considered the fine head of iron-gray hair, the unwrinkled face framed in carefully kept sideburns and short beard, the curled mustache above an unsunken mouth, the blue eyes under brows that had not yet gone completely gray.

"Bien?" the old man said testily.

"I am glad to see you looking so well, Papa."

"You are not glad. You are surprised."

"A pleasant surprise, then."

"Diabetes is never a pleasant surprise. I have diabetes."

Victor looked at his father critically.

"You were never a diabetic type."

"Heh? You forget—I was a physician long before you were born, my boy. You think my diagnosis incorrect? You think this an illusion?" He pointed to his left foot with his cane.

Victor studied the swollen toes bursting from an old slipper from which the end had been cut. Enlarged veins in the instep showed through the thin white sock.

"I know what you are thinking. Don't be an ass. It is not gout."

"I would recommend a regimen of colchicum, nevertheless."

"Then I would recommend that you go back to your books!" The old man beat the cane furiously on the floor.

"Come, Mr. Michel," Bazile said, gently taking him by the arm. "It is getting too cool for you out here."

The old doctor's sister had neither moved nor joined the conversation. She stood, a striking figure in her dark foulard, hands crossed at the wrists and composed at her waist, in an attitude of smug serenity that Victor knew. Nanaine was still handsome at sixty-eight. She was, as her friends admitted enviously, well preserved. The five years since he had last seen her had brought no gray to her black hair; Victor suspected that the hairdresser had seen to that. The pompadour, correctly marcelled with hot irons, showed luxuriantly from under her veiled turban, and her alert black eyes needed no glasses. She had, however, grown fleshier, and since she was not tall, the added weight fell just short of making her fat; but this she overcame with the help of an excellent corsetière. Despite her lack of height, she achieved a regal bearing by holding herself proudly erect, and the effort gave her mouth a hard set and made her lips thinner than they really were. My aunt is a remarkable woman, Victor thought, with a surge of warmth. But it was the warmth of anger, not of pride.

"You cabled my father was gravely ill?"

"I cabled you to come at once."

You deliberately led me to believe— He checked himself, and said coldly, "I gathered the wrong impression."

"Your father has been very sick. He has had a slight hemiplegia."

Victor dismissed the contradiction in the words "very" and "slight."

"When was that?"

"On the day of our arrival. When I cabled."

"Did you have a doctor?"

"Dr. Jolivet. But he is a fool."

"What did he say?"

"That Michel did not have a stroke. That all he had was hallucinations."

"We have known that since my father retired from practice, for over a year. Why is Jolivet a fool?"

"Because Michel *has* had a stroke."

Nanaine looked at Victor steadily. He remembered that look. He had known it since he was seven years old. It said, "I, Nanaine duRocher, have spoken, and the matter is settled." When he was small, he had stood before her bewildered, his fists clenched at his sides in painful confusion, tears of fury often burning his eyes. Then she would sweep past him, her skirts rustling with an air of efficiency, leaving him to smolder with humiliation and resentment.

She was sweeping past him now, the train of her skirt with its heavy satin folds swishing toward the salon.

"We will have supper as usual at seven."

The old helplessness was upon him. Unconsciously, his hands tensed into fists, but he unknotted them quickly. He was no longer a child. He could not be dictated to, pulled here and there by the hand. He would find out what his father's condition was in short order, and if it was as good as he believed, he would return to Panama on the next ship. Whatever his aunt's motive in trapping him into coming home, it interested him very little.

Meanwhile, he could very well do with a bath and a shave. He went down to the servants' quarters in search of Zeph.

Zulime was sitting on the kitchen steps. The hair showing from under her red-and-blue tignon was white, and her face so thin that her tan skin seemed to be pasted onto her bones. Victor saw as he came closer that the whites of her eyes had become yellow and veined, and over one a visible film had grown. Her shrunken breasts were deposited in her full-skirted lap, and her calico waist had slipped away from one withered shoulder, showing where she had been branded with the flower-de-luce the initial time she ran away from her first master. To look at her now, without ears—penalty for the second time she ran away—no one would think that once she had sold on the slave mart at seven thousand dollars; but then she was fifteen, and now she was eighty-seven. She was a mulattress, and her beauty had brought a good price from the man who had bought her for a mistress. He sold her to Victor's grandfather for seven hundred and fifty dollars at the age of thirty-nine, and threw in her sickly son for good measure.

"Eh là bas, Zuzu!"

The old woman got up unsteadily. "Who dat callin' Zuzu?"

"You don't know?"

She squinted her dim eyes.

"You can't see?" Victor stood before her.

With a gasp, she threw herself from the step into his arms.

"It Ti Toto! At last you come! Ah, pou l'amou du bon Dieu! You one fine gen'l'man now!"

She was hysterical with joy. The women in the kitchen came running to the door. Zulime felt like a rag doll in his arms, so boneless and light. The claw that clutched his shoulder was a sad remnant of the soft hand that used to bathe him when he was a child. He carried her past the sill and put her down by the chimney.

"No longer my little Toto. You a man!" She began to cry.

"I was a man before I went away, Zuzu."

"Non, non! Ma little Toto wen' away. Big man come back. Me, I know!"

"Look, Ma Zuzu, you working up to a smothering spell. You sit down and let Glad make you your hot sweet water." A Negro girl the doctor did not know pushed Zulime into a chair by the window. The young woman was pregnant and her stomach was so large that her cotton wrapper, stretched over it, seemed about to split. This must be Zeph's wife.

"She *like* dat sweet water, but it don't save her wastin' away. She *crossed*, her." Victor recognized Cumba, her eyes rolling to heaven. "Li ouanga! She's bewitched!"

The old woman trembled. Cumba was her widowed daughter-in-law, Zeph's grandmother. She had come from Martinique, and her West Indian blood was steeped in voodooism.

"Mama Cumba, you let Ma Zuzu have her hot sweet water."

Glad took an iron pot from the back of the wood stove and poured boiling water over a spoonful of brown sugar in a mug. The belly of the pot was red hot and nearly empty, and she placed it hissing in a dishpan full of cold well water. There was a sound as sharp as a shot, and when they looked, the pot had cracked in two.

"Ah! Grand Dieu!" Zulime's hand shook so violently she could hardly complete the sign of the cross.

"You see? You see?" Cumba screamed. "It Zombie who make dat!"

"Be quiet, Cumba," the doctor said impatiently. "Drink your sugar water, Zulime."

"That pot been in this family before I come," Zulime wailed in the Negro patois. "Miss Nanaine, she going to be upset, her. Ah, bon Dieu, bon Dieu!" Moaning, she rocked back and forth, her folded arms pressed against her ribs as if she were in agony.

"Quick. I make grigri," Cumba said, her voice shaking. She reached for a coffee can filled with powdered red brick and began to strew handfuls on the unpainted cypress floor, worn so clean with daily scourings that it looked like ivory satin.

"Oh, God. Oh, God. My nice floor I just scrub," Glad objected.

"That's enough, Cumba!" the doctor ordered sharply. "Bring water. I want a bath. And call Zeph to shave me." He turned to the old woman. "Zulime, I'm coming back to see you. You're not well."

"Ti Toto never come back. Ti Toto gone—forever. Beau miché come back . . . big man. . . ."

She closed her eyes and wagged her head from right to left.

Three

Supper was served in the basement. Twilight was deepening, and Bazile lit the lanterns fixed against the brick pillars. Then he came back and took his place behind the old doctor's chair, beating the air gently with a large palmetto fan to dispel the mosquitoes.

Nanaine served the bisque from the tureen. Victor knew it had been made especially for him. It took hours to clean the crawfish and prepare the highly seasoned forcemeat to stuff the heads. He forgot his earlier rancor against Nanaine. She loved him very much. He had been seven when his mother died of yellow fever, in the same year as Zeph's, and Nanaine had come to live with her brother and raise his son. Victor knew her better than he had known his own mother.

"Gladys asked me to tell you—she has broken the great iron pot."

"What!" Nanaine stopped, spoon in mid-air. "Not the one given to Grand'mère by *her* grand'mère!"

They knew the pot as they knew the face of a close relative. It was the only one Grand'mère had kept when iron was being requisitioned to make bullets for the War; she could not bear to think of the heirloom reduced to so base a destiny as becoming embedded in Yankees.

"How did she break it?"

"She put it red hot in very cold water."

"One of the smart things taught her by the Americans she used to work for, no doubt," Nanaine said bitterly. Of a sudden, she looked alarmed. "The pot must not be thrown away."

"I have some souvenirs from the Canal Zone." Victor wished to avoid the superstitious subject of omens. "I should like to distribute them after dinner."

"You will have time for that later," Nanaine answered shortly. "There is a lawn fete at the Roussels' tonight. You must go."

The old doctor had said nothing since coming to the table. He ate heartily of the rich gravies and spiced meats, and helped himself heavily to the Madeira. There was no question in Victor's mind about his father's self-diagnosis. If he had diabetes, habitual indulgence such as this would have induced coma long ago.

Nanaine suggested that they take coffee at the card table and allow Bazile to clear the cloth. She folded her serviette and drew it through her napkin ring. The rings, Victor remembered, had been saved with the spoons and other silver by the foresight of Zulime. When General Butler came to New Orleans and billeted several of his lieutenants in the duRocher house on Royal Street, Zulime had buried piece by piece in the parterres of the courtyard. For years afterward, the gardener, when planting, dug silver up with the soil. There was probably some still under the bricks that bordered the flower beds.

"Olympe and Julien," Nanaine resumed, "are entertaining Colette's friends. Your cousin, the youngest daughter of Alcide Larouche, will also be there." Nanaine rang a silver bell to let the kitchen know they had finished supper. "I have something to say to you about your cousin."

"Which one?" Victor inquired.

"Colette Roussel."

Victor helped his father to the hammock, and sat down opposite his aunt. He gave Bazile his empty cup and waited for her to begin. Something of a serious nature was impending. Now, he thought, we shall know the real reason why I was called home. . . .

"Julien has spoken to your father. Colette would bring a dowry of fifty thousand dollars."

"Do we need money?" His voice sounded hard against her. The question was sheer sarcasm.

"No. But you need a wife."

"I need a haircut more." He passed his hand over the back of his neck.

"Don't be facetious. Who is this Dolores Salazar at whose house you have dined in Panama City?"

"I thought I wrote you. The daughter of a surgeon. I met her at a dance at the Tivoli Hotel. A beautiful and charming girl."

"You wrote me that much. You are entertaining none of this newfangled nonsense about a love match, I hope?"

"I'm not in love, if that's what you mean."

"Good." She drew a breath of relief. "There is enough Spanish blood in this family already." Actually, there was very little, coming from his great-great-grandmother whose people had come to Louisiana in 1766 when Ulloa took possession for Spain. "Then you have no objections to Colette?"

"None whatsoever. Tell her she may continue to live next door as long as she likes."

"Stop your foolishness." She stamped her foot. "You know what I mean."

"She is my cousin," Victor said more seriously.

"Three times removed. She is your father's brother's daughter's daughter."

He smiled. Nanaine could name every twig of their huge and complicated family tree.

"How is my father's brother? Is he here yet? I should go to see him." His property, which he had named "Shiloh," adjoined the duRochers' on the left.

"He came yesterday morning. Six months too soon." She meant she would have preferred his coming after they had left. She and her brother Ulysse had never agreed. "I believe we were saying it was time you were married?"

"Well, *you* were."

"And to your cousin Colette."

"If she survives the surprise of finding herself affianced to me."

"It is no surprise. Julien and Olympe have told her. Colette has always admired you. She used to stare at you as if you were a god."

Victor wished to say, "She stared at me on the boat today—not as if I were a god," but he remained silent. His aunt had already inquired if they had met; and he had told her no. After a moment, he asked, "What did she say?"

"What *could* she say? You are the cream of the crop. Olympe duRocher regrets she has become a Roussel. When her daughter marries you, people will forget Julien's unfortunate connection with the Louisiana lottery."

It was not so unfortunate. He became rich."

"It was unfortunate," Nanaine insisted. "But for that, Colette might have been Queen of the Carnival this season. Her name was mentioned."

"Poor Olympe." What he really meant was poor Julien. He remembered Olympe's martyred airs, a constant reminder that she, a duRocher, had favored the family Roussel by allowing their son to become her husband. It was a privilege Julien had never been able to live up to, strive as he might.

"Now, with you as his brother-in-law, Colette's brother Leon can eventually be King of Comus. Olympe would be delighted with that."

"Great things are expected of me," Victor commented, half joking, half annoyed. The years spent on the Isthmus, in the tremendous task of cleaning the Canal Zone and insuring the health of thousands of men, had dulled his interest in the trivial intrigues of society.

"Yes," Nanaine said emphatically. "Great things. It is hoped that you will exceed even your father's reputation as a physician. As the colleague of your cousin Dr. Alcide Larouche, you will achieve this easily."

A flush of anger colored Victor's face. Dr. Larouche enjoyed a lucrative career as a fashionable gynecologist in New Orleans. Victor considered him more a fad than a physician.

"Good God! Am I affianced to my cousin Alcide, too?" The effort to cover his anger with a pleasantry did not deceive his aunt.

"You want to spend your life in that hole down there?" She leaned forward in her chair, gripping the armrests. "That's what it is—a *hole!* It will never come to anything—never! If de Lesseps and the French could do nothing with it, the Americans will do less. The papers are full of it. 'Millions for Mud.' 'Throwing Our Money into the Ditch.' It is the joke of the century! 'Connecting the Oceans'— Bah!" She slapped her hand against the chair arm so loudly that the old doctor in the hammock stopped snoring.

Victor could have argued with her. Despite the attitude of the press, he believed in the Canal and in his work. The victory over

yellow fever alone was worth the fight. There were still malaria
and smallpox and beriberi to overcome, accidents from dynamite
and steam shovels and concrete mixers to suture and splint, snake
bite and scorpion sting to battle. These were real challenges.

"I helped dig that hole with a scalpel and a thermometer," he
said, "and I'm proud of it."

"Prouder than you are of us," she retorted. "If you had come
back after two years, as you promised, you could have married
Minerve de Gerbeau. Her splendid connections are wasted entirely on Sylvain Vignaud."

Nanaine was at times pathetically transparent. This was why
she had brought him home, to arrange for him what she considered a proper marriage, to see him making what she considered
maximum use of his profession. It was such a childish piece of
scheming that he resolved to ignore it.

Four

The Roussel place was called "Beaux Arbres," and its trees were
indeed beautiful. Tonight, every door and window was thrown
wide open and every lamp and candelabrum lit. To one side of
the garden, a low floor had been erected for dancing. Lines of
swaying Chinese lanterns crisscrossed between the trees and connected the corner posts of the uncovered platform. A string band
was playing, and the bright colors of young ladies' dresses and
the white coats of young men bobbed about to a two-step. The
sound of people enjoying themselves came from every direction
—gay talking and high ripples of laughter.

Julien and Olympe were in the drawing room, greeting guests
who were by now arriving in smaller groups and at longer intervals. Victor and his aunt found them alone.

Olympe was as he remembered her. She was professionally
pale; she made a career of circled eyes and sunken cheeks. Despite this, she had a reputation, studiously acquired, as a charm-

26

ing and gracious hostess. Olympe was convinced that generously to do her part in the upper circles of society, amiably to dispense the pleasures of the salon and the dining room with frequency and captivating taste, was the duty of a lady. She dressed with a severe elegance that dramatized her pallid features. Tonight she was wearing a princess gown, lavish with insertions, and around her throat she affected a velvet band to which she had pinned a small pearl brooch.

The doctor performed the formalities expected of him.

"Mes hommages, ma cousine," he said, bending over her hand ringed with pearls. He thought, Pearls are for tears, of course. He could never embrace her. Without raising a finger, somehow she held off even the men who were related to her—even her husband, Julien—at arm's length. She sighed, "Well, my cousin, you come home at last," making Victor feel that his absence had personally abused her, but that she nobly forgave him.

Julien embraced him warmly—too warmly, in fact; the backslapping savored of a politician. In five years, Julien had grown fifteen years older. He was bald, except for a fringe of hair that ended at his temples. He wore glasses now, and his black mustache had become grizzled. The diamond stud in his bright tie and his expensive Shantung suit seemed defiant of something. Julien was only forty, but he looked fifty-five.

"Well, it's coming—it's coming!" He rubbed his hands together, smiling with satisfaction.

"What's coming?" Nanaine asked suspiciously.

"The causeway. The great bridge between New Orleans and Mandeville."

"Ah—*pf-f-f!*"

Nanaine's disbelief was emphasized by a spasmodic gesture of one hand, thumb pointed outward.

"It's here," Julien insisted. "At least, the engineer for the corporation interested is here. Once Northern capital gets interested. . . ."

"*Northern!*" Nanaine's face hardened.

"Well, the South has neither the money nor the ambition.

27

When something needs doing, it's the North—" He stopped, seeing himself on dangerous ground. "Anyway"—he took a newspaper clipping from his pocket—"he's here—Harry Lockwood. From Chicago. Stopping at the St. Charles Hotel. I've written him promising my political support in getting State permission to build."

Olympe looked bored. Her expression said that any woman married to an asinine lawyer who thought it something to be an influential Democrat deserved the compassion of the world.

Nanaine carried on the conversation. "So! That is why you are buying up all the property here. You expect a boom!"

"This is just between us, you understand," Julien cautioned. "If the town gets wind of it, nobody will sell. Only myself and the mayor know so far."

"And they are fighting over real estate like two pigs over a bone!" Olympe lifted her nose in disgust.

"It is two *dogs* that fight over a bone," Julien corrected gently. "But there is no denying that Bidault is a pig."

"Is he mayor?" Victor asked. "The Bidault who runs the dairy and the livery stable?"

"Yes. And the drugstore, too. He owns everything."

There was no reason for Julien to be envious. He himself owned a large interest in the Mandeville Boat Company. Recently he had acquired the sawmill on the Bayou Castain. Now he was thinking of starting an electric-light plant and an ice factory. But Bidault, who was a notorious miser, was goaded by sheer greed, whereas Julien's grabbing was an attempt to fill the vacuum in his private life. It was plain to Victor that money was his means of giving himself importance in his wife's eyes, and making it had become a mania with him.

"The mayor nearly bought the Delamare property," Olympe contributed with a spark of malice. "He was negotiating with the Delamare brothers for weeks before Julien even had their address. They are in New York."

"Well, neither of us got the place." Julien bit his lip. "It was sold to the sister who has been living in Paris."

"Ah!" Nanaine straightened as if she had received a shock. "Then I am right. Then she is here. I was not sure it was she—it's been so long—and she had a girl with her. I saw her get off the boat this evening."

"Yes. I hear from Mugnier she's staying at his hotel until the house is cleaned up. It's been closed for years. The girl is her daughter."

"Ah!" Nanaine said again. "Her daughter."

Victor wondered if they were talking about the pair who had lent him the binoculars and who he had supposed were sisters. But could so young-looking a woman have been the girl's mother?

"Ah, speaking of the boat, you had a little excitement aboard, I hear?" Julien turned to Victor. "Judge Chambert?"

"*Judge Chambert!*" gasped Nanaine. Breathlessly, "What happened?"

"Why, don't you know? He fell dead at the head of the stairs." Julien spread out his palms and raised his shoulders.

"*But no! What. . . .*"

"Apoplexy," Victor said. "I was there, but I could do nothing for him."

"How is it you told me nothing?" Nanaine turned angrily on Victor. "We knew the Judge well!"

"In the excitement of seeing you. . . . And later, we had other things to talk about. You remember?"

"Yes, yes," his aunt conceded. "Olympe, where is Colette?"

Olympe pulled a bell rope, and brown Doudouce, grown much stouter, answered promptly.

"Find Miss Colette. Tell her to come here."

"Apoplexy, eh?" Nanaine clung to the story of the Judge. "But what caused the attack, eh? What caused it?"

"I heard he had been having an exciting game of poker. And he had been drinking heavily, as usual," Julien answered.

"Ah, it was not that. I know better. I know better." She added under her breath, "Palmyre Delamare, after twenty years. And on the same boat with the Judge. . . ."

Colette appeared with her brother Leon and a tall young man, whose reddish-brown hair and blue eyes indicated that he was a stranger. She was dramatically beautiful tonight, the pale-yellow bodice of her organdy dress molded to her slim waist, the short sleeves and low neck revealing superb arms and shoulders. A necklace and bracelets of jet heightened the ivory tone of her skin, and in the blue-black mass of her curling hair she wore a yellow rose.

Leon presented the young man. Harry Lockwood, the son. . . .

"Well!" Julien rubbed his hands together, obviously pleased. "I wrote your father at the St. Charles."

"We *were* there, sir. We came here this evening on the freight boat, bringing our automobile."

"I met him in the bar at the Mugnier Hotel," Leon explained. "He was drinking himself to death over a short-haired girl."

Leon in the hotel bar, and talking of girls. . . . Well, he was twenty-one now. He was graduating from Loyola Academy in June and had all the marks, Victor observed, of the popular fraternity man. Striped linen suit, bow tie, silk shirt—he was what was called a "snappy dresser." The small mustache probably helped his ego, for he was not tall, but stocky like his father.

"I imagine one drink won't kill me." Harry laughed. "And besides, I know the young lady only by sight. She. . . ."

"Colette, you remember your Cousin Victor," Nanaine cut in rudely.

Olympe had forgotten them. When Leon was near, she saw only Leon.

"Good evening, Cousin," Colette smiled. Her eyes were brown, and the dark pupils gave them depth. She had been staring at him in much the same way she had as a child.

"How are you, Colette?"

"Go on, go on." Nanaine made a wagging gesture with her hand. "Embrace each other. You are not two sticks!"

Victor put his hands on her shoulders and kissed her cheek. Her skin flushed warm to his lips and he felt her tremble.

Her program was full, and between dances she was surrounded by so many young men that a word with her was impossible. Victor danced with his cousin Féfé Larouche, who had shed her convent uniform for a smart party dress somewhat beyond her fifteen years. She talked more than she observed, else she might have recognized the *Camelia's* bearded passenger, now cleanly shaved. After giving Féfé to her next partner, Victor wandered over to the basement, where an extravagant buffet was laid. Fauvette d'Eaubonne was pouring coffee, and the other chaperones sat around beating their skirts with palmetto fans to chase the mosquitoes, and talking so fast that Victor was reminded of the French Market in the city on Saturday morning. When he appeared, the talk subsided noticeably, giving way to a whispering behind fans. He joined Harry Lockwood, who was standing at the table with a group of Leon's friends.

"I'm another candidate for an alcoholic death. Colette's program is full."

"She's your fiancée, isn't she?" Harry asked. Leon had been gossiping.

"Well—it seems to amount to that."

"She's honored me twice. I'll share with you." He consulted his card. "The fifteenth?"

"There is some mistake." Colette puzzled over her program.

"I threatened to cut my throat if Lockwood didn't surrender this dance with you."

The music had started, and couples were circling about them. He took her hand and they fell in step.

He talked to her about the fete and she answered in monosyllables, her head turned aside. At length, she faced him, eyes laughing. "You have come out of the bushes!"

"I thought it time—when on the boat my own cousin didn't know me."

"I knew you," she said, almost solemnly. "I remembered your black hair and hazel eyes, and your tallness. . . ." She stopped, confused.

31

Their Spanish ancestress echoed loudly in Colette's coloring, the dimpled oval of her face, the dark masses of hair. The black lace fan for her, Victor thought, remembering the Panamanian souvenirs.

"Then why were you so wicked? You should have made me some sign of recognition." He pressed the hand lying on his.

"Why do you suppose I made that loud ridiculous remark about you?" She looked up at him, and confessed, "It was to attract your attention."

"I was a fool. . . ."

"No. You were too busy flirting yourself."

"I was . . . ?"

"Oh, we all saw you!" she laughed. "With the girl who has so much impressed Mr. Lockwood."

"I only borrowed her binoculars."

The set of her mouth was serious.

"Is she a friend of yours?"

"I never saw her before."

"Even with so little hair, she is very pretty," Colette said thoughtfully. "There is something about her—"

"Perhaps. But the most beautiful young lady on the boat was my cousin!"

"For that, you are forgiven! I was punishing you, giving all my dances away. But now I relent. Will you dance with me?"

"You said—your program is full. . . ."

She freed her hand from his, removing the card hanging on its silken cord from her wrist.

"Shall we say—these?"

He looked closely where her finger pointed, and saw his name written, in a delicate feminine hand, three times in a row.

He drew her close, suddenly, searching her face. The music stopped and they broke apart.

He had only time to say, "You are an angel, Colette!" before the young bachelors closed in around her again. But he had all evening to consider himself the luckiest of men.

Five

A week passed before Victor was able to talk to Dr. Jolivet about his father. Dr. Jolivet had been on the Bayou Lafourche, called in consultation by Aurélie Blanque, widow of Henri Coulon. Her uncle was dying of cancer of the throat, and Aurélie had great confidence in Dr. Jolivet. He had kept her tubercular husband alive for five years after every other doctor had given him up.

When Victor, coming from the post office, saw the dusty buggy before the bank building, he went up to the doctor's office at once. He passed Madame Naquin, wife of the postmaster, and her son Hippolyte on the stairs. Hippolyte had been kicked in the head by a mule when he was small and had never been quite right since; but he was happier than most people, and there were those who questioned whether the mule had done him foul or favor.

"Good morning, Madame. Good morning, 'Polyte. How are things going?"

"Very well," Hippolyte grinned. "Fine!" though he had a bandaged hand which smelled of iodoform.

As Victor opened the waiting-room door, the woman his aunt had referred to as Palmyre Delamare and her daughter were just entering the doctor's office.

He took a seat and looked around. The old leather-upholstered furnishings were shabby, but clean; a leg of contrasting wood had been supplied a crippled table where some stale copies of the Mandeville *Trumpet* and a worn volume of French lithographs lay strewn. The doctor's diplomas hung framed on the walls: his sheepskin from Tulane, his certificate from Charity Hospital, the testimony of his degree in pharmacy. A reproduction of "The Doctor," by Sir Luke Fildes, graced the wall on one side of the room, and Dean Cornweller's "Conquerors of Yellow Fever" the other.

The mother and daughter did not stay long. As they reentered the waiting room and Victor rose, the girl glanced his way and smiled. She recognized him despite the vanished Vandyke. They said good morning. Her eyes were of deep blue and had that wide-open look of the very young.

"Well!" The doctor shook Victor's hand with both his own. "I hear you had a patient even before getting off the boat."

"I didn't keep him long," Victor said wryly.

"Apoplexy, heh? Well, that is what we doctors would say." He drew a chair for Victor. "The ladies have a different verdict. They have elected themselves coroner and have held an autopsy at their coffee tables. They say it was something else killed him."

"Have they named it?"

"They leave that to us, but it will tax our Latin. They say it was—the sight of a beautiful woman." The doctor's gray eyes snapped. He was a slight man, past seventy, but the precision of the middle part in his white hair, his neat mustache, each end waxed to a fine point, and his general good grooming indicated something of the beau beneath his years. "And they are making a scandal of it. You know the ladies love a scandal, when it is not about themselves. In fact, the daughters of the Judge, with whom he was in the habit of spending his week ends here, have packed up and returned to the city, as well to escape the scandal as to attend the funeral."

"She must have been a very beautiful woman," Victor said.

"She is. You saw her just now. The auburn-haired one. Good God, my boy"—the doctor jabbed Victor in the ribs with his thumb—"don't you know a beauty when you see one?"

"I was looking at the girl."

"Yes. The daughter is just over a siege of typhoid. Came here to recuperate. I prescribed a tonic. That's all she needs—the ozone air and spring water will do the rest."

Victor heard the arrival of another patient in the outer office. He broached the subject of his father.

"You are thoroughly correct as far as I know," Dr. Jolivet concurred. "There is nothing wrong with him—except that he thinks there is. Senile hallucinosis, I would say."

"My aunt claims he had a stroke. It was at the time you were called in."

"Resulting in the imagined paralysis of the left leg. But he did not have a stroke. All he had was an attack of gout."

"I know. I've already put him on colchicum, but I doubt if it will do him any good as long as he fails to control his diet."

Victor got up to go, but the doctor put a hand on his arm.

"Wait a minute. I'll see who it is. I would like to talk to you a little longer."

He opened the door and looked into the waiting room.

"Come here, Masoom," he said, making a beckoning motion with two fingers.

An Indian girl entered the office. There must be, Victor thought, an epidemic of beautiful women around here. She was lithe as a cat in the full calico skirt that fell down to her bare feet. Her copper-colored arms were bare to the shoulders. An artist would have reveled in her heart-shaped face, full red lips, large black eyes that timidity and a nuance of fear made larger. Her hair was gleaming black and straight and hung down her back below her knees. She carried a Choctaw basket filled with deer's-tongue and vetiver, with which ladies liked to sachet their clothes and bed linens.

"Have you been selling that stuff in the town again?" the doctor asked harshly. "Didn't I tell you not to?"

"I think doctor say gombo filé only." She held the basket behind her back.

"Well, I mean that, too. I mean *everything!* Do you understand?"

"Yes." She hung her head.

"Now go empty that stuff in the wastebasket."

She pattered across the floor and did as she was told, while the doctor went to a medicine cabinet behind a screen and returned wrapping up a bottle of amber-colored fluid.

"You keep on selling stuff in town and I won't give you any more of this," he threatened. "What do you do it for? Don't you hunt and raise enough to eat?"

"Tobacco," she murmured. "Buy tobacco."

"Oh, Christ," the doctor said in English.

He gave her the bottle, and shyly she slipped her fingers into a hidden pocket at her waistline and took out two bits. She laid it on his desk.

"Pick that up again," he commanded. "I told you I didn't want any money."

She reached out hesitantly for the coin and stuck it back in her pocket.

"Now let me catch you selling anything again and you know what I'll have to do, don't you?"

"Won't sell," she promised.

The doctor opened the door for her. After she left, he went to the medicine cabinet again and returned with a swab soaked in a solution of carbolic acid. Standing before the desk with his back turned to Victor to screen his action, he rubbed the spot where the coin had rested, leaving a new scar. The younger doctor had been reading the faded titles in the dingy bookcase: Gray's *Anatomy*, Chapman's *Therapeutics*, Dewees's *Obstetrics*, Thompson's *Practice*, Neill's *Outline of the Nerves*. . . . He turned suddenly, startled by Jolivet's abrupt question:

"Do you believe in love?"

"As a cause or a cure?" Victor joked.

Dr. Jolivet looked serious. "I should never have been a physician. I'm too damned sentimental."

"Sentiment is no asset in any trade."

"I prefer pharmacy. Steady hours—and you don't have to go out in bad weather, or the middle of the night. Clean. Fascinating. The drama in belladonna, opium, hemlock. The romance in herbs and roots—senna, jalap, ipecac."

Victor smiled. He had never thought of emetics and purges as romantic. He supposed the doctor referred to their origin rather than their application.

"Listen, my boy. How would you like to take over my practice? An easy way to get poor quick. No results positively guaranteed in fifty years. I wish to retire. All my bellyaches and bad hearts are yours for the taking."

"No, thank you," Victor laughed. "I always wanted to be a

college professor, myself. You don't have to jump up in the middle of the night to give a class in Greek, either."

"Well, that's that." Dr. Jolivet sighed. "Perhaps I made my offer sound so tempting that you could not resist refusing it. To tell you the truth, the minute you stepped in here, I liked you enough to *give* you my confounded practice. But now I find I like you enough *not* to."

In the waiting room sat the Widow Aurélie Blanque-Coulon, her two daughters, and their five children. The group looked like a silhouette; they were all in black, relieved by the neat white collars and cuffs permissible in the second year of mourning. The widow still wore her crepe veil. Victor remarked mentally that mourning was extremely becoming to Aurélie. At middle age, it gave her a grace and distinction which he did not recall her having before. Black lent her plain face interest and had a refining effect on her figure. It was odd that the mourning that was meant to efface Aurélie achieved exactly the opposite effect.

"Ah! Good morning, Aurélie. Come in, my dear."

Victor thought he detected in the way "Aurélie" was pronounced the excessive sentiment of which Dr. Jolivet had accused himself.

When he got back to the house, he went down to the kitchen where Cumba was breaking in a new iron pot. She rubbed red brick dust into it, washed it, then smeared the inside with pork fat and put the pot on the fire.

"Cumba, tell me what this is."

The doctor drew from his coat pocket a trio of voodoo charms. He had found them in his pillow. The lumps had puzzled him, and opening the ticking, he had extracted the assorted grigri. One was a hard ball of pine needles mixed with mud from a wasp nest and rolled in powdered brick; the second, a red-flannel bag containing sugar and the dried hearts of birds; and the third, a black bag filled with cat hair and minute bones.

At the sight of the charms, Cumba emitted a low wail.

"*You* put them there," he accused.

37

"I didn't do it! I swear befo' God!" Cumba's few teeth began to chatter.

"Tell me what it means," the doctor ordered.

"Dat wanga! Powerful charm!"

"Come on! Tell me!"

Cumba pointed with a trembling finger.

"Dat ball keep you home. Dat lil red bag make you love. And dat black 'un keep away love."

"You didn't do it, and yet you know all about it. What is it you want, exactly?"

"I don't want nothing! Sacred word of honor!"

Glad came in from the adjoining room.

"Go on, Mama Cumba. You *scared*. You say Doctor Vic bring death smell the evening he come. True he come from a dead man, but dead man don't smell *that* quick!" Glad laughed loudly, stirring her gumbo.

"Dat lake smood' when Miché leave odder side?" Cumba wanted to know. "She kick up big befo' Miché get here?"

"Well, what of it?"

"Den ol' pot break. . . . Oh God, God. Dis family goin' see rough times—dis family goin' break up someways!" Her voice rose in a shriek.

Victor moved toward the stove.

"Miché t'row four bits after 'em fo' Papa LàBas!" Cumba pleaded.

"I can find a better way of throwing my money to the devil than that," the doctor said. He lifted a stove lid and dropped the trash in with the burning pine.

"Aie, aie!" Cumba wailed.

"Glad, where is Zulime?"

"She over home, Doc' Vic."

Cumba followed the doctor across the yard, whimpering.

The servants' quarters were a three-room frame building with a narrow porch running along the front. Two bushes of sweet basil, "male" and "female," were planted close together at one side of the steps. As Victor approached, the hounds, cooling their bellies in the dust, got up and stretched, arching their backs.

Zulime sat in an old rocking chair, practically lost in her cotton matinée and shirred skirt. Something odd hung on a piece of twine around her shriveled neck. Victor recognized it as a mojo, the leg bone of a cat purported to have been killed in a graveyard at midnight.

"How are you, Zuzu?"

"Poorly, thank God," Zulime replied. She was very religious, and thanked heaven for both good and bad.

"Did you take your medicine?" He knew there was no help for her, but he would keep her alive as long as he could. Her trouble was progressive pernicious anemia, in which iron had been found of little use; even arsenic would bring no more than a transient improvement. Science still had a long way to go in the treatment of the blood and its diseases.

"I been voodooed," Zuzu mumbled, "and medicine will do me no good."

"You take it anyway. You understand?" He tried to reason with her. "Who would cross a good woman like you, Zuzu? For what reason?"

"I don't know."

"How is your rheumatism today?"

"It better," Cumba interrupted, "sence she stop takin' Miché's pills and rub herse'f wit alligator fat an' buzzard grease."

"I'm sure it is." The doctor drummed his fingers on his knees and sighed. He got up to go.

He remembered, during his internship at Charity Hospital, how some patients cried and fought to keep the knotted strings, mystic stones and teeth, bones and roots that were found on their persons. One man died after his charm had been taken away— from fright, no doubt. Perhaps Dr. Jolivet's weariness and wish to retire were due in large measure to his futile fifty years' struggle with grigri. The work it would require to stamp out voodoo and supplant it with science seemed at that moment incalculable to the younger man. He walked rapidly back toward the house as if he were hurrying out of the way of a monster. I thank heaven, he thought, that *I* am not called upon to grapple with this problem.

Six

Father Guichard's ten-o'clock Mass was the most popular, for it put his parishioners home in time for their second breakfast at eleven. A large attendance streamed out of the church and fell into groups in the churchyard or stood on the banquette talking, following a time-honored custom of visiting on the street.

The duRochers and the Roussels lingered with the rest on their way to their carriages. None was so beautiful or so exquisitely dressed as Colette, standing at Victor's side. Looking down at her cheek, made rosy by the reflection of her pink parasol, he felt a thrill of pride as people passed and stared at her. He was aware that the old ladies opposite were remarking that they made a handsome pair. He felt Colette slip her hand through his arm, and reached over to press her gloved fingers.

Father Guichard wove in and out of the groups, shaking hands here and there. A circle of mouse-colored hair showed from under his black biretta. His full, round face was stamped with a continuous smile, and his large waistline was girded by an embroidered sash over his silk cassock. His parish supported him well and gave him few worries.

One of his worries, however, was Uncle Ulysse, and seeing the duRochers, the priest hurried over and addressed himself to Nanaine.

"Miss Nanaine, your brother is absent again today? You promised me. . . ."

Nanaine had promised the priest she would prevail on Ulysse to come to Mass, but since she and her brother were not on speaking terms, she had sent Colette to urge him.

"Colette, what did your grandfather say?" Nanaine asked, furious that Ulysse dared to stay away.

"He is fighting the Battle of Bull Run today, and could not leave," Colette explained, repressing a smile.

"Bah!" Nanaine said disgustedly. "It is too bad he could not be killed at one of his everlasting battles."

"M'sieur Vic, is there nothing you can do?" the priest asked.

"I'll see. I'll talk to him."

"If you please, without delay." The priest's ever-moving eyes came to rest on Dr. Jolivet, who was engaged in what appeared to be an unfriendly argument with Mayor Bidault. He hastened to interrupt it. "Ah, Dr. Jolivet—is it true that the uncle of Aurélie Coulon—? I will say a Mass for the repose of his soul."

"Poor Aurélie!" Madame Larouche sympathized. "She does nothing but attend funerals."

"Poor, nothing!" her mother, Madame Vigée, contradicted. "She comes into a considerable inheritance through her uncle."

"I mean, she is always in mourning," Madame Larouche explained.

"Which again is to her advantage, since mourning becomes her. If her family continues to favor her by dying off at the rate of one every two years, her black may catch her a second husband." Madame Vigée had a rasping voice, the result not so much of age as of attitude. She never went anywhere without Coucou, her fat fox terrier, who accepted his fate with mute misery. Father Guichard had to tolerate him even in church.

"I have it from good authority that Dr. Jolivet has failed to appear at his wife's tomb for three Sunday afternoons running," Nanaine contributed.

"He has shed no tears for six months," Madame Larouche added.

How do they know all these things . . . ? Victor wondered at the clairvoyance of women.

"Look—it is barely a year, and he no longer wears the black mourning band on his coat sleeve."

All the ladies looked, but as at that moment the mayor left Dr. Jolivet and started in their direction, they began to fan themselves industriously.

"Let us go home." Victor's father was beginning to feel the need of breakfast.

"No, no, Michel. Just a little longer," Madame Larouche insisted. "But Mama, are you *sure?*"

"Positive," Madame Vigée declared. "She is with Fauvette d'Eaubonne, I tell you."

"Incredible!" Nanaine said under her breath. "I cannot believe she would *dare*. . . ."

"If she does *this,* she will surely call on us before long. And *then* what will we do?" Madame Larouche worried.

"She will probably follow the American custom, where the new neighbor is called on by the old ones," Nanaine assured her. "And she will wait until she rots for *that,* I can tell you!"

The talk was disrupted by the arrival of Mayor Bidault, who came directly to Victor. Remembering his manners, the mayor bowed to the ladies, making quick business of it. In Bidault, the pig Julien had referred to was apparent. He was short and fat, and his tan linen suit called for laundering. There were spots on the front of his checked vest. He wore a shaggy brown mustache, and his eyes were little and close-set in his fleshy face. His collar was the cheap, shiny celluloid kind designed to save washing and resist wear.

"We *need* a new doctor here." The mayor wiped his hatband with a crumpled handkerchief. Evidently he did not get along well with Dr. Jolivet. "Back in the States to stay, I hope?"

"I don't think so," Victor said. "There is still a lot to be done in Panama."

Colette's fingers tightened on his arm.

"Stick around here for a while. You'll find enough to do," the mayor suggested.

"I don't doubt it," Victor said pleasantly.

From the banquette someone called the mayor. It was Guy Chauvin, the druggist. He had difficulty in walking straight, and held himself more erect than was necessary. Sunday morning or no, he looked to Victor like a man who had been drinking.

"Excuse me." Mayor Bidault left and joined the druggist. They rode off together in the mayor's buggy.

At that moment, a sudden hush fell upon the chatter in the churchyard. Only Father Guichard's voice sounded in the calm. "You have burned your candle, my little one? I shall pray with you that your prayer be answered."

"Thank you, Father." It was Palmyre Delamare's daughter. Her mother and Fauvette were behind her.

Several ladies broke the silence with a gasp. Madame Larouche had her hand to her heart. Olympe reached into her Irish crochet bag and, bringing out her smelling salts, passed them under Madame's nose. Nanaine's face was hard, her lips tight, her eyes outraged. Julien's, beside hers, was an odd contrast: it lit up, came to life. A slight frown troubled Colette's smooth forehead.

"Who *are* they?" she asked curiously.

"It is better for a nice girl not to know," Olympe said.

The three descended the steps of the church and walked the gamut of stares that lined the pathway to the banquette. They got into Fauvette's barouche, the black boy snapped the whip, and the carriage started off.

"Well!" Olympe was too shocked to think of fainting. She fanned herself furiously. "The career of Fauvette d'Eaubonne as a young ladies' chaperone is ended, as far as *I* am concerned!"

Victor felt himself isolated in his own confusion. What was it about the girl with cropped hair and her beautiful mother that struck such consternation into the hearts of Nanaine and her friends?

Uncle Ulysse took breakfast in the open, at a table set in the shade of his pecan trees. The sun through the leaves made patterns of shine and shadow on the damask cloth and silver coffee service. A parrot perched on the back of the old gentleman's chair.

Uncle Ulysse was thin to the point of appearing emaciated. He wore a mustache and a Napoleon III Imperial, locally called a "goatee." His scant white hair fell in wisps over his high brow, and in his dark eyes the fired warehouses and wharves of New Orleans in the spring of 1862 seemed still to smolder. He always wore a black frock coat and light-tan trousers.

Uncle Ulysse's leanness was not due to lack of appetite, for he helped himself generously to the grillades and grits, while a platter of fried plantain waited at his elbow. He was sipping his claret as Victor came up. He rose to pull his nephew into his arms, kissing both his cheeks and then his mouth.

"No, I've had breakfast," Victor refused. Nevertheless, Uncle Ulysse clapped his hands, and when his servant, Noonoon, came, instructed her to bring a cup and saucer for coffee.

"Before I forget," Victor began, "Father Guichard has commissioned me to save your soul."

"You might just as well have forgotten." Uncle Ulysse cut a piece of gristle from his grillade. "I am heading for hell purposely. General Butler is there, and I have something to say to him in person. Eh, Bragg?" He held his fork over his shoulder to the parrot, and the bird took the gristle in his claw.

"Well, since you have business there—I shall tell Father Guichard, 'Business before pleasure.'"

"If you please."

"Tell me, how is the war?"

"Wonderful, wonderful!" The old man's eyes gleamed. "We are winning." He reached to the chair beside him and picked up a cardboard map of the Confederacy into which varicolored pins had been stuck. He was in the habit of studying his maps while he ate, deciding on his next moves as if he were dealing with pawns on a chessboard. "Now here we are at Corinth, General Johnston commanding. If the Confederates could defeat Grant before Buell could join him, and then defeat Buell, the ground lost by the fall of Donelson could be regained. . . ."

The old man went on and on, explaining, pushing in and pulling out pins, his excitement bringing the claret to his bony cheeks. For twenty years, Uncle Ulysse had been writing a history of the War Between the States, or, rather, a hypothesis. For it was entirely an account of what would have happened *if* this

44

had happened, or that had not. *If* the Union, having seized John Slidell of Louisiana from the British vessel *Trent,* had refused to give him up. *If* Britain had thus been drawn into the war against the North. *If* Jackson, after the successes at McDowell and Front Royal, had had reinforcements. *If* Lee's Maryland campaign had not failed. . . . Ever since Victor could remember, Uncle Ulysse had been fighting the War over again from the beginning, working gradually but surely to victory for the South. It was one thing, he said, to be defeated, and another to *accept* defeat.

". . . the failure of the Federal campaign on the Peninsula," his uncle was saying with satisfaction. "In the seven days of fighting, the Union loss was sixteen thousand, the Confederate loss twenty thousand."

Twenty thousand men. . . .

"So who won?" Victor asked wryly.

"Heh? Heh?" The old man was a little hard of hearing. "Who *won?* Why, the Confederates, of course."

The futility and fanaticism of his uncle's work depressed the doctor. It seemed a tragic waste to have spent twenty years in studying how to change the course of a war that had already been fought. Hate, it seemed to Victor, was not a happy hobby. "I never forget a wrong," Uncle Ulysse was accustomed to claim with pride. He had been an active Knight of the White Camelia, fighting during and after the War with equal violence.

Nanaine was similarly accomplished. She had not spoken to her brother in forty years. She had never forgiven him for relinquishing law for the rice business, thus smudging his du-Rocher hands with the taint of trade. Uncle Ulysse had been a huge success on the Rice Row—a power on the New Orleans Board of Trade, president of this, chairman of that. He had made a fortune, retiring at the age of fifty-eight to live in ease as a rich *rentier,* while his agent clipped his coupons and collected his rents, giving the old gentleman unlimited leisure in which to re-wage his War and enjoy his grudges. Uncle Ulysse was acutely sensitive to his sister Nanaine's preference for her professional brother Michel, Victor's father.

"Nanaine and her lady friends must be having a fit, heh?" His expression changed, and his eyes twinkled. "I hear Palmyre Delamare is back. And with a pretty daughter, by God!"

"Yes. But Uncle Ulysse, who are they? Why are they so offensive?"

"That's right—you wouldn't remember. You were a child when Palmyre left." He leaned closer to the doctor. "I know the daughter's name. Noonoon got it from Doudouce, who works for Olympe, and Doudouce got it from the housegirl of Madame Dufour, wife of the baker, who was told by Madame Naquin, wife of the postmaster, who saw it on a letter which the young lady received yesterday from New York."

Good heavens! Victor thought. The neatness of the network aroused his admiration. At the same time, he remembered a maxim inspired by Madame Naquin's notorious tongue. "Who knows Madame Naquin, knows all."

"Well, what is the girl's name?" he inquired.

"Miriam Mendel."

"Pretty." He repeated it slowly.

"Doesn't that name tell you anything?"

"A young lady's name usually tells who her father was."

"In this case, that is far from all. Now, my boy. . . ." Uncle Ulysse pushed his chair back. "I have no time to tell you more. It is too long a story. If you want to hear it all, ask your cousin, Alcide Larouche. As for me, I must return to work." He rose and reached for his map.

General Bragg spread his wings and flew to Uncle Ulysse's shoulder, emitting a bloodcurdling noise. It was the Confederate Yell.

Uncle Ulysse had said his last for the day about Palmyre Delamare. The doctor stood for a moment looking at the old man's back bent over the map. His cousin, Alcide Larouche—the wealthy Dr. Larouche of New Orleans with whom Nanaine wanted him to go into practice. Dr. Larouche and Palmyre Delamare. . . .

Seven

Dinner at the Roussels' lacked the vivacity that customarily distinguished a family gathering. Everybody's thoughts seemed to be elsewhere. At ten minutes before the three-o'clock dinner hour, Leon appeared with Harry Lockwood, an impromptu and reluctant guest. Julien had been with the young man's father all morning at the hotel and had not dared to ask the Northerner to his home; but Leon was in the habit of doing and getting what he wanted. It was evident that his imperative methods worked with Harry.

"He wanted to stick there at the Mugnier and moon over that short-haired girl. He has managed to meet her."

"Well, I wouldn't say it was a very brilliant maneuver on my part. My father met her mother at an art exhibit in New York some years ago, and he remembered her. He'd bought one of her husband's paintings."

"Her *husband's* paintings—" Olympe paled and closed her eyes.

"Of course, even at that, Mrs. Mendel is not the kind of person you'd forget," Harry added quickly. He wondered why he had upset Olympe.

"Indeed not!" It was the only thing Nanaine had said to him since dinner began.

"In any case, I haven't much more time to moon," Harry laughed. "She's moving into her own house tomorrow."

" 'Belle Pointe.' " Julien sighed. "It is a beautiful piece of property."

"Papa," Leon said irritably, "for the love of God stop buying property. All it's good for is to paint and repair. Buy an automobile, and save taxes."

"Later, later." Julien waved a harassed hand. Leon had brought up the subject of an automobile at every meal since the Lockwoods appeared with their Packard.

"*That,*" Olympe said through tight lips, "is what you told Leon when he wanted the yacht."

47

"He got the yacht," Julien said doggedly.

"After six months of waiting. It took all the pleasure out of getting it, having to wait so long."

Leon cast his mother a tender glance. She glowed to it, as much as Olympe was capable of glowing. She went on to mention in a complaining voice all those among their friends who had or were getting automobiles. Julien subsided into silence.

"Papa has ordered the nineteen-ten Oldsmobile to be ready soon," Féfé Larouche announced.

"We'll get a Packard like Harry's," Leon said confidently.

Julien, pompous all morning with plans for the causeway, looked shrunken and dejected. "Shall we have coffee in the garden?" he suggested timidly.

On the way to the garden, Leon persisted. "Papa is so inconsistent. He talks nothing but causeway. Then he expects us to be satisfied with a yacht. Why, the causeway will make boats obsolete! Are we to cross the causeway in carriages, for God's sake? Times are changing. This is the automobile age. We live in a new world. Wake up, Papa!" He slapped his father on the back.

"Because the world is changing, is precisely the reason why we should *not* change!" Nanaine said angrily. "Let the world fall apart if it wishes—it is the duty of people like us to remain the same!"

Victor sighed. It had not been a pleasant meal, yet he was unable to put his finger on the undercurrents of feeling.

"We'll see, we'll see." Julien seemed to be considering the purchase of an automobile.

Followed by a boy bearing the tray with china and silver, Doudouce brought the coffee. Doudouce was in her Sunday finery. She wore the large breast pin willed her by Olympe's mother, and gold rings in the pierced lobes of her ears. The slight mustache on her upper lip was glistening, for the day was warm.

"I'll need some years of experience before I'm qualified to give an opinion. You see, I just graduated from the engineering school last June, and I've been with my father barely a year," Harry Lockwood apologized.

This was in answer to Julien's probing. He could not get the elder Lockwood to commit himself on the erection of the causeway. He did not know whether the engineer was inclined to recommend the project to his superiors or not. The most Lockwood would say was that it looked feasible, was possible, and would most certainly be profitable. Julien wishfully envisioned Mandeville as a flourishing suburb of New Orleans, and himself as tycoon of the town. One thing was certain: he was not going to sink any more money in the Mandeville Boat Company, or in the wharf, either. Leon was right: boats and the wharf would be superfluous once the causeway was built. The wharf, in particular, was a source of woe. It was always in need of repairs.

"The one thing that does worry my father is the problem of the seasonal hurricanes you have down here," Harry went on. "I mean, the terrific storms of the autumn equinox. If they can toss giant steamers up on the docks at New Orleans, and twist the steel girders of concrete buildings into pretzels. . . ." He smiled, not wanting to go too far.

"Nonsense," Julien said impatiently. "It is not as bad as all that."

When the younger members of the party had retired to the croquet court behind the house, with Madame Larouche filling the role of chaperone, Nanaine and Olympe turned on each other with the impetus of floods breaking their dams.

"My dear, did you hear! Her *husband's* paintings. . . ."

"His father remembered her!"

"As who could forget!"

"Still speaking to strange men!"

"As if buying *one* picture made him a friend of her family!"

"Her *family*, my dear!"

"Did Judge Chambert *paint?*" Julien inquired, frowning in his effort to remember.

"Don't be a fool!" Olympe scolded. "Have you forgotten?"

"What?"

"*We* have not forgotten!" Nanaine declared, beating her breast with a clenched hand.

"Papa," Colette came to her father's rescue, "she was Judge Chambert's *wife*."

"*Colette!*" Olympe gasped. "How do you *know* such things. . . ."

"Doudouce. . . ." Colette bit her lip.

"Yes, I know, I know," Julien said. "That is why, when you said her husband's *paintings*. . . ."

"You are stupid!" Olympe said, stamping her foot.

"Ah! Oh yes. Yes, of course. . . ." Julien recollected. "I see. I remember. An artist. . . ."

"Was she divorced?" Victor asked. He recalled Judge Chambert's purple face, the glazed expression—as if he had seen a ghost.

A hush fell on the ladies at the mention of divorce.

"You see. . . ." Julien cleared his throat.

"Julien!" Olympe reprimanded. She cast a quick glance at Colette and then turned large fierce eyes on her husband. He understood at once that some things were not to be discussed in the presence of pure young ladies.

Nanaine was too aroused to bother with a strict observance of the proprieties.

"If you want to know the truth," she blurted out to Victor, "she ran off with some godless Bohemian—while still married to the Judge—and they lived all over Europe together! *As man and wife!*"

"Oh." Victor smiled. "I was beginning to think she had committed some horrible crime."

"You don't think that a horrible crime?" Her black eyes snapped.

"Moving into 'Belle Pointe' tomorrow. . . ." Julien mused. "Then she means to stay."

"She has no right to live among us!" Olympe cried dramatically.

"What you want to say, my dear," Julien said coldly, his narrowed eyes boring into hers, "is that she has no right to *live*."

Olympe's pale lips parted in surprise. It was the first time Julien had spoken to her like that in Victor's memory. She fell back as if struck and began to fumble in her bag for her salts.

Colette was unable to sleep. Through the leaves of the magnolia that grew outside her room, Victor could see her dimly at her prie-dieu. Her lamp was turned low, and a candle, set in a glass of water, burned on a small table before her as if she were petitioning heaven to grant a wish. She was late at her prayers. It was after twelve o'clock.

Victor himself had no desire to sleep. He had been annoyed to find red brick around the legs of his four-poster, and between the sheets, leaves of the male and female basil bushes. In his irritation, he cursed Cumba. The day had passed none too pleasantly, and the depression he had felt in the morning, when contemplating Uncle Ulysse and his stubborn refusal to live in the present, now returned, without apparent reason, to nag him.

The night was sultry, giving fair warning of the heat to come. The mosquito bar, visible through the open doors of his bedroom, hung limp; not a breath of air stirred its net folds. Victor walked around to the front gallery and looked out over the lake. The water had a smooth, oily sheen in the starlight. Here and there patches of phosphorus glowed on the swells. The moon was rising, a bright ball behind the trees.

A sense of suffocation assailed him. He had a fantastic idea that the walls of "Clair de Lune" were invisibly coming toward him, closing around him, crowding the air out of his lungs. He went down the stairs and walked aimlessly about the lawn.

His mind slipped back to the long hot days in the hospital at Ancon. The fevered faces of Hungarians, West Indians, Spaniards, Italians, Frenchmen, Chinese passed his inner eye in unending parade. On the Isthmus he had known all kinds of men— all races, religions, creeds and colors. He had had acquaintance with all kinds of minds; and he had come to recognize that the brain that controlled the pile driver and electric drill, or merely

51

coordinated the simple movements involved in slinging a shovel, was as important to the mutual endeavor as the brain of the skilled technician, the engineer, and the doctor. There no man was negligible, none lacked the dignity of a calling.

He wondered why he thought of all this now. Homesick for the hospital, perhaps. He smiled. . . . There was a shadow of irony there that evaded the grasp. On the trip home he had been looking for a freedom he had not found. Here was the summer house he loved—the same; here the town of his happiest days, unchanged; here his people, and the townspeople he had always known. Yet everything was different, he could not say how or why. The elusive transformation distressed him, leaving the taste of disappointment in his mouth. This was his first vacation in five years, and at the moment, at any rate, he was not enjoying it. Perhaps it was wrong to try to recapture the freedom of youth, or, if not wrong, at least unwise.

His thoughts progressed from past to present to future. Somehow the increasing mistiness of what lay ahead made him uneasy. He could not pin the years to come to any definite background of place, and his mind shifted quickly from an impressive office in New Orleans to the carbolic-smelling wards of Ancon. He knew from his conversations with Colette about Panama that she entertained, like so many, a revolting picture of snakes and sickness and heat and jungle. Would even the neat screened bungalows of the Married Quarters make an adequate home for her? He wondered. . . . Besides, Colette, like all of them, already considered him the colleague of their cousin, Dr. Alcide Larouche. Julien had said, "You're handsome enough, my boy. You'll be a great success. You'll outshine Alcide with that ugly scar of his, I can tell you!" His "bright future" suddenly shone with the spurious glitter of carnival tinsel.

He was startled by the rustle of skirts behind him. It was Colette. She had slipped through the gate in the Cherokee hedge, holding up the train of her long silk wrapper from the dew that already covered the grass. As she came closer he noticed that the ruffled neck of her nightgown protruded, and her hair hung in a curling mass down her back to the waist. She laid her hand on his arm.

"Vic dear, is something troubling you? What are you thinking about?"

"I was just thinking—well—of the men I worked with at Ancon. It's hard to explain. They worked with their hands, most of them, but it was important work. . . ." His voice trailed off.

"Is that all?"

"Not quite." He smiled, showing her the sprays of basil he had been absently twirling in his fingers. "I've been crossed."

"No, you haven't. That means *good* luck. Abundance, happiness, completion."

"Don't tell me *you* believe in grigri?"

"Well"—she looked down at her clasped hands—"if I wanted something very badly, and I was afraid I wouldn't get it, I would try voodoo, for want of anything better." She raised her eyes to his face again. "There *is* something troubling you, Vic."

"Nothing important." He hesitated a moment before he said slowly, "It's just that I expected to find things the same here, and somehow—I don't know how—they've changed."

"*They* are the same. It's you who have changed."

"If they were the same, I'd be happy here as I always was."

"It is because they are the same that you are unhappy."

He reverted playfully to a common gesture of bewilderment, frowning and knocking his knuckles against his forehead.

"Zulime is right," she went on. "You have grown big, oh, so big. Doudouce tells me she mutters continually, 'Old Zuzu's Ti Toto gone.' She knew it the minute she saw you." She added softly, "And so did I."

He laughed. "And what has caused this unanimous conviction?"

"Your mouth has a stronger set to it, and there are lines. Your eyes are kinder, and your face has a new, serious quality." She went on in a rush. "You care what happens to your fellow beings."

"A bad habit for a doctor."

"The rest of us," she continued, as if she had not heard him, "only care what happens to ourselves. Like Papa, buying up all the land before people know about the causeway. Like Nanaine, cutting out your life to fit her pride. Like me. . . ."

". . . worrying about my worries!"

He drew her into his arms. In her heelless slippers, the top of her head reached only to his chin. He buried his face in her sweet-smelling hair. Her hands crept to his shoulders, her fingers curling over them in a tight grip.

"Oh, Vic—" she sounded close to tears—"I don't mind that you've grown. You are more wonderful than ever, and to me, you were wonderful ever since I can remember! But I have the most frightful feeling sometimes. I can't explain it. . . . It's as if—as if you'd somehow grown *away* from us. Oh, Vic, suppose you've grown so far away that we can't reach you! Suppose. . . ."

"Suppose Doudouce finds you here!" Over her head he could see a shadow moving about in Colette's room.

The dew was dripping from the trees now, glistening like tiny eyes on the grass. He picked her up and carried her as far as the hedge. Her arms wound around his neck—close, strong—as if she wished to make of them an enduring wall.

Eight

It was late afternoon of the first Sunday in June. Victor was lying in the hammock. The lake was as smooth as skin; there had been no wind all day. Everywhere there was a sense of waiting for sunset and the cool relief of dusk. In the stillness the band playing for the picnic in Jackson Park could be heard faintly.

The music made the doctor think of the Saturday-night dances at the Tivoli Hotel in Ancon. From that point his mind moved into a groove of indecision that day by day was growing deeper. Only Colette had kept him from returning. . . . Three weeks had already elapsed.

54

Tallyhos and surreys from Bidault's livery stable were passing as the picnic headed for the boat back to the city. He heard the whistle of the *Marguerite* as she approached the Cape Charles wharf.

The wheels rolled away and his thoughts fell back into their rut. Three weeks more would bring him to July. Should he return to Ancon then? Counting his sick leave, which he had never used, and nine holidays, which he had never been able to take, he had due eighty-one days, approximately three months. Until the middle of August.

He would use more leave, accumulated over the past five years, in November, when the summer exodus moved back to the city from resorts and abroad. The formal announcement of his engagement was to be made in New Orleans. At that time he would give Colette the large ruby surrounded by diamonds that his father had given his mother, and the date of the wedding would be set, probably sometime after Lent. He could return to Ancon at the end of November, but by Easter he would be compelled to come to a definite decision between Panama and his partnership with Larouche.

He rose impatiently from the hammock and went into the salon. There he found Nanaine mending a music album. She looked up.

"Weren't you to go to the Roussels' this evening?"

"For supper with Colette and Olympe, later."

"So they got off all right?"

"Yes." She was referring to Julien and Leon, who had left on the yacht *Le Cygne* an hour before. Leon, having graduated the previous Friday, was to start slaving, as he described the negligible duties to be assigned him, in his father's office. "They took the Lockwoods with them. A meeting is slated with the politicians who are going to push the State's permission for the causeway."

"Did Madame Larouche go, too?"

The doctor was thinking that Harry would probably have preferred to stay, if Leon was right. "He is completely gone on that girl with the short hair. . . ."

55

"Madame Larouche, did you ask? Yes, she went, and Féfé, too, of course."

"Then Madame Vigée is in that big house alone?"

"Madame Larouche behaves as if she were fleeing the small-pox," the doctor said irritably. "What is the matter with her?"

"She cannot endure the thought of . . ." Nanaine's mouth set in a hard line. She slapped with unnecessary vigor at a patch she had pasted on the reverse of a torn sheet. ". . . of those people at 'Belle Pointe,' " she finished.

"Why, for the love of God?" He was more annoyed than ever. "The mother can't be such a monster, and as for the girl, she looks like an angel!"

Nanaine's hands came to a sudden dead stop. "You think so, do you?"

"Yes, I do. They seemed human enough on the boat. I borrowed their binoculars."

She slammed the album shut. "So I have heard. That chatter-box of a Féfé Larouche has scattered the pretty story of your incognito—and other details of your eccentric behavior—to the four winds!"

"I confess I showed none of her mother's inclination to flee two charming ladies."

"Indeed! Must we consider you, then, among that woman's admirers?" She turned her black eyes on him with the sharpness of a searchlight.

At that moment they heard the screaming on the lake.

From the gallery he could see the wild confusion at the end of the Cape Charles wharf. A glance told him that the *Marguerite* was in an odd position; but it was the splashing and struggling, the cries of hundreds of people at her water line that held him for a full minute paralyzed with horror.

He ran without stopping from the house to the pier's end. He was conscious of others running from shore with him, and he knew that crippled Zeph, hampered by his heavy shoe, was somewhere behind. Skiffs and pirogues were putting out from all directions. All at once, the church bells began to jangle insanely, announcing disaster.

He paused only long enough to strip off his coat and kick off his shoes, then threw himself into the water. He had no idea what had happened, but was aware that an apron of the wharf was floating and that people were grabbing for its ragged edges. The weight of numbers submerged the platform and as many fell away or were knocked off by the stronger, and as the lightened platform surged again to the surface, he saw that women and children had been pinned underneath. He dove and took hold of a young girl by her hair; perhaps she was already dead. Swimming toward the torn pier, he clung to a piling with one arm while downreaching hands took the girl from his other. Then he struggled back through the nightmare, returning with a second burden. This happened again and again.

In a short time he had established a kind of system, and now he no longer had to concentrate desperately on his route from the drowning back to the dock; he went about it as from habit. He became conscious of life preservers being fought for, lifeboats hitting the water; he could distinguish the shouting on deck and the hoarse cursing of the crew from the shrieking and strangling around him. Inane details stood out and caught the corner of his eye: a woman's soggy pompadour falling into her eyes; a picnic basket floating past his shoulder. Once he caught sight of Zeph swimming toward the pilings with a limp child under his arm.

A round object, gaudy with red and gold braid, bobbed about, a young girl clinging to it with a bleeding arm. It was the drum, lately used in the band that had played in Jackson Park. She is all right for a while, Victor thought. He swam back and dove under the debris of the apron, keeping his eyes open under water. He came to the surface again with an old woman. She was unconscious, perhaps dead, but he could not stop to decide. He delivered her up to the hands on the wharf. When he returned, the drum was drifting out into the thick of the struggle. Immediately a tangle of desperate hands rose around it, clawing and clutching. The drum went under with its heavy freight. The girl let go; she sank slowly bottomward like a water-soaked rag. Victor caught at her. The arm that was not bleeding was broken. She had fainted and it was easy to swim back with her. Most of them were like frantic cats, scratching and kicking, and once he had had to strike a boy insensible with his fist.

This time, among the hands stretched to help were the age-spotted pair of Dr. Jolivet.

"Careful," Victor cautioned. "Care with that arm."

The old doctor's voice came back at him in hoarse English.

"Goddammit, get out of that lake and come up here!"

"They're drowning. . . ." He didn't hear himself. Jolivet must have read his lips.

"They're drowning up here, too! I can't put breath back into all these bodies alone!"

The lifeboats were filled now. Skiffs, loaded down, were making for shore. The splashing and struggling had diminished, the screaming had become shouts interspersed with intelligible words. Those who were still afloat were safe, those who were not were by now beyond saving. Victor caught hold of the studding between piles and raised himself out of the water. Hands came down to assist him. He was not above needing them. His shirt was torn from his shoulders, his sleeves in tatters. All at once, he felt tired. He got a knee hold on the studding and had all he could do to pull himself up on the wharf.

Dozens of dripping men, women, and children lay scattered about, crumpled and inert. There was a desperate lot of work to be done. A great deal of it would be futile. Where to start . . . where to start. . . . He got down on his knees beside the young girl with the broken arm. Her clothes had been ripped half off in the fight for the drum, and one firm breast was bared. He drew a remnant of lace over her chest, pushed back the light-brown hair that stuck to her forehead and cheeks.

Grasp both arms near the elbows, sweep them upward above the head. . . . The fracture—he could work only with the good arm.

Presently he saw that it no longer mattered. She was dead.

At the close of twilight, the townspeople brought lanterns and lamps out to the end of the wharf.

The two doctors had never stopped, going from one to the other of the victims, repeating the same ministrations in the same methodical fashion until they appeared more like machines than men. Victor had used the last strip of his shirt for a swab, wrapping it around his forefinger to wipe still another mouth free of froth and mucus. He pulled off his damp undershirt and tore it into fresh pieces.

By now, the various versions of what had happened came out of the clutter of voices around him. The apron of the wharf had collapsed under the weight of numbers when the crowd rushed forward, all eager to be first to board the *Marguerite* and get the best places on her decks. . . . Positively not. The platform had been wrenched from the pier when the *Marguerite's* cables pulled a piling loose. . . . Nonsense. The *Marguerite* had not yet landed; her line had been thrown, but not made fast. The disaster had been caused by her bumping into the apron. Somebody saw the platform sway when the boat struck; somebody else heard the crack of the shattering piles.

Victor remembered Julien's saying the wharf was in need of repairs. *But with the causeway coming, the wharf will be obsolete. Not one penny more will my company spend. . . .*

There was no use trying with this one, or that, or that. They were too far gone when taken out of the water. He lifted a rigid child. Her head lolled on a broken neck. On one side of the wharf, in a neat row, lay the dead. Victor had an insane desire to stop and count them. Father Guichard got in his way. The priest was closing open eyes, folding hands before they stiffened, making the sign of the cross with his long arm outstretched. Two Sisters from the Catholic school threw sheets over the half-naked dead.

Victor wiped the sweat out of his eyes. He was tired. He was so tired that he did not see Nanaine until Cumba, who accompanied her, cried out at the sight of the covered bodies. He looked up into his aunt's face in surprise. In his arms lay the

59

dead girl with the light-brown hair whom he was about to carry over and place with the others.

Nanaine's eyes moved over him coldly.

"Have you forgotten you were to have supper tonight with the Roussels?"

"Yes. Yes, I have forgotten."

The dead girl's shoe lay at the hem of Nanaine's skirt. She stepped around it.

"I shall explain to them that a good memory is not among your many gifts."

She turned and walked away.

Victor carried the girl over to the lengthening row and laid her down gently. He was too tired for anger. He only felt sick.

The *Marguerite*, due to leave for New Orleans at six o'clock, left at nine with as many bodies as could be identified. The dead whose families were not known were put in the care of Mr. Ovide Clouzat, undertaker and son-in-law of Dr. Jolivet. Shortly before midnight, the *Camelia*, requisitioned for the emergency, returned to the city with a number of survivors. But a good many, dazed and horror-stricken, refused to board a boat, and to these Mr. Mugnier threw open his hotel, while the sufferers from broken bones, shock, sprains, and lesser injuries were taken into private homes. Every carriage and wagon was put to use, even some from the livery stable of Mayor Bidault, who usually was more careful to make sure his patrons could pay the fee.

The two doctors and volunteers from the town worked all night. Zeph, on his uneven legs, wheeled barrows of sand the length of the pier, together with flatirons collected from the neighborhood, to be heated and applied to numb limbs and feet. The charcoal furnaces that on Mondays supported boilers full of wash glowed until dawn at the end of the wharf. The ladies had sent their servants with as many blankets and coats as were available in a climate which seldom required such equipment, and Bazile had brought the medical supplies ordered by Victor from the druggist, Guy Chauvin.

Victor had a confused recollection of stopping once to drink the hot, strong coffee Doudouce handed him with some reference to Colette. He needed the coffee, but refused food. On the beach, the ladies had established a headquarters of their own, supplying the rescuers with refreshment. Lamps set on impromptu tables flickered among the trees.

Dr. Jolivet went home around four o'clock. The points of his mustache drooped, his eyes were bloodshot, and his habitually neat clothes were soggy with lake water. Reluctantly, Victor gave up a woman on whom he had been working for several hours. She was the last in whom he had hoped to revive a lingering breath of life. He pulled a sheet over her face, and went to join the men who were still searching for bodies.

By lantern light they dragged the lake until dawn. The fisherman Alceste Moreau and his eleven sons strained the waters nearer shore with their seines; they found two drowned that had drifted beachward. The *Camelia,* some hours before, had gone close to land, stirring up the lake bottom with her propeller to dislodge bodies buried in the mud, and skiffs ablaze with pine flares searched for any that might have floated out. There was hardly any tide; the water continued to be calm, and so clear that peering closely with a flare one could see the ribbed sand of its floor. Zeph found a dead man hugging a pile. The grip of the corpse on the barnacled wood was so tight that the knuckles had to be broken to release him.

The grappling-hook crew started work at daylight.

Nine

The sensational fact of Dr. Jolivet's change of domicile to the house of the Widow Aurélie Coulon soon became common property. There was no one who did not acknowledge the doctor's need of a woman's presence, particularly in view of the increased ardors of his profession during and after the accident. Although he had a good housegirl and a fine cook, they could not, of course, supply that sense of home essential to a man's morale. What people did not discuss was the doctor's failure to go, if loneliness weighed on him, to his daughter and son-in-law, the Clouzats.

Since the wharf disaster, however, in reporting which the New Orleans *Picayune* had lavishly praised the valiant work done by Dr. Cyprien Jolivet and his young colleague but lately arrived from Panama, the old doctor had become the man of the hour, and no one dreamed of censuring the reigning hero. Instead blame fell heavily on Mr. Ovide Clouzat, who was accused of barring his door, out of spite, to this worthy man. Everybody knew Mr. Clouzat's jovial saying: Jolivet was a good doctor, but a bad father-in-law—too many cures, too few coffins. He gave the undertaker little business. The truth was that Mr. Clouzat was not temperamentally suited to his vocation: he had a round, red face prone to crack into laughter at the slightest joke, and a luxuriant black mustache which, indecorously for an undertaker, did not droop. People resented being buried by an entrepreneur who had the appearance of someone at a party. They wanted a man who wore black cravats and a mournful air. Yet, though many a corpse cheated Mr. Clouzat by taking the *Camelia* to the city, the Clouzats were not destitute. Madame Clouzat, seizing the bull by the tail since, as the townspeople said, her husband would not take him by the horns, catered to christenings, and her cakes and punches brought in a good income, where babies could not be counted on the fingers of one hand.

It was the undertaker who spread the rumor, in self-defense, that the doctor had removed to Aurélie's because she was so sick as to require his presence day and night. And when reproached by his father-in-law for a liar and a fool, he had replied, "If I were a fool, I would not be smart enough to lie. And she *is* sick. Lovesick."

"I speak to you frankly," Dr. Jolivet continued. It was not yet ten o'clock. Bazile had brought coffee, and the two physicians sat in the latticed basement at "Clair de Lune," talking over their cups. "It is you who deserve the honors. You did more by far.

Perhaps if I were younger. . . . No, even so, I don't think I would have entered that hell in the water. I would have kept myself high and dry, in readiness to revive them, instead of pulling them out so they wouldn't *have* to be revived. But of course I don't swim."

"You helped enormously by staying where you were, then," Victor laughed.

"I had thought to make a public statement of the true facts. Then Aurélie came, and when I saw how greatly the newspapers had influenced her in my direction, when all these months I could not budge her an inch. . . ." He turned his palms up, fingers spread wide.

"The facts are true enough as they're known."

"She convinced herself I was exhausted and insisted on taking me home to care for me," he said. "With her two daughters and their families in the house, we are naturally well chaperoned." The doctor sighed.

"No doubt it will do you no harm." Dr. Jolivet's eyebrows shot upward, and the younger man hastened to explain, "I mean, to be cared for."

"I accept her favors under false pretense, but"—with a shrug— "all is fair in love and war." He allowed Bazile to refill his cup. "Wait!" The older man's face lit up. "Surely you would like to wear your laurels for—some lady of your own?"

Victor dodged his meaning. "My aunt does not appreciate laurels soaked in sweat and sand."

"Ah!" Jolivet winked. "I was not thinking of. . . ."

Victor could not complain, however, about Nanaine's attitude toward the survivors. It was impeccably gracious. Three frightened women had occupied the east wing until this morning, when Nanaine's efforts to prevail on them to remain longer had met with polite promises to come again. She herself accompanied them in her carriage to the railway station, and saw them on the train with a hamper of lunch and a bottle of wine. Her generous conduct was in extraordinary contrast to her cool treatment of him when he had returned from the lake after having been away for nearly forty-eight hours, the black beginning of a beard showing on his face and his bare torso burned darker by the sun. He had reflected with bitter amusement that while she exerted herself on a grand scale to succor the victims, she considered it demeaning to soil the hands or bend the back to save them.

"I was thinking," Jolivet persisted, "of Mamzelle Colette."

"I believe she has enough laurels of her own." He smiled, recalling how Colette, always accompanied by Doudouce, who adored her, came out to the end of the wharf and herself carried home an injured child. There were still five people at "Beaux Arbres" receiving Colette's care.

"Thank you for looking in at the Roussels'," Dr. Jolivet continued. "How is the boy's leg?"

"Only an ecchymosis. They'll be going home tomorrow."

"Would that free you sufficiently to take on a few more cases?" The old doctor looked at him slyly from the side.

"I'm busy night and day wasting time," Victor bantered, "but I'll see what I can do."

"*I'm* not exhausted, but my patience is." Jolivet's mouth set firm. "It does me a lot of good to be at Aurélie's house when I have to be out of it most of the time."

"Well?"

"You might look after the people Fauvette d'Eaubonne took in."

"All right."

"Ah," he said, rising, "and Fauvette d'Eaubonne is so close to 'Belle Pointe,' and there are half a dozen cases of cuts and a fracture there. The Delamare woman and her daughter are taking care of them. Would you mind if I stole your leisure as well as your laurels?"

"Belle Pointe" was named for the beautiful point of land on which it stood at the extreme east end of the beach. A triangle heavily wooded with live oaks jutted sharply out where the Bayou Castain flowed into the lake, and somewhat back from its apex stood the old Delamare place in all its white majesty. It was built in the Greek revival style, Doric columns rising to the height of its two stories on three sides. The white-marble shaft of a sundial gleamed in a garden that had lost its formality through lack of attention, and as Victor approached, gardeners were busy with shears and clippers at the box-bordered walks and the hedges.

He remembered "Belle Pointe" as being much more spacious. The exposed point had receded, gnawed away on two sides by the continual lap and lash of water. He had come here as a boy to watch fascinatedly from the bayou's bank the big whirlpools that would open and wheel about below, and the savage eddies that would suck at the earth until chunks of soft loam fell away into the stream. Inch by inch, foot by foot, this had gone on for years, and now the oaks along the bend showed naked roots, and moss from the overhanging branches dragged in the water.

Descending at the gate, Victor noticed that scarcely three yards remained between the east wing of the house and the bayou's brink. The greedy current had bitten off fence and trees.

He was amazed to find Julien taking coffee with Palmyre Delamare at a table laid in the piazza. Julien was equally surprised to see him, the surgeon's satchel belonging to Jolivet in hand.

"I cannot induce Madame to sell," Julien hastened to explain. Though the afternoon was mild, he took out his handkerchief and mopped at his forehead and temples.

"On the contrary," Palmyre Delamare said. "Instead of selling, I wish to buy. Doctor, do you know of a piece of land I could acquire to pin under my bedroom window? If I don't, I shall soon be sleeping in the bayou."

She laughed apologetically for her little piece of foolery. He saw that her eyes were almost green, and startlingly clear. Her fair skin was emphasized by the gleaming auburn hair. Wasp waist, rounded hips, and full bust gave her the figure of fashion. Without doubt she was a rarely beautiful woman, perhaps the most beautiful he had ever seen. Colette . . . yes. But there was something about Palmyre that surpassed Colette. He could not name it. A deeper warmth. A fullness.

"The breakwater preserves the beach, to a degree," the doctor remarked. "I don't know why the town has never extended it around the point."

"Taxes," Julien said. "It would require more taxes. But I shall speak to the Council about extending the breakwater," he volunteered briskly. "I shall let Madame know what is said."

"Thank you." She smiled. "Then I shall sleep much better, I'm sure. The other night I was awakened by a horrid noise. *Boom!* like an explosion. I ran to the window. It was moonlight, and I was just in time to see two more of my trees topple into the water. The birds flew out of them shrieking."

"I observed when I came in," Victor said. "Part of your fence, too."

"Something must be done." Julien seemed quite anxious. He wiped the moisture from his forehead again. "We'll see, we'll see."

"Will you show me to the patients?" the doctor addressed Palmyre.

She rang a small silver bell, and a black girl came slapping along in house slippers.

"Bibi, take the doctor upstairs," she said in Negro French. "Ou Mamzelle Miyám?"

"Li courri dans boutique de l'apothécaire."

"My daughter went to the drugstore, but Bibi. . . ." She broke off, laughing. "There! You are a Louisianian, too. You understood her as well as I."

"Miyám?"

"Miriam." She laughed again, a deep, rich sound. "You cannot expect our people here to say that. I have almost fallen into the habit of calling her Miyám myself."

"I must go." Julien rose nervously. "I have not yet been home."

The doctor followed Bibi to the stairs. Behind him, he heard Palmyre say, "If ever I decide to sell, M'sieur, it will be to you that I shall offer first."

Glancing down from the first landing, he saw Julien's bald head in its black fringe bent over her beautiful hands.

He regretted that he was not going to see Miriam. She had not inherited the vivid coloring of her mother, but she had a pastel prettiness, the more fascinating because it held an elusive charm. He recalled that she was slightly taller, and more slender. She was only seventeen. Jolivet had mentioned her age casually that morning in his office. She had an air of originality about her, probably because of her short hair. It struck the eye startlingly in a feminine society devoted exclusively to pompadours, puffs, and plaits.

These irrelevancies ran through his head as his practiced hands strapped a sprained ankle, eased a splint. The cases of shock were recovering rapidly. All these people could, in his opinion, return to their homes tomorrow. They were beginning to worry about their families, who they knew were worried about them. They inquired about train schedules and the hiring of carriages to take them to the station.

He was following Bibi down the stairs when the stir of a commotion on the other side of the piazza reached them. Bibi stiffened; she stopped so short that the doctor nearly collided with her. The skin of her black neck puckered under her tiny tight braids. "Allons, allons." He had to say it twice before she would budge.

Miriam had returned. She stood with Palmyre and the gardeners before some repulsive object that lay on the flagstones.

"That wanga bad . . . ," one of the men was saying over and over, his eyes sticking out.

"Baptiste, who did that!" Palmyre demanded of the oldest. "Didn't you see? You were around here trimming the grass!"

"God knows, Mist'ess." The old fellow shook his gray woolly head vehemently.

As the doctor came closer, he saw a skinned cat. The hair remaining on its head and tail indicated that it had been black. Its teeth, locked tight in its last agony, were bared. A shriveled lemon that had been dipped in red wax was pierced through with a black cord and tied around its bloody neck.

Miriam looked at him without speaking. Her dark blue eyes filled with tears.

"Bibi! Come here!" Palmyre ordered.

The girl hung back, flattened against the wall. "I din' do dat! It wa'n't me!"

"Tell me what it means," Palmyre said more kindly.

"It mean somebody wan' mek Mist'ess move fum yeh." She put her hands to her face and burst into frightened sobbing.

"Baptiste, take it away and bury it."

The old fellow stepped back. His mouth fell open and he shook all over.

"Lemme at it." The youngest of the three grinned. "Ah might be 'fraid of a *live* cat, it show me its teet' like dat, but Ah'm not 'fraid no old *daid* cat, not me!" He scooped it up on his shovel and carried it off.

Miriam walked with the doctor to the gate. She looked crisp and cool in her starched white waist with the low collar and billowing elbow sleeves. Her gored skirt brushed him once or twice as they walked side by side.

"What is it all about?" She faced him in the middle of the path. "I don't understand. . . ."

"Don't try to. It's just some nonsense that began in the jungles of Africa and grew in the West Indies and was transplanted here among our servants—and many of ourselves."

"But it must have some meaning. . . ."

"What makes it dangerous is that sometimes it *seems* to work. Like the time a jealous milkman milked a wet towel and all the cows of his competitors went dry."

She threw her head back and laughed. Then she grew suddenly serious.

"It is a shame, though. That innocent little animal. . . ."

"Don't feel sorry for the cat. To be effective he had to be in the cemetery at midnight. And he was probably stalking sleeping birds."

He smiled down at her. She smiled back.

"If you say so. . . ."

They reached the gate.

68

"I think I am a little superstitious, myself," she said thoughtfully. "You see, one Sunday I burned a candle in church and instead of saying a prayer, I made a wish. And it has come true."

"I shall know what to do when next I want something."

"The wish—it was to see *you* again."

The confession amazed him. It was made with the candor of a child.

"I hope all your wishes come true so easily," he said. "But you must wish for something better next time."

Latching the gate for her, he asked, "Who are your servants?"

"Bibi. Baptiste the gardener. The other men are just temporary helpers. And this week we hired a new cook. She used to work for Dr. Jolivet."

"Did his housegirl come, too?"

"No. She was taken by Madame Dufour, wife of the baker."

"Ah"—the doctor laughed—"from now on, our bread will be flavored strongly with everything that happens in your house."

Zeph was waiting for him in the surrey. The doctor looked back as they turned onto the beach road. She was still standing at the gate.

Olympe had fainted.

Leon, returning with Julien and the Lockwoods on *Le Cygne*, said Papa had stayed on the wharf to look over the things recovered from the drowned for possible identification marks. Instead, Julien had hired a carriage from Bidault and gone to "Belle Pointe." The news was reported to Olympe by Doudouce, who had brought it home with the daily bread.

Victor found Olympe's pulse steady, her heart regular. He was not sure what to prescribe for tantrums. If she wished to remain in her carved mahogany bed, gazing with tear-drenched eyes at the blue satin tester, fingering her gold and crystal rosary, frail as a lily of the valley in her Paris negligee frothing with Valenciennes and ribbons—well, that was as good a sedative as any. She turned her face into her pillow and cried silently when the doctor was not alarmed at her condition.

Leon came and sat on the edge of the bed and held her hand. He tried to cheer her with a report of the rich and well-connected young ladies with whom he had danced in New Orleans at the Grunewald, with the letters he had from other young ladies traveling with their mothers in Europe this summer, of the cable from Elise Deschamps, who hated Biarritz because he was not there. He kissed her fingers tenderly, held them to his cheek, and casually mentioned the superior advantages of the Packard Elise's father had bought.

Julien drank brandy and perspired. He walked the length of the drawing room, his handkerchief every minute to his face. "I *told* her I went there only on *business*. What the devil! Let Bidault have 'Belle Pointe,' then." In the few words he had with Victor afterward, he confessed that he had been to "Belle Pointe" many times before. Did Olympe tell Victor that? No? Well, thank God she didn't know. . . . He put his handkerchief in his high, starched collar and wiped around his neck.

Colette was waiting for him at the end of the long hall, startlingly lovely in the cool shadow. She ran toward him, and for a few moments stood breathless in the circle of his arms, as if she had been fleeing something and had at last found safety.

"Let's go in here," she said, leading him into a small sitting room adjoining.

They remained standing by the curtained window. He took her chin in his hand and, raising her face, saw a little frown of fear, or anxiety, or puzzlement between her eyes, and the faint rings beneath them. He was reminded that he had noticed a light in her room until late the night before.

"I ought to scold you for not going to bed earlier," he said, "but instead. . . ." He kissed her.

The frown vanished and she smiled. "I was talking to Doudouce. . . ."

"Until one o'clock in the morning?"

"I couldn't sleep, so I called Doudouce, and we talked."

"Why couldn't you sleep? And what did you talk about?" There was real concern for her behind his bantering tone.

She looked up at him gravely. "I don't know—so many things. . . ." Suddenly she put up her arms and clung to him. "Oh, Vic. What is happening to us? We can't be sure of anything any more! The other night I dreamed it was spring, and the Mississippi River was at flood tide, and it was eating away at the levee without our knowing it, and all at once the levee went. . . ."

"And it was only a dream." He drew his fingers slowly through the heavy wefts of her hair, which today she was wearing unbound.

"No. It wasn't—it isn't—a dream. . . ." The frown came back. "I feel something happening around us, Vic. I don't know exactly what. Something that only some magic can stop. . . ."

"You *have* been talking to Doudouce!"—he laughed quietly— "I suppose she knows just the right kind of charm to use?"

"Vic, don't. . . ." She colored self-consciously. "Don't make fun. . . ."

"Ma mignonne. . . ." He used the French tenderly, softly, and added in English, "You *are* my darling."

"Am I, Vic?" She looked deep into his eyes. "Will I always be?"

"As long as you promise not to worry about dreams."

"I promise." She brightened, then at once grew serious again. "But some of it is so real, so—so frightening! Like— Oh, Vic, what is happening to my mother and father?"

They heard Doudouce in another part of the house, asking loudly, "Anybody see Miché Vic? Miché Vic still 'round here?"

Colette's hand tightened about his arm in a grip that felt strangely frantic.

"Nanaine is angry with you, Vic."

"What is it now?" Impatience made his voice sharp.

"She is furious with you for going to 'Belle Pointe.' " Her eyes, searching his, were deeply troubled.

"So that's abroad already!" He snapped his fingers, and his lips set in a line of annoyance.

Her mouth trembled. "We knew about it here even before you went. Bazile heard Dr. Jolivet ask you, and carried the news back to the kitchen. And from your kitchen to ours. . . ." She spread out her hands.

"Are *you* angry with me?" He could not have said why he asked her that.

She shook her head, he thought a little sadly. "How could I be angry with you for doing your duty?"

He drew a deep breath. "Then everything is all right! I can go home and get my head knocked off with perfect peace of mind!"

An urgent step sounded in the hall. They looked around into Doudouce's face, shining moistly with exertion.

"Good Lor', I been looking ev'where fo' Miché. His aunt want see him right away. La! La!" She raised her hands alongside her ears and wagged them vigorously, her eyes rolling to heaven.

Ten

Finally the family furor caused by Victor's visit to "Belle Pointe" died down. The injured had all returned to the city, and now, almost two weeks having passed since the day of the disaster, even that was pushed into the background by new events.

Great things were happening in the world. The *Picayune* reported the successful flight of an airplane at Brownsville, Texas. In Panama, half the excavation had been completed, and concrete work was beginning on the locks. In France, a young man named Blériot was planning to cross the English Channel in something called a "monoplane." But these miracles made little impression in Mandeville. The event of real importance to summer society was the hanging of a sign in the arched iron gateway of Fauvette d'Eaubonne's "Joli Bois."

The scandal which presently occupied the ladies was comprised in a simple motto painted in Spencerian script against a background of pine boughs.

Chambres à louer
Pension

Underneath, brazenly defying any possibility of doubt, it was explained in English. ROOMS AND BOARD. Fauvette, last of the d'Eaubonnes—they who had danced at the ball given for Lafayette on his visit to New Orleans in 1825, they who had eaten from golden plates with Henry Clay at the St. Louis Hotel, they who had a carte de visite of Mr. and Mrs. Jeff Davis, and (if Fauvette had not pawned it) a daguerreotype of General Beauregard in a velvet-lined case—Fauvette d'Eaubonne dared to advertise the predicament of her purse in two languages.

Once the d'Eaubonne purse had been proud and fat. Its present state of deflation was due to a sinister chain of circumstances. First, their lands above New Orleans on the Mississippi were swept by a calamitous crevasse. Houses, cattle, slaves, crops—all, with a number of d'Eaubonnes, were lost in the flood. The remnant clan had scarcely recovered when the War broke out between the states. Fauvette, until recently, had a rosewood piano that had been used as a horse trough by the Federals; most of the carved mahogany parlor suite had furnished them firewood on chilly evenings. Then, even the lowly insect had conspired against the d'Eaubonnes. One night the dread borer came upon the cane, and between sunset and sunrise not a stalk was left whole. Finally, Fauvette's father died of a heart attack on the floor of the Cotton Exchange in the Panic of January 1894.

Fauvette's mother spent the rest of her life fighting her poverty and preserving her pride. In this way she "kept up appearances." Madame d'Eaubonne's dinners continued to be the talk of downtown society. Sometimes one of the guests missed a hand-painted vase or reached for a silver tobacco box which was not there; but nobody, including Madame, really minded that the lavish Sunday soirées were a prelude to starvation for the rest of the week. Madame always managed to wear a wealthy smile, which was more visible to an astigmatic world than an empty stomach.

The little that Fauvette inherited from her mother included a large list of pawnshops and mortgage brokers, and to this legacy Fauvette herself added the variable fortunes of raffle and auction. It was a Northerner, loitering along Royal Street and attracted by the auctioneer's red flag and the colored man sitting on the banquette beating a tom-tom, who bought the framed bouquet of flowers made entirely from the hair of deceased d'Eaubonnes. "Ah!" said scandalized friends, "Fauvette's heart does not beat any more. It goes boom, boom! boom, boom! like an auctioneer's drum!"

Those who were most sentimental about the fate of the d'Eaubonne relics were troubled by no sentiment at all when dining on the proceeds of an ancestral wardrobe or some great-aunt's whatnot. Only Madame Vigée, whose summer home was next to "Joli Bois," and who never spoke except to criticize, said in her rasping voice, "Things have come to a sorry pass when a guest doesn't know whether she is eating the leg of a fowl or the leg of a chair!" But that was before it was known that Fauvette had taken the marble mantel from the parlor of the d'Eaubonnes' city house to make her mother's tombstone. This fact came out when the father of Alcide Larouche, who collected the house when he could not collect the mortgage, took possession. After that, Madame Vigée said, "Things have come to a sorry pass when a guest doesn't know whether she is looking at a mantelpiece or a mortuary tablet!"

Fauvette, at the moment the doctor came, was engaged in a game of poker with Mr. Néron Paviot, the nucleus and inspiration of her new enterprise. Mr. Paviot had come on the ill-fated picnic; he frequented crowds, sifting them for purchasers of his oil stock. But, until yesterday, when the youngest son of Alceste Moreau caught it in the seine with a mess of mullets, Mr. Paviot's portfolio, with all the crisp green certificates, had rested at the bottom of the lake, while Mr. Paviot himself, with a nail in his hand, had been resting at "Joli Bois." All the others had gone home, but Mr. Paviot, who had no home in particular, had put the idea into Fauvette's head of taking summer boarders, establishing himself as her first. It was a singular tribute to Fauvette's homely freckled face, red hair, and flat figure that none of the ladies talked about her—at least not for being alone in the house with a strange man.

"Good evening, M'sieur le docteur," Mr. Paviot said, rising.

The lake water and sand had been pressed out of his formal gray-striped trousers and Prince Albert, but he still grieved for his shoes and silk hat. Privately, the doctor thought him lucky to have kept his toupee, which he center-parted and combed in bangs over his forehead. For his lost patent leathers he had substituted a pair of canvas tennis shoes. "You see, my hand is well enough to hold a full house." He spread out on the card table three queens and a pair of tens, and raked in the chips.

Victor dressed the hand, and Mr. Paviot excused himself to go to the post office. He was expecting mail from Caddo Parish, where the drilling was about to begin.

"You come on foot?" Fauvette inquired. "I didn't hear a carriage stop."

"I walked. The weather is so fine."

He did not explain that Zeph had been penalized for taking the surrey to "Belle Pointe" without his aunt's permission. The doctor had overheard Glad and Cumba talking on his way to Zulime this morning. He knew Zeph better than to offer him the amount his aunt withheld from his wages. He would have to make it up to Zeph in some other way.

Fauvette was not fooled.

"You have not returned to 'Belle Pointe.'"

"I had no occasion to. All my charges there considered themselves well after my one visit. I don't know whether I cured them or scared them."

"Miriam painted that sign," Fauvette said irrelevantly. "It is not the sort of thing she does, but she did it for me."

"What sort of thing does she do?" He was aware of a feeling of interest.

"Landscapes. And stills. Her father taught her."

"Where is her father?" The question leaped out of him.

"He was taken with typhoid and died. It happened in Froissy, that little village near Paris."

They fell silent. The doctor sensed that Fauvette was considering how much she should tell. For his part, he was considering how much he could ask.

"Who do you suppose wants them to leave?" he asked at length. "I was there when a disgusting grigri. . . ."

"Who . . . oh, you mean Palmyre and her daughter. Practically everybody. But in particular. . . ." She hesitated.

"Go on."

"Well, your cousin Julien, who wants to buy the place. Bidault, for the same reason. Judge Chambert's daughters, like Madame Larouche, who have fled to New Orleans and won't come back till they have gone. Or Madame Vigée. . . ."

Or Olympe? the doctor asked himself. Or Nanaine? He put the latter idea aside with conviction. Nanaine was too religious to dabble in charms and conjuring.

"Maybe it is the Grand Zombie himself"—Fauvette laughed—"maybe he believes, like so many others, that seeing Palmyre again caused the Judge's death. The Zombie may have wanted the pleasure of killing off an old devil like the Judge without interference."

Victor frowned. "The Judge's youngest daughter is old enough to be Palmyre Delamare's mother."

"Of course." A carriage ground to a stop on the shelled road, and Fauvette rose to look out. "Ask your cousin, Alcide Larouche, to tell you the rest of the story," she said, recognizing her visitors. "Or don't you know why he cut his throat?"

It was Fauvette's barouche, driven by Fauvette's black boy, Narcisse. The top was thrown back, and in it on the same seat sat two ladies, one holding a parasol with a deep fringe. The other wore a wide-brimmed straw, and as she had no pompadour to pin it on to, she had it tied on with a veil.

The doctor reached the banquette just as they had gotten out. He removed his hat and bowed.

"M'sieur le docteur, one moment, please?"

Miriam put her hand into the raffia bag she carried and brought forth the last thing expected—a joint of cornstalk.

"Is it another of those grigri, M'sieur le docteur?"

He took it from her. The pith had been replaced at the ends to

76

cork up the cavity scooped from the middle. The space was filled with parings from the callous spot near a horse's knee known as the "nail."

"I found it under my pillow this morning."

Then it was the girl who was not wanted.

"Don't trouble about it." He threw it in the ditch.

"I have discharged Bibi," Palmyre announced. "She has gone back to her mother, who works for Madame Vigée."

The doctor saw the sullen look on Narcisse, who was loitering near Madame Vigée's fence.

"You aren't going to be superstitious, are you?" he said to Miriam, whose eyes were on the engine of mischief lying in the drain.

"No. Only. . . ." She gave him that open look of hers. "Doctor," she said in English, "I burned another candle, and now look —today. . . ."

"Darling, our friend is waiting." Palmyre reached for the gate latch.

Fauvette was on the gallery. The doctor understood now why she had said, "I am sorry I cannot offer to send you home in my carriage." She no longer owned a carriage. Fauvette had her mother's magic knack for transforming furniture into food, and other assets into practically anything. He wondered if the carriage had been converted into some of Mr. Néron Paviot's oil stock.

At "Clair de Lune," Victor went directly to the kitchen in search of Cumba. She was grinding chicory to add to coffee.

"Cumba, tell me the meaning of a joint of cornstalk filled with parings from a horse's knee."

Cumba's eyes bulged. Her head stood out on her neck like a turtle's.

"Miché Vic, it not a bad charm! It only mean dat person who get it, dat person heart stay empty like dat joint, or if anybody say love, dat heart fill up hard an' dry, like wit' dose parin's, and don' say love back."

The doctor lost patience. He cursed between his teeth. It must be Olympe; the grigri must have been meant for Palmyre, after all. He would find some excuse to go to the Roussel stables, and examine the horses there.

On his way back to the house he passed his own stables. Zeph was currying Blanchette, one of the pair of white Arabians that drew Nanaine's carriage to church on Sundays.

"Miché Vic, I want tell you something." Zeph pointed to Blanchette's knee. "Somebody been foolin' round wit dis horse."

Though the night was warm, Olympe lay swathed in a cashmere shawl on the chaise longue that had been dragged into the drawing room especially for her. Leon was not at her side; no doubt he considered the gesture superfluous since the automobile had been ordered. Julien hoped, in buying the Packard, to purchase his own peace; but the reproach in his wife's cavernous eyes only acceded to a noble state of repressed suffering.

The room was quiet. Colette, a vision in a Directoire gown of flowered mousseline, was engaged on a piece of eyelet embroidery which was presently "all the rage," as the ladies allowed themselves to say in English. At intervals, she picked up a sharp pointed instrument and punched a hole in the linen. Then in, out —in, out went her needle again, trailing its long silken thread. . . . Victor, playing dominoes with Julien, noticed that several times she paused in her work to stare at the wall, and once she sighed audibly. Something was troubling Colette. . . . He wished to go to her and ask her what it was, to comfort her; but such conduct was out of the question in the presence of her parents.

Julien dropped a domino and reached under the table for it, coming up with a perspiring face. Mopping his brow and jowls seemed to have become as necessary to him as breathing, and frequently he made the wrong play or forgot to play at all. He, too, had something on his mind. Victor might have thought it was the recent wharf disaster, but he knew that Julien did not worry about it in the least.

The custom, the doctor reflected with impatience, of never

78

leaving a young lady alone with her fiancé was cruel and insulting. He would have said so openly if Colette had not helped by contriving to meet him when he came to call, waiting for him after his visits to her mother, walking to the gate with him when he left. Now, as he looked her way, her eyes met his longingly, and he knew she wanted as much as he to talk in private.

Presently, Olympe's heavy sighs and the tantalizing sight of Colette sitting there in all her beauty became unbearable to him. He rose and made his excuses. Colette got up at once and followed him to the gallery.

"I feel so depressed tonight," she said hurriedly. "I wish. . . ."

"Can I help?" He pressed her hand.

"That's just it." That little frown settled between her eyes. "Can anybody help? Could anybody help King Canute when he ordered the waves of the ocean to stand back? Things"—a tremor crept into her voice—"things just keep on happening, the way they have to, and all we can do is stand by and watch. . . ."

"No." He reached out for her. "That's not all we can do. . . ."

"*Colette!*" Olympe's call came shrilly, startling them. "Get me my bottle of lavender, chère!"

She kissed him hurriedly and returned inside.

He went down and took a long walk on the beach, feeling thwarted and irritable. He thought with distaste of going home to "Clair de Lune." What would he talk to his aunt about? It was becoming increasingly obvious that they two had very little in common. Besides, tonight, he felt it would be impossible to face her agreeably, after the discovery involving Blanchette, the horse. He shrank from accusing her, and from the inevitable argument that would follow. He could not reconcile himself to the evidence that she was at the bottom of the voodoo business. . . . He knew she disapproved and even feared his interest, however impersonal, in the people at "Belle Pointe," and would enlist any and every means to discourage it. But it was too bitter a thing to believe that she would stoop to the hokum of grigri. . . .

It grew late, and he was turning back when a great hubbub, louder as it came closer, caught his ear. Then a disorderly parade rounded the corner, making a noise that brought people from their beds. Boys shouted, dogs barked, men laughed, whooped, made loud jokes. They were blowing horns, ringing cowbells, and banging on pots and pans. Leading the rough music was Mr. Ovide Clouzat, the undertaker, who beat on a wash boiler with an iron poker.

"*M'sieur le docteur!*" he yelled. "Come on! Get in the crowd! Give him a tin pan, a piece of pipe!"

"No, no!" the doctor protested. "No, thank you, Ovide. But for whom is the shivaree?"

"For my father-in-law, by thunder!"

"Dr. Jolivet has married?"

"Today! To the Widow Aurélie Coulon! They wanted to be married quiet! *We* make it quiet for them, all right!" He punished the wash boiler with great blows of the poker.

The head of the column was already over the bridge and pouring into Aurélie's yard beyond the ravine. Without consciously willing it, Victor moved along with the party. It must be nearly midnight, but he was not tired. He would drink a glass to the doctor's happiness.

Lamps were already lit in the house. The bride and groom were not surprised. Bottles of scuppernong wine and baskets of anise cakes on the dining-room table showed that the couple expected to be shivareed. It was Ovide Clouzat and his attendants who were surprised. They found not only their hosts, fully dressed, but Aurélie's daughters and their husbands besides, all wearing their Sunday-best black. The grandchildren of the bride appeared in their long nightgowns to smear their sleepy faces with anise-cake crumbs.

Ovide toasted the new Madame Jolivet. She looked very handsome in her best mourning outfit of black-net shirtwaist and satin skirt. Victor congratulated Dr. Jolivet.

"I was coming to see you in the morning," the old doctor said. "I wish to go on a honeymoon. You see how it is here. . . ." He looked around at his new relatives, who flitted among the guests like a flock of ravens.

"Where are you going?"

"To the place Aurélie inherited from her uncle Blanque on the Bayou Lafourche."

"For how long?"

"Only a couple of weeks." The old doctor's voice held both plea and apology.

Victor knew what Dr. Jolivet wanted to ask. No, he did not care to take over Jolivet's practice in his absence. He himself did not know how long it would be before he returned to Panama. Perhaps he would decide to be off in that couple of weeks. He started to say so.

"I have not had a vacation in fifty years," Dr. Jolivet said wistfully.

The younger man looked at the thin, lined face, the tired eyes.

"Very well"—he cursed himself for a sentimental fool—"but don't forget to come back."

Eleven

On Sunday morning, Dr. Jolivet acquainted him with his dossiers and current cases, and on Monday from nine to eleven, Victor was at the old nicked desk in the second-story office of the bank building.

As the native townsfolk generally waited until they were too sick to walk, Dr. Jolivet's practice consisted mainly of house calls. For making these, Victor had accepted the old man's bay and shabby buggy. Nanaine was displeased over the arrangement made with Jolivet, for she considered the ills of his patients beneath the dignity of a duRocher—as if the virus of the same disease were more vulgar in ordinary people than in persons of her class. She refused to allow the unkempt horse and rickety vehicle at "Clair de Lune." To avoid further argument, Victor was using Uncle Ulysse's stable and carriage house. Uncle Ulysse concerned himself neither with his nephew's problem nor Jolivet's property;

his sole interest in the matter was the opportunity to defy his sister. Nanaine bit her lip and waited.

Jolivet's fee for an office visit was fifty cents, while a call at the house ranged from one dollar to five, depending on the circumstances. There were, of course, some clients who thought more of their pocketbooks than of themselves, like Madame Naquin, wife of the postmaster, who came this morning with an attack of malaria that should have been put to bed. Her happy son Hippolyte, the one who had been kicked by the mule, was with her.

'Polyte was developing another bone felon. He had a passion for fishing and, obviously, an equal passion for getting the hooks more often into his fingers than into the fish.

"My poor boy has passed a white night," Madame Naquin deplored, meaning that he had not slept. Though it was a hot morning, her store teeth chattered with every chill, and she hugged herself in her gray shawl.

"How are you feeling, 'Polyte?" the doctor asked kindly. 'Polyte's face was peaked and his eyes were bloodshot.

"Fine!"—'Polyte grinned—"all right!"

Her son's hand was dressed and Madame Naquin clutched her quinine, but she was still unsatisfied, though she had already received two treatments for the price of one. She took pride in her reputation for driving a shrewd bargain. Now she bent her talents toward getting a prescription for her husband, who, she said, had recently been complaining of sudden headaches followed by nausea.

"Tell him to come see me," the doctor advised, "and I'll test his blood pressure."

"Perhaps it is overwork?" Madame was disappointed that the doctor had not reached at once for his pad.

"I cannot tell until I see him."

She lingered, groping for a craftier approach while dispensing the latest news.

"Do you know that Fauvette d'Eaubonne has ordered a *bicycle?* But yes! My husband saw the card giving notice of shipment. And why do you suppose she is getting so much mail from the

North? It is because she has been soliciting in a Yankee paper for boarders. But yes! My husband saw the bill for the advertisement. By holding the envelope to the light. . . . Well, she can afford it, since she sold her horse and carriage to that pair at 'Belle Pointe.' Do you know how Palmyre Delamare gets her mail? Madame *Mendel.* What cheek! Does she think she can make a fool of us all the way she did of the Judge, heh? My husband says. . . ."

"Your husband is indeed overworked, Madame," the doctor interrupted. "Tell him to come see me when he can spare the time from other people's mail."

"Yes, yes!" Madame Naquin missed the barb. "That's it! The poor man has devoted all his life to other people's mail, and now that he has fallen sick with those sudden headaches. . . ."

"Perhaps if he would strain his eyes less. . . ."

"You think so?" She snatched eagerly at the diagnosis. She sighed contentedly. If that were all, she would not even have to pay for the filling of a prescription. "I'll tell him."

"You had better tell him to come see me," the doctor insisted.

She rose petulantly. He held the door open for her. As she stomped down the stairs, he heard her say to 'Polyte, "Well! What do you think of that!" "Fine. Very pretty!" 'Polyte approved.

The next patient did not stay as long. The doctor recognized the Choctaw girl, Masoom.

"Will you come in?"

She shrank against the wall at sight of him. Her large eyes widened with anxiety.

"Ol' doctor, he not here?"

"He has gone away. He won't be back for two weeks."

"I come again."

She picked up her basket and ran. He heard the swift slap of her bare feet on the stairs. In her haste, she had dropped a small book of oblong brown papers used to roll cigarettes. Mingled with the customary office odor of carbolic was the sweet scent of vetiver.

Colette was at the piano. Nanaine, rocking on the gallery outside the open door, had taken up her shuttle and was idly adding inches to her roll of tatted lace, and Papa was dozing in the hammock. It was late afternoon; the lake was a serene glow under the paling westward sun. The hour seemed suited to the delicate melancholy of Chopin, and Colette's sure fingers were gliding through a nocturne.

The doctor sat on the sofa beside the mantel, over which hung the full-length portrait of his grandfather. Grand-père was seventy-eight at the time of the portrait. His lean figure was emphasized by a pair of pea-green, skin-tight trousers drawn taut over the shoe. The tails of his mauve claw-hammer coat hung to his knees behind, and the stiff black stock made his neck look abnormally long. Bristling white brows overhung eyes that looked like inkwells and gave him a fierceness that had frightened Victor as a child. The eyes seemed to follow the boy all around the big dim parlor on Royal Street, and he used to confuse his grandfather with God, Who, Nanaine said, saw everything.

There was no escaping Grand-père because Nanaine took him every season to the summer house across the lake. She had a strange fear that something might happen to him if he were left in the city until the fall. Fire, theft, lightning—she could imagine all sorts of hazards. His was the last of the ancestral portraits; the others, including the Sieur duRocher who had been an officer in the navy of Louis XIV, and Grand'mère who was related to a vicomtesse lost in the Revolution, had been stolen or destroyed by the Yankees. The naval officer, it was said, had been used for target practice; and a lonely and romantic young captain had taken a fancy to Grand'mère, painted at the age of twenty, and carried her off to the North. . . .

The nocturne came to an end, and with it the doctor's musing; but he continued to stare at the old gentleman above the mantel. Colette's voice roused him.

"Isn't he splendid? I've always loved Grand-père!" She had twirled around on the black haircloth stool and sat there looking up at the portrait, her hands clasped in her lap.

84

"He was your great-grandfather, and he died before you were born." He teased her, "Did you happen to know him very well?"

"Yes," she said gravely, "I have always known him."

"Then you have the advantage over me."

"No—you have always known him, too. I don't mean the way he walked, or talked. I mean—what he stands for—all the fine, big things that run through our lives."

"It is too bad"—for some reason his temper was ruffled—"more common sense doesn't run through our lives!"

"Why, Vic!" His outburst startled her.

"Louisiana has belonged to the Union for over a hundred years now, and we still live on a self-created island populated with ostriches!"

"Ostriches!"—she managed a little laugh—"what on earth are you talking about!"

"We bury our heads in the sands of our pride in order not to see the outside world rushing in on us. We think that by closing our eyes we can keep it out. We tolerate no intrusion, admit no advance. But the world is coming in whether we will or no, and if we don't accept it we will be stampeded, trampled out!"

Colette looked alarmed. She put her hand over her heart as if to quiet it.

"But if we let the world in, we would no longer be the same, Vic! Who was it complaining just the other night that he found things changed here? Don't you see now it is *you* who have changed?"

He shifted his position. "I don't know what's the matter with me," he said more calmly. "I only know that lately there are times when I feel constricted, bound, and I have a frantic urge to burst my bindings."

"I have seen that feeling in your face." She had become very serious. "I lie awake at night and think about it. It worries me—I don't understand. What is it you wish to fight, Vic?"

"Among other things, the intolerance and self-centeredness and prejudice I find among us now," he said with distaste.

85

"Those things"—she looked at him half reproachfully—"Vic, you find them in anybody, anywhere. You don't want to fight any special people, or any one place, or any one period. You want to fight the world, forever."

For a few moments he was silent, hands dug deep in his pockets, chin on his chest.

"Perhaps you are right." He shrugged. "Entire countries have lost that kind of fight. Any man who tries it is a confounded fool."

He rose and began to walk up and down, his hands still in his pockets. He felt the fierce eyes in the portrait following him, reproving, challenging, threatening. He turned and met them defiantly. "We have got to realize that God has created other people besides ourselves. We have got to live with them, work with them, suffer with them. The past decade has pushed the whole world forward, whether for good or bad remains to be seen. We are face to face with change. What we need is not a dull-witted determination to stay put, but the will to meet what lies ahead!"

"Vic!" She ran over to him, caught his arm. "Don't talk like that!"

They almost missed hearing what was going on outside.

"Allez, allez!" Nanaine was shouting. "No, I tell you he is not at home!"

"Will you please tell him when he returns, Madame"—a boy's voice—"that my mother is very sick. Our house is back of the Chinchuba road, just before the swamp."

"He has gone away."

"No, it is Dr. Jolivet who has gone away."

"They have *all* gone away, I tell you!" she said angrily.

Victor came out on the gallery. The boy was going down the shelled walk. The shells cut his bare feet, but he dared not walk on the grass.

"Wait a minute!" Victor started for the stairs. "I'm here. I'll go back with you." A look of animation came into his face.

"What is your name?"

The boy beside him on the buggy seat was about ten or eleven

86

years old. He was as brown, from the sun, as roasted coffee; his blue denim shirt was faded, and his jeans, belted with the skin of a rattler, hung ragged around his ankles.

"I am called Numa, third son of Alphonse Gaspard."

Gaspard. Jolivet had referred ironically to Madame Gaspard as one of his pets. "She is in her seventh month. Bad kidneys. She runs into a dirty mess of autotoxemia with every child. . . ."

"How is your mother sick?"

"She has had headache and bad pains." He pressed his hands below his chest. "And she could not ——." He used a vulgar French word because he knew no other. "Now she has been sleeping a long time, and we cannot wake her up."

Victor turned in at the bank corner to go to the apothecary, located next to the post office. There was a long queue extending from the General Delivery window out into the street. The evening mail was in. He had no time to go to his box, though he was expecting a letter from Ancon. Guy Chauvin, the pharmacist, was nowhere in sight. The doctor went in the back and helped himself to the drugs he needed. Vaguely, through his haste, he noticed the long shelves of voodoo cures and the jars and bottles whose contents went into their composition. Romarin. Calamus. Cannelle. . . .

Ten minutes later, the wheels of the buggy were biting into the dust of the Chinchuba road. The boy indicated an unpainted frame house through the trees. Children were playing on the low porch and in the yard. The rail fence that rambled around the clearing was covered with moss, grown black in the process of curing. To one side of the house stood a patch of corn.

As the doctor turned his buggy off the main road into a wagon-rutted path, he was startled to see Miriam, with a canvas under her arm and brushes in her hand, walking toward him. "She is making a picture of our house," Numa said. "She comes very often. A carriage brings her and comes to get her." Then the doctor noticed Narcisse, following with Miriam's easel and a square satchel.

She stood at the side of the path, surprised, then smiling. He was not sure whether he would have stopped and spoken to her, even if he had had the time. He raised his hat and passed on.

Madame Gaspard lay deep in eclamptic coma. He found, as he expected, a high-tension pulse. Her unconsciousness was so profound that it would have been impossible to get her to swallow anything. With some difficulty, he managed to place two drops of croton oil under her tongue. Within two hours the woman would either wake or sleep forever. Meanwhile, half-hourly hypodermics of veratrum viride should bring the pulse down. He settled himself as well as he could in the homemade chair and prepared to wait. . . .

The sun was setting; through the uncurtained window he could see it going down behind the clump of gums at the edge of the swamp. The last rays gleamed on the brown waters of the Bayou Chinchuba, making a bronze glare through the trees. Soon the swamp was aflame. Then slowly it blackened, as if the fire had been put out, and only charred tree trunks remained. Mosquitoes began to hum around the doctor's head. He fanned them from Madame Gaspard's face with his hand.

Sophronie, the oldest girl, came back to offer him coffee and corn bread. "We have squirrel stew," she said, "if Miché le docteur. . . ." He shook his head. He accepted the agate cup of coffee not to offend her and drank the weak brew.

It grew dark. Alphonse, the husband, carried in a lamp. He was tall and thin; his long bony arms seemed stretched from reaching for moss. The light flaring into his face and over his hands showed the red scaly eruptions found on the skin of pellagrants. Poverty and corn pone spelled pellagra all through the South.

Two drops of croton oil—two lives. He took out his watch. Eight-thirty. Toward nine o'clock Madame Gaspard stirred. The doctor went to the door and called Sophronie.

Eclampsia was always dangerous and dirty. Now the purging and vomiting were over, and the patient was conscious and clean of toxins; but the pulse had fallen below seventy, and a condition worse than the imminence of convulsions had to be overcome. He lowered the head and administered an opiate. He resumed his waiting on the uncomfortable chair.

After a while, the straight back became a torture, and he rose and stretched and walked out to the porch for a breath of air. It was a hot night. He had taken off his coat, but his shirt was sticking to his back like wrinkled skin. The dank air of the woods carried the smell of the nearby swamp. An owl hooted, and there was a continuous chirping and croaking among the cypresses.

"My wife, she won't die?" Alphonse Gaspard was sitting on the step. His voice was hoarse.

The doctor evaded saying "I don't know" by asking a question. "Why didn't you send for me this morning?"

"I had no one to send."

"You have several children."

"All day they mus' pick moss. It is our living."

"You couldn't spare one?"

"Not today. The big ones, they help make the moss to bales. Every other Monday the buyer, he come."

"You could have let one of your boys ride to town with the buyer."

"He go d'other way. He say he telephone Miché le docteur from the Convent at Chinchuba. You get no message?"

"I have no telephone."

"Ah!" said Alphonse. "Dat is d' trouble wit dese new thing d' telephone. *One* is no good. Dere mus' be two."

"I shall get one," the doctor decided.

"If Miché le docteur had dese telephone, my wife, she maybe was save'?" Alphonse put his face down in the crook of his arm and began to sob.

It was after one o'clock when Victor got home. Madame Gaspard was saved—no doubt for another attack. But Jolivet would be back to handle the next one. . . . He fed Rougette before putting her up for the night in Uncle Ulysse's stables. He himself had had nothing to eat since noon.

There was a bright light in the salon at "Clair de Lune." As he reached the top of the stairs, he saw that Nanaine was still up. She sat erect beside the center table, one arm resting on the marble top, fingering her rosary. Her lips were tight closed. Her whole attitude indicated taut fury.

"Well!" she snapped, "you have remembered where you live?"

"We must get a telephone," the doctor announced.

"What! A telephone? For what?" She stood up suddenly.

"I need it. In cases of emergency, time is important."

"For two weeks? It is ridiculous! You promised that fool"—she meant Jolivet—"for two weeks. . . ."

"For two weeks, or two days, or two hours, if it saved a life, it would be justified."

"I will not have that modern monstrosity in our house!"

"Very well!"—he was tired and hungry, in no mood for argument—"you will not have me in the house either!"

"Ha!"—she laughed shortly—"if you are thinking of moving to Jolivet's hovel, you are wasting your time. I will see to that. Julien bought the house Saturday!"

He remembered Madame Naquin's gossip of the morning. Fauvette d'Eaubonne was soliciting paying guests.

"I am thinking of moving to 'Joli Bois.' "

"What! You would not dare!"

Their voices had become loud.

"We will see if I dare!"

The specter of scandal leered at Nanaine duRocher. Madame Naquin would make a pretty piece of talk out of the young doctor's moving from his own house into Fauvette d'Eaubonne's, with carpetbaggers and confidence men.

"You dare to say these insulting things, in the presence of your grandfather!" She pointed dramatically to the old man above the mantel.

"Yes! I don't give a picayune for the presence of my grandfather!"

It was the doctor, this time, who turned and stalked from the room. Nanaine continued to stand there, stunned.

Twelve

It was the night of the midseason musicale at "Bon Repos," a home supported by local ladies of good family and reasonable fortune for salesgirls and working women who otherwise would never have known what it was to escape the city heat. Olympe was on her way to her carriage when Leon came up the walk, staggering, an ugly cut on his forehead.

She sent the girl Coco for Victor. The color of Coco's skin was proof that her father was a white man. It was golden, and she had yellow eyes like a cat; her hair was tar black and hung to her shoulders in oily ripples. She stood on the threshold of Leon's bedroom, her red lips parted over white teeth in a sidelong smile for the doctor.

"Get to your work!" Olympe ordered. The girl had been taken to help in the kitchen, since the Roussels had a dozen guests, all friends of Leon. The garçonnière, the two-story brick building in the garden designed to house the young bachelor and his company, was crowded.

The doctor cleaned the cut, and found it inconsequential. As he leaned over Leon, a strong reek of absinthe told him that Leon's unsteady gait had been due much more to inebriation than to injury.

"How did it happen?" He took gauze and adhesive from his satchel.

"I slipped in dismounting from my horse," Leon said sullenly.

"And you fell head first into the basin of an artesian well?"

"None of your business where I fell."

The doctor removed a bit of green scum from Leon's wet hair.

"If I want to have a little fun on St. John's Eve, it's my own affair," Leon muttered.

"Certainly, old man. And your own head, too." He snapped the satchel shut.

Olympe was back with her checkbook. "Are you really all right, my darling? Are you sure you don't want me to stay with you?"

She pressed a bank draft into his hand. She knew better than any doctor how to salve her son's wounds.

In the enormous basement at "Bon Repos," the city guests were already seated, the old ladies in rockers, mothers with children on their laps. The local people took the chairs reserved for them at one side of the space where the piano had been pushed out. There was a bright confusion of voices, and a perpetual palpitation of fans.

Colette was prominent on the program. She carried the black lace fan Victor had given her as a souvenir of Panama. She wore a saffron lace gown with deep-pointed waistline and flounced skirt, the décolletage revealing arms and throat. A single red rose bloomed between her breasts and another in her jet hair.

The doctor sat next to Harry Lockwood, who, rather ill at ease under the glare of Madame Vigée's lorgnette, was included as a guest of the absent Leon.

"Where is he?" Harry asked. "I'm beginning to believe he can't be depended on for anything."

"Leon's had an accident. He says he fell from his horse. But he's not seriously hurt."

"Well, he *will* get hurt one of these days, if he doesn't stop his foolishness." Harry was searching the company with anxious eyes.

"Did you want to see him tonight?"

"Great heavens, no! Frankly, I didn't come for Leon," he confessed dismally. "I came thinking *she* would be here." His honest face lengthened.

Zeph, with his basketful of invitations, undoubtedly had no reason to call at "Belle Pointe." Certainly if the other ladies, looking through the lot for theirs, had seen an envelope addressed to Palmyre Delamare, that envelope would never have reached its destination. Neither was Fauvette d'Eaubonne present.

"Do you think she has gone to the Bamboula instead? She mentioned she'd like to see it."

"No decent white woman goes there." Victor stopped, surprised at the prudish sound of his own words.

"I understand white women are frequently among the on-lookers. If they're asking Zombie for help, they have to do him homage on St. John's Eve, don't they?"

"I suppose any woman will do something silly when she's desperate, or in love. Well!"—the doctor laughed—"you seem to know a lot about it!"

"I've been inquiring of Zabette, who takes care of my room at the hotel."

"O-ho! So Zabette works at the hotel, does she? We will know all your secrets now!"

"There is one secret I would share with you on the spot."

"What is it?"

"I would like to go to the Bamboula."

"Well. . . ." He hesitated. Then, "All right. If you insist. But you won't find your ladies there, I'm sure."

Colette sang the "Habanera" from *Carmen*. Her contralto was rich and flawless. "Bon Repos" sounded to the rafters with a clapping of hands that continued on and on, reluctant to let her go. She gave them "Les Filles de Cadiz," and again hands clapped till they stung. The doctor tingled with pride.

One of the sudden heavy showers characteristic of a Louisiana summer had detained them, and it was after midnight when they reached the swamp at the end of the beach. Several carriage lamps glowed among the trees, and the doctor was ashamed to admit that white people of quality helped voodoo to survive. He felt depressed as he got out of the buggy. Harry, on the contrary, was elated. The presence of carriages allowed him to hope that curiosity had drawn Miriam and her mother.

Rougette whinnied at sight of bonfires blazing on the opposite rim of the swamp. The doctor tied her to the trunk of a gum, in whose branches tree frogs trilled like thousands of tiny bells. The soggy ground underfoot crept and creaked with insects, and around his head bats circled. He picked up the lantern and, holding it so that its light fell both front and behind, led Harry across a narrow catwalk that spanned the swamp. As they came closer, the throb of drums grew louder, and now they heard a low moaning song, punctuated by shrieks. *"Aie! Aie! Dance the Bamboula! Badoum! Badoum!"*

The crowd formed a circle before the Mamaloi's shack, those in front sitting on the ground. The trees were alive with dark figures that had climbed among their branches to see better. The doctor and Harry found an untenanted oak and hoisted themselves onto a limb.

On either side of the circle sat an old drummer beating a tomtom. Their voices pierced the singing with sharp yells. The drumsticks were the customary thighbones of an ass. Beside the drummers sat boys naked except for a red cloth about their loins; each boy held a pair of bleached bones, which he rattled together by movements of the fingers of one hand. In the broad space between the musicians gyrated the dancers, in couples, a few at a time. They jerked their bodies into sensual postures, twisted wildly, stomped their bare feet, and threw their arms about. The sweat gleamed on their black skins in the glow of the bonfires, and their shadows slithered across the front of the shack. The circle of onlookers, aroused by the throbbing music and violent contortions of the dancers, groaned and writhed and swayed, slapping their breasts, palms, and thighs in time with the drums.

"Aie! Aie! Voudou Magnan! Aie! Aie! Dansez Bamboula!"

The musicians formed two points of a triangle, at whose apex a rude dais and altar were erected. The Mamaloi and her consort sat on the platform in rough pine chairs, decorated with branches of basil. She was a shrunken old woman, almost lost in a red calico wrapper girded with the blue cord that distinguished her as voodoo queen. Around her head she had twined a black snake, which, when it became restless, she exchanged for another from the basketful she held on her lap. Her king was a young Negro, not over twenty, whose ebony beauty was bared save for a red kerchief binding his loins. He likewise wore a blue cord, and a living serpent about his muscular neck. Small bright bells were tied in his hair, a necklace of alligator's teeth hung down to his navel, and his ankles were girded with pieces of red cloth and more bells.

On the altar stood the grilled box containing Zombie, the holy serpent, the great god of voodoo. One by one, suppliants approached, swearing devotion, pledging secrecy, making their prayers for love or revenge. Sometimes they consulted the Mamaloi, who placed her hands in her basket of snakes and received from them the "power," evidenced by a trembling that she communicated by a touch of her fingers to her king. Such suppliants received a charm, produced from the voluminous folds of her red wrapper, and threw an offering of silver on the floor of the platform. As those who had realized favors from Zombie in the past year also went through the ceremony of paying the floor, there was soon a carpet of coins at the Mamaloi's feet.

Throughout the rite, the Mamaloi screamed at the top of her cracked voice:

> L'appé vini, le grand Zombie!
> L'appé vini pou fé grigri!

"What does she say?" Harry asked.

"That the Great Zombie has come. That he has come to bewitch people."

The doctor recognized some of the suppliants. The woman Noonoon, who worked for Uncle Ulysse. Tawny Coco from the Roussels'. Dr. Jolivet's former cook, now in the kitchen at "Belle Pointe." The girl Bibi, recently taken into the service of Madame Vigée. . . .

Now it was the duRochers' Cumba who paid the floor. She threw a shower of silver at the Mamaloi's feet, begged an audience, received a wanga from the depths of the red wrapper. The Mamaloi made cabalistic signs over it, spat on it, rubbed it dry with the palm of her hand. Cumba threw down another handful of silver more generous than the first. She would have had to deprive herself of her gin and tobacco for weeks to have saved that much from her wages. Yet the doctor was sure he had seen her smoking her strong perique only yesterday. She must have got the money from Nanaine. . . . The thought persisted, persecuting him.

Finally, no more suppliants came. The bonfires had been fed several times during the rites, but now all save one was allowed to die down. It was nearing two o'clock, and the moon was rising behind the grizzly mosses of the swamp. Two women placed a wash boiler over the remaining fire, and the devotees tossed in their contributions: toads, frogs, cats, snails, a hoot owl's head, live turtles. The drums continued their barbaric beat, but now with a drowsy throb that swung in the brain like the onset of hypnosis. The songs had become monotonous chants and mechanical whines. A crate was brought before the king. He took from it live pigeons and roosters, which he proceeded to tear limb from limb, licking the blood from his hands. The Mamaloi surrendered her basket of snakes, and the cook poured them into the boiler. He stirred the gumbo with a broomstick, from time to time lifting out a snake that had been boiled limp.

The assembly ate the fantastic food, supposed to impart mystic power, and drank great quantities of tafia. The doctor's gorge rose in disgust. He looked to see how his friend was faring, but Harry's eyes were fixed on the woods beyond.

"Did you see that? Looked like a white woman—in a cloak and veil."

"It's quite possible." He thought with revulsion: Even probable. . . .

"She disappeared with a Negress. . . ." Despite the grisly ceremony, Harry's mind was still on Miriam.

The music and the dancing started up again. All singing had ceased, but fanatic yells broke here and there from the dancers. By now the moon had risen, flooding the clearing with light. The drums rolled faster. Men stripped themselves of all their clothing, women were disheveled, waists falling from shoulders, skirts twisted and torn.

Until now, the king, despite his fine physique, had appeared a dull-witted fellow, mechanical in all his motions. Suddenly his face grew tense and his lips drew back from pointed white teeth.

With a prodigious yell he leaped into the arena, ripping off the snake he still had around his neck and brandishing it aloft before he tossed it over the shack. Jingling with bells from head to foot, he knocked a male dancer aside with a thrust of his magnificent body, and fell upon the girl partner, sinking his teeth into her bare arm. The girl was Coco. The Mamaloi threw her head back, closed her eyes, opened her toothless mouth until it was a cavern in her face, and gave out a bloodcurdling screech. Casting off her wrapper, she, too, plunged her obscene old body into the stomping and writhing.

The Bamboula had reached its height. Some of the dancers, exhausted, had to be dragged to the side to avoid being trampled on; one fell foaming at the mouth. Clawing and biting couples fell rolling on the ground. The drums raced into an insane staccato, and the bodies of the bone-rattling boys streamed with sweat.

"Enough," Victor said. "Let's go."

It was dawn by the time he had put up the buggy and stabled Rougette. He still heard the hypnotic pattern of the Bamboula, the stomping of bare feet on bare earth.

The Mamaloi and her black magic was a disease—a virus engendered by the universal urges to be happy, healthy, prosperous; to hate, to love, to revenge. Eradicating voodoo would be as difficult as uprooting the human compulsions that fed it. Yet if medicine were to make any progress in Louisiana, it would have to be done. Once again he congratulated himself that he was not called upon to assume any responsibility in the tremendous task. He had a letter from Ancon in his pocket. The head of the hospital staff was inquiring when he would be back.

As he crossed his own lawn, his attention was drawn to "Beaux Arbres" by a light in the wing where Colette slept. He had seen her lamp burning after midnight many a time, and wondered about it, but she had never before been up so late as this. She must be ill, he thought with quick concern. He hurried through the Cherokee hedge and called quietly below the French windows. She came to the railing in a long white negligee, though the elaborate coiffure she had worn the evening before was still intact.

"Colette, are you sick?"

"No. It's Leon—Leon was so sick. . . ."

The doctor grunted. "That is to be expected."

His glance fell on the saffron gown Colette held over her arm. The hem was wet and soiled.

"You looked lovely in that tonight," he told her. "I hope it's not ruined. Didn't you get home before the shower?"

"I splashed my skirt going across the yard to Leon." She went on nervously, "I haven't been able to sleep. I'm worried about him—drinking so much. I didn't tell Mama."

"Go to bed now, darling. I'm so glad you're all right. Try to get some rest." Starting off, he turned back to her. "You sang magnificently tonight, Colette."

"It was for you," she said. Her voice grew tense, trembled. "Everything I do is for you, Vic! Do you hear me, darling? Everything!"

He pressed his lips to the back of his hand, and waved it to her.

For some time after he left, she stood at the railing, unmindful of the soiled flounce brushing against her white robe. It was only when Doudouce came back with a cup of hot milk that she moved.

"You drink dis it make you sleep nice. Come now, let Doudouce undo your pretty hair—my po' tired liddle lady."

Thirteen

Dr. Jolivet returned a week before he was due. Nanaine, who attended Mass every morning, brought the news from church.

"Aurélie was there. She says they arrived last night. Thank God! Now you can give him back his precious Gaspards."

The doctor shrugged.

"It is time you were seeing Alcide Larouche," she went on, "to discuss the arrangements for your partnership. I thought"—her voice hardened—"you two could have had your conference here. Alcide always spent his summer week ends with his family at the house of his mother-in-law, Madame Vigée. But now that Madame Larouche has gone back to the city, and refuses to return while that Delamare woman is here, or to allow Alcide. . . ." She beckoned to Bazile to take the coffeepot back to the kitchen for refilling. "You will have to go to New Orleans to talk to him."

Victor considered it superfluous to start a discussion at the table. Privately, he had decided it would be unnecessary to see his cousin, at least about the partnership. He remained silent.

"I *said*," Nanaine repeated with emphasis, "you will have to see him in New Orleans."

The one-sided conversation was interrupted by a formidable voice that came from the fig tree outside the basement lattice. It was Bragg practicing the Confederate Yell. Uncle Ulysse gave him the freedom of the neighborhood, but of all places he preferred the fig tree next door. Nanaine's expression changed completely.

"I want you to go at once to your uncle. Tell him"—her eyes narrowed—"that he must do something about that parrot. If he refuses, I shall have the bird shot. The pest disturbs Michel's sleep."

Her brother Michel, as a matter of fact, had been sound asleep at the head of the table for some time. He was the only one who had not started at the hellish noise. A plate piled to a peak with fig skins was before him, the leisurely climax of a heavy meal. To eat and sleep were Papa's prime concerns, in which the parrot had no part. But that was beside the point. In forcing Uncle Ulysse to cage Bragg, Nanaine would have at last found a way to pay him back for letting Victor keep Jolivet's horse and buggy in his carriage house.

Uncle Ulysse was busy in his basement with his maps, rewaging the unsuccessful Maryland Campaign. If McClellan's army had not outnumbered Lee's two to one . . . if Lee had not recrossed the Potomac into Virginia. . . . The old man sat at a table littered with the paraphernalia of his futile dreams, his nose in a box of crayons, searching nearsightedly for a wanted color.

"Battle of Sharpsburg," he mumbled, in greeting to his nephew. "Sit down."

The doctor removed a heap of manuscript from a chair and with difficulty found space for it on the table. He was more interested in the battle of brother and sister than in Sharpsburg. It was juvenile in a way, but it could become bitter and bloody. Nanaine would not hesitate to have the parrot shot, and Zeph would be ordered to do it. It would be against Zeph's nature to kill the old gentleman's pet, but he would obey his mistress. Then Uncle Ulysse's Noonoon, out of loyalty, would retaliate—perhaps against Glad. And Cumba, avenging Glad. . . . The feud could be endless.

"I suggest that you have Bragg caged," the doctor said.

"What? What?" Uncle Ulysse cupped his deaf ear.

"The parrot, of course."

"Because he disturbs your Papa's sleep, heh?"

"Who told you?" Already. . . .

"Your Cumba told the Roussels' Doudouce, who informed my Noonoon, who lost no time in advising me."

"Then I need not explain."

"Not explain, heh? Will you kindly explain how the voice of an innocent bird can affect your father's rest more than the voice of his conscience? We all know he was a rake, finding no need to marry until middle age."

"My father had nothing to say."

"Ah, then it is your aunt who says it all! I might have known! What else does she say?"

Victor avoided announcing that she wanted the parrot shot. This is getting nowhere, he thought wearily.

"At any rate, allow me to insist that you cage your bird—if you wish to keep him."

"Ah, so? She has told you to say that, heh?" Sudden alarm flashed across the old man's face. He gave the Yell, and a flapping of wings outside the lattice preceded Bragg's appearance. He lighted on his master's wrist, and from the black frock-coat pocket received a lump of sugar. He ate it sloppily, showering Sharpsburg with sugar crumbs. Uncle Ulysse scratched the bird's head and throat. "Very well, General," he said fondly. "I will retreat. And you will become a prisoner of war. Behind the bars with you. But we are not beaten. No. We will see what kind of strategists we are!" He turned to Victor. "You may tell your aunt the bird will be caged."

"It is best, uncle."

"Tell her also"—the old man's eyes twinkled as he prepared the counterattack—"that I shall invite Palmyre Delamare to dine with me. A duRocher and the granddaughter of a cabaret keeper! Ho, ho, ho! How your aunt will enjoy our little feast!"

It was a worthy counterthrust.

The doctor was about to go, but the mention of the cabaret interested him.

"Did Palmyre's father, too, keep a saloon?"

"Not far from it. He imported wines and went in the wholesale business. The sons are now doing the same in New York. Anyway, they moved from New Orleans when Delamare, the father, died. Their wives could not stand the scandal. He was said to have died of a broken heart over the behavior of Palmyre. The ladies love a pretty story. But actually it was acute indigestion from pork sausage and raw onions that killed him."

"For the sake of the ladies, he could at least have chosen caviar," the doctor commented. "How did Delamare, grand-père, come by the capital to set up in business?"

"From his father before him. A Gascon, from the cattle country near Opelousas."

He laughed at his uncle's ready answers. "Depend on a duRocher to dig up family trees."

"Ah, but no. In this case it was the family Larouche that did the gardening. Alcide had an interest there, you know."

The old man began to fumble among his maps, nervous to get back to the Battle of Sharpsburg.

"The family Larouche was very thorough," the doctor prompted, hoping to get him to say more.

Uncle Ulysse tittered. "The best of it was that the family Larouche drew their richest revenue from blocks of property they owned in an unsavory neighborhood. The Delamare skeletons did not live in closets—they lived in bottles. But the Larouche skeletons lived on Basin Street. And very well-fleshed skeletons they were, too!" He threw back his head and laughed till his eyes watered.

Victor would have liked to know about the mysterious connection between these two families. Several times he had been on the point of asking his aunt about it, but the idea that she already considered him too much interested in the women at "Belle Pointe," and would cut him short with some sarcastic remark, always held him back. Now, as Uncle Ulysse, eager to return to his work, told him good morning, he left "Shiloh" with an annoying sense of disappointment.

The waiting room was empty except for the girl Miriam and a young hound whimpering on the floor with a bloody hind leg. She seemed surprised when he entered.

"I thought—I heard Dr. Jolivet was back."

"He is in town. Is there anything I can do?"

She looked down at the suffering dog. A piece of bone was protruding from the lacerated flesh.

"The pharmacist wanted to chloroform her. But I—it seemed such a pity. . . ."

"How did you get her up here?"

"Narcisse helped me carry her. He's downstairs in the carriage."

He looked at her soiled frock and the scratches on her arms.

"You could have been bitten. Is the dog yours?"

"No. One day I fed her, and now she follows me around. She even runs after the carriage."

The dog howled suddenly and pitifully.

"Wait a minute," the doctor said. "We'll give her just enough chloroform to carry her inside, if we don't want any more scratches. Then we'll see what we can do."

She held the gauze for him, and handed him the splint, and reeled off the sticking plaster. Her hand was steady and sure. Any other young lady of his acquaintance would have paled and grown faint, but Miriam might have been watching the progress of an interesting piece of art.

"Well," he said when he had finished, "we'll hope for perfect primary union." She was so serious that he tried to tease her. "Do you think we may anticipate a tendency to anchylosis?"

She took him in earnest. "Yes. I suppose there is bound to be some stiffening."

He had not expected her to understand the medical term.

"I've had some Greek," she said, guessing his thought.

"How did it happen? No"—he grinned—"the accident, I mean."

"A carriage wheel."

"Well, if she's a sensible dog and minds the voice of experience, she'll never run after your carriage again."

"Oh, it wasn't *our* carriage. It was a pony cart." She added pensively, "Perhaps it was revenge."

"On *you?*"

"Do you know the public drinking well on the beach near the point?"

"Yes. . . ."

"The other day I was sitting there sketching when a young man came up and—well, I pushed him—and he fell against the curb of the basin. It was he who was driving the pony cart. He dashed by so swiftly his wheel caught the dog running alongside us."

"I see. . . ." The doctor frowned. "That was my cousin, Leon Roussel."

Miriam turned her candid eyes on him.

"Is he the brother of the young lady you are going to marry?"

"Yes."

"Her father, Mr. Julien Roussel, mentioned it only this morning. He called on my mother."

"Is she reconsidering her decision not to sell 'Belle Pointe'?" He was surprised that Julien would persist in visiting Palmyre since her answer had seemed so final.

"No, it was about extending the breakwater around the point. Mr. Roussel says he would like to see the breakwater brought all the way to his sawmill back of us, but the mayor won't have it."

As Julien had said, the more breakwater, the more taxes. The more taxes, the fewer votes in the next election. Mayor Bidault would rather see the whole point washed away than lose an inch of his political prestige.

"Well, I think our patient can go home now. Provided she has a home."

"I'm going to take her to mine."

"You had better get Narcisse to help you."

He opened the door for her. The waiting room was no longer empty. She hesitated, and then came resolutely back into the office.

"Doctor, are you going away soon?"

"Perhaps. Who told you that?"

"Our cook says Madame Naquin said you received a letter from Ancon. . . ."

He shook his head. "Wonderful! Wonderful!"

"Since you're going away," she came up to him, "Doctor, will you kiss me? It would be a memory for the rest of my life."

The childlike request startled him. She stood there, waiting for his consent or refusal. An anxious tremor disturbed her chin. Her dark-blue eyes seemed bigger than ever in her upturned face.

He put his hands on her shoulders, bent his head. Her lips under his were soft and moist. She closed her eyes, her arms at her sides.

"Thank you, Doctor," she said.

"Thank *you*, Mamzelle."

She was such a child . . . only two years older than Féfé Larouche.

But she was only two years younger than Colette.

"Now you had better get Narcisse."

On the chair facing the door was a gray shawl. It looked like Madame Naquin's.

He was getting ready to leave when Dr. Jolivet appeared. In a week, the old practitioner had become years younger. There was a spark in his eyes and a spring in his step.

"Well, my boy," he said briskly, "bonjour and adieu. I hoped to see you earlier, but I had so much to do. I have just come from signing the act of sale for my house. Everything else I bequeath to my successor, whoever he may be. All I shall need is my diploma in pharmacy. But I shall unembarrass the walls of the other guarantees of my wisdom also."

He had taken a chair and was already on it, sprightly as a cricket.

"Wait a minute"—Victor had never seen such a remarkable change in a man—"what is all this about?"

"Haven't you heard? My, my! Don't tell me that somebody in this town is allowed to have a secret? Or have they all been stricken with lockjaw?"

He took down his sheepskin in medicine. The removal left a blank square on the dingy walls.

"They will all be stricken with hysteria if you mean this."

Dr. Jolivet stacked the peeling frames one on top of the other. He blew the dust off of his diploma in pharmacy.

"They will survive. I leave them a good supply of valerian on my shelves."

"What do you intend to do?"

"First, retire from our unprofitable profession, my boy. Then set up in pharmacy for myself. Aurélie loves the Bayou Lafourche. It is just the right distance from her children, both for personal privacy and the proper exercise of parental affection. And I love Aurélie. I will not be dragged from her side in the middle of the night because some old bluffer has a pain in the belly."

"Who will continue your practice here?"

"Now don't try to corner my conscience. The town will find a new doctor. What would they do if I died? Some young fellow will come, burning with a holy zeal for serving humanity, and work his fool head off as I have. He can have all this"—the old doctor made a circular sweep of his hand—"and I include Rougette and the buggy for good measure."

"That's generous of you, Doctor."

"When you're giving somebody nothing, the least you can do is furnish them something to put it in." He screwed up his nose. "Country practice, my boy, was invented for fools and idealists. If at any time you feel yourself pursued by ideals, for God's sake, run. Think of me at seventy-two—and run like hell."

"Then I would have to think of you a week ago."

"There *is* a Fountain of Youth, boy. It is love. Love makes us young—keeps us young." He became brisk again. "Now before we go into the physiological phenomena of increased circulation and nerve stimuli incident to the mystery of the emotions, let me show you something that will amuse you in your spare time"—he winked—"and give you something to think about when you are too tired to sleep."

They went into the inner office, and Dr. Jolivet opened a narrow door that had been locked. The alcove was a small laboratory. He lit a lamp fitted with a reflector, and a strong white light fell on vessels containing fungus-grown corn, glass slides, a micrographic camera, a Zeiss microscope, test tubes, syphons, and various other pieces of equipment used to record the steps of research and experiment. He pointed with pride to a thermostatic arrangement for accurate temperature control.

"These are my toys. Let somebody else play with them for a while. Pellagra is lots of fun—except for the fellow who has it. A grand game. Find the cause—then, if you have any energy left, invent the cure. And the prize? Maybe you get a nasty germ named after you." He laughed loudly.

"I'm sorry I won't be here to play. I'm going back to Ancon."

"Well, if you happen still to be around when the next man

comes, tell him what it's all about, will you? Maybe he'll be ass enough to play."

When Victor stepped out of the alcove, Masoom was standing in the office doorway. She had, as always, her Choctaw basket, and her hair was braided against the heat.

"Ev'body say, ol' doctor, he back."

"Yes, he's here."

Dr. Jolivet came in.

"Well, Masoom, have you been behaving yourself?"

She looked down at her bare feet. "Don't sell anything," she murmured.

He went to the cabinet behind the screen and took down a large brown bottle.

"Listen, Masoom"—Victor could see him searching on the bottom shelf for a smaller, empty vessel—"I'm going away. You understand?"

"You come back?"

He hesitated before he said, "No, I'm not coming back. Somebody else will be here."

Her face became a mask of horror. She stood there woodenly, saying nothing. He came from behind the screen with both vessels in his hands, preparing to transfer the liquid, and saw her face. "Oh, hell," he said, reverting as always to English to swear. "Here. Take the whole damned thing."

She took the big bottle from him slowly, and placed it with utmost care in her basket. She turned and went out without saying a word.

Victor's curiosity was stirred. "What's the matter with her?" he asked bluntly.

"Oh, she's in love." Jolivet flipped his hand in a gesture of irritation. "When you see a love as big as that, it makes you scared to touch it. You let it alone." Dismissing the subject, he went to the desk and picked up the framed diplomas he had left there, tucking them under his arm. "Well, my boy, good-by and good luck. Drop me a postcard from Panama."

Victor put out his hand.

"Before you go, Doctor"—he cleared his throat—"there's something I want to say. I know how you feel about it, but personally I think you've done a magnificent piece of work here."

The younger man felt the increased pressure in the handclasp.

"I haven't always done my duty, my boy. I could have been suspended for some of the things I've done—or rather, *not* done."

His eyes went to a piece of moss that had fallen from Masoom's basket. He picked it up on the end of a match and dropped it in the waste pail.

Victor remained at the desk for some time after Dr. Jolivet had gone.

He turned in the creaking swivel chair and looked around the shabby office. For the first time, he noticed such details as the rusty hinges on the folding screen, the cracks in the worn leather pad on the obsolete operating chair. From where he sat he could see, behind the screen, the chipped white-enameled surgical cabinet and the shelves cluttered with instruments that had been used so long that the underlying metal showed where the nickel had rubbed off. A stained tin washstand occupied a corner; beside it stood a table supporting a metal sterilizer over an alcohol lamp. Along part of the rear wall stretched a ledge burdened with drugs whose labels were spotted and dim.

His eyes moved to the side wall hung with anatomical charts, lithographed in colors that had once been violent, but now were subdued and soiled. On one, the Latin names of the bones had become too faint to read. To his right hung a human skeleton in a dusty glass case; specks of mildew dotted the bleached bones. Next to the skeleton stood a bookcase containing yellowed copies of medical journals, and texts whose leather bindings were rotten and ragged. He noticed one of the volumes was reversed; he went over and took it out. It was a work on syphilis. No doubt some lady had been shocked.

He reached for his Panama from the battered hatrack beside the desk. In the short space to the door, something arrested him—

some one thing in the melancholy and decrepit atmosphere of Dr. Jolivet's office that was fresh and bright and young. He stopped, searching for it, groping for it in his mind. A slow smile erased his frown.

Doctor, will you. . . ? a memory for the rest of my life. . . .

Fourteen

On the afternoon of Sunday, July Fourth, a great crowd was gathered on the beach. A cart from the mayor's dairy advertised Bidault's Better Buttermilk and was doing a brisk business. Colored women went through the crowds with baskets of rice wafers and sweet-potato cakes on their heads, and barefoot Choctaws squatted on the ground offering Indian wares. Apart from the others was Masoom with her sheaves of vetiver. "Ol' doc' not gone? He here today?" she asked Victor, her eyes big and frightened. When he said, "No—he's gone. He's not around," she seemed relieved.

Conspicuous among waiting carriages was Leon Roussel's brand-new automobile, from which, with his friends, he stepped in a sporty linen duster, checked cap, and motoring goggles. Uncle Ulysse was present in the gray uniform which he wore on holidays and all special occasions. "Ha!" he was saying to Julien, "you see what happened yesterday to this Orville Wright at Fort Meyer? The motor stopped when his confounded machine was sixty feet in the air. And you say the aeroplane will replace the cavalry. *Pfui!* That for your new weapon!" He lifted one foot and administered a kick to the inoffensive air.

Father Guichard was surrounded by a group of ladies, including Nanaine, Olympe, and Madame Vigée leading Coucou, who wore, with a disgusted air, a pink-satin pompon on his bridle. Old Dr. duRocher stood with them, erect above his gold-headed walking stick. He was bewildered by the crowd, and kept asking, "Where are we?" He had been especially perplexed when, a little earlier, Colin Menard, publisher of the *Trumpet,* read the

Declaration of Independence, followed by Madame Dufour, wife of the baker, singing the "Marseillaise."

Fauvette d'Eaubonne caused a sensation by riding up on her bicycle. Afterward, she was observed in the company of Mr. Néron Paviot, in his formals and tennis shoes, and several of her Yankee boarders. Even if Fauvette could have been forgiven all this, it would have been impossible to overlook the latest desecration of "Joli Bois." The English-speaking Northerners pronounced it "Jolly Boys." This piece of news Madame Naquin scattered in scandalized whispers after one of them had asked at the post office for the mail.

The undertaker, Ovide Clouzat, and his wife were there with their seven children. As Madame had had so much practice at home, it was small wonder that she could handle christening parties capably for others. As for Alceste Moreau, it was one of the few times in his life that the old fisherman was wearing shoes. "Yas," he was telling Ovide, "I am a success, me. I make eleven sons, I eat every day, I got me a good bed and a good wife. Me, I got nuttin' to be mad wit God fo'." He was elated that his youngest, Hercule, had won the greased pig in the morning races. "That Justin, son of Dufour, say my boy he put sand on his hand—he cheat. No, not my Hercule. Tha's a lie. I *know*, me!"

Madame Naquin was with her husband and their son Hippolyte. Mr. Naquin was a slight man with a large rusty mustache and watery eyes. He was not the type one would suspect of hypertension, Victor thought. Perhaps his headaches came from his wife's nagging. It was due to Madame Naquin that young Dr. duRocher was the target of whispers and widened eyes. Madame had been in such haste to report the outrageously long time Palmyre Delamare's daughter had been with the doctor Saturday morning a week ago that she had left her shawl on the waiting-room chair.

As Glad, with a large grin, remarked to the doctor, "The fireworks sure started early 'round *here*, Doc' Vic!" It enraged his aunt only the more to hear the story of the hound. "This is the last time"—she beat the palm of her left hand vigorously with the back of her right—"the last time I will hear of your disgraceful nonsense! Do you understand?"

Colette had neither questioned nor commented, though the talk must have caused her embarrassment and perhaps pain. When Victor himself brought up the subject, she said jokingly, "Part of being a doctor is being locked up with lovely ladies. I might as well get used to it." He had caught her in his arms and blessed her for her understanding. And when he released her, he had found tears in her eyes.

The sun had gone down, and the hot breeze cooled. Parasols closed and fans now worked more for effect than comfort.

Ovide Clouzat, the undertaker, announced through his megaphone elaborate fireworks, including pieces titled "The Liberty Bell" and "The Fall of the Bastille," to take place at nine o'clock. July Fourth, 1776, and July Fourteenth, 1789, were very much confused at the Mandeville fete. Even those like Fauvette d'Eaubonne, some of whose forebears had lost their heads to the guillotine on the Day of Wrath, forgot the past and applauded. Next on the program, Ovide bellowed, was the bidding for the Mystery Boxes.

The young men, and some widowers and bachelors, flocked to the foot of the speakers' platform. Behind Ovide and his megaphone was a heap of gaily decorated boxes. They contained suppers prepared by the young women, and the man who had a sweetheart, and was able to identify her box by some article in trimming, bid desperately for it, since getting the box meant getting the girl for the first dance and enjoying the supper with her afterward. Annually the money from the auction was given to the colored Sisters of the Holy Family for their orphanage, and since it was for a charitable cause, young ladies of the best families were allowed to forget for an evening that it was unrefined to dance in public.

The doctor came across Harry Lockwood, looking as if he had lost something.

"I can't find her," Harry said miserably. "She promised she'd come. I talked her into fixing a box so I could bid for it."

"She's probably gone to the pavilion to wait with the other girls. Do you know how to play the game? How are you going to know her box from the others?"

"I'm not worried about that. She sent me a note, giving a full description."

Leon sauntered by. He had shed his motoring outfit. His stylish pedestrian attire was climaxed by a slender sword cane tucked jauntily under the arm.

"Come on!" he called. "Let's get in the swim!" A slight deviation in his step indicated the aid of absinthe in Leon's observance of Independence Day.

"Look at Leon," Harry said on a note of disgust. "Can't he see what he's doing to himself? It's getting so I hate to meet him any more."

Leon elbowed into the crowd, heedless of the hard looks he earned from the other young men. The doctor followed him. Pushing toward the speakers' platform, they became separated from Harry Lockwood somewhere along the way.

At length, Colette's box came up for bidding. It was impossible to mistake its round shape, its red ribbon tied in a bow and mixed with tinsel. The doctor offered a bid, and was raised at once. He looked around to see who his competitor might be and was astonished to meet the bewildered face of Harry Lockwood. The doctor bid higher. Harry, puzzled and desperate, exceeded him. What was the matter with the fellow? The doctor doubled him.

"What in hell are you doing!"—Leon gripped the doctor's uplifted arm—"Let him alone, damn it!"

"That's Colette's box!"

"I know it is. But *he* thinks it's. . . ." Leon laughed unsteadily.

"Leon!"—the doctor grabbed him by the lapel, turning him around—"what have you been up to?"

"Fifteen dollars!" Ovide roared. "Mr. Lockwood bids fifteen. . . ."

"I got Coco to talk her mother, Zabette, into a deal." Leon's laugh was silly with absinthe. "Coco," he boasted, "would do anything for me. You see"—he grew confidential, tapping the doctor's shoulder with his forefinger—"Harry said she would send him a note. So I paid Zabette to turn it over to me and give him one I wrote instead. I described Colette's masterpiece with minute detail in the most delicate hand. . . ."

"*Gone!*" thundered Ovide. "Gone to Mr. Lockwood for fifteen dollars!"

"You see, he will get Colette and I will get the girl from 'Belle Pointe.' " Leon choked with laughter that died in surprise as the doctor shook free of him.

"Harry! *Harry!*"

The young man was headed jubilantly for the dancing pavilion to claim the girl with the matching ribbon. The doctor started after him. But at that moment, Leon's voice rose confidently to bid. Ovide was holding up a square box wrapped in pink paper and tied with blue water silk. The doctor stopped, turning back toward the platform.

"Five!"

"Seven!"

"Seven four bits!"

The heap was going down, and the young men who saw themselves without a supper or a partner for the evening began to bid more actively, but as the figure grew beyond their pockets, they dropped out, leaving the contest to Leon and the doctor.

"Ten!"

"Fifteen!"

Leon was in no condition to dance, and Victor was determined not to have Miriam humiliated. Moreover, he visualized with something akin to terror Olympe's reaction if the future King of Comus. . . .

"Sixteen!"

The bidding reached thirty, climbed to forty. Ovide's excitement soared with the increasing sum; he jumped about, pointing dramatically to the coveted prize, bellowed through his megaphone urging the rivals onward and upward. The competition took on the aspect of a spectacle. An audience gathered, curious and amused.

"Forty-five!" Leon was red in the face.

"Fifty!"

Some in the crowd whistled softly. There were exclamations and profane comments. Ovide was all but hysterical.

"Miché le docteur bids fifty! Do I hear somebody bid fifty-five?"

Leon swore. He had reached his limit. He must be short of money, thanks to bribing Zabette and his drinking parties at Paul's Exchange. He looked at the ring on his little finger, then at the doctor. The doctor smiled. He took out his watch and swung it idly on its chain.

"Does nobody bid fifty-five?" Ovide sounded surprised and disappointed. The crowd held their breath. "Gone!" Ovide admitted, reluctant to end so good a game. "Gone to Miché le docteur. . . ."

Leon burst into a string of curses. He struck his cane against the platform with such force that the slender stick broke in half, exposing a comically crooked point of steel. The onlookers laughed.

He had never had a partner like this before. Dancing with her was like floating. Their feet hardly touched the roughly waxed boards. He could feel the froth of her full wide skirts whipping his legs. Her short, heavy hair was a flash in the dusk of the lanterns. She threw her head back joyously, her lips parted, eyes shining. Her uncorseted waist was lithe under his touch and her hand in his was cool and confident.

The musicians caught the fever of their dancing. The violins sang, the bass fiddle thumped like the beat of a wildly happy heart, the brass shouted. Couples, one after the other, stopped dancing to watch the pair. Finally they were alone on the floor. They wove together, they circled till his head swam. She followed him perfectly. The blaze of bonfires on the beach and the glare of rockets and flares became streaks before his eyes as he whirled her, faster and faster. The noise of cannon crackers burst through the music, and their world became a carnival of sound, motion, color, light.

Their step ended precisely on the last note. They held their dancing position a moment longer, then dropped hands.

A thunder of applause came from the side lines. Shouts and stamping shook the pavilion.

"Bravo! Bravo, Miché le docteur! Bravo, Miché Vic!"

He felt embarrassed, but at the same time elated, knowing in a vague way that the approval of the townspeople was not alone for the waltz, but for him as an individual. He had enjoyed himself in their midst, and according to their simple code this made him one of them.

Abruptly the drum began to roll, and as all attention turned from the doctor and his partner to the corner where the band sat, Ovide Clouzat took up his megaphone.

"Miché le docteur, please step outside! Somebody has been hurt!"

A cannon cracker had exploded in Hippolyte's right hand. His forefinger was a bleeding stump to which a piece of the dressing left from the bone felon still stuck with ironic stubbornness.

A crowd had gathered around him. A little way off, Madame, his mother, lay on the grass, unconscious. She had fainted. Mr. Naquin was begging her to speak to him, the first time anybody had ever had to beg Madame to talk. The baker's wife was bathing her head and face with water from the public spring.

"Stand back!" the doctor pleaded. If Hippolyte fainted it would be harder to get him to the office.

Comments from the crowd dropped thick and fast.

" 'Polyte is a fool. He should have blown his head off. It's no good to him anyhow."

"No, he is not a fool. He picked the thing up just as it was going to explode under Madame Vignaud, who is enceinte."

"Yes, I saw her skirt sweep it. Neither she nor her husband was looking at the ground."

" 'Polyte is a fool, all the same. Does he think Madame Vignaud will give a fig for his finger?"

"Me, I still say 'Polyte is a *hero.*"

A loud argument arose.

"Stand aside!" the doctor ordered. In the light of the bonfire near by, 'Polyte's face was glistening with great drops of sweat. "How do you feel, 'Polyte? Do you think you can get to a carriage? Shall we carry you?"

"Fine!" Hippolyte grinned, gritting his teeth. He looked at his piece of finger. "Very pretty."

Ovide Clouzat drove them to the bank building.

"Well," said Ovide, never at a loss for an optimistic word, "that is the *fastest* way to get rid of a bone felon!"

Fifteen

Monday morning his aunt failed to appear for breakfast. "Nanaine is not feeling well," Papa muttered. "She has a headache. She was unable to sleep."

The doctor, himself, had neither slept nor rested. On returning home after attending Hippolyte, he found the telephone, installed at his bedside, ringing insanely. It was the first of a chain of ptomaine cases he had been called to treat during the night. Télémaque Moreau, eldest son of Alceste the fisherman, and his whole family were down. Questioning revealed they had all drunk Bidault's Better Buttermilk the evening before at the Fourth of July fete. It developed that every one of the victims had been customers of Mayor Bidault. Among them was Madame Vigée, who, as she herself was accustomed to observe, was never slighted when unpleasant things were passed around. God ignored her on all other occasions.

"I must see the mayor," the doctor remarked. "I have a com-

plaint to make about his dairy. I wonder where I can find him."
The mayor's headquarters were at the Town Hall, but as Bidault
had so many other interests, he was seldom there.

"He goes over to his stable mornings, Miché Vic. That what
my friend Lazare tell me." Bazile stood behind Papa's chair waving the palmetto fan.

"Thank you, Bazile." The doctor decided privately that it
might be wiser to visit the dairy first.

"Mamzelle Nanaine wish to see you, Miché Vic."
He expected that.

"Come in!" His aunt's voice was crisp and efficient.

He was surprised at the evidence of her having eaten a hearty
breakfast. A tray of empty dishes waited on the dresser to be
taken down to the kitchen.

A door of the armoire was open. She stood before it, replacing
on the bottom shelf the black bag that she carried regularly every
summer from the city, and back again in the fall. The bag held
the corals and cameos, the tasseled and enameled brooches and
earrings accumulated from generations of duRochers.

"Good morning, Nanaine."

She neither acknowledged his greeting nor turned, busying
herself with tucking the satchel behind a stack of sheets. The
scent of vetiver with which the bed linens were sacheted floated
out into the room.

He waited for her to finish, meanwhile observing details of
activity incompatible with her sick headache. Fresh candles
burned on the small table covered with a lace cloth, the votive
lights had been renewed, the holy-water fount on the wall had
been recently filled, and on the shelf beside it his aunt's favorite
saints and the branch of Blessed Palm looked recently dusted.
He knew she attended to these duties herself. He wondered what
important business had induced her to forego Father Guichard's
early Mass.

At length she closed the armoire door and locked it.

"Well! You have made us all sick by making a show of yourself!" She sat down at a table littered with signs of a vigorous correspondence. "I have written your cousin Alcide and have his reply. He is ready to take you into partnership at once."

Her announcement startled him. It still amazed him that she should take such liberties in arranging his life. What did Alcide think—that he was incapable of handling his affairs alone? He was not interested in any proposition that involved him with the prosperous Dr. Larouche. But he was in no mood to argue, so he merely said, "I cannot leave here until the new doctor comes."

She brought her hands to a clasp with a loud smack, lifting her eyes ceilingward as if imploring heaven for patience.

"Are you out of your mind? Has that ass of a Jolivet pushed you into making him another ridiculous promise?"

"He's asked me nothing. But there are certain things a physician promises himself." He thought of Madame Gaspard and the difficult delivery she faced, of Hippolyte's hand, of the family of Télémaque Moreau.

"And the good Dr. Jolivet has promised himself to make a fool of you, no doubt?"

"He is seventy-two. He has earned a right to whatever promises he makes himself."

"Nonsense!" She stamped her foot. "Well, has the town applied for another man?"

"The Council has notified the Board of Health and informed the Charity Hospital of the opening."

"The young men today are too smart to come to a poor-paying community like this, the middle-aged are established where they are, and the old ones are thinking of stopping instead of starting again. They will have to find a failure or a fool."

Or an idealist, Jolivet had said. Perhaps idealists were fools. Quite often they were failures.

"Then we may expect the place to be filled soon. It would take longer to find a success or a sage."

"Soon or late, genius or idiot, *you* must leave!"

He believed he understood the reason for her urgency. He resented her presumption.

"I may have lost the regard of my relatives, but I have not lost my head over a child—however," he felt constrained to add in fairness to Miriam, "charming."

"Let us hope not." She looked at him steadily. "A duRocher loses his heart, but never his head."

She was referring to the well-known fact that his father and grandfather had indulged the vices of gentlemen of their class, but in the matter of marriage they had chosen carefully and well.

"Head or heart—one is not much good without the other," he said dryly, wishing the conversation over.

"That foolish girl has lost both over you!" She raised her fist and brought it down on the table with a bang that shook the ink-well. "That the daughter of Palmyre Delamare would *dare!*"

He half turned toward the window, fingering his watch chain, frowning.

"Can no one," he asked grimly, "ignore the theories of the gifted Madame Naquin?"

"No. Nor the ingenuity of your equally gifted uncle." Her lips set smugly. "Do you know that he had the gall to invite them to dinner? To create a scandal to spite *me,* of course. Well, what do you think happened?" She threw her head back and laughed. "Palmyre Delamare declined. She is still in mourning, she regrets. For the girl's father, no doubt. Or do you imagine it is for Judge Chambert?" She laughed again, shortly.

So Uncle Ulysse had failed. Nanaine could indeed laugh at him. She was ahead again.

"What has all this to do with the girl?"

"Ask Madame Vigée! She got it from. . . ." Again the vicious circle of wagging tongues. Victor tried to shut out her voice. "The girl begged Palmyre to accept. She told her mother shamelessly she wanted to go because she thought *you* might be there."

"And my working with Alcide in the city would prevent my being there, should Palmyre change her mind."

"It will also prevent your being *here,* and wasting your profession on the Gaspards and imbeciles who go around carrying a lit firecracker as if it were a bouquet!"

"I shall more than make up for the waste when I am partner to Alcide."

She failed to see his smile. She had picked up from the table a sheet of foolscap and was looking at it with an air of triumph.

"Now you talk sense," she said tersely. "I shall advise him to expect you for a conference. You should be able to make all arrangements by the end of the month."

By the end of the month I shall be on my way back to Ancon. . . .

"Please also advise him that it is not because I do not know how to write that my aunt finds herself forced to handle my correspondence."

"I shall say that you are too occupied with the waltz to write for yourself."

He was infuriated despite himself. Never had he been able to match her sarcasm. It was futile to try.

"I was not concerned with the waltz," he said hotly, "or with the young woman, either! I was concerned with saving several people from an unpleasant situation!"

"You succeeded very nicely in saving *Leon* from an unpleasant situation, I assure you. Do you think Olympe appreciated the way your fine Northerner humiliated him before the crowd on the beach?"

She was referring to the tussle Harry had had with Leon after the dance. In a bad humor, Leon was complaining loudly to all who would listen that his clever scheme had been ruined, and Harry, overhearing, had grabbed him by the shirt front and all but shaken the life out of him, to the amusement of onlookers. There would have been a fight if Leon had been able to stand.

"Yankee barbarian!" Nanaine said under her breath. "Well, it does not matter what concerned you," she continued to Victor. "The result remains the same. And you may save your explanations for your cousin Colette." She reached into the bosom of her negligee and brought out a velvet jewel box. "You may have need of these. Give them to her." She snapped the box open, revealing earrings and matching pendant and bracelet fashioned of red gold and studded with coral roses and diamonds. "Zulime saved them by hiding them in her mattress when your friends"—her lip curled in allusion to Harry Lockwood—"the Yankees came. They belonged to the Spanish ancestress common to your cousin and yourself. It is fitting for her to have them."

"Thank you." His anger left. He thought of the pleasure he would have in presenting Colette with the jewels.

"You may go now," she said as if she were dismissing a child. "No—wait a minute." She bent her attention to the foolscap sheet before her. "Julien Roussel. Ulysse duRocher. Fauvette d'Eaubonne," she read off. "Three signatures. Three simpletons. Do you know what this is?"

"The petition to the Council to continue the breakwater around the point, no doubt."

Julien had told him. The mayor would do nothing unless the property holders requested it; he would have done nothing at all if Julien, influential in securing the causeway, had not pressed him. Julien said he wanted the breakwater for the protection of his own interests, since it was proposed to carry it past the Roussel sawmill back of "Belle Pointe."

"I wish you would return this idiotic paper to Julien and tell him he has all the signatures he is going to get. I have seen to that." She glanced at a pile of letters inscribed in her flourishing hand. "I have written my friends. As for the tradespeople, I have given them to understand we will all stop dealing with them if they dare to sign."

"But the breakwater is needed! 'Belle Pointe' is falling into the bayou. The point is being washed away!"

Her smile was cold.

"You seem to know all about it. I wish you would tell Zeph to come. I have some important notes for him to deliver."

She gathered up the letters and placed them in a basket. She must have been writing since dawn.

Zulime was worse. The doctor was not prepared for the change in her appearance. When he saw her on Saturday, her tawny skin had become yellow, the color of a shriveled lemon. This morning her face was gray. She had removed her tignon, and he was shocked to see that her hair had fallen out in tufts, leaving bare spots on her skull and temples. Her eyelids were swollen and had lost their lashes. The cheekbones showed prominently, giving her a queer, Chinese look, and for a flash he had the feeling that he was back in the hospital at Ancon looking down upon the face of a dying Oriental.

"Zuzu. . . ." He knelt on the scrubbed floor, unmindful of the brick dust against his white trousers. He took her hands, no heavier than dry leaves. "Zuzu. . . ."

She opened her eyes.

"Ti Vic. . . ." Her fingers closed around his, clung with all their remaining strength. "You don' go away again? My l'il boy he stay wit Zuzu? You see, Ah speak Eenglish to please him. He like dat, no? After Zuzu dead, ev'body speak Eenglish. . . ."

She had half risen, his arm supporting her. Now she fell back, exhausted. *She realizes in her untaught way that her world is obsolete,* he thought. He looked at the delicate head shorn of its ears, and the fleur-de-lis branded into the crinkled shoulder. *It is good—it is good that it's finished. . . .*

"Ma Zuzu, you got no right to be talkin'," Glad admonished. "She got one of her weak spells this mornin'. Near scare me outa my skin."

"Cumba, come here," the doctor commanded. "Take this thing from around her neck." It was a fresh eelskin tied in nine knots.

Cumba whimpered. "I can't, I can't. . . ."

"Mama Cumba, you put it there," Glad accused. "But you ain't fryin' no toad frogs and boilin' no red worms fo' Ma Zuzu on *my* stove—no *ma'am*, you ain't!"

"*Cumba!*" The doctor pointed to the loathsome necklace. Cumba came over and untied it with trembling fingers. He made her throw it out, suspecting she would pick it up as soon as his back was turned.

"Did you get her medicine renewed?"

"Ouai," Cumba answered, quivering. "Me, Ah got dat med'-cine."

"Not *that* medicine, you didn't, Mama Cumba. If you ain't goin' to tell the truth, me, I will." Glad turned to the doctor. "She let that Mr. Chauvin, the druggist, give her goofer dust in capsules, and she pay the same price as for your pills. And goofer dust is jest plain dirt off o' graves."

"Give them to me." He held out his hand. "Allez, allez! Get them!" His tone was sharp.

Cumba reached into a hole in the mattress and brought out a pillbox. He dropped it into his coat pocket.

"I'll be back, Zuzu." He stroked her cheek. "Eat what Glad gives you, and sleep all you can."

"I can't sleep," Zulime sighed. "I got me a bad mem'ry. It won' let me fo'get."

He started to rise, but she caught his coat and held on tightly.

"Ti Vic won't go dat faraway place—not till Zuzu go?"

He hesitated to promise. He had a letter to mail in his pocket, advising the Ancon Hospital he would be back by the middle of the month. Zulime might linger till August. He shook off his reluctance. What did a fortnight matter?

"I'll stay, Zuzu."

"She worryin'," Glad said. "I tell her, 'You still *here*—don't bother 'bout here*after*.' But Ah know how it is—me, myself. When Ah'm bad Ah'm afraid they *is* a hereafter. And when Ah'm good, Ah'm afraid they *ain't*."

He went straight to the apothecary. He found Guy Chauvin in the prescription room, compounding a Dobell's solution.

"Young Justin, son of Dufour, the baker, has a sore throat," Guy remarked. The doctor smelled whisky.

"Someday your hand will slip on the carbolic and somebody will have no throat at all," he commented. "Or the arsenic. Or the chloral."

"Heh? Heh?" Guy's hand shook. "You say—what's that about chloral?" The druggist's mind was not clear enough to detect the anger in the doctor's voice.

"Well, you need no longer worry about your hand slipping on this."

Victor went to the shelf stacked with mystic herbs and love potions. He filled his arms with jars and bottles. Devil's Shoestring. Infernal Stone. Virgin's Milk. Salep Root. He crossed to the window and threw them out, one by one, each shattering against the iron hitching post. He returned for more.

"Name of a name! What're you doing?" The druggist lunged at him, but the doctor pushed him back.

In the street, a crowd was gathering. It was the hour for the distribution of the morning mail, and the queue before the post office adjoining had dissolved and gathered at a careful distance from the smashing glass. At first, they were puzzled; then, seeing Dr. duRocher, astounded. Gradually their good humor converted the act of destruction into a game, and they laughed and nudged each other, urging the doctor to aim at various parts of the cast-iron horsehead that topped the post.

"Bravo, Miché le docteur! Soak him on the nose!"

"Give him one in the eye! Give him a close view, the poor beast!"

Their jokes became coarse. "Throw him a bottle of castor oil and make him run, yas!"

"Ha!" shouted the barber, Alex Gravois. "It's the voodoo cures he is throwing out! My poor wife will have nothing to waste her money on!"

On the edge of the crowd Victor saw Miriam, the lame hound at her side. Her eyes were fixed on him, her face excited.

"Ho-ho!" Ovide Clouzat screamed with mirth. "A horse so full of charms should be one charming horse!"

The crowd laughed. The blacks and whites who believed in the cures and potions gazed in bewilderment at the mess in the street. They were amazed that nothing more magical came from it than an acrid stench.

The doctor found Mayor Bidault breaking in a Creole pony. His stableman, Lazare, watched from the gate, a serious set to his black face.

"Miché le maire not goin' far on *dat* hawse." He shook his head.

"What's wrong with the horse?" The animal, a dark-brown stallion, beautifully starred, looked familiar to the doctor.

"Noddin' wrong wit *him*. Sump'n wrong wit Miché le maire. Dat hawse hate dat man."

"He'll hate him more if the mayor doesn't use a different means of persuasion."

Bidault was flaying the pony with his crop, digging his heels into the animal's sides, and swearing to the skies. The pony, with splayed legs, stood ground and refused to budge. The fat and furious figure of the mayor would have been comic if there had been less venom in him.

"Dat Miché Clouzat's hawse. He name 'Pluton.' Miché le maire take him fo' pay a bill. Dat hawse don't like dose doin'."

The few funerals Ovide got were those of people in the woods who were too poor to mind the undertaker's irrepressibly gay temperament. Since he obtained so little business, Ovide was bent on handling it impressively when he did, and hired carriages from Bidault for which he could not pay since he could not collect. Bidault was more successful in getting what was owed him.

The doctor walked over toward the horse. "I have just come from looking over your dairy." He looked up at the mayor. "It is dirty and dangerous."

"What!" Bidault half raised his crop. His face, already red from struggling with the horse, turned a shade darker. The sweat streamed down his jowls and fleshy short neck, soaking into his shirt. His arm dropped. "On what authority have you inspected my dairy?"

"On the authority of fifteen cases of ptomaine, all caused by buttermilk sold from foul containers."

"My man showed you the cans?" He knocked the crop angrily against a tree. "What right had you. . . ."

"He was too busy to show me anything. I showed myself. The reason the cans are unsanitary is that one man can't run a place like that and still have time to clean cans. You need two additional men."

"You're telling me how to run my business, are you? What the devil. . . ."

"I'm telling you how to run it *right*."

"Right or wrong, it's *my* business!"

"When the community is endangered, it's everybody's business."

"Listen, you young fool! You stop meddling with me or I'll run you out of town. Do you understand that?" He spat out an obscene French oath. "I'll report you to the State Board of Health for practicing without a license!"

"Very well. I'll report you to the Board of Health for violating the pure-food law."

"You dare! You dare!" A vein stood out on his forehead.

"You can do better than that. You can have me arrested. I've just thrown your whole drugstore stock of voodoo into the street. As soon as Aristide Préjean gets up from his ptomaine, you can have him put me in jail."

"You did *what*?" He sputtered through his thick lips. "You threw. . . . Where was that ass, Chauvin?"

"He was there. While on the subject of Chauvin, you need a new druggist. He's even more dangerous than milk cans coated with vertigris."

"Need a new . . . !" He spat on the ground. "That cousin of a jackass!" His pig eyes looked at the doctor from between narrowed lids. "You'll pay, all right!" he promised through his teeth. "You'll vomit up a pretty fine!"

"So will you." The doctor drew from his pocket the pillbox Cumba had surrendered earlier. "The State Board of Pharmacy will be interested to know that Bidault's Apothecary fills my prescriptions for Blaud's with goofer dust—while accepting the price of iron."

The mayor's arm flew shoulder high. The doctor put up his hands in self-defense and the crop caught him across the forearm. Bidault, off balance, pulled himself back into the saddle and the crop fell on the grass. The doctor kicked it away.

"You don't want to add assault to your list," he said angrily, rubbing his arm.

The mayor was having trouble with the skittish horse again. Besides, he was too furious to speak.

"Meanwhile, you get two more men over at that dairy. And get rid of that druggist of yours. He's murderous."

Bidault's rage seemed to reach a peak, then, visibly, it began to subside. Slowly, his face relaxed into an oily smile.

"Let us compromise, Miché le docteur. I'll get the two helpers at the dairy. But the druggist stays. I couldn't get another one."

"Dr. Jolivet might be induced to come back and take his place."

The mayor appeared to go mad at the mention of Jolivet.

"I don't want him back!" he shouted. "Only too damn lucky to get rid of that smart-aleck sonofabitch!"

"I am sorry my suggestion annoys you so greatly."

Bidault got himself under control.

"I'll speak to Chauvin. I'll forbid him the bottle, or else. . . ." He kicked the air. "Are we agreed?"

The doctor carried the mayor's unpleasant smile away with him. It stuck to his mind like a plaster.

Sixteen

By dusk of the same day, the story of what had happened at the apothecary had spread to all the houses on the beach. The doctor's aunt, returning from her euchre at the home of Madame de Gerbeau, had gone to bed with a migraine, this time unfeigned. She refused the doctor's sedative, preferring to suffer. "Are you out of your mind?" she ranted. "What business is it of yours what Bidault sells, or who buys it?"

The doctor felt discouraged. It was not enough to destroy the powders and potions. It was essential to obliterate the belief in them. He could readily see why the mayor, pretending cooperation, suggested that they work together to rout the Mamaloi from her swamp. Without her competition, Bidault's Apothecary would monopolize the sale of grigri. The doctor knew it was only a matter of days before the stock would be restored, this time in some secret place, to be dispensed in whispers from under the counter. He was puzzled by Bidault's insistence on retaining an incompetent sot like Chauvin, but a more scrupulous and sober pharmacist would probably have refused to sell the trash. Certainly Jolivet would.

Bidault's sudden show of friendship was confusing. It was the fisherman, Alceste Moreau, who inadvertently had shed light on the subject. "Miché le maire is making a list of the people you are treating in this town. Is it true that one needs a written permission to cure the sick, Miché le docteur?" The doctor's application to the State Board of Health went out within the hour. The license could be revoked on his return to the Isthmus. Meantime, it would checkmate the mayor's malicious move. When in a few weeks Dr. duRocher left the whole sorry mess, he could at least say to himself that Bidault had not gotten the better of him.

From the front gallery he looked out over the lake, roughened this morning by a northeast wind. *Sans Souci,* the skiff he had lately given Zeph, bobbed alongside the landing attached to "Clair de Lune's" pier. He turned and saw Olympe and two of her friends sitting in the Roussel pavilion enjoying the breeze.

Now, he thought, would be a good time to give Colette the corals. He had seen Julien leave in his trap, and Leon was out in the automobile. Victor had been waiting all week for the opportunity of clasping the necklace around Colette's beautiful throat without an audience.

Colette lifted the earrings from their velvet case eagerly. She ran to the pier glass above the mantel, her fingers trembling as she slipped the gold loops through her pierced ears.

"There!" She smiled at her reflection. The coral roses were exquisite against her creamy skin; the diamonds shone along with her eyes.

"We have not finished."

He fastened the bracelet about her arm.

"Oh!" Her smile deepened. A thrill went through her shoulders. . . .

He was trembling himself as, standing behind her, he draped the necklace, with its deep scalloped fringe, around her throat. For a minute they both stared into the mirror. She laughed with delight.

He slipped his hands down around her waist and drew her back against him. He bent his head and pressed his mouth to the delicious curve between throat and shoulder. She raised a hand and stroked his hair.

"Oh, Vic. If only. . . ."

"If only what, my darling?"

She whirled around and faced him.

"If only you belonged to me alone!"

"But I do!" He paused. "Don't you believe what I told you—about the night of the Fourth?"

"Yes." A rueful little smile. "We all know about that." Her expression changed as she added humorously, "Harry Lockwood's comical surprise when he saw he had drawn me was proof enough! Papa has made Leon apologize to him for such a horrid joke."

The way Leon was flourishing bank notes at Paul's Exchange indicated that Julien had paid a high price for the apology. But he had heard Harry Lockwood's good-natured admission of his own hot temper and seen the two young men shake hands; no doubt Julien considered the renewed good will worth the money.

"If you believe me. . . ." Victor took her hand, caressing it gently. "Then to whom else might I belong?"

"A man can belong to ideas, and special interests, and places—as well as to people . . . ," she said, gazing at the floor. "Or he can belong to his conscience, or his convictions."

"And a woman—can't she belong to the same things?"

"Yes," she admitted slowly, "and to her fears, and doubts, and intuitions."

"So, then I, too, can expect competition?"

"Oh, Vic," she rushed on, unheeding, "I've been thinking—people have so many worlds—it's so hard to decide in which world one belongs! There are the past worlds, like the home where you were born, and childhood . . . and you carry them around with you . . . you never let them go. Or maybe *they* never let *you* go. . . ."

Her seriousness sobered him, and he studied her face and the anxiety he saw there. He believed he understood what she was trying to say. All her life she had been sheltered, kept close, walled up in a private domain untouched by anything beyond. Now, like any who were not too blind to see, she was aware that the walls were trembling, and she was instinctively frightened.

"Come." He gathered her in his arms. "Nothing is going to hurt you, dearest."

"But Vic," she pressed her fingers to her temples, "in my mind, I can't face things. I *want* to be brave, but I can't. I am always running away. . . . I wish," she finished lamely, "I could run away from myself."

He groped for a way to restore her peace, but all he could do at the moment was try to bring back her smile. "As long as you always run to *me*," he said.

Her gravity broke in a nervous little laugh.

"Oh, Vic! I don't want to be gloomy today. I want to be happy!" She twirled around once on her toes, stopped, wound her arms around his neck. "I shall have Papa cable Paris to make me a special gown to wear with these"—she fondled the necklace—"on my feast day, the fifteenth of August."

"I shall wish I were here to see you."

"You won't be here?" All the light went out of her face.

"I have my duties in Ancon, Colette."

"Oh. . . ." Her voice caught. "Ancon. . . ."

"I'll come back in November for our announcement, and again at Easter for our marriage. Then we will return together."

"Oh, Vic." The anxious look was back. "I've heard the most

fearful stories about snakes and fever and scorpions and filth. . . ."

"Not now! You'd be surprised. It is more modern than here!" He laughed. "Screened houses and sanitary bathrooms!"

"You also have a French Opera and a Mardi Gras in your jungle?"

"Well—not exactly. But we do have opera and plays. Yes, and a Carnival, too."

"Still. . . ." She remained troubled. "Vic, dear, there is so much more for you here—for both of us! We *belong* here, where our roots are!" She pressed her cheek against his and whispered, "Yes, darling. *This* is where I want to belong—with you. . . ."

He sighed. Perhaps he could persuade her when the time came.

"We'll see," he said.

"Let us see whether you will be at my fete." She searched his eyes. "I believe I see *yes*."

For an instant he was irritated at the idea of changing his plans. Then he felt exultant that his presence meant so much to her.

"You really want me here?"

"Yes!"

"Then I shall stay."

Two weeks longer for Zulime . . . two weeks longer for Colette. . . .

In the afternoon, he went to Jolivet's office with a sample of Zulime's blood.

An odor of mold filled the crude laboratory where Jolivet had played, as he termed it, with pellagra. The smell came from vessels containing different kinds of corn: shucked and dried, yellow and white, boiled and raw. In the crowded space Victor stumbled against miniature replicas of bins such as were found throughout parts of the South where maize was the mainstay of diet. He lit the lamp and turned the reflector so that its full light fell upon the work table. He moved to one side an incubator in which racks grown over with corn fungi were neatly lined up and labeled, and set the microscope in position. He smeared a slide with Zulime's blood, slipped it into place under the instrument, and focused the lens. The specimen contained hardly a quarter of the normal number of red corpuscles.

A pall of sadness settled on him. For some time he sat there, drumming his fingers on his knee, staring at the stained floor.

Determined to think of something else, he reached toward the file cabinet that stood beside the table, and drew out a drawer. It contained an alphabetical index of case histories on pellagra, all laboriously detailed in Jolivet's minute handwriting. Under the *G's*, he found the dossier on the moss picker, Alphonse Gaspard. The notes were strewn with cross references to pages of medical works on the subject, with marginal jottings, and with Jolivet's own groping and sometimes contradictory conclusions.

The material was absorbing and tremendous in volume, and he went through folder after folder, sifting obvious fact from doubtful theory, consulting the cross files and footnotes, digesting great blocks of assorted data and drawing his own inferences. Jolivet inclined again and again to the likelihood of an insect carrier as the cause of the disease. In one place, he suggested the stable fly, citing observations of pellagrologers nearly a hundred years before, and quoting Strambio's claims based on the prevalence of pellagra among those associated with stables. This accounted for Jolivet's collection of bugs and beetles, even colonies of the infinitesimal sandfly. Then it seemed that later evidence had forced him to drop this idea, while he still adhered to the belief in an undiscovered microorganism as the responsible agent, theorizing on the possibility of the carrier being bred in stored corn. No matter how far afield he went or in what direction, his patients, almost all belonging to that section of society which Jolivet called the "Cornbread Belt," each time had led him back to corn products at least as a contributing factor.

Yet nowhere, as far as Victor had read, was there any case of a pellagrant among the Choctaws, notably a corn-consuming people. Perhaps Jolivet had remarked this, and, because of the observation, returned to the premise that methods of storage and preparation among whites were involved rather than anything inherent in the grain itself. But the case of the lay Sister at the Chinchuba Convent struck the younger doctor's attention with especial force. She was recorded never to have eaten corn in any form. The lay Sisters' diet included white flour, oatmeal, molasses, sweet potatoes, salt pork, lard, cottonseed oil, milk, and fruits. Soeur Cécile, however, disliked milk and rarely ate fruit. She had advanced to the eruptive stage of the disease, suffering lesions of the hands and face.

He picked up the pad and pencil at his elbow and began making notes. It would be interesting to see if there were any indications of pellagra in families that kept cows. He had a hunch that it was not what was *in* the corn that produced pellagra, but what was *not* in the corn. It was the absence of a needed nutritional element in certain foods, not the presence of a harmful unknown in any one of them. . . .

He had been studying for hours, unconscious of the uncomfortable temperature of the room. His shirt stuck to his back. He had forgotten to remove his linen coat and it was damp between the shoulders.

Outside, twilight had deepened to dusk. Homère was lighting the street lamps. The doctor stood for a while watching him at his task. Homère, atop his long ladder, opened the window of the lantern, removed the lamp globe, applied a match to the wick, and adjusted the flame. Then he came down, shouldered his ladder, and trudged on to the next corner.

So much patience, so much labor, to produce a little light.

Seventeen

By the middle of July, the wave of transition that was sweeping the world reached Louisiana. It was lapping at the columns of newspapers, flooding the analytic mind with fancies and conjectures. While due respect was expressed for the steam engine, the telegraph, telephone, electric light, and automobile, a note of fear sounded for the future. "What will be our new discoveries?" demanded an editorial. "We have invented submarines. We are on the eve of solving completely the mystery of the air. Will we keep forever at this speed, and if so, where will we end?"

This morning the tide of change murmured even at the threshold of "Clair de Lune." A registered letter had been delivered by Mr. Naquin containing an order from the New Orleans Board of Health that all cisterns on the duRocher city properties be screened.

"Ha!" Nanaine struck the paper with the back of her hand. "The insolence of them! *Third notice*, heh? Well, third or thirtieth, it will not be done!"

"You needn't worry about receiving thirty. We shall be fined or in jail long before then," Victor said.

Nanaine waved the threat aside. "As when we were charged with unsanitary vaults. Julien fixed it. It came to nothing."

"Julien should be called upon to fix the seventy-two cases of typhoid in the city at present."

"Obviously it is expecting too much to assume that you would ever uphold your own family?" Nanaine smiled bitterly.

"Yes. It is expecting too much when they are wrong."

"What! *We* are wrong! Is it right for their inspectors to enter our houses at any time of the day or night? I ask you—is it right for them to take such liberties with our property?"

"It is right if we are taking liberties with the lives of our tenants."

"Bah! You talk like a fool."

"Don't mistake me. I am not in favor of screening. It may keep drinking water fairly free of larvae and prevent the breeding of malarial mosquitoes, but all it does beyond that is filter the filth that washes in from the roof with every rain."

"There, you see!" Nanaine agreed.

"So I am in favor of abolishing the cisterns entirely and installing city water."

"*City water!* Mississippi River *mud*, you mean!"

"The new purification plant takes care of that."

"How about lead poisoning from the pipes? Madame de Gerbeau had a tenant who *moved*, when Madame's agent, unknown to her, installed. . . ."

"That only proves Madame's agent was more intelligent than her tenant."

"And look at what happened when Madame Vigée's friend had illuminating gas put in her house. Her old mother blew the light out, as she was in the habit of extinguishing her lamp, and the next morning she was found stretched out stiff in her bed."

"I can think of no more powerful argument for the installation of electricity."

"And what else? Pray go on."

"Bathtubs and water closets."

"My God, my God, listen to him!" Nanaine implored heaven. "He has gone completely crazy! And what do you think all that would cost?"

"We have the money. What good is it, piling up in the banks and homesteads? Lately we haven't even bothered to invest it. The bank box is stuffed with bonds and securities as it is."

"I refuse to continue this revolting discussion of sewage," Nanaine declared. "Today is Friday—Julien should be here this evening. Victor, bring him this notice and tell him. . . ."

"I am sorry. I must ask you to do that yourself."

A glacier slipped between them. Upstairs the telephone, representing the one instance in which he and modernity had won at "Clair de Lune," was ringing insistently.

Dropping by the office to pick up his bag, he found several patients waiting to see him, among them Justin Dufour, son of the baker, and Madame Naquin with Hippolyte. He explained his urgency and promised to be back.

The case was more serious than he had expected. A charcoal maker by the name of Philo Fanchon had been badly burned on the face, arms, and feet when accumulated gases exploded the kiln near which he was working. Nothing had been done for the man besides some typical hocus-pocus that would have been better left undone. He lived on the Bayou Tête l'Ours and claimed that it was too hard, without a horse, to get to town for medical aid.

"You could have sent for me, as you sent for Father Guichard this morning."

Philo made a slight painful movement intended as a shrug.

"It was Père Guichard w'at tell you my husban' he so bad?" the wife inquired. She scowled at the doctor and his bag suspiciously. "You cut Philo arm off an' I kill you. He goin' to die, he die wit' dat arm on, him."

"Shut your trap!" Philo ordered. "If I am goin' to die, I wish to die comfortable. Cut it off, Doctor—it hurt like hell." The unburned side of his face twisted into an agonized wince.

The forearm was in as foul shape as the doctor had ever seen. Some of the seared flesh came off with the crude canvas bandage, soaked with a discharge of pus and blood. The odor was revolting. Ordinarily he would not have hesitated to remove the arm above the elbow, but the squalor of the room, the insuperable difficulties of operating in such a place held him back. He thought of the clean and completely appointed surgical ward at Ancon, of the alert and intelligent assistants, then looked around at the cobwebbed walls and the dull faces of the wife and her brood, who had come in to stand and stare. The man had one chance in ten to live if he amputated, and the same chance if he did not amputate at all. If he lived in the latter case, he would still have his arm, however badly damaged.

The doctor administered an opiate and prepared to excise only the gangrenous area.

"What's this?" He indicated with his thumb a strange scapula worn around the man's neck. It seemed to crawl.

"Dat a grigri to keep 'im from harm," the wife said.

"Was he wearing one the day of the accident?"

"Yas, he wear one all de time."

"H'm. . . ."

"If he didn't, he burn *worse*, yas!"

"What is it?"

"Nine live sow bugs inside dat," the biggest boy said. "It cure my sister of sores. It cure anyt'ing. Das one fine grigri!"

The sister's sores undoubtedly cured themselves. It was one of those coincidences that made grigri so popular.

The boy shook his head. "Maybe some dose bug die. Maybe it wear out."

"If we took it off and my medicine cured your father, then medicine would be better than sow bugs, wouldn't it?"

"Sais pas. I don't know," the boy said grudgingly.

The mother sneered.

"You do know," the doctor insisted. "You are an intelligent fellow. Come over here and take it off."

"Felix, you let dat be!" the mother screamed.

The doctor took from his kit a pair of sterile scissors he would not need again that day and snipped the dirty cord. He picked the thing up with the points of the shears, went over to the wood stove where grits was cooking, and dropped it in the flame. He came back and washed his hands in alcohol.

Philo had grown too drowsy to protest. He was now almost unconscious under the opium.

"Dat firs' sleep he get in long time," Felix murmured. He looked with awe at the wood stove where the grigri had been consumed.

"He dead! Dead!" the woman shrieked. "Took away grigri and he die!" All the children, save Felix, began to wail with her. The din was horrible.

"Shut your trap!" Felix sounded exactly like his father. "He is *breathing*."

Meanwhile, the doctor went about his task. The group against the wall grew quiet, absorbed in watching. When he had finished, he cleansed the feet and the side of the face and sprayed the burns with tannic acid.

"If ever something like this happens again, you must call a doctor at once," he advised the wife as he gathered up his instruments.

She looked at him sullenly.

"Don't depend on grigri of any sort," he appealed to the boy. "You saw what that one was worth just now, didn't you?"

Felix brought one shoulder up to his cheek, puckering his mouth. "Doctor cos' money. Medicine cos' money. Grigri of sow bugs don' cos' noddin'."

The doctor paused in closing his satchel and looked at the boy for a long moment. Here was a basic economic fact in the fight against superstition and ignorance, and he hadn't even given it a thought.

On the right side of the road going back to town stood the frame buildings of the Chinchuba Convent, maintained by Sisters of Notre Dame. They conducted a school for deaf-and-dumb children, who were sent them from all parts of the South. On the left, just before the Chinchuba Bridge, lay the swamp with all its strange majesty and desolation. On the other side of the bridge, the woods ran to oak and gum. It was in a clearing in these woods that Alphonse Gaspard, the moss picker, lived. Then the land tapered off to pine again, tapped for resin; each of hundreds of trees showed an arrow-shaped wound that bled into a cup attached to its trunk. Mayor Bidault owned this land, on which he operated a turpentine works. The buildings of the distillery could be seen from the road.

The doctor's buggy rattled across the bridge. The bayou water looked inviting after his work in the hot, musty cabin of the Fanchons. The July sun stung through the roof of the buggy. His job had been nasty and he had not washed his hands. It had been difficult enough to procure soap and water for the patient.

Dropping Rougette the rein, he descended from the buggy and went down to the bayou's edge. He stooped and cupped up the water in his hands, rubbing them together vigorously. Then he splashed the sweat and the dust of the road from his face, sighing with pleasure.

"May I offer you a towel?"

He was startled, even though he knew the voice. It came from the woods. The lame hound was beside him, wagging her tail giddily, the injured leg tucked up. The dog ran back along the shore, he followed, and then he saw Miriam. She was sitting before her easel in the shade of an oak whose trunk walled her off from view of the road.

He could feel the water dripping from his chin, and strands of his black hair dangled before his eyes. He took the towel from her and dried his face.

"Comb?"

"You're very kind."

She went with an agate cup to a natural spring a little way off and returned with it brimming.

"Drink?"

He laughed. "For a dryad, you're very well equipped!"

"I'm a working girl," she said, indicating the half-finished canvas. "If you had come a little sooner, I could have given you lunch." She glanced at a wicker basket that contained only a rumpled napkin. "Dixie didn't leave a crumb." She explained, "The dog."

"She seems to be getting along all right. She'll know when to put down that leg. It might not match exactly."

"Do you know who she is? A thoroughbred from the constable's kennels! But she wouldn't stay with him. And now, since she limps, he says I may keep her."

"She probably objected to becoming a professional bloodhound."

"I don't blame her. It must be a horrid career."

She showed him her work. She had chosen as her subject a portion of the farther side of the bayou with its background of swamp. A pirogue lay moored at the end of a plank walk, weather-beaten to silvery gray. Large patches of lavender water-hyacinth moved slowly with the current. The low bank was fringed with bristling palmetto and purple iris, and long streamers of moss dipped into the water, vaguely disturbing the reflection of cypress and creepers and the vivid scarlet of the poison-ivy trumpet. On higher ground farther back, through a

139

maze of sunshine and shadow, a shack on pilings was visible, blue smoke rising from its red-clay chimney.

"You see that little house back there? A Choctaw girl lives in it. That's her pirogue. I wanted to paint her, but she's too shy. I paid her to stand a couple of times, then she never came back. Wait, I'll show you." She bent over her square satchel and brought out an unfinished canvas of a girl holding an Indian basket filled with vetiver and deer's-tongue.

"I know her. That's Masoom. Sometimes she sells those things in town."

"There's a man there, too. One day I was studying through my binoculars and I saw them." She hesitated. "I felt as if I were eavesdropping."

He found himself telling her about his morning with the charcoal maker. She listened attentively but without comment. Then he changed the subject.

"And you, Mamzelle, have you been troubled with any more grigri?"

"Oh, yes! We came across a dead black chicken on the staircase. Narcisse said it was another charm to get rid of us."

"Someone must want to get rid of me, too. I found this little statue of St. Expedite in my bed, in the center of a ball of wax." He produced the figurine from his coat pocket. "He gets things done quickly. Cumba tells me I am to cross water before the month is out."

"I shall miss you. I see you every day, you know."

"Where?"

"At the post office. You go to the boxes. I am at the General Delivery window. We cannot get a box. They are all taken."

"I would like to give you St. Expedite," the doctor smiled. "Perhaps he will help you to get a box."

"Oh, please!" She took it from him greedily. "I shall keep it forever."

"It is not worth such an honor."

She looked him in the eyes, and said without shame or hesitation, "I love you."

He stepped back quickly, as if the steadiness of her gaze was a physical force, pushing him. He managed to say more lightly than he felt, "Then it is I who am honored."

"We should tell people when we love them," she went on. "Have you ever noticed how easily we let them know it when we hate them? Why are we ashamed to show love, and so ready to show hate? It should be the other way 'round!"

Justin Dufour passed by in the bakery wagon. It occurred to the doctor that it was odd for him to be back here. The only customer to whom he could have been delivering was the Convent, and it was known that the Sisters baked their own bread.

"Are you not afraid to be alone in this place?" The doctor was suddenly concerned for her. And he was relieved to be able to change the subject.

"I'm not alone. Dixie is here. You don't know Dixie. It's a good thing she knew you!"

"How will you get back?"

"Narcisse will come with the carriage. He brought us here."

Before climbing into the buggy, he turned and waved. She was a picture, herself, there under the oak, the hound at her side. A remarkable, and somewhat disturbing, child. . . .

By the time he reached town his mind was so busy with the idea inspired by Felix Fanchon, the charcoal maker's son, that he forgot he had not lunched. He went directly to the office. Several hours had elapsed, and the patients to whom he had made a promise to return had vanished long ago.

He sat down at the desk, without removing his hat, and drafted the announcement of his clinic. A placard at the post office, one at the bank—he smiled when he thought of placing one even in the window of the apothecary—a notice in the *Trumpet* . . . and a sign next to Jolivet's black shingle on the entrance door: FREE CLINIC. EVERY DAY, INCLUDING SUNDAYS. FROM 3:00 TO 5:00. The Sundays were for workers. He must remember in all cases to have the "free" stand out in bold letters that assaulted the eye. It would induce the poor and intrigue the frugal. And no peeling gilt on dull black. It must be glaring red on gleaming white.

His spirits rose as he thought about it. He would need many cures to set science above superstition. But tongues wagged fast and furiously in this town where talking was the principal pastime. He should have thought of it before: people would try practically anything if it cost them nothing.

Now, if he could strengthen his plan with the cooperation of the priest: an occasional sermon; the Sisters exerting their influence among the children at school; Father Guichard, himself, bringing patient pressure to bear on such as the Fanchons and Gaspards. . . .

Father Guichard listened politely, but without enthusiasm. He would have to get permission from his superior for such a campaign. He had been bothering the archbishop with so many matters lately that he hesitated. . . . Besides, they had tried all the doctor's suggestions in years gone by. Perhaps, by the time the weather tempered in November, December—if the doctor were still here. But now, the heat, and with so much to do since the swelling of his congregation with summer residents: confessions, sick calls. . . .

As the priest spoke, he seemed to grow older. It was strange. He was no more than sixty but he sounded like seventy-five. He looked like Dr. Jolivet before his marriage to Aurélie Coulon.

Ignorance had defeated them, the doctor thought, and for a moment he was shaken. Then in his own uneasiness he recognized the cause of their failure. *No,* he amended—they had *let* ignorance defeat them. . . .

Eighteen

He spoke to Miriam every day in the week that followed, at the post office, or returning from his visits to Philo Franchon. He was especially concerned about the outcome in the case of the charcoal maker. If he lost the man, Madame Fanchon would swear to the country round that her husband would have been alive and well if the doctor had but allowed the bag of sow bugs to stay where it was. If Fanchon recovered, since so much tissue had been destroyed, there would inevitably be deformity and some nerve damage for Madame to interpret as retaliation from offended powers. It was on the days when he felt discouraged that he got out at the bridge and went down to the oak where she was at work. A half hour's conversation with the girl refreshed and cheered him.

He found her an intensely interesting and contradictory young person, combining the freshness of a child with the wisdom of a woman of fifty. In the beginning, her mature mind, against the background of her years, startled, even shocked him. As he became accustomed to it, it fascinated him. She had read books, seen plays, heard music; she had been in Paris, Rome, London, Berlin. She moved, spoke, smiled, in all things was different from any girl—or woman—he had ever known.

At home, he was made uncomfortably aware that people had "noticed." Madame Naquin's comment had become a current classic. "He lets us stand there to die in our tracks while he goes off in the woods with that girl!" Justin Dufour, who had driven by in the bakery wagon, had told Madame his mother, who promptly told. . . . The doctor cast the endless chain aside in disgust. Nobody had "noticed" that he was not officially the town's physician, that he was not compelled except by his own conscience to treat any of them, though, for the benefit of the mayor, he had hung his license up in the waiting room. In particular, nobody had "noticed" that he sent no bills.

"You have real talent," he had told her yesterday at the bayou. She was not only copying, she had managed somehow to capture the spirit of the swamp—its sadness and splendor, its beauty and decay.

"I don't know." She shrugged. "My father had. That's what the critics said. My mother has a scrapbook full of clippings." She looked at him squarely. "*You* have talent, too, Doctor."

"I have remarked a special genius in myself lately"—he

grunted—"for making enemies." The mayor. Chauvin, the druggist. Those who believed in the voodoo cures he had shattered in the street. Madame Fanchon. . . .

"No. For gentleness. It is more important to be gentle than anything else."

"More important than being honest?"

"Oh, if you are gentle, you will be honest. Stealing is a form of violence."

He laughed. "Is that why you like me, Miriam?" It was the first time he had used her name. "Because I don't steal?"

"I don't know why I love you," she said solemnly, changing his word without a trace of self-consciousness. "It is not good for a woman to know why she loves a man. She must love him without knowing the reason. That is the surest love. If she loves him for anything in particular, that may not last, and then. . . ."

Today he had been too busy to see her, and he found himself missing something—he felt a definite sense of loss. When he realized what it was, he was surprised. He smiled. So quickly is a habit formed. . . .

He sat at Jolivet's desk poring over the pellagra files. It was nearly five o'clock. No one else would come now. His red-lettered sign had been up for several days, his placards at the post office and in every store. He had gone at night to place one in the apothecary, when Guy Chauvin was too drunk to bother about what the doctor was doing. The clinic was launched and the first timid souls had trickled in with their backaches, boils, and kidney troubles. A collection of grigri on top the bookcase showed that progress had been made; he would keep them there, to encourage those yet to come to surrender theirs. Each day since the beginning, the meager clientele was increased by one or two. Today there had been eight.

He reached for another dossier from the stack at his elbow. One thing was positive: pellagra was not communicable. Despite the fact that sporadic cases were unusual, and that the disease nearly always occurred in groups, there would be, if it were contagious, some record of epidemic. Nowhere in Jolivet's many years of research was there such evidence. Endemic, yes, but no violent outbreaks pointing to the presence of a transmissible virus.

He went again over all proofs adduced to support the theory of a responsible fungus. Ceni, an Italian, claimed to have produced the disease in poultry with an organism developed in moldy Indian corn; but if Ceni's *aspergillus fumigatus* was the cause, how could he account for the fact that pellagra was known in Italy in 1771, many years before American maize was introduced in that country? Frappoli, writing in that year, was persuaded that pellagra was a disease of the leprous group, microbic in etiology, perhaps aggravated by altered corn, but by no means caused by it. Having come thus far, Frappoli abruptly stopped, giving no indication of the character of the unsolved microbe.

More and more the young Dr. duRocher inclined to his earlier opinion that the disease was, if not entirely dissociated from corn products, at least not directly derived from them.

His intense concentration flagged. Fragments of Miriam's talk echoed in his mind. . . .

People make a mistake, thinking it is easy to fall in love. It is really very hard to find someone who can awaken in you a deep affection. . . .

The heat had him. The bank building was of brick, and the July sun, beating full on it all day, had made an oven of the office. Besides, he had been busy since early morning. Shortly after daybreak, Gaspard's boy telephoned for him from the railway station. Madame was going to have one of her convulsions. He brought her through a second eclamptic attack, and wondered what sort of confinement was imminent. The prudish customs of the locality had never allowed him an adequate examination. Groping under the dingy sheet that covered the perspiring woman, while he engaged in general conversation with the husband, Alphonse, to prove the absence of carnal design in the procedure, gave him at best the poorest guess on position. The doctor's sense of touch, however, indicated trouble.

*I think Romain Rolland is right. We should be grateful to any-
one who inspires love in us. . . .*

He bent his head over a fresh dossier. His temples throbbed.
Sister Cécile at Chinchuba—he must see her again. . . .

*Why is it always new? How can it be always the same and yet
different? . . . I listen for your horse. . . .*

He closed the file with a snap. His inability to fix his attention
was due to fatigue, need of fresh air. He put on his coat, reached
for his hat.

Then the door to the waiting room opened.

It was Leon. His checked suit was rumpled and soiled, one
trouser leg torn at the knee. His hair was disarrayed, his mustache had lost its precision. A monogrammed lavender handkerchief soaked with blood enveloped his left hand.

"I saw your horse and buggy downstairs."

"What happened to you?"

"A goddamned dog bit me." Leon, too, preferred English as a
medium of profanity.

"Let me see it."

The doctor led him behind the screen, to the side of the room
reserved for surgery. He examined the hand in the light from the
window.

"He did a good job on you. What kind of dog was it?" He
went to the cabinet for the nitrous acid, brought out cotton and
gauze.

"A hound." Leon was not talkative.

"I think we can handle this without stitches." He went on
with the cauterization. "Did the animal give any indication of
rabies?"

"What?" Leon gritted his teeth as the acid ate into the
wound.

"Was the dog mad?"

"With *me,* she was—the bastard of a bitch."

"Was it a female? They're usually not vicious. Did she attack
you without provocation?"

146

Leon maintained a sulky silence. The doctor dressed the hand, winding the gauze into a neat mitt.

"I said, did she attack you without provocation?" he repeated when he had finished.

"That's none of your business!"

"I'm sorry, but it is," Victor said calmly. "If the dog was rabid, I'd want you to go to the hospital for treatment. If there is any doubt, I might insist on having the head of the dog. Whose hound is it?"

Leon, confronted with the possibility of hydrophobia, reconsidered.

"It was the hound from 'Belle Pointe.'" He avoided the use of names.

"Mamzelle Miriam's?"

"Yes."

"You were at 'Belle Pointe'?"

"What's that got to do with it?"

"You are right," Victor admitted. "Nothing." He saw Dixie only yesterday. The dog was healthy. "When that wound begins to heal, we'll treat it with the nitrate-of-silver stick and see if we can't avoid a hypertrophied scar." It would be a pity to mar Leon's elegant hands.

"You needn't mention at home that I was at 'Belle Pointe,'" Leon said, anticipating his mother's reaction, "because I wasn't. I was out at Chinchuba."

"What were you doing around there?" Leon certainly was not visiting the Convent.

"I was taking a drive. Any objection?"

"I suppose," Victor said coldly, "the hound leaped into your automobile as you sped by?"

"No." Leon's eyes narrowed at him. "I saw the girl and I got out. I suppose, when *you* want to kiss her, you chloroform the beast first? Or doesn't the girl fight you off? Maybe she orders the hound to go bury itself in the bushes?"

Victor did not see Leon's face at all. He saw only a red blur. He wondered afterward how he had ever struck him so accurately. Leon crashed against the screen, falling with it to the floor.

"You want to be the only one to go out in the woods with her, heh?" He tried to pull himself up, grabbing with his good hand at the leg of the operating chair. But he was tangled with the screen and was having difficulty.

"Get out!" the doctor ordered. *"Quick!"* He got a grip on Leon's coat collar and jerked him to his feet.

"If my hand wasn't crippled. . . ."

"There's nothing wrong with your *right* hand."

Leon made an attempt to brush himself off without much effect. He sought desperately to recapture his usual jaunty air.

"The family will be interested in your various activities, I'm sure!" His exit was as nonchalant as he could manage.

Add to my list of enemies: my cousin, Leon Roussel. Victor stood in the center of the room, feeling the anger die within him. He had not meant to hit Leon, especially when the boy was injured. What's the matter with me? Why can't I get along with these people?

"Olympe has had some kind of attack," Nanaine greeted him at the gate. "Julien asks that you come at once." Her eyes, hard and cold, asked, "Where have you been? What have you been doing all day?" He had missed dinner, coming home only for a quick collation which Bazile served in his room while he changed his saturated shirt.

Olympe had managed to throw herself into hysterics. She paced the handsomely appointed matrimonial bedroom, the train of her negligee dramatically sweeping the matting. She wrung her ringed hands, she pressed a Valenciennes handkerchief to her eyes to stem the tears, to her mouth to stay the sobs, to her drumming temples. Her hair had become tragically disheveled.

Doudouce stalked after her, holding the cut-glass bottle containing her smelling salts. Leon, smoking a cigarette, implored his mother from the ease of a rattan armchair, "Darling, darling!

Please stop! You will wear yourself out. Then what will become of me?"

"My son. . . ." Olympe closed her eyes, beat her clasped hands against her brow. "And to think that it was while gathering wild flowers for *me* that the fiend of an animal jumped out from behind the trees. . . ."

"Here, cousin," the doctor interrupted curtly. "Take this, please." He handed her the dose of valerian he had been mixing.

She looked at him astounded and with some hostility. She had never understood his lack of sympathy, and deeply resented it. "Please," he repeated firmly. She took the glass from him as if hypnotized.

"Bank the chaise longue with pillows and have Madame recline," he told Doudouce. Olympe would be very pleased if she could see herself, an hour hence, in a profound sleep simulating death.

Leon sat on the edge of the chaise beside her, taking her hand in his. "Darling, don't send me away," he begged superfluously. "Your illness has upset me horribly." He ordered Doudouce to bring up his father's cognac.

The sight of the driveling Leon sickened the doctor. No wonder lately that Harry Lockwood stayed out of his way whenever he could manage it. The doctor paused with his hand on the doorknob, a cutting comment on the end of his tongue. But what was the use? Any criticism directed at Leon would only arouse Olympe again. He pulled the door open brusquely, to find Colette waiting for him in the hall.

"Papa wants to see you."

As they passed the sitting room, the light through the open doorway fell full on Colette's face, and Victor stopped short.

"Colette—have you been crying?"

Her chin trembled. "I. . . ." She tried to hold back the tears, then suddenly buried her face on his shoulder. "Oh, Vic. . . ."

"Come. . . ." His arm held her close. "What in the world is the matter?"

"Oh, Vic. I don't know. . . ."

"You don't know!" He sought to cheer her. "Then we'd better find out!"

"Is my mother very sick, Vic?"

"Of course not." Was it only that? "She'll be all right in a few hours."

"No." She shook her head, pressing her face deeper against his chest. "No. She—none of us will ever be all right again."

"Of all the nonsense!" He tilted her chin and made her look up at him. "If you're going to let these silly ideas upset you, I'm going to have another patient. And I promise you, I give nasty medicine." He kissed her.

She would not be comforted. "Oh, Vic—something strange and terrible is happening to all of us. Our lives used to be so—so even and calm and peaceful. And now—nearly every day something comes up. Even when it's nothing I can see, I can *feel* it."

"For example?" he smiled at her.

"For example, nobody has to tell me what is happening between Papa and Mama—I can guess. And it's just part of every thing—everything going to pieces—if we let it. . . ." The tears welled again.

"Then we won't let it," he said, stroking her hair.

"No." She pulled herself together. "We won't let it—we *won't*. Please go to Papa now, Vic. He's waiting."

She walked with him to Julien's study, her hand clinging to his as if afraid to let it go.

Julien was walking the floor with as much energy, though without histrionics, as his wife. He took Victor into the small room he used as an office and closed the door.

"This notice from the Board of Health." Julien motioned to the envelope on his desk. "I haven't yet had time. . . ."

"Don't bother. I'll attend to it."

"But you don't know anybody. . . ."

"I mean—I intend to have the screening done."

"I understood from Nanaine. . . ."

"I'll pay for it out of my own pocket."

"As you wish. But you don't have to. You could be that much money in. . . ."

The doctor thought of the wharf disaster in June.

"Thank you. But I've decided."

Julien drummed on the table with his fingers. He was obviously not thinking about the notice. Something else was on his mind.

"How is she—Olympe?"

"There is nothing wrong with her organically. She is unnerved by Leon's accident."

Julien drummed more rapidly.

"No. It isn't that. She started before he appeared. It's"—he took out his handkerchief and began the familiar business of mopping behind his ears—"I'm to blame."

Poor Julien. The more he tried to please her, the more she despised him.

"It's about the breakwater," he went on. "Nanaine has brought her influence to bear adversely. I asked Olympe to counteract it. She has as much prestige as your aunt. I pointed out the advantage to my property, the sawmill. She refused. I insisted. She began to cry and accused me of wanting it for the benefit of 'Belle Pointe.' At length I lost patience. I said yes, I wanted it for 'Belle Pointe' as well."

The doctor made no comment.

"She turned on me like a tigress. She would have clawed me if I had not controlled her. She said I was interested in Palmyre Delamare." He ran the handkerchief around the inside of his collar. "I did not deny it. I. . . ." His voice thickened. "I am."

Poor Julien. Poor Julien.

"I told Olympe the truth. I cannot stay away from 'Belle Pointe.' I go there on the slightest pretext. If I can only look at Palmyre, talk to her, be in her presence. She gives me no encouragement, not the least. On the contrary. She is kind, but inaccessible. She is still in love with the girl's father. I swore to Olympe that there was nothing between us but what I am powerless to help, but she will not believe me."

"No," Victor said. He added to himself, She does not want to believe you. She wants to dramatize herself: *After giving you the best years of my life, a loyal wife and devoted mother.* . . .

Julien was unable to stop. "I don't know how it happened. I am tortured, possessed. I eat, sleep, breathe Palmyre. Knowing it is hopeless does not help. . . ."

He rushed headlong to unburden himself.

"Perhaps if Olympe were different. . . . You are a doctor. You will understand. She is one of those women who have never derived any satisfaction from the marriage relationship. There is nothing wrong—it is her mental attitude. You see? She regards physical love an unfortunate necessity, on the part of the man, like—like relieving the bowels. She gives herself as a grim duty. She would consider it sinful, shameful to enjoy—I don't know if I make myself clear . . . ?"

"Yes," Victor nodded. "I know what you mean." He thought of the little Panamanians in the countryside, rolling in the shadow of the bush on a moonlight night, laughing, grunting like healthy pigs. . . .

"Not that it will matter in the future." Julien's expression relaxed somewhat, now that he had told his story. "She has barred me from our bedroom. Henceforth, I am to sleep in the right wing, she at the opposite end of the house."

It was the conventional arrangement for couples who were estranged. There was never any outward show of separation. Society was spared the shock. Husband and wife agreed to live under the same roof in different rooms. And so, by keeping apart, they remained together.

Nineteen

The following Monday, Nanaine came to the breakfast table with a letter.

"Your cousin Alcide will see you on Wednesday," she informed him.

"I am sorry. I cannot see my cousin Alcide on Wednesday. It is not convenient."

"I should like to know why? You are on vacation. You have nothing else to do." At his bland smile, she added, "Nothing of *importance!*"

"I am expecting a difficult confinement. I cannot leave here until my patient is delivered."

"Ah!" She brightened. "Minerve de Gerbeau-Vignaud?"

"No. Madame Gaspard, wife of the moss picker."

"*Pf-f-f!*" scornfully. "Your career must be held up because a moss picker's wife is having a baby?"

"It will hold up my visit to the city, not my career."

"We will not split hairs on the subject. Well, when is this woman due?"

"Any minute."

"Very good. Since you are obliging enough to treat her, I hope she will be obliging enough to have her child before Wednesday. I shall advise your cousin to expect you."

"I cannot guarantee it."

"While you are in New Orleans," she ignored his firmness, "you can make arrangements—since you say Zulime is so low—to have the family tomb unsealed. We will bury her there."

"Yes." On this point, at least, he could agree. "I have just seen her. It is only a question of days."

Zulime, who had served the duRochers for nearly half a century, would be laid away in a manner befitting a faithful servant.

The charcoal maker's arm was no worse, but it was no better. Suppuration persisted, despite the doctor's most minute precautions. He sprayed carbolic into the air every time he dressed the wound, spent hours sterilizing and disinfecting. He had come to regard Philo Fanchon as a fight he had to win, and this morning he felt disturbed that so little ground had been gained.

On his way back to town, he stopped at the bayou to talk to Miriam. She came to meet him, the hound bounding ahead.

"Have you been busy?"

"Yes. How did you know?"

"For several days you drove by hurriedly. I know the sound of your wheels on the road. I know Rougette's gait."

"How is your work getting on?"

"All right. I am in no rush to finish."

"Yet you stayed very late last Saturday."

"Narcisse forgot to come for me. He stopped on the way to visit Bibi at Madame Vigée's. He came at last, full of funny excuses. He is in love." She raised her eyes to him. "Was he badly hurt?"

"No more than he deserved." They referred to Leon.

"Shall I tell you the truth?"

"Yes."

"I set the dog on him. I don't want anyone to kiss me. No one ever did, before you. No one shall ever kiss me after."

Such a solemn vow from one so young was amusing. But she no longer surprised him. He had become accustomed to her refusal to indulge in small talk.

"Come now. A young and pretty girl like you must expect more than one man to kiss her before she becomes an old lady."

"No. No," she insisted. "I don't wish to change the change in me. Since then, I am different. The whole world is different."

"When I am gone for a few months, you will forget these differences."

"I know what you think, but you are wrong. I will never forget you."

"We will see."

She walked back to the road with him. They were silent. At one place in their path an oak branch spread so low that it almost touched the ground. He took her hand and helped her over it. He kept her hand in his; it was cool and soft, and yet he sensed strength in the slender fingers.

At the bridge she said again, "No, I shall not forget you. You are all of Louisiana to me."

"Including the mosquitoes and the malaria," he added grimly.

"Aren't you happy here?"

"A physician's life is not very gay anywhere."

154

"But his heart can be gay! The way you live and the way you feel—you can separate them if you have to!"

He was about to object, "That is easier said than done." But at sight of her intense face, something inside him melted and he said with a tenderness he had never before heard in his own voice, "You are a sweet child. . . ."

He kissed her fingers lightly, withdrew his hand from hers. The next moment he was in the buggy. The wheels crunched against the hot sand. He had a quick pang of conscience—why was he encouraging her childish adoration? Was it to satisfy his own bruised ego . . . ? He did not look back.

As he drove past the bank building, the moss picker's son, Numa Gaspard, rushed out into the street and hailed him frantically.

"My mother sends me to say it has begun."

He went up to the office to get the obstetrical bag. It was heavy, and as he came quickly down the stairs the old instruments inside rattled and clinked like a collection of can openers. He hoped desperately he would not have to use Jolivet's worn forceps from which the nickel had rubbed off in spots, showing the iron beneath.

Rougette started back over the road she had just covered. They passed the pines where the distillery stood, and turned in at the fork that led to Gaspard's clearing. The doctor did not have to tie the horse. She would still be there in the morning if he had to stay all night.

He walked across the yard, where the steamy odor of raw moss, spread to cure in the sun, filled every breath of air. Barefoot children stood beside their skinny dogs and stared at him with round eyes. He was a strange god. He was fate. In the wise but wordless way of woodspeople, they knew that all their future depended on him. If the mother died, the entire course of their lives would be changed. Their eyes, even the eyes of the dogs, followed him to the house.

Madame, in a voluminous cotton nightgown, under coarse sheets kept especially for such occasions, was sweating furiously.

The doctor saw at once that he would have to deal not only with a difficult presentation but with the false modesty that was as much a disease of his people, high born and low, as malaria and pellagra. It was out of the question for any respectable woman to expose herself to the eyes of a doctor, even in childbirth; the fact that she had a man at all, instead of a midwife, was in itself a startling deviation from accepted form. The moss picker's wife had a doctor because the local midwife, an old Choctaw medicine woman, had recently died and none had taken her place. He was impatient with prudery after his years of practice among the sensible wives of European immigrants in the Canal Zone, and the frank attitude of the Panamanian women who saw nothing wrong where wrong was not intended. But here he knew he would have to tolerate Madame's coverings and the hawk-eyed presence of the husband, Alphonse.

He insinuated an arm under the sheets and made his blind survey. One hand placed on the abdomen showed the woman was already in the second stage of labor. He withdrew his hand and took off his coat, rolling up his sleeves. He went back to the kitchen and washed his hands with the bar of yellow soap he found beside the dishpan. Sophronie, the eldest, had water heating on the wood stove.

Back at Madame's bedside, he palpated the abdomen again, palms flat, his finger tips pressing down firmly. He continued feeling at several points within the pelvic brim. When he had finished, he knew he had an abnormal position to handle. Madame did little more than sweat and grunt. To her, childbirth was like Christmas. It came once a year, and it was a great deal of bother, and much expense, but it was a custom of mankind that could not be helped.

He swabbed his hands and his arms up to the elbow in alcohol. He sent Alphonse to the kitchen for cooking lard, and using it as a lubricant, made an internal examination. He found that the oncoming fetus presented a hand and arm.

If he had been called earlier, he might have been able to convert the position into normal by manipulation. There was no time, however, to waste on past possibilities. It was the present that was important. He might try turning by the ratchet method, but he dreaded a permanently injured child.

Madame, meanwhile, was beginning to suspect that all the practice she had had still did not make perfect, and she was surprised and puzzled by her long suffering. Under the husband's watchful eyes the doctor threw back the top sheets, religiously leaving the last in place; but Madame was perspiring more now from pain than from temperature. She was a stoic woman and did not scream. Only great balls of moisture rolled from her brow into her oily black hair.

With infinite patience, he strove to improve the position. The hard work and the heat drew sweat from him now; he removed his collar and tie, then stripped off his shirt. After a while, he went to the kitchen and again washed his hands, returned and dipped each of his instruments in a carbolic-acid solution and laid them out on a sterile towel. It had become obvious that he would need them.

He would have to give chloroform, as much as he disliked the idea. It interfered with nature. Besides, he had no one to help him. He considered the husband, dull and drooping, his pellagrant hands rough and red. He looked at Sophronie's sad, stupid young face. Numa—he was only eleven; one misunderstood direction would be enough. The others were too small, even if he had found a bright one among them.

Miriam might still be at the bayou. . . .

"Numa."

The boy came in promptly from the kitchen adjoining.

"Go down to the bridge. Take my horse. You will see a young lady there. Ask her to come back with you. Tell her I sent you."

Miriam would not doubt the boy's good faith, because she knew the horse and buggy.

Not a Caesarean. Not in this squalor. Not with these tools—for that was what they were, as clumsy as brace and bit. Even if the woman did not die at once from shock, it would be practically impossible to avoid septic poisoning later. He knew what he had to do. It became momentarily more obvious, more urgent, but the thought of it was repugnant.

"I want to talk to you."

He beckoned to Alphonse. They went out on the porch. He tried to explain in simple words.

"There are times when we have to take a life to save a life."

The husband understood, and considered. Another child meant another pair of hands to pick moss. Often these people procreated with that definite purpose in mind. They did not reason that another child meant another stomach to fill, because the proceeds from the sale of the moss amounted to a few pennies more than the cost of corn seed, or the shot to bring down squirrel and 'possum. Having children was a profitable investment.

"It would be hard for me, yes, to get anodder wife. But I can ged anodder bébé nex' year," Alphonse decided.

Miriam was coming across the yard with Numa.

He placed folds of lint over the cage. "Keep it wet, but not dripping," he instructed her.

"I know how to feel a pulse. I used to test my own when I was ill."

"Then you can count the beat. If it seems irregular, take away the anesthetic at once and call me."

He poured the chloroform. The odor filled the room.

"Watch the breathing. And the lips. If the breathing lags, or the lips get blue, remove the cage and call me."

The woman's grunting stopped. She was unconscious. He handed the bottle over to Miriam.

He turned to the grim instruments waiting on the chair. He picked up a Simpson's basilyst, plunged it once more into the carbolic solution. He could no longer cater to the ridiculous standards of modesty. The child's lot was already cast, but to fumble might be fatal to the mother as well. No physician on earth could be expected to perform a basiotripsy blindfolded. He threw back the last covering.

"Sacré!" Gaspard breathed. He took an uncertain step forward. "Leave the room. All of you."

Sophronie and Numa had come in to stand and stare, cringing in a corner. They went out silently.

"*All* of you," the doctor repeated, looking at Alphonse.

His voice was as hard and sharp as steel, though he spoke quietly. The wet hair had fallen over his forehead and he could feel the sweat trickling down his back and over his shoulders. He would throw the man out if he had to; he waited for him to go, muscles tense. Every minute of delay counted dangerously. Gaspard gaped at him. His hands dropped loosely at his sides. He shuffled out sideways, glancing from the doctor to Miriam. It was easy to read his narrow thought: As long as another woman is there. . . .

The doctor inserted the basilyst. He turned the screw at the end of the handle and felt the soft smashing up of the small skull.

Afterward, he put on his shirt and went out into the yard where he found a bench under a tree. He tried to get some air into his lungs, but they felt locked. Beads of sweat were on his eyelashes and his vision was blurred by the sudden sunlight, but he could still see the bruised and swollen and broken thing that was Gaspard's baby. He had only a hazy recollection of cutting the cord and bundling the body up in a sheet.

The children who had looked at him as if he were a god when he came in romped under the trees, the dogs yelping at their spindly legs. They were playing statues, whirling till they were dizzy and then striking some fanciful pose. They no longer paid any attention to him.

After a while, Miriam came out and sat down. She put her hand on his shoulder and for a minute said nothing.

"She's feeling better. Don't worry." A long silence. "You threw down a stupid barrier when you threw back that sheet!"

Oh, God . . . there were too many barriers—ignorance, superstition, poverty. . . . He was tired, very tired.

"It was the first time I ever. . . ." He felt slightly sick.

She knew what he meant. The basilyst. She leaned over and drew his head to her shoulder. Gratefully he rested against her bosom. He knew that he had failed. Not in losing the child; that was inevitable, but in losing the detached scientific attitude a doctor must at all times maintain.

"I'm a sentimental jackass," he accused himself bitterly.

"Don't be ashamed." She stroked his hair. "Don't be ashamed of being yourself. It's when anybody tries *not* to be himself that he ought to be ashamed."

As he lay against her breast, listening to her heartbeat, she seemed to him no longer a child but as old as he—older, really. He saw her again bending over the woman in labor. He saw her cool, her steady hand. He saw into the depths of her understanding. Perhaps women, no matter what their age, were always older than men.

After the clinic was over, he stayed for a while to transfer some fungus from the corn crib to the incubator, and by the time he started for home, Homère, the lamplighter, was making his rounds.

The doctor had had nothing to eat since breakfast. He wanted nothing. His suit was wrinkled and soiled, his shirt had never dried. A dark beard was beginning to show as a blue shadow on cheeks and chin.

Papa and Nanaine were on the gallery rocking, awaiting Bazile's summons to supper.

"Well!" Nanaine brought her palmetto fan to a sudden halt. "All this killing yourself at that foolish clinic will soon be stopped! The mayor has been looking for you! You can't start a free clinic here without the town's permission! Are you insane?"

So. The secret sales of voodoo cures at Bidault's Apothecary must be falling off. It was good news, after all.

"I am licensed to practice by the State Board."

"Ah! Perhaps! But you are not licensed by the town to set up a *free circus!* For that you must have the mayor's approval!"

"Very well." He was too fatigued to argue. "Those who come to the clinic can be considered regular patients. I shall send them bills. But they will not be paid, and I shall not press collection."

He went to his room, removed his coat and shoes and threw himself on the bed. He would have to blot out the "free" on the signboard. He would have to explain to those who came that the bill sent them was a matter of form, for their protection. So many stupid, unnecessary things to do, to think of; so many people, prejudices to fight. . . .

His aunt's voice came up through the basement lattice, shrill with fury. "Ah, all that education wasted on a clinic! But *wasted*, I tell you!"

Twenty

Wednesday morning he went to New Orleans. Added to the day's agenda was a call at the offices of the United Fruit Company to reserve passage to Panama for the third Saturday in August. By then he would leave whether the town had secured another doctor or not; but he hoped the new man would come while he was still there. He wished to explain the pellagra data to him, to enlist his interest in continuing the clinic.

He had decided to see his cousin, Dr. Alcide Larouche, not to discuss the partnership, but as a matter of courtesy. Indeed, he found himself eager to see Alcide, for he expected to get from him a full account of Palmyre Delamare once and for all. By now he knew enough of her story to understand why the mere mention of her name was a token of scandal, but he had not yet been able to uncover Dr. Larouche's part in it; and while in the beginning he had not cared a picayune about Palmyre's past, lately he had become curious. "It's too long a story," Uncle Ulysse had said. "Get your cousin Alcide Larouche to tell you." And Fauvette d'Eaubonne had asked in some surprise, "Don't you know why Alcide tried to cut his throat?"

He went directly to the leading confectioner to order the centerpiece for Colette's fete on August fifteenth. From there he called at the Board of Health and made arrangements for their contractor to screen all cisterns on the duRocher city properties. He reached Dr. Larouche's suite in the Maison Blanche a little before eleven o'clock.

Not a chair was empty in the handsomely furnished waiting room. Nottingham lace curtains draped the windows, wicker furniture graced the cocoa carpet, signed paintings hung on the moiré-papered walls. A humming wave of feminine conversation met him as he stepped inside the door. It broke and receded abruptly when his presence became apparent. There was a hiatus of complete silence, during which he noted he was the only man in the midst of many elegant ladies. He stood near a pedestal on which was set a jardiniere holding a potted palm, his broad-brimmed Panama in his hand. The ladies became aware that they were staring, and engaged suddenly in self-conscious talk.

"But yes!" She wore a dashing hat trimmed with a black ostrich plume. "The paper says 'Sacrifices his position for love'!"

"Who? Who?" asked an old lady wearing diamond earrings and an ear trumpet.

"The Infante Alfonso of Orleans," supplied a blonde leaning on a silk-fringed parasol.

"He was deprived of his honors and the regiment!"

"Shocking!" A hand-painted fan wagged more vigorously. "Whom did he marry?"

"Beatrice of Saxe-Coburg, without permission!"

"Poor Spain! She is going to the dogs!"

"*To the dogs!* My dear Anaïs! *Where* did you acquire that filthy American expression?"

Their attention was distracted by the reappearance of a fat matron encrusted in Irish point lace. Following her exit, an angular woman in starched white poked her head out of the inner office. She seemed startled at sight of a man. Her raised brows inquired sternly who he might be.

"I am Dr. duRocher, cousin of Dr. Larouche," Victor said across the room.

"Ah!" Her brows slid back into position. "The new partner!"

Alcide appeared at once and embraced him warmly. "My dear

fellow, at last, at last!" He propelled the younger man toward his office, keeping an arm around his shoulder.

As the door closed, the wave of talk, which had subsided again during the greetings, rose once more and crashed in exclamations. There was considerable excitement among the wealthy ladies who had nothing to do but be sick.

"Excellent, excellent!" Dr. Larouche had a way of saying things twice. "You come just in time to save me from a death of exhaustion. You see I am overworked." He spread a hand toward the outer room. His hand was white and fat, and the black hair on it made it look whiter. "So many pregnancies," he said, annoyed. "I declare, I believe there is something to the claim that this Mississippi River water is responsible for the phenomenal fecundity of our women. It seems to me that when women were drinking rain water we had fewer babies."

"And more typhoid," Victor said. He swore to himself that when he returned from Ancon for his visit in the fall the cisterns would go.

"Ah, but we can treat typhoid," Dr. Larouche winked, "while the only ethical way to cure having a baby is to have it." He laughed loudly at his joke. He wore an unusually high silk cravat fastened with a pearl stick pin; but when he threw back his head, the ropy scar around his throat showed.

He went on briskly to discuss the arrangements for the partnership. Dr. Larouche was a man of many words, and Victor found it difficult to get in any of his own. ". . . an extensive suite in the new building that was going up at St. Charles and Gravier. The very latest surgical equipment. . . ." Victor's eyes showed a spark of interest for the first time, and Alcide rattled on, encouraged. "Entirely new appointments—and a new face and physique, such as yours, my dear fellow, and we may"—he chuckled—"have to lease a whole floor. . . ."

Victor managed at last to wedge in, "Well, I must be frank. I don't know that I'd be at all interested. . . ."

"Oh, all this," Dr. Larouche cut him short, wagging his white hand, "is purely tentative, purely tentative, my boy. You think it over. You write me your reactions, give me your own ideas. We can then thrash out our final terms." That would be best, Victor thought. A diplomatically worded letter would dull the edge of his refusal.

He was wondering how he could introduce the subject of Palmyre Delamare, when suddenly the tone of his cousin's voice changed. "Tell me, is she still there?"

Victor did not pretend to be perplexed. "Yes," he said.

A twitch seemed to pass over Alcide's face. "I would have come occasionally for a week end, but it was no use starting all that again."

"She is very beautiful." He could think of nothing else to say.

"I remember the first time I saw her. It was on a Sunday at church. I was twenty-five then. She was sixteen."

"She still looks quite young."

"I suppose you know?" He looked surprised when Victor shook his head. "I wanted to marry her. If the Larouche family"—his voice became bitter—"had not created such a fuss because her grandfather was a cabaretier, I could have had her—and several lives would have been better, or at least different."

"I understand she married Judge Chambert."

"Who was nearly four times her age. Her father accepted him to slap the face of the family Larouche. The Judge was equally well connected, you know."

"Judge Chambert had something of a reputation as a rake, as I remember."

"With good reason. Even while his first two wives lived, he had his quadroons on the side. He was worn out. It was said he needed a young and beautiful girl to stimulate—you know what I mean?"

Victor shrugged. "It may be that youth and beauty can do more in such cases than science."

"I pictured all the details of her wedding night." Alcide was naturally talkative; nervousness now increased that tendency. "You know what our customs are. . . . I pictured her escorted to the bedroom by her mother, disrobing and putting on the white nightgown and negligee. Then left—propped against the pillows in the big bed—to await her husband. You can guess how it must have been for a sixteen-year-old girl, just out of the Convent, to lie there trembling, afraid of the unknown, finally to find herself alone with. . . . A young girl you love madly, to distraction. . . ." He broke off and resumed recklessly, "Oh, there need be no secrets between you and me. I tried to kill myself."

"I was a small boy at the time." Victor felt uncomfortable. "I didn't know. . . ."

"There was, of course, a great scandal. He took her to New York. One day they were in the Metropolitan Museum. There, while the Judge was examining a Rembrandt, she spoke to a young Jew. He was an artist, twenty-one years old, just starting his career. It was a case of love at first sight. He said, referring to Chambert, 'I thought you were his granddaughter.' She induced the Judge to take her again to the museum. He was there —this David Mendel. He had come every day, same place, same time. They left the Judge gaping before a Gainsborough and ran away. When at last his detectives found them, they were in Paris, and she was enceinte."

"The daughter's name is Miriam," Victor said. "Down here, the servants call her 'Miyám.' "

"The Judge did not divorce her. Divorce, then as now, was not mentioned in polite circles. *He* gave, as his reason, religion. But those who knew him well called it revenge."

Victor shook his head, looking at the floor. All this had happened over twenty years ago. But so firmly did his people cling to their ways that it was not impossible for something similar to happen even today. So much unnecessary suffering, even cruelty. He could not, looking around this sumptuous office, feel sorry for Dr. Larouche. His cousin had done well, and his days seemed full enough of life's favors. But Palmyre—and then, Miriam—who no doubt was unaware that she was a victim of old prejudices and foolish prides. . . .

The silence that had fallen between the two men sitting opposite each other reached the point of embarrassment, and Victor hastened to talk of other things, but his cousin's interest seemed to have waned. Victor declined his invitation to dinner. Taking a cab, he ordered the driver to the St. Louis Cemetery. He got out at the gate on Claiborne Street, and went in search of the sexton to arrange for opening the family tomb. Early this morning when he had looked in on Zulime, he knew that the end was very close.

When he got back to "Clair de Lune" that evening, Zulime was dying. Her mind, however, was still lucid, and when she saw him, she tried to raise herself. He took her gently by the shoulders and laid her back on her pillows. She felt like a shell in his hands.

"I wait till Ti Vic come," she said in Negro French. He sat down on the edge of her mattress, and bent his ear close to hear her. "If mitraise say it all right, I go now." She was beyond the will of any mistress, but she had been so long accustomed to taking orders that she asked permission even to die.

"Zuzu, you're not suffering?" he asked her tenderly.

"Zuzu suffer nice now." Perhaps she was comparing her present weakness with the iron collar and the whip. She had known both during her rebellious service as concubine to her Baton Rouge master.

"Is there anything you want?"

She did not hear him.

"Zuzu run away for last time, forever." A spark of malice showed in her dim eyes. "Dis time, can't catch Zuzu cut off ears, bran' shoulder. . . ."

"Is there anything you want?" he repeated.

"Maybe I see my Mama again." She stared at the whitewashed ceiling. "My Mama, she bring big money at auction. Zuzu seven year ol' den. Zuzu never see, hear her since. Zuzu got lot to tell her Mama now."

He leaned very close to the shriveled scar where her ear should have been.

"Tell me if there is anything you want, Zulime." The sun was

166

setting. A pale glow came through the window and fell on the white iron bed.

"Yas, yas. I wish to ride train." She knew wagons and boats; she had never been on a train in her life. "Even dead, Zuzu wish to take train ride."

"Very well, Zulime. It will be arranged." He stroked her yellow forehead. She talked on, as much to herself as to him.

"My firs' son die, he bury in box like chicken coop. He neck too long, boss man break neck, make head roll over. Den dey nail on top, and big nail stick in eye. Toted off in wagon dey haul slops. Me, I go right on work, same as other day."

"That was long ago, Zulime." He knew now what she meant when she said, so often, "Zuzu got a bad mem'ry. It won' let her forget."

"Zuzu wish ride to train in carriage like lady. Miché Clouzat, he got fine shiny black carriage, glass sides." She meant the hearse. "See pretty flowers through. No?"

"Yes, of course, Zulime. As you wish."

Father Guichard was summoned. He stayed alone with the dying woman for some time. Then Victor and Nanaine joined him to pray. Papa remained in the big house. "I have seen enough of death," he said. "What sight I have left I shall save to witness my own."

Zulime's progeny were called in: the grandson Bazile; the great-grandson Zeph, and his wife Glad; even the two great-great-grandchildren, silent and scared. They all kneeled on the bare floor. Nanaine prayed intensely, fingering her rosary with an efficient progress from one black bead to the next. Her mouth set hard, and she frowned a little when she prayed. Glad once had said, "She don't *ask* God *kin He please*. She *tell* God He *got to*." Looking toward Glad now, the doctor noticed how heavy her abdomen was with her pregnancy. The weight hung over her bent knees like a huge melon. Her time was near.

All were there save Cumba. The West Indian woman was engaged in weird incantations over a wash boiler which she had set on a fire in the yard. The doctor could see her from his place near the door. From time to time she dropped some eerie ingredient into her witch's brew and stirred it with a broomstick, muttering and shaking from head to foot.

It grew dark. "Notre Père, qui êtes aux cieux . . . ," the priest prayed, and the others made the quiet responses. Outside, the flames leaped up from the charcoal and kindling, writhing about the base of the boiler, and Cumba's black face in their red light glistened with sweat. A disgusting odor floated in over the fragrance of night jasmine. Cumba was reaching up and tearing handfuls of moss from the limbs of the pecan tree and dropping it into the kettle. She shrieked once, hoarsely.

Victor slipped out into the yard.

"Cumba! Be quiet. Let Zulime die in peace."

"She dying!" Cumba screamed. "I knew it. I knew it when dat swallow fly in her window! Ol' woman die, sign of bad storm, big trouble! Aie! Aie!" She bent over as if she had horrible cramps, holding her elbows against her stomach, wailing.

"Be quiet! Or I'll drive you off the place!"

"Wanga say Miché Vic cross water. He cross water today!"

He had forgotten about the ball of wax enclosing St. Expedite. He made an impatient gesture and went back to Zulime. Cumba cringed against the tree, moaning.

He was alone with her when she opened her eyes for the last time.

"Beau miché. . . ."

"Zulime. . . ." He raised the mosquito bar and placed his hand over both of hers, clasped over a crucifix.

"Zuzu . . . tried. . . . She done her best. . . ."

"Then you succeeded, Zulime." He bent over and in a surge of affection kissed her cheek.

He sat there helplessly watching her struggle for oxygen. She was shut off from him now in coma. No matter how close he came, he could never get near her. A trickle of saliva came from the corner of her mouth. He wiped it away. Her hard breathing became irregular, stopped, and did not start again. The face that had once been beautiful became beautiful once more with an expression of freedom that war and statutes had never been able to confer.

He looked at his watch. It was midnight. Zulime's long day was ended. The moon, rising, flooded the room with silver. Victor straightened the limbs, drew the sheet all the way up over the body, over the face. He had the feeling that he was drawing the sheet over an era, a finished age.

Twenty-one

The doctor had collected enough charms to make a bonfire, and in the street before the bank he had made short ceremony of them with kerosene and match. Even the barber's wife, who had come to him with her backache, surrendered her bottle of Four Thieves' Vinegar purchased from Guy Chauvin, and found herself improved. The grateful barber had given the doctor a shaving mug that now rested with the private cups of other citizens on the barbershop shelf.

Victor liked these people. Even their faults and their foibles, while trying his patience, endeared them to him. As, for example, the vice of the storekeeper, who, with two cents' worth of black pepper, so often gave lagniappe worth three that eventually Bidault held a mortgage on his store. As Glad said, "They not all *good* people here, but they good-*natured*. That's what I *rather*." The doctor found their large grins and warm greetings pleasant as he went through town. "Good morning, M'sieu' le docteur. Comment ça va?" The old men and women who had known him since he was a child called him "Miché Vic." He would miss them when, in little more than a fortnight, he left for the Isthmus. He would even miss, he thought with a chuckle, the pellagra records that had been his companions through the long hot hours of the afternoon and night.

It bothered him that he had not yet found time to draft a diplomatic refusal to Dr. Larouche. The arrangements for Zulime's burial on the Friday previous had kept him busy. Ovide Clouzat had prepared the body, and Zulime was laid out in the room where she died. "Do your best," Victor ordered, and the undertaker answered jovially, "I will perform a miracle. I will give her back her ears." He had parted the rippling hair in the center and combed it down softly over the sides, so that one who did not know would never guess what lay beneath. Her coffin was made of enduring cypress. "Even Madame the Mayoress was buried in plain pine," Ovide said. "But then," he winked, "Miché le maire was no more interested in keeping Madame in death than in life. Died in the morning and buried in the evening. *Zut!* just like that. Without benefit of embalming. Perhaps he considered Madame embalmed enough?" He winked again. The doctor did not ask the undertaker to explain his joke. He was watching him stuff Zulime's shrunken cheek with sawdust.

This morning, Victor had received a letter from Dr. Larouche, asking him to attend Madame Minerve de Gerbeau-Vignaud in her imminent confinement. "She is due in less than two weeks," his cousin wrote, "and your being on the scene will save the whole family's moving back to the city in this insufferable heat. I cannot come myself, you understand." Victor decided that in staying away, his cousin was not virtuously resisting temptation, but cautiously avoiding a domestic explosion. There was a wistful note of regret between the lines. "Madame de Gerbeau, the mother, will send for a competent midwife to assist you. I am sure you won't mind, my dear boy. . . ."

He sat at Jolivet's old desk pondering his reply. Perhaps now was the moment to frame a definitive *no* to Larouche's partnership proposition. He made an attempt, but found that he was not in a writing mood. He could not, however, refuse to attend Minerve Vignaud, and her accouchement would in no way interfere with his present plans. If need be, he could leave her next day in the hands of the midwife. He ended by scribbling his acceptance briefly on a prescription blank and apologizing for a haste that did not exist.

When he had dismissed his last patient, he drove out to Chin-chuba to visit the charcoal maker, whom he had not seen in several days. An agreeable surprise awaited him. The suppurated area in the arm showed signs of clearing; there was definite improvement in the surrounding tissue. He knew that Philo Fanchon was saved, and the arm as well.

"You are a better doctor than I," he said to the boy Felix. "Your treatment while I couldn't come seems to have saved your father."

"I only did w'at you tell me. An' I kept my hands clean." He turned them over for the doctor to see the close-clipped nails.

"You did fine work."

Felix rubbed his bare big toe against the floor, embarrassed.

"I invite you to my shack behin' the swamp. It is a very fine shack wit a mud floor an' a palmetto roof an' I have a rifle an' five 'coon skins." He said it all in one breath and panted a little when he had finished.

Victor smiled down at him. "I will be glad to come some day when I have more time."

Madame Fanchon sat in a corner and said nothing. But the doctor knew he had a friend in her son Felix.

He whistled as he drove back to town. Rougette twitched her ears, unaccustomed to such sounds. No doubt Jolivet had always been too weary to whistle.

From the bridge he saw Miriam working away at her easel. He would celebrate his success by having a few words with her.

"I missed you," she said at once.

"We lost an old servant. We buried her in the city."

"Yes. I saw the black-bordered notice on all the lampposts. It said, 'Zulime, F.W.C.' What does F.W.C. mean?"

"Free woman of color. She was part white. She was proud of that designation and wanted it on her funeral poster. Of course it is obsolete now."

"It is sad." Miriam stroked the hound's head. "I mean, it is really freedom that is obsolete."

"Yes, Mamzelle Philosophe?"

"Oh, you may laugh at my philosophy, but if you look around, you will see that I am right. Slavery was never abolished. People, particularly white people, are still slaves—everybody being not what they are, not what they want to be, but what they think they ought to be, or even what other people think they ought to be!"

"What a splendid little suffragette you would make!"

"Well, it is true." Her cheeks flushed. "To select, to think for oneself—that is the greatest privilege. Spiritual freedom. Physical freedom is nothing compared with it. And so few people exercise the right to be an individual, to be—different. I mean, to be a *person!*" She peered up at him, anxious that he understand.

"Well! I see I should have brought you a pulpit instead of a present."

"You brought me a present?" She jumped up from her folding stool.

In New Orleans the Wednesday previous, he had come across a hand-painted scarf he thought would become Miriam's blondness. He purchased it on impulse, then, on the boat back, almost cast it into the lake, knowing he had neither right nor reason to encourage her affection. But in the end he had kept it—indeed, he had been carrying it in his coat pocket ever since—arguing with himself that he owed her some token of appreciation for her help with Madame Gaspard. He knew, however, that it would take the joy out of it for her if he gave it in the nature of a reward.

He handed her the gossamer thing wrapped in tissue paper. "We will call it a present for want of a better name."

She shook out the folds, threw the scarf over her head and shoulders. The pale green made a beautiful contrast with her tawny skin and hair. He smiled, admiring her.

"Oh!" Her fingers crept up over the soft stuff. "It's lovely!"

Suddenly she threw her arms around his neck and kissed him hard on the lips.

He put her from him gently.

"Until tomorrow," he said.

He did not realize he had made a promise until he was nearly back in town.

Bazile had a message for him. Nanaine's friend, Madame Vigée, wished to see him at once. He ate from a tray in his room, changed his linen, and set out again.

Madame's home, named "Tranquilité"—though she could hardly be said to lead a tranquil life there—stood on a spacious lawn between Fauvette d'Eaubonne's and the de Gerbeaus'. As the doctor reached the top of the stairs, the open door of the salon revealed the servant girl Bibi putting a starched Mother Hubbard on the Venus de Milo. Madame's husband on his frequent trips to Europe had brought back nymphs and goddesses that on his death Madame had transported to "Tranquilité" because she was too disturbed by their nakedness to keep them in her city house, and too sentimental to destroy them. M'sieur Vigée had valued them highly. His penchant for nude art had always pained and puzzled Madame.

Bibi was having trouble. Venus seemed to resent clothes, and the voluptuous sloping shoulder kept slipping out of the stiff garment. The girl produced a safety pin and restrained the shoulder under a deft pleat.

"Mitraise know herse'f got a belly now because it hurt." The girl giggled.

Madame was sitting in her bedroom, hemming a small apron, probably for some marble sylph. Fat old Coucou, her ever-present fox terrier, lay on a pillow at her feet.

"I do not digest my food," Madame complained. "I have a continual lump in my throat, and I belch sourly."

Time had touched his aunt's other friends lightly, but on Madame Vigée it had trampled with hobnailed boots. It was another instance of God's partiality. Today, without her wig, she was a revolting old hag, and the diamonds in her shriveled ears and on her knotty fingers only underlined her ugliness. The doctor made the routine test of tongue and pulse, asked questions.

"How can I hope to remain well when my meals are constantly interrupted by the coarse shouts of *boarders?*" She gestured with the apron toward "Joli Bois." "They play a crude game called 'baseball.' They run and shriek. This morning—*sp-lllllsh!*"—she sprayed the air with saliva—"the ball falls into my birdbath. Ah!"

It was soon apparent that Madame Vigée was not suffering from faulty digestion. She was suffering from Fauvette d'Eaubonne.

"Do you know what those hoodlums call her? Miss 'Doughbones.' It is enough to make her forebears burst their shrouds! So now she has translated her name, and she calls herself 'Goodwater.' Do you hear?" She leaned forward and shook her finger in his face, as if he had something to do with it. *"Goodwater!"*

He wrote out a prescription for Madame's heartburn and another for her nerves.

"She has sold her silver gong, and now rings for dinner with a *cowbell*," Madame went on furiously. "Such noise! And they all go herding into the house like cattle."

"A teaspoon in half a glass of water after every meal." He handed Madame the prescriptions. "One pellet on rising and retiring."

"And she has absolutely no modesty. She rides that bicycle astride." Madame reached down, plucked a flea from Coucou's corrugated neck, and cracked it between her thumbnails.

"It is the only way to ride a bicycle," the doctor said somewhat wearily.

"In *my* day, a lady *had* no legs. My sainted mother"—she crossed herself—"even wore a nightgown when she took a bath. She was a shining example of modesty."

"But not of hygiene, Madame."

"As for myself, on my wedding night, I insisted that M'sieur Vigée undress behind the door."

Madame's modesty, the doctor thought, might have accounted for M'sieur's interest in art.

"You should be all right by tomorrow, Madame. I shall not return unless you send for me."

"And do you know who plays baseball with those beasts? Your friend—ah, ah, ah. . . ." She beat her brow for the name.

"Harry Lockwood."

"But he does not go there to play. Ah, no!" She wagged her hairless head. "He goes there because Palmyre Delamare and her daughter go there. 'Joli Bois' is but one step from a house of assigna. . . ."

"Good morning, Madame."

"Wait!" She caught his arm. "You must look at Coucou."

At the sound of his name, the terrier raised his head, then laid it again between his paws and resumed snoring with his eyes open. Coucou's eunuch existence was made more miserable by overfeeding. Madame stuffed him, and when the dog had eaten so much he could hold no more, and refused the proffered dainties, Madame feared immediately that he was sick. She would then force him to eat, and presently the poor creature would be sick of necessity.

"He vomited all his brioche this morning."

"That was probably good for him."

"Kindly examine him."

"I am not a veterinarian, Madame."

"No?" She sharpened a barb for him. "But perhaps you specialize in hounds?" So she, too, had heard about his setting Dixie's leg.

"I specialize in being humane when the occasion offers, Madame."

She turned from him, a knowing smirk on her ugly face. At that moment, Bibi burst into the room.

"Zeph—sa femme é tombé!"

Zeph was there to fetch the doctor. Glad had fallen.

Glad's child had light brown skin, Zulime's legacy. Victor went out to the carriage house where Zeph was waiting with the two other children. They jumped up and down when they saw him coming, shouting and clapping their hands. Zeph had promised them a brother. He looked at the doctor dumbly.

"Ouai," Victor said in Gombo French. "A fine boy."

Zeph grinned. "Ma femme?"

"She's all right." After a moment, he asked, "How did it happen?"

"She slip on boardwalk to our well."

"Well, no harm has been done. You have your baby a few days sooner, that's all. What would you like for his gift?"

"I would like—" Zeph began and stopped. "Non, non. It is too big one to ask."

"Let's see what it is, anyway."

"I do not wish *thing*." Zeph sweated and stammered in the effort to express himself. "Thing do not last. Thing—they wear out, they break, like us. I would like"—his eyes shone—"I would like that you make my son a doctor for his people. Then he teach and make more doctor. Then w'at he do live—it last for alway."

The two men looked at each other.

"It *is* a big thing. Not the asking, but the idea." He paused. No casual promise would suffice. And doing what Zeph wanted would not be easy. "I shall try, Zeph. I shall try as hard as I can."

Twenty-two

This morning Miriam was waiting for him at the side of the road. She wore her wide-brimmed straw and a simple blue dimity dress. She had dispensed with her smock.

"I heard Rougette's hoofs."

"Aren't you working today?"

"No—the painting is finished." She hesitated. "I would like to give it to you, but. . . ." She did not have to conclude, "But it would only embarrass you for an explanation, to your family, to your fiancée."

"What are you going to do next?"

"I would like to do something to justify my existence."

"Great heavens!" He smiled. "You sound as serious as a sermon."

"I am. My father always said, 'To do nothing constructive with one's self, one's time, constitutes the greatest degree of immorality.' He said, 'It is more immoral to do nothing good than it is to do something bad.'" She quoted him exactly, as if reciting a catechism.

"Well, you are painting."

"That is just passing time. It isn't *using* it. I mean—*do* something—like my mother used to do. There was a little charity hospital in Froissy. She worked there two afternoons every week."

"We have the school for deaf-mutes here." He glanced toward the roofs of the convent buildings. "Perhaps you could teach them to draw."

She jumped at his suggestion. "I would like that! I know a little sign language!" She made rapid movements with her fingers.

He shook his head, wonderingly. "Is there anything you don't know?"

"I learned it from a girl whose brother was mute."

"Perhaps I can arrange with the Mother Superior. I am treating one of the Sisters there."

"Please!" she begged. "Today?"

They drove back along the sandy road, leaving Dixie behind to guard her painting paraphernalia. The wind was blowing from the north, and the clean smell of pine swept away the odor of the swamp. She held on to her hat, as the breeze was tearing at it.

"You never wear your scarf?"

"No. . . ." After a moment, she added, "It holds the scent of your person. I do not wish to lose that."

"Carbolic and arnica."

"Perhaps. But it is yours."

"Miriam"—he hesitated—"I am going away soon."

She was silent.

"Child, what are you thinking?"

"Oh, I am thinking of all the things we will *never* do together.

. . . And I am *not* a child!" It was the first time he had ever heard anything approaching anger in her voice.

He did not reply.

Suddenly she blurted out in English, "I hate that word *never!* It is horrid in every language! It is hard, cold, heavy—like a stone falling on the heart!"

"You are too young to say 'never', Miriam."

"Oh, you—you know all about women's bodies, but you don't know anything about their minds! I am as old as Methuselah. I am old because I am a woman."

Abruptly her voice calmed. "You love your cousin very much?"

"She is to be my wife."

"But do you love her?"

"What is love? Do you know that, too, Mamzelle Philosophe?"

"Yes." She took her hat off and laid it in her lap, letting her short hair blow. "I talk to you all day long, I wake up in the night and talk to you. And no matter what I do, no matter where I am, you are there, in the back of my mind, in the bottom of my heart. And I would give you anything I have, I would work for you, I would be glad to suffer for you. I would do anything for you. Anything!"

He could feel the fire in her body beside him. For a brief moment he longed to touch it, to burn himself in it. He waited a while before he said, "Then do this for me, Miriam. Be happy. You deserve to be."

They had turned in at the gates of the convent. Some children were playing tag on the lawn. The sight of such a merry game without shouts or sound of any kind had the odd quality of a dream.

"I'll try."

She let him help her down from the buggy. He pretended not to see her tears.

The Saturday clinic was heavy. He forgot the morning in the pressing routine of the afternoon, and presently the memory of Miriam's face and voice slipped from his mind, leaving him with

178

a sense of relief. A steady stream of patients came and went, and a number of new grigri had been added to the heap that filled the washbasket. The last for the day was a diminutive doll stuffed with the ashes of the water moccasin and the powdered, dried hearts of hummingbirds. The girl Coco had worn it around her waist.

"It is for good luck in love," her mother Zabette said. She was a tall, handsome Negress, an air of intelligence in her bearing.

Coco's strange topaz eyes left the grigri she had been persuaded to give up and settled on the doctor's face. She gave him a sidewise look full of coquetry.

"Mamaloi is ver' angry wit Miché le docteur. He take her people away. Me, I think Miché le docteur ver' nice man."

"How are you sick?" the doctor asked. He was more concerned with what Coco felt than what she thought. He remembered her sensual dancing at the St. John's Eve rites and a strong suspicion of her trouble came to him.

"She have headache all de time," Zabette spoke for her. "She leave good place at Roussel because she sick."

"I cannot eat," Coco whimpered. "My t'roat it 'urt w'en I swallow."

He put on his reflector and had her open her mouth. She complied readily, throwing back her head so that the oily ripples of black hair fell behind her gold-ringed ears. Ulcers showed on both tonsils. Then he took her temperature, the thermometer recording a little over a hundred.

"Take off your waist," he ordered.

The girl giggled. Her fingers flew down the buttons, she pulled her arms from the sleeves, and the blouse fell over her round hips, leaving tan arms and shoulders bare of her chemise. The expected eruption appeared in a copper-colored patch above the left breast.

"You may put on your waist now."

She rebuttoned reluctantly, her red lips screwed into a little pout.

"She got measles?" Zabette inquired in surprise.

He delayed replying. Looking once more in her mouth, and using a tongue depressor, he found a gray lesion on the inside of one cheek. The mucous patch was conclusive. He turned to Zabette.

"How are this girl's morals?" he asked in English.

Zabette, sensing the situation, drew her bosom up proudly. "She got no morals—she got *measles!*"

The pathetic humor of Zabette's reply made him shake his head and smile gently.

"She must discontinue seeing men," he told the mother firmly. "Do you understand?" Coco was in the secondary stage of the disease, when it was actively contagious.

He went behind the screen and returned with a loaded syringe. Coco cringed. She began to cry and scream at sight of the needle. This time he had difficulty in inducing her to lift her skirt. She continued to whimper for some time after he had given her the painful intramuscular injection.

"You must keep going to the doctor for two years," he told her. "You must let him do that to you twice a week. If you don't," he thought of some fitting threat, "you will become covered with ugly sores and people will put you away to starve to death in the swamp."

"I'll come! I'll come!" She was sobbing now.

He went again to the medicine cabinet and put up a mouthwash and a jar of mercurial ointment, and gave them to Zabette with detailed instructions. "For a few weeks she can spread this sickness through contact, even through dishes and glasses, so be careful. Keep her at home, and above all don't allow her any—visitors." Zabette understood his emphasis. She shook her head affirmatively.

"Come back next Wednesday," he told Coco. "And even when I am not here, you must come back to the new doctor."

As he was about to dismiss them, he asked, "Who has been coming to see you?"

Coco stopped crying and became sullenly silent.

"They are sick, too," he coaxed her. "And if you tell me, we can help them."

"Nobody," she said stubbornly.

He saw the futility of pressing her.

"Where do you live, Coco?"

"On the Chinchuba road, jus' pas' the convent."

"Well, you must receive nobody from now on. If you do, we will have to arrest you, put you in jail."

Zabette flared up at him. "You can't do dat! The law say a white man can't cohabit wit a colored woman. But it say he can *go* wit her. According to *you* folks' law, it a crime if we marry you, but not if we sleep wit you. God's law is different. According to *Him,* it's a sin d'other way 'round!"

He could not argue with her about the concubinage statute. She knew more about it than he. *God's law is different.* . . .

After they left, he thought of something trivial in itself but big with possibility. Justin Dufour had been to see him on the morning he was called away to treat Philo Fanchon's burns. Returning from his call, he had seen Justin going up the Chinchuba road in the bakery wagon. The young man had not come back to see him.

He found Justin frosting brioches. The odor of baking bread spread far over the town when the wind was blowing from the north, and several customers, drawn by the smell, were waiting at the door for hot loaves for their supper. Among them was Madame Naquin, shivering in her shawl. Her malarial chills found comfort near the ovens where Dufour the father worked with his long wooden shovels. Dufour was dusted with flour from head to foot. Even his eyebrows were whitened.

"Miché le docteur comes for bread? Only the flutes are ready," he said.

"I come to see Justin."

The father shrugged and returned to his baking. He opened the iron door and threw more pine into the furnace. The blaze leaped out, and he locked it in again with a loud slam.

Justin came forward, licking his fingers.

"I'm sorry I was called away on an emergency the morning you came to see me," the doctor said.

"That's all right." Justin smiled. He was big and bearish like his father and blond and ruddy like Madame, his mother. "Myself, I well understand such emergencies."

The doctor disregarded the innuendo. "Can we go into the shop? I wish to talk to you."

"I am not sick," Justin said. "I only had a sore throat. It has passed."

"It is imperative that I see you alone."

"What is this with my son?" the baker demanded. The others had been served and were gone, but Madame Naquin lingered, waiting for a French twist.

"Only answer me this," the doctor said to Justin. "Have you seen the girl Coco? I wish to help you."

"What business is it of yours?"

"What is going on here?" The father came forward, wiping the sweat from his neck with a flour sack.

"If you have, it is everybody's business. You are a purveyor of food to the public, and if you have been with her, you must stop your occupation at once."

"Ah!" Justin's red face grew redder with anger. "It is only the cream-of-the-cream that have privileges with Coco, is it? Sellers of bread have no rights!"

"What do you mean?"

"I am as good as Leon Roussel!" Justin shouted. "And you can tell him for me, if he does not stay away. . . ."

The doctor noticed Madame Naquin's greedy eyes, and was silent. He said only, "Come to see me at the office tomorrow."

"You'll see me in hell first!"

"You go, do you hear, you——?" The father used an obscene French word. "I am tired of your ailing around here. A headache today—a rash yesterday—a this, a that! Lazy, complaining, trying to get out of work! Spending your time God knows where!"

Madame Naquin's wise wagging of the head indicated that

she knew where. But yes! From such a conversation, any fool could guess. . . .

"I shall wait for you tomorrow. If you don't come, I shall be back."

As he went away, he heard loud, angry talk, in which Madame Dufour's voice, defending her son, was uppermost.

The garçonnière was filled again with Leon's friends from the city. A poker game was going on in the ground-floor apartment. As the doctor walked in, a large pool of chips lay in the middle of the table, and Leon and a young man in a plaid suit were bidding against each other, while the others, out of the game for the time, watched tensely. When Leon called his opponent's hand and the cards were spread on the table, he muttered an oath, and the young man in plaid smiled and raked in the chips with both hands. The others broke their silence with a laugh of relief.

Leon was in a bad humor and what the doctor had to say to him was not calculated to improve his mood.

"Is it important?"

"It is to you," the doctor said.

Leon threw his cigarette into a brass cuspidor and drained his absinthe. "Play my hand, Marcel," he said to young Lavalle, who had the dejected air of one who had already lost all his money.

They went up to the house, to Julien's study. Julien was not there. He was busy moving into the bank building, having rented all the space adjoining Jolivet's office for his all-important project, the New Orleans-Mandeville Causeway Corporation. The senior Lockwood was inclined to report favorably to his Northern superiors; as an engineering scheme, the causeway seemed sound, except for one hazard over which no degree of mechanical genius had any control: the equinoctial hurricanes that from time to time threw the lake into convulsive havoc, and tore and twisted and splintered and smashed every structure yet devised by men. It was the history of hurricanes that Lockwood was investigating now, studying the strength of tides, tabulating the momentum of winds. Meanwhile, Julien assured himself of senatorial support at the State capitol, prepared to sell stock, and planned an ambitious real-estate program.

"Well?" Leon said, picking up a map from his father's desk and looking at it upside down.

The doctor went straight to the point. "Have you been seeing the girl Coco?"

Leon dropped the map and scowled. He had had a little too much absinthe again.

"How can I convince you that my life is my own?"

"Coco has a social disease," the doctor said quietly.

Leon was visibly shaken.

"I got to her only once. That bastard of a baker's son. . . ."

"He has done you an inestimable service by keeping you away."

Leon swore under his breath.

"You are probably lucky in more ways than one. But you had better come with me to the office, anyhow."

"For what?" He looked alarmed.

"You'll see. A matter of precaution."

"I'll be damned if I will! Who are you to. . . ."

"Do you want me to tell your mother?"

"Sacré! You . . . !"

He saw the doctor's eyes narrow. Leon realized that this was no idle bluff.

"Come on, Leon."

Leon rose, taking his time. "Since coming back from the Isthmus, you've put your nose in many people's affairs." He followed Victor out of Julien's study. "Has it over occurred to you that it might get cut off?"

Twenty-three

"Madame Vigée is furious!" Nanaine informed him three days later. "She is telling everybody you left her to go to a Negro servant!"

"I left her dog to deliver Zeph's wife," Victor said. "I am sorry if Madame's ideas of protocol were violated."

Not only God, but now Dr. duRocher had neglected Madame Vigée. Both doctor and Deity placed even black babies before her. She felt sorry for herself from one end of the beach to the other. And when Victor called to see Minerve de Gerbeau-Vignaud, Madame her mother advised him her daughter was sleeping. He detected a coolness in the air that indubitably blew from the direction of "Tranquilité."

Summer society was further shaken by his scandalous attitude in the case of the girl Coco. Madame Naquin's account of the scene in the bakery was all asterisks, but she managed to say more with suggestive silence than if she had adhered to the facts and shouted. Cautious people stopped buying bread, and Dufour's business was badly hurt. For this he did not thank the doctor, any more than he appreciated the doctor's insistence that Justin's help be withdrawn from all work involving direct contact with their product. Madame Dufour hated Dr. duRocher for the lie he had pinned on her pure and virginal son. The doctor had made for himself two excellent enemies at the bakery. But he did not stop there.

"Of course," Nanaine said, "we expect you to have the girl run out of town."

Olympe, who had come to call—and not really to discuss the disgusting affair—shook her head approvingly.

"Why?" the doctor asked.

"Why? Why?" his aunt sputtered. "For the sake of society. That's why!"

"*Society!*" Her limited point of view preyed on his patience. "There is a society beyond your card tables and coffee urns! It is better to keep her here where she can be watched and compelled to be treated! If she goes somewhere else, she will neglect herself and spread her syphilis!"

At the sound of the word that was never mentioned except in medical books, Olympe swayed. She fumbled in her silver mesh bag for her smelling salts.

185

"It is a crime!" raged Nanaine. "If she stays here, she may contaminate one of our own young men!"

"One of our own young men may have contaminated her! And what," he demanded, "do you call a crime?"

"Is—is it so contagious?" Olympe asked in a weak voice. Perhaps she suspected. . . .

The doctor was too angry to answer.

"Where is the crime?" he persisted.

"That she should dare. . . ."

"That she should dare to be born, perhaps." His eyes flashed. "The crime is the father's who bred her. Who made her neither white nor black! The crime is yours—and yours!" In his anger, he flipped his hand at his aunt, at Olympe.

"Ah!" breathed Nanaine, aghast. "Listen to him! He has gone mad!"

"It is your crime because you are part of the society that made the laws that made such creatures as Coco! Oh, yes—you read in the papers with self-righteous satisfaction: 'The inspector issues orders to the police to enforce the concubinage law.' 'Our police are doing their duty!' you smile. Their duty! What is it? To punish persons of the Caucasian and Negro races for cohabitation, while condoning casual intercourse between them!"

At the word "intercourse," Olympe closed her eyes and clapped a hand over her heart. She clutched her smelling salts tighter.

"It is a good law!" Nanaine insisted. "Otherwise a white man could be held responsible for the support. . . ."

"It is a bad law!" he contradicted hotly. "Any law that is not good for everybody, white or black, is bad!"

Bazile appeared to announce Madame Morel, wife of the banker. M'sieur Morel was of no importance, beyond financing such things as the purchase of cows, but Madame descended from a courtier of Louis XIV; and while it was claimed by some that her relative remained in royal favor only because of his faculty for entertaining the king with amusing gossip, the fact that he had been at court at all was sufficient to admit Madame at least as far as the circumference of Nanaine's circle. Besides,

Madame had inherited from her ancestor one distinction beyond the pale of doubt: a long tongue and the ability to wag it.

The doctor, wishing he had left earlier, excused himself.

The next evening he did not stay after the clinic, as was his custom, to "play" with the pellagra files. What at first was a curious game had become an absorbing interest, and some correspondence with the Surgeon General had resulted in a request for a monograph on Dr. duRocher's claims of noncommunicability. He laid aside, with some reluctance, the statistics he was drafting to write the article.

It was Olympe's receiving day, and he had promised Colette at least to put in an appearance. When he arrived at "Beaux Arbres," a squall was rising. The customary calm that preceded a blow lay on the lake, and the water gleamed weirdly under a low black sky that flashed green and growled and flashed again. Servants were hurrying children off the beach, rushing ahead of the threatening downpour. It was the first of the thunder-and-lightning storms that every year announced the onset of the equinoctial season.

Colette, seeing him, crossed the room toward the drawn folding doors. She wore a strikingly becoming gown of blue net and voile, and every eye followed her. Her sparkling smile rejoiced him, and he was pleased to find no traces of the moody spells that he had been striving to banish with his love and reassurances. She laid her fingers on his arm. "Come, let me give you coffee. You look tired, darling." A deep tenderness for him showed in her face. His heart warmed to her. She was as fine as she was lovely. Certainly she must have heard—*he leaves us to die in our tracks while he goes off to the woods.* . . . But she was above the malicious murmurings of such as Madame Naquin.

Olympe received him coolly. He presented his compliments to the company. There were assembled Mesdames Vigée and Morel, Madame de Gerbeau and her eldest daughter Celeste, Nanaine, and Father Guichard. Several other ladies who had called had already left, fleeing in their carriages before the squall. Olympe sat beside the coffee table, where a silver urn swung in a rack above an alcohol flame, and almost depleted trays of cakes and cut-glass dishes of dragées and bonbons showed that the afternoon was wearing to a successful close. Olympe poured black coffee into a Sèvres cup for the doctor.

"As I was saying," Madame Morel resumed, "I go, once a week, to see my niece, Sister Augustine, at the convent. And yesterday I was much amazed at some astonishing news she gave me."

"Tell them! Tell them, dear Madame Morel!" Olympe urged. It became at once evident to the doctor that Madame Morel, never actively sought, had been invited today with deliberate purpose.

Madame needed little coaxing.

"With great joy Sister Augustine informs me that the mutes now have a drawing teacher." She waited for effect.

"Go on, go on, dear Madame." Olympe clasped her hands so tightly that her diamonds gouged her flesh.

"So far, so good. But who do you imagine the drawing teacher is?" She tortured them by slowly sipping her anisette.

The storm broke. Somewhere a batten blind banged, and the shouts of running servants were heard from below. The wind swept from the gallery into the drawing room and troubled the skirts of the ladies. Doudouce and another girl appeared to close doors and windows. Presently the rain came roaring down, and the thunder continued to crack and rumble. It had grown dark, and the closed room smelled of burning lamps.

"Well, who is it?" inquired Madame de Gerbeau impatiently. She always dressed in black, with a cameo on her bosom, and sat erect, never allowing her back to touch the chair.

Madame Morel obliged eagerly.

"The daughter of that woman at 'Belle Pointe'!"

"Palmyre Delamare!" Olympe left no room for doubt.

"Mon Dieu!" exclaimed Madame Vigée, clapping her bony hand to her bony cheek.

188

"Ah!" said Madame de Gerbeau and Celeste in unison.

Nanaine, who had probably known for the past twenty-four hours, began to fan herself vigorously, lips compressed. Colette looked surprised and disturbed. Father Guichard, suddenly finding it warm, took out a handkerchief and wiped his forehead.

"Our poor little mutes," Madame Morel observed, "who have no voices to defend themselves from such an outrage!"

"Are we going to stand for this?" Olympe demanded, looking at the priest. "Can we allow this horror to continue?"

"I think," Madame Vigée rasped worse than ever, "that the Mother Superior should be instructed to send the girl away at once. And I also think, as I thought once before to no avail"— she stabbed at the priest with her sharp eyes—"that the Delamare woman should be barred from church."

"She has never had the decency to call on me," Madame de Gerbeau said icily. The ladies resented Palmyre so much the more because she had not given them the opportunity to snub her.

"She is shaking the very foundations of our society!" Nanaine claimed.

"Well, what are we going to do?" Olympe's voice was hard, her face vindictive. With great dignity, she adjusted the dog collar of pearls she wore about her thin throat. "Are we going to allow this woman and her daughter not only to invade our own lives, but the lives of our children as well?"

The doctor winced. Poor Olympe. How big she wanted to be, and how small she actually was. He looked around the circle at the women who had spoken. Madame de Gerbeau, fat and flabby, her arms spreading on the rests of the chair like soft wax. Her daughter, Celeste, past forty, a drab spinster under her tulle scarves. Madame Morel and her warts. Madame Vigée and her wig. Olympe, the widow with a living husband. Nanaine, who had never married because no man was good enough, living barrenly with her pride. "She would have refused Jesus Himself," Uncle Ulysse once said profanely, "because Joseph's family tree had no noble roots in France." These women whose womanhood was wasted, whom love had cast aside, or never touched, could not forgive Palmyre Delamare her passion. They could not pardon her having known that exquisite insanity of the heart.

They could, the doctor thought, perhaps even have forgiven her sin, but not her happiness and peace. Sinners should suffer and be miserable, and here was this scandalous woman living in apparent contentment. Further, she had no right to be beautiful still when she had been bad. She broke all the rules of retribution. If she had been withered, shattered, it would have been something they could understand. But it puzzled and piqued them that she had not grown ugly in her wickedness.

Finally, they could not, he suspected, forgive God for forgiving Palmyre. God had failed—because He had failed to punish her. It was an oversight, a delinquency on His part, a negligence in the administration of heaven which aroused their resentment and violated all their notions of right. The wages of sin had not been paid and God was guilty of keeping a set of books that did not balance.

They turned to Father Guichard to help God out with his tangled accounts.

"I cannot forbid her the church." The priest's face was red and worried. "On the contrary. There is more rejoicing. . . ."

"But she is not repentant!" Olympe objected.

"She should at least be told to come to the first Mass and made to sit with the servants!" Madame Vigée insisted. "My daughter, Madame Larouche, when last here, was mortified to find herself at the same Mass with that woman. If it is to happen again, I shall see that no more money of mine finds its way into the parochial-school fund!"

Father Guichard looked even more harassed and unhappy.

"And the girl must be dismissed at once from the convent," Madame Morel reminded him.

"Yes. Yes, of course." He complied under Madame Vigée's beady stare. "I cannot imagine how she got there."

The doctor deposited cup and serviette on the table. Outside, the rain continued with a loud hum, punctured by peals of thunder.

"*I* brought her there," he announced.

"You!" Nanaine snapped her folding fan shut. "What for, in the name of heaven?"

Colette's hand flew quickly to her throat.

"She has a talent. She wished to use it. For the good of others." He looked around at the circle of ladies. "She can paint and she also knows their sign language." But even as he spoke, he knew it was in a lost cause.

"But she is—she is. . . ." Olympe could not bring herself to use even the euphemistic French term, "enfant naturel."

"A bastard," the doctor said angrily. "Some of the best people. . . ."

"Colette. . . ."

Olympe signaled weakly with her hand, and, after a moment's hesitation, Colette got up and slipped from the room.

". . . were bastards. The Duc de Toulouse. The Duc du-Maine. Both sons of Louis XIV by Madame de Montespan. In New Orleans, we do them honor by having named streets after them."

"Indeed!" Madame Vigée glared.

"Madame would naturally be interested. Since the family Larouche owns a great deal of property on those streets." He cared little what he said now. Anything to hurt them, cut them, lay bare their useless lives and ridicule their narrow minds.

"Oh! Oh!" gasped Madame Vigée.

"Are we to understand, then," asked Celeste de Gerbeau, curling her lip, "that virtue in a woman is no longer its own reward?"

"I would not say so." The doctor met her eye. "No doubt the sense of chastity is consoling to those who have never had the opportunity of losing it."

"We digress from our subject," said Madame, her mother, quickly, "which is, as I understand it, what measures we should take to free ourselves of an immoral influence. . . ."

"Morality is often a matter of circumstance," the doctor snapped. "Not what people do, but *why* they do it—we should find that out before we dare to call them immoral."

"The circumstances in this case do not condone . . ." Father Guichard began, goaded by Madame Vigée's repeated glance in his direction. He should say something crushing, but he could not finish.

Victor made an effort to control his mounting anger. "What has the girl done? How is she to blame?"

"But she—the mother—is an assassin!" Nanaine beat the palm of her hand with the fan. "She is responsible for the death of the Judge. . . ."

Their voices had risen. Their sharp words became part of the storm outside.

"Society is the assassin! *We* are the criminals—because we have set up a code which compels anyone to do what she did. It is she who should point an accusing finger at us!"

"We—the de Gerbeaus—criminals and assassins! Ah!" Madame rose, fumbling with shaking fingers at her hatpin. "Come, Celeste. It is time to go!"

"But dear Madame—the storm. . . ." Olympe was too horrified to hunt for her smelling salts.

"No matter what," Father Guichard proffered weakly, "it was wrong. . . ."

The doctor looked at him long and hard. The priest turned aside, without finishing his sentence.

The ladies left in the rain, preferring to be drenched rather than remain for an instant longer subjected to insults and indignities. Olympe had not looked for such a dismal dénouement when she wrote Madame Morel a special invitation that morning.

Twenty-four

On returning from church the following Sunday, the doctor went to see Uncle Ulysse, who had stuck a thumbtack in his hand and acquired an infection. The old gentleman was seated in his library, a confusion of open books on the floor, before him a draftsman's board with a map of Virginia pinned to it. A greasy spot of Victor's unguent covered Cold Harbor. Uncle Ulysse's eyes were growing dimmer, and this morning his hearing was particularly bad. He became aware of a presence only when Victor stubbed his toe on Volume II of Patton's *Butler in New Orleans* and Bragg, perched on his shoulder, gave a shrill yell.

"Ha!" said the old man. "Sit down, sit down."

Every conceivable sitting space in the room was strewn with books, maps and papers. Of necessity, Victor remained standing.

"Well, my boy"—Uncle Ulysse chuckled—"what do you think of the ignominious rout of the carpetbaggers through the crushing strategy of our brave Bidault, heh?"

"Pardon?" Perhaps Uncle Ulysse was wandering a little.

"You don't know the news? Noonoon brought it back from the bakery. Fauvette d'Eaubonne cannot meet her mortgage. Bidault forecloses. 'Joli Bois' is his, and the Federals must retreat."

"Where are they going?"

"Why, where they came from, where they belong. On their own side of the Mason-Dixon line."

"And Fauvette?"

"She is moving to 'Belle Pointe.' Palmyre Delamare has taken her in, together with a Mr. Néron Paviot, who, it seems, has no roots but a deck of cards and a bundle of oil stock."

"Why, I just saw them in church. They looked calm enough."

"They were probably praying for their next meal."

For some weeks there had been rumors of a crisis in Fauvette's chronic state of financial distress. She had had to pay her bread bill with her great-grandfather's snuffbox. It was puzzling, since Fauvette's venture was apparently a great success; "Joli Bois" overflowed with boarders. The truth of the matter was that Fauvette fed them too lavishly, setting her table with an open hand inherited from her mother. She could not distinguish between banquets and board, and those famous Sunday suppers on Bourbon Street were an everyday event at "Joli Bois."

The doctor, knowing Fauvette's capacity for converting even calamity into some sort of success, did not stop to waste his sympathy. He changed the subject.

"Well, Uncle, we used the right weapons against the poison. Your hand is much improved."

"Weapons? Improved?" Uncle Ulysse in his deafness misunderstood. "Nonsense! A foolish fad, nothing more! Wait. I'll show you. Get me that portfolio off my desk."

Victor had to dig it out from under a landslide of manuscript. The old man extracted a sheaf of newspaper clippings. "Read, read!" He shook with indignation.

The doctor scanned an editorial.

The tremor which seized Britain when Blériot made his historic descent on British soil causes one to smile. For it is evident that none of the machines brought before the public so far contains the slightest menace, in the military sense. It is truly wonderful that men should succeed in flying at all, but it does not follow that the airship will ever be used in commerce or war. . . .

"Go on, go on!" Uncle Ulysse urged. "See what the next one says!"

Despite the development of airships [Victor read], *there should be no letup in the construction of battleships. We are told a man in an airship could drop a bomb the size of a croquet ball on the deck of a dreadnought and demolish her, but those engaged in warship construction have no knowledge of any such explosive and do not believe in the efficacy of the fabulous croquet ball. . . .*

"You see!" Uncle Ulysse crowed.

What the doctor saw was a world in the throes of convulsive change. He wondered how long his people could continue to insulate themselves in this tragic way. His uncle's vision, mental like physical, was too weak to see the present, much less the future, and even the past was for him obscured with bigotry. There was no point in exciting him to argument. One must admire Uncle Ulysse for his indomitable spirit, and ignore the rest.

"Well"—Victor handed back the portfolio—"I must be going."

"Yes?" Uncle Ulysse cupped his ear. "You are leaving for the Isthmus?"

"Next Saturday. I have a cabin engaged on the *Cartago*."

"A waste of time and taxpayers' money—that Canal," grumbled the old man. "Of all the worthless, crazy, impractical notions . . . !"

He went back to his voluminous work on how the War Between the States could have been won for the Confederacy.

The doctor had time, before the hour of Colette's fete, to call on the moss picker, Alphonse Gaspard. The man's pellagra was responding appreciably to a diet of fruit juice, broth, and milk, and while the gain of a pound or two was not sensational, it was encouraging. He was indeed improving faster than the eldest child, Sophronie, who, though the disease in her case had made less headway, was reacting indifferently to a tonic treatment of iron and manganese compounds.

"Ah, but Miché le docteur should see Joe, husband of Masoom!" Sophronie said. "I saw him when we were washing on the bayou. He came looking for her. He has more bobo"—she used the childish word for sores—"than all of us put together!"

The doctor looked up from his examination of Gaspard's hands.

"Is he a Choctaw?"

"I have heard he is part white," Alphonse said. "He never comes out. Nobody knows him."

The information was interesting, and perhaps far-reaching. There was no file on Joe in Jolivet's records. Victor knew them all by heart. He remembered having been impressed by the absence of pellagra among the Choctaws, despite their addiction to corn. He had theorized that the Indian method of preparation might be the differentiating factor. But if Joe had pellagra, not only was this premise shattered, but likewise the doctor's claim—which he thought all but proved—that corn of itself was an innocent agent and that the lack of some essential nutrient in the general diet of poor whites induced the pellagra evil. It was of extreme importance to him to investigate.

"I would like to see this Joe," he said.

"It is not easy, but you can try. Go along the Chinchuba road past the bridge. Turn in at the fork to Fanchon's. Midway you will see the house on pilings, to your right, in the swamp. But I cannot tell you how to reach it."

It was after five o'clock, and the doctor was on his way to the swamp. He was amazed to see Miriam at her old place under the oak. She came running toward the road.

"Ah!" she laughed. "St. Expedite must have sent you. I made him"—she pointed to the little statuette dangling from the top of her easel—"my mascot. You see, Narcisse has not come. It is Sunday, and his Bibi is free, because Madame Vigée is going to your fiancée's fete. I suppose Narcisse has forgotten me."

The doctor looked at the sky. Another electrical storm was coming out of the purple northwest. Since the squall on Wednesday, the weather had been swerving fitfully from sudden rain and high winds to periods of bright and sunny calm, typical symptoms of the coming equinox. The blow now gathering might pass over.

"I am going to make a short call. On my return, I'll drive you back to town," he offered.

She smiled delightedly.

"I am no longer angry with Narcisse."

A lightning flash split the blackness in the north, followed at once by a peal of thunder.

"We may get some of it, after all," he reconsidered. "Perhaps you had best come with me. You've no shelter here."

"You're going to the Fanchons'?"

"No. To Masoom's place."

"Why, she was with me a while ago. I found her on the bayou, washing, the other day, and persuaded her to let me finish painting her. I had to double her fee for posing."

"It is her husband I wish to see."

"Ah, yes. Her husband. That's why she wants money. To buy him tobacco."

Together they carried her easel, stool, and satchel to the buggy and placed them under the seat. They drove off, Dixie huddled at her feet.

As they passed the convent, she remarked regretfully, "I taught there only a few days. On Thursday, the Mother Superior told me they found the little mutes would have no time for drawing. It interfered with their other lessons."

He covered his anger with a joke.

"If Narcisse is going to neglect fetching you like this, it is just as well."

"Unless St. Expedite was as efficient as he was today."

"I am sailing next Saturday, Mamzelle Miriam."

"Ah!" Her breath came out in a little gasp.

An automobile went by. It was certainly Leon's, and the two men in it were Leon and his friend, Marcel Lavalle. The doctor had supposed the young bachelors from the Roussels' garçon-nière were by now well steeped in absinthe at Paul's Exchange, where he had seen them earlier. He frowned at the presence of Leon in the forbidden neighborhood of the girl Coco, but Marcel's company reassured him.

A fierce crack of thunder came out of the pinelands ahead. The sky darkened and a strange half-luminous light descended on the road. As they turned into the rutted wagon path that led to Fanchon the charcoal maker's place, Felix came running from the woods with his rifle and a gamebag of plaited palmetto swung over his shoulder. At sight of the approaching buggy and familiar horse, he stopped short.

"Miché le docteur will never make it to the house!" He had to shout to be heard, for now the wind had rushed down upon them, bending the trees. He presumed the doctor was going to see his father.

"I am looking for Masoom!" The doctor pointed a thumb toward the swamp.

"Ho! Even on good days, you would 'ave to wade. Nobody ever go there!"

The convent was too far behind, and the Fanchons' house too far ahead.

"You will 'ave to come wit me to my shack!" Felix jumped on the footstep, pointing straight up the wagon path. "If you drive fas', it is jus' t'ree minute away!"

The storm fell like a burst of gigantic applause. The tiny cabin was intermittently lit with green flashes, and the wind tore at the palmetto-thatched roof weighted down with stones. There was a sudden lull, and then the clouds opened and the flood came. The little shelter quivered, the tall pines around it groaned; now and then a tree could be heard crashing before the blast. Rougette, exposed to the storm, whinnied in fright.

Felix had wisely built on a rise and had dug a draining ditch around his den, so that the mud floor, covered with brown pine needles, remained dry, though here and there a leak appeared where the gale ripped pieces from the roof. The temperature fell amazingly. Miriam shivered and hugged the hound for warmth. The doctor took off his coat and put it around her shoulders.

Felix was well fitted for such emergencies. A single shelf supplied all his needs. Taking down a lantern, he lit it and began to dress the birds from his hunting pouch. He had made a barbecue pit in a corner of the cabin. There he spitted and roasted his kill.

The storm lasted longer than an hour. Afterward, the drenched buggy made slow progress through the puddled ruts of the wagon path, and it was dark when they turned into the road to town.

He was late in arriving at Colette's fete. In consideration of the weather, plans for a garden party had been abandoned, and the spacious basement at "Beaux Arbres" converted into an enormous ballroom. Lanterns glowed, and through foliage and latticework dancers could be seen in the gay figures of a polka.

The musicians came to a stop as the doctor entered, and the couples milled about, talking and laughing, the ladies fluttering their fans. He looked for Colette, but could not find her. He even searched the least likely places—the circle of gossiping chaperones and the row of stiffly suffering wallflowers. A number of guests had moved toward the end of the basement where the buffet was spread. Perhaps she was there.

He was pleased to see that the confectioners had produced the masterpiece promised. From the spun-taffy rigging of a simulated ship waved a sugar flag on which was written "Bonne Fête." "Colette Marie" was spelled out across the prow in small pink roses. He had been apprehensive about so much fragile art being delivered from New Orleans by the *Camelia*, but not a wave of the foundation piece was crushed. The cake would be cut at midnight. At present, the guests were helping themselves to the lavish array of cold meats and fowl and fish, sauces and salads and sweets, fruits and bonbons. Victor thought fleetingly of Felix's little hut, so crude and bare. Yet how warm and cheerful it had been with the three of them huddled about the barbecue pit.

The doctor saw Féfé Larouche among the cakes and candies. Harry Lockwood was with her, not eating, his face flushed and stamped with a look of consternation. Victor noticed that his black bow tie was slightly crooked.

"Where is Colette?"

Féfé answered. "She went up to her Papa's study—with Leon."

Harry Lockwood's sullen behavior was totally unlike him. Victor asked, "Something wrong, Harry?"

"Some day Leon is going to get me when he's sober—or when I'm not a guest at his home," Harry said thickly, "and I'm going to knock his head off."

"If it wasn't for *me*," Féfé babbled, her mouth full of ladyfingers, "Mr. Lockwood would have punched Leon for what he said about that girl at 'Belle Pointe.' But I hung on his arm and wouldn't let him. It was simply awful!" Féfé had obviously loved every minute of it.

Victor's jaw set. "I'll see you later, Harry." *In Julien's study. . . .*

Féfé ran after him. "Mr. Lockwood wanted to leave the party. But Cousin Julien made him promise to stay. And Cousin Olympe is sick. It was simply. . . ."

"I'm in a hurry, Féfé."

"Colette was in a hurry, too." She giggled. "Leon said he had something to tell her."

The door was partly open.

"Marcel! Didn't we see them go together into the cabin?"

"Yes." Marcel sounded confused. "But. . . ."

"I followed them for your sake, Colette. It is for you that my auto is ruined with rain and broke a spring on that damnable road. It is for you that I risked my life in the lightning. I shall need at least two hundred dollars. . . ."

"I'm afraid you wouldn't spend it on repairs, Leon. You know quite well Mama will see that the automobile is fixed."

"It would not be fair," Leon objected, "to require Mama to pay damages incurred solely for your sake. Do you think I was personally interested in what we saw?"

The doctor stepped into the room, closing the door with a bang.

"Tell *all* you saw!" he demanded.

"Eavesdropping," Leon sneered. "A fine business. . . ."

"As fine as spying! Tell her the rest of it!"

"We saw you meet her. Didn't we, Marcel? Where you have met her before in the morning. . . ."

"I had no idea she would be there at five o'clock. Narcisse failed to bring the carriage for her."

"Why should he bring the carriage, when your buggy is cozier?"

"I took her in my buggy because she had no way of getting home!"

"Was it because you were taking her *home* that you drove up the road in the opposite direction from town? Didn't he, Marcel?"

"Yes," Marcel said hoarsely.

"I was making a call. I could not leave her there in the threatening storm."

"Ho! A call in the swamp? On an ailing alligator, no doubt? You think we did not see you go directly to your rendezvous, into the cabin?"

"We went there to get out of the storm."

Leon laughed. He managed to say a great deal by saying so little.

"Were we alone? Tell your sister. Were we alone?"

"Must I count the hound you keep to warn you of intruders?"

"You know the boy Felix was with us! Tell her!"

Leon's lip curled. "May I tell her also that you pay him for the use of his cabin, and to keep guard for you with a rifle?"

Anger was like bile in the doctor's throat. He could have taken the younger man and hurled him against the wall. He clenched his fists. Colette, still as a statue, said nothing. She was watching the scene with a curious numbness, her eyes moving from one speaker to the other. Only the vivid flush in her cheeks indicated that she felt anything at all.

But she could not believe her brother! She must see through his scheme to kill two birds with one stone: to settle accounts with the doctor, and have money in his pocket besides. Victor turned and addressed her quietly.

"Colette, do you believe all this?"

Her lips twitched as if she were going to cry.

"Yes," she said.

Leon brushed imaginary dust from his coat sleeve. "Come on, Marcel." He took his bewildered friend briskly by the arm. "I'm thirsty."

The doctor looked at her, stunned by her loss of faith in him. Until now, he had assured himself that she was too fine to let gossip mar their relationship, and the sudden change in her attitude took him by surprise. She returned his look coldly, her chin high, and with a start he recognized in her something of the hard pride of his aunt and the penetrating stare of Grandpère in the portrait. At the same time her beauty was never so dazzling. Her low-cut bodice revealed the perfection of bust and shoulders, and she was wearing the antique set of corals he had given her. He recalled how different their meeting that day had been from this, and he longed to bring back the warmth of the moment he had clasped the necklace about her throat.

"Colette"—he went close to her—"I can prove to you. . . ."

Her forbidding reserve held him off. "Have I asked you for proof? Have I *ever* asked you? When I heard of your excursions into the woods—when I heard of the sessions in your office—did I ask you for proof that it was not so? I think too much of our family"—her soft red lips curled—"to let a member of it shame us with falsehoods!"

He had never seen this side of her before. All the hauteur of the generations that had produced her seemed concentrated in the flash of her glance. He felt helpless before her. . . . And God, how beautiful she was—this girl who had been chosen for his bride. . . .

"Colette—listen to me," he begged. "I can get the boy Felix. . . ."

She turned her back to him.

"And pay him for supporting your story, too?"

"Colette!"

A painful silence piled up between them. Then he said, "If you believe these lies about me, you can't love me, Colette."

She whirled about and faced him, her hands clenched at her sides.

"I do love you—I do! It is because I love you that it matters so much!"

"There is nothing to matter, my dear—except Leon's imagination." The hurt she had given him showed in every line of his face.

Her tension broke. Tears started in her eyes, and she was once more the Colette he knew—kind, yielding, full of love and understanding. She flew to him, grateful for his arms.

"Oh, Vic! I am only human! I can't help being jealous! So many little things—people talking—the way you danced with her the night of the Fourth—taking her to teach at the convent. . . . Don't you see—they grow so big when they are all thrown together! Oh, Vic"—her eyes brimmed over—"I am miserable—so miserable. . . ."

He cradled her head on his shoulder and dried her cheeks with his handkerchief.

"I must ask you to forgive me," he said tenderly. "I should have been more careful. I can see now how it looked."

She tried to smile.

"I am sorry I was so jealous."

"I am glad. It shows you love me."

"Do *you* love *me?*"

"Yes." He kissed her softly on the corner of her mouth. "Oh, yes, Colette."

"Then if you want to prove anything," she said against his lips, "prove that."

"In any way you wish!"

"You promise?" Her arms crept around his neck. His hands went up eagerly to cover them.

"Anything! I promise."

"Then you will not leave me. You will not return to Panama next Saturday. You will not return at all. You will stay here in Louisiana and be a successful physician with Dr. Larouche!"

His hands dropped. After a minute, he said, "Does it mean that much to you?"

"Yes, oh, yes!" She held him closer. "Promise me, Vic. Promise!"

He stood there, staring at the wall over her head, biting his lip.

"Give me your promise for my feast day, darling. It would be the most precious present of all. Please. . . ." Her hands caressed his shoulders, his arms. *"Please. . . ."*

Perhaps—perhaps something could be done with Larouche's practice, after all. At least, for her sake, he could give it a trial. He was signing no contract. He could always withdraw. . . .

He drew a deep breath. "Very well, my dear. If that is what you want."

She pulled his head down and met his mouth with hers, giving it freely, fiercely, as if she knew the extent of the sacrifice he was making.

Twenty-five

Tuesday morning he put three letters in the mail. One was to the steamship company canceling his passage. The second, containing his resignation, was addressed to Colonel Gorgas of the Medical Division of the Isthmian Canal Commission. The third was to his cousin Dr. Larouche; it was a brief letter, as he found no heart to go into details. He merely indicated his acceptance of the proposed partnership, and stated he would be in New Orleans toward the end of the month to conclude the necessary arrangements.

For some time after the last patient had left, he sat in Jolivet's office, drumming his fingers on the old nicked desk. He felt an odd sense of depletion after mailing the letters. Until this morning, he had concentrated on the decision itself, and the pleasure he was giving Colette. Now, suddenly he thought of his future . . . ready-made for him, bought like a suit of clothes in a store. No excitement. No struggle. No anticipation. No element of the unknown. Already it had the cut-and-dried quality of the past.

He jumped up as if to run away from himself, and faced Miriam standing in the doorway.

"I came to say good-by." Pain made her deep blue eyes enormous. "I saw Rougette, so I knew you were still here."

He took a step toward her.

"I am not going, Miriam."

She fell back against the doorframe, incredulous. For the space of several seconds her eyes swept his face, relief and honest hunger in their depths. At length, she said in a whisper, "You are not going at all?"

"No. Never." The words tasted of gall. He knew now the full savor of the *never* she despised.

Of a sudden she threw herself against him, her arms tight around his neck. She laughed, she cried. She clung to him, as if what he said were untrue, and something was going to tear him away.

"There, there!" He patted her short hair as he would a little girl's.

"I can't help it!" She looked up at him and smiled through her tears. "I was dead, and I have come back to life!"

"Then I must be glad instead of sorry that I am staying."

She released him. Her face became grave.

"Why are you sorry?"

"Because in a few weeks I shall go to the city to assume a practice I care nothing about."

"*She* wants it?"

"Yes."

"Then she loves something else more than you—she would never belong to you first—and completely!"

His sense of loyalty to Colette was aroused by Miriam's criticism, delivered with the fiery petulance of the young. Yet he could think of nothing to answer. There was a long silence. Out of it she continued more calmly.

"I know how you feel. I've been reading Thoreau. He detested living out the ideas of others—secondhand living, he calls it. He says in *Walden* he wished to live deliberately and not, when he came to die, discover that he had not lived at all."

He was used to her chameleon changes from child to woman. Her mind never failed to delight him. But in his present mood he was disturbed by what she had just said. He tried to shrug off the feeling.

"You would have me, like Thoreau, take to the woods?"

"Yes!" she said vehemently. "A man's place in the world is where he is needed. And you are needed in the woods!"

She was so earnest. He laughed, trying to dispel his depression.

"Very well. But I shall need you with me in case there are many more like Madame Gaspard!"

"I have never told you—it was so shameful—but I was grateful to Madame Gaspard for losing her baby. Because that one time you did really need me—not only my hands to help—but *me*."

He remembered that afternoon well, sitting on the bench in the Gaspards' yard—his misery—his head on her breast. He would not tell her, but he needed her that way now, in his uncertainty and self-reproach. . . . A strange loneliness came over him. His hands went to her shoulders, he bent his head and felt the mingling of her breath with his. Slowly his arms slipped around her and he gathered her against him, pressing her close to his heart. . . .

He took his mouth away from hers and looked down into her face. It was a little dazed, filled with wonder. She put the tips of her fingers against his lips. "How beautiful!" she said in a whisper.

A stone came crashing through the window of the waiting room adjoining. Victor's arms dropped from Miriam. He ran to the window and, standing behind the curtain, saw a crowd in the street. A figure he recognized as Colin Menard, editor of the *Trumpet,* was brandishing above his head a long sheet of copy and shouting at the top of his voice. For a moment he could not make out the meaning of the harangue. Then he began to understand.

"We have been cheated, swindled! Roussel knew all along the causeway was coming! That is why he bought our property right and left! Now he has the gall to expect me to publish the announcement in my paper!"

"He buys from us at bottom prices," raged another whom Victor did not recognize, "and then expects us to invest the money in his stock to make him richer! Ha! These lawyers! They are all slickers!" It was he who had thrown the rock, apparently mistaking the doctor's window for one of the Causeway Corporation. He picked up another stone from the side of the street and hurled it with telling accuracy. A smashing of glass was heard next door.

"What's going on here?" The marshal, Aristide Préjean, rode into the crowd on his horse. Victor saw that Mayor Bidault rode beside him.

"A great bridge is going up across the lake!" Hercule, son of the fisherman Alceste Moreau, spoke up. "Our town will grow rich, and we who have sold our homes will be put out to grow poor!"

"Listen! Listen!" sputtered Colin Menard. "I'll read you—'There are men who have the vision to realize the importance of a bridge across Lake Pontchartrain from Mandeville to New Orleans. A group of these are Chicago men who are willing to put up half the capital required. The other half must be supplied by local interests. Buy stock! Be men of vision! See the savings in time, the outpourings of cramped city offices into the sun-kissed gardens of suburban homes, the gay throngs of rural pleasure seekers called by the lure of bright lights and city amusements. Share in the tremendous tolls! Live on your dividends!' "

"We could have gotten ten times the price for our property!"

"He pulled the wool over our eyes! Now he wants us to be men of vision!"

"What are you talking about, you dolts?" Bidault shouted. His horse reared and he pulled down on the bit sharply. He had bought up as much property as Julien, and wanted the bridge as badly, but none of the crowd associated craft with a greed they had become accustomed to accept. "You got your money! Invest in the bridge and enjoy the profits! If you hadn't sold, you'd have no money to invest!"

His smooth logic confused them. There was murmuring and mumbling.

"Me, I 'ave no property to sell," Télémaque Moreau, Hercule's eldest brother, contributed. "But I don't believe in dat causeway. A big storm come, she blow it clean away."

"You!" The mayor cracked his nervous mount with his crop. "You'd better watch that featherweight brain of yours in the next wind, or *it* will blow away. You know as much about bridges as you do about buttermilk—claiming mine poisoned you!"

"I was not the only one." Télémaque was wary of what he said. Bidault could take away his fishing license.

"You believe every word that damn dog doctor says?"

"He is our friend," said Alex Gravois, the barber. "He cured my wife. . . ."

"If he is your friend, why didn't he tell you about the causeway?"

"Why, he didn't know. . . ."

"The prospective son-in-law of Julien Roussel, and he didn't know? Come now, Alex. You are a smarter man than that!"

"Yes!" cried the druggist, Guy Chauvin. "He could have told us!" He was half drunk, but managed to draw a long face to denote his loss of faith in humanity.

"It's true!" The baker, Emile Dufour, had not forgotten the recent events that had hurt both his business and his son's good name. "The doctor is the biggest scoundrel of all. With the money he has squeezed out of people in sickness, he has probably bought up a lot of the stock!"

The rumble of voices rose in pitch. Victor, from the second-story window, could look down into their faces. He saw how easily they were swayed from reason to wrath. They were men who believed themselves betrayed, they were convinced that they had been duped out of their due. A few well-calculated words had fallen on their resentment, all that was needed to inflame them to violence. In the crowd were many who followed voodoo and had never forgiven him for destroying charms and offending the Grand Zombie. Some of them attributed their subsequent misfortunes to his dreadful defiance of their beliefs. Now, if they went against him, they would perhaps regain the favor of vengeful powers.

"Well, what are you going to do?" demanded the mayor. "Let him make jackasses of you and ride you, too?"

208

"We'll see him about this!" Dufour shouted. "He's upstairs. There's his horse and buggy!"

"We'll smash every goddamn thing he has up there!" Guy Chauvin made a lunge toward the entrance.

The mob pressed forward. Aristide Préjean shouted, but no one heard him. He whipped his horse onto the banquette to block their passage, but they flowed around him like water. Victor saw that the mayor stayed in the background on the edge of the crowd.

"Gentlemen!" shouted Ovide Clouzat who, with others holding no grudge against the doctor, had remained in the street. "Those of you who will be killed, please do not forget my excellent services!"

"Go into the office and lock the door," he told Miriam quietly. His calmness was a front. His stomach was knotted with fear and his hand shook.

He met them halfway up the stairs. Dufour was in the lead. He raised his huge hand to shove the doctor aside. Victor stepped back out of reach, flattening himself against the wall to give them passage. He could not possibly bar their entrance. His only chance was to talk, loud and fast.

"Go on!" he yelled at them. "Wreck the place! But don't forget —none of it is mine! It belongs to Jolivet—or the next man you're lucky enough to get here. And in the meantime, some of you—or your families—may need the things you're going to destroy. You're not destroying *my* property—you're destroying yourselves! And if you're stupid enough to do that, you're not worth stopping! Go ahead! Smash everything up there! But you're only hurting yourselves!" He hoped the tremor in his voice was lost to them in the noise and confusion.

They stood jammed up on the staircase like bewildered cattle.

"My wife is eight mont's." Hercule Moreau rubbed his cheek. "I can't afford to take chances. . . ."

"Are we going to let him bully us?" snarled the baker. But he made no attempt to charge again.

"Don't let him call us stupid! We're not stupid!" Guy Chauvin slobbered.

At least he had stopped them momentarily, divided their ranks. He drew a deep breath. "I don't own a single share in that causeway. Not one! What's more, I think there are bigger things to be done around here than building causeways!" He stopped for a second, searching desperately for ideas to divert them. "You don't want a causeway! Save your shouting for what you really need— a decent system of drainage, a way to fill your open ditches, a plan to reclaim your swamps. Where does all your sickness come from, your malaria?" They were listening now, it was talk they understood. "From the mosquitoes that breed in those ditches and swamps, that's where! Get your mayor to do something about that!"

"I been trouble wit that sonofabitch malaria it make twenty year," Télémaque Moreau said. "Time dose bastard drain dey was close up."

"Next meeting of the Council is the first week in September."

"I am an alderman, me."

"Miché le maire, he don' like to tax people. It make him lose votes."

"People lose deir healt'—hit's less impo'tant, heh?"

They were backing down the stairs. The crowd was breaking up. Dufour snarled something obscene, and several advised him urgently to shut up. Guy Chauvin grumbled to himself. Aristide Préjean, belatedly down from his horse, ordered the men to return to their businesses. The mayor was nowhere in sight.

Victor stayed a moment on the stairs, leaning against the wall, trembling and short of breath. Then he remembered Miriam in Jolivet's office and walked slowly back up the steps.

Twenty-six

A week passed. During that time he had purposely not seen Miriam at all, and yet, in a way, he saw no one else. The remembrance of their last meeting crouched always in the corners of his mind, springing at him in every unguarded moment. He thrust it aside, often angrily. She was disturbing him more than he had thought possible, and he found it difficult to analyze his feeling for her, trying to dissect it into component parts of curiosity, perhaps pity, and no doubt passion. It was something that had crept up on him unawares, like an animal out of ambush; something to be fought and strangled. He did not deceive himself. He was drawn to her with a force he had never before felt, and he would be careful not to let it trick either of them into some absurd folly.

He threw himself into work, finishing his paper for the *Medical Journal,* sifting and assorting data he had gathered but had had no time to file, welcoming the growing clinic with its manifold problems. Whooping cough was going the rounds, and he was grateful for the hours of drudgery he had to put in at the colored Convent of the Holy Family, among the little coffee-colored girls and boys. Lately he had not been able to sleep, and he was glad for night calls; a long trip through the woods to a croupy child or a man suffering from snake bite was better than tossing in bed, or reading until daybreak. But no matter what he did, he caught himself thinking of her again and again—between the lines of a book, cauterizing a hand finned by a catfish, on his way to the post office, where now he went at a deliberately different hour. It was as if the germ of her was in his blood, and there were times when he was almost sick with it. When this happened, he dosed himself with more work, staying until all hours in Jolivet's hot little laboratory and coming home worn out and soaked to the skin.

Tonight, at least, his longing to be with her, to talk to her, to touch her, was quiet, and he experienced a sense of triumph in the certainty that he had successfully starved his fever. Yet he was restless, and though it was late and he had had a full, fatiguing day, he had no desire to go to bed. He walked the length of the front gallery, keeping his thoughts in disciplined paths. He tried to interest himself in the scene along the lake shore, where to a stranger it might have appeared that a carnival was in progress.

The shrimp were running. The wind, coming from the east, had brought them in just after sunset and by now the breakwater was thronged with shrimpers casting their nets, and the bathing piers were alive with activity. From one end of the beach to the other, pine torches flared and smoked, casting a weird red glow on the women and children who had come to help with the catch. Mothers had brought their babies, and where there was not a gocart, there was a cot, fully equipped with a bar against mosquitoes. Wagons and buggies stood about, while horses, unhitched, grazed under the trees. Families had coffee in jugs, and sandwiches and watermelons, and picnicked in the light of the blazing flares.

He watched the shrimping in front of "Clair de Lune." The graceful lacy skirt of the cast net . . . the quiet plop of sinkers as it hit the water . . . and then the slow hauling in, the pulling up of the dripping tangle, and the shaking out of the shrimp into tubs and buckets. He could see Zeph in silhouette, busy on the boat landing of the duRocher bathing pier. When she heard the shrimp were in, Glad had made balls of cornmeal and flour to bait them, and the first big catch was already boiling on the furnace in the back yard. Others used clam bait. Farther out, the diving for clams was still going on, while the shrimpers already supplied broke up their clams and poured them into the lake to draw the swarm to their stakes.

It was after midnight. Perhaps he could sleep now. He went to his room, and had half undressed when he heard Zeph's uneven step on the gallery.

"Miché Vic! Quick! Somethin' terrible happen!"

Hercule Moreau lay on the beach where they had dragged him out of the water. His head was a bloody mass, and one look by the light of a flare indicated that his skull was cracked and a portion of the parietal bone badly splintered. He had gotten into an argument with Justin Dufour over a stake Hercule claimed to have baited, and Justin had picked up the flatiron he had been using to smash clams and gone for Hercule like a maniac. There were several shrimping near them who had seen the whole thing.

It was clearly a hospital case, but it was nearly one o'clock, and there would be neither train nor boat to New Orleans until morning. Opiates might wall out the pain until they got Hercule to the city, but meanwhile there was danger of infection and complications. The fracture required an operation and the doctor remembered no trepan among Jolivet's outmoded instruments. He hesitated, weighing the situation, reluctant to accept a responsibility he was doubtful of discharging.

Alceste Moreau, the father, had been found. The crowd opened for him, and for a minute or two he stood there bewildered, looking from his unconscious son to the doctor.

"You will fix my boy? You can do it, heh?" His wrinkled face twisted with anxiety. *I am a success, me. I make eleven son, I got me a good wife, a good bed. . . . I got noddin' to be mad wit God fo'.* Hercule was his father's favorite. It would be a tragedy if, in his old age, Alceste were given cause to be on bad terms with God.

"Take nim to your house," the doctor made his decision. "I'll follow at once with the things I need."

It would be unwise to send Hercule home to his wife who was, as Hercule had said, eight months. Besides, at Alceste Moreau's there would be many hands to hold lamps, heat water, find and fetch things. But there would be no hand to administer the chloroform while the doctor performed the operation, no hand that he could trust. They would be hands that hauled seines, rowed boats, cleaned fish—strong hands and skilled in their trade, but wanting the delicate precision governed by intelligence that it took to handle an anesthetic cone. Miriam hovering at the head of Madame Gaspard. . . . He shut out the image quickly. He would not see her again. He was not going to allow this incident to shatter the peace of mind for which he had fought for so many days and nights. All the Moreaus were stoics. They had a reputation for being able to stand pain with the immunity of stones.

An alligator bite, a slipping fish knife—to them such things were no more than pinpricks.

As the men lifted Hercule into a wagon, the doctor heard his moan. This was no knife cut. *I can't do it, I can't do it. . . .* He had to have help, no matter what the consequences.

"Zeph. . . ." He scribbled a note on a prescription blank. "Take this to 'Belle Pointe'. . . . Somebody will give you a ride. Hurry."

It was four o'clock when they came out of Alceste Moreau's neat white house in its neat plot of trees and garden. The work on Hercule had been difficult and tedious, involving the removal of a piece of bone to relieve pressure on a vital area of the brain and, as the doctor had suspected, there was nowhere in Jolivet's odds and ends of equipment anything like the cylindrical saw needed for such a task. He had to use what the old doctor's kit offered, relying on impromptu devices in technique to make up the difference. But he was satisfied with what he had accomplished. Hercule was all right, and Alceste could continue on good terms with God.

Colin Menard and a number of sensation-mongers were at the gate.

"Is Hercule going to die?" Colin wanted to know. Apparently he was hoping for a murder case to fill the lagging pages of the *Trumpet*.

"We are all going to die," the doctor said, "someday. But I hardly think you need headline it."

"He got his head bashed in, didn't he?" Colin argued. "A man can't live with a cracked head, can he?"

"A great many do." He grinned. "It's the people who have to live with them that find it difficult."

"You don't want to talk, that's it, heh?" Colin's face grew ugly. "Afraid to open your mouth, heh?"

The doctor thought caution as good an excuse as any. "Yes. I'm terrified."

The sensation seekers began to drift away, disappointed.

There would be talk enough for Colin, if the doctor drove off in the buggy with Miriam. "Belle Pointe" was about a mile away. In a society where it was as great a disgrace for a woman to ride in a buggy with a man as to be seen coming out of a brothel with him, the best policy, the doctor reflected, and the only choice, was to walk.

She spoke lightly of casual things to relieve the tension of the past hours. Last night's stars were paling, and the new morning was calm and cool. In the trees and hedges along the sandy banquettes, the birds were waking.

"Narcisse is not to be depended on any more. Do you know where he was that Sunday afternoon of the thunderstorm? He was getting married. To Bibi. Miss Fauvette says"—she laughed—"that it is the first *voluntary* activity Narcisse has ever committed in his life."

"So you have Bibi back again?"

"Yes. Madame Vigée would not keep her an instant after she knew. She seemed to think there was something immoral about Bibi's marrying."

He understood. Madame Vigée, who put a breechcloth on the Apollo Belvedere and a blouse on the Venus de Milo, would not have in her employ a girl married to a man who worked for a woman like Palmyre Delamare. It would not be respectable.

"Though Narcisse and Bibi had a legal ceremony," she continued. "They went in great style, in our carriage, all the way to the county judge. Father Guichard made his excuses, since he did not have Madame Vigée's permission. Narcisse didn't want to get married like his mother and father, you see, with no other ceremony than jumping over a broomstick. 'Me, I wanted to get married out of a book,' he said."

"That's an old custom left over from slavery times, when Negroes who wanted to marry merely jumped over a broom with the master's consent. It is still practiced in some places by the very poor." He was enjoying Miriam's gay chatter. He felt himself relax.

"But—Narcisse told me—his parents saved up some money and finally got a priest. His mother was going to have another baby, but she dressed like a bride, and his father wore a boutonniere, and all their nine children were there, himself included, and they had a wonderful time at the wedding. Then, after they were married a few months—her husband left her."

"Obviously out of the book was less binding than over the broomstick."

They laughed together.

"Book or broomstick, they were pretty well bound together by nine children, it seems to me."

He wondered if she knew about herself—if Palmyre had ever had the courage to tell her.

They reached the beach and turned toward the point. The carnival scene had vanished. A few tired torches were still burning, but the wind had changed and the shrimp gone with the tide. Now, as far out as the bathhouses, the lake was a stretch of sandbars and puddles; here and there a gray figure walked the waste, hunting for soft-shell crabs. Tonight the returning tide would bring back the swarm and the crowd, and so it would go on for weeks, until the shrimping season ended.

"It is strange," he mused, "what a man will kill another for. A few pounds more of shrimp. . . ."

They walked the rest of the way in silence. When they reached "Belle Pointe," the sky behind the eastern trees was growing red. Homère appeared, starting on his faithful rounds. Leaning his ladder against the corner lamppost, he climbed up, blew out the light, descended, and trudged on.

At the gate, the doctor said, "Thank you, Mamzelle. Without you, there might have been one pair of eyes less to see the sun today."

He wished to go, but he found himself standing there unwilling to take the first step.

"When I do not see you," she told him, "I say to myself: He is busy building his prison."

"My prison?"

"Yes. That practice in the city you are going to set up, and which you care nothing about."

He had not been able to interest himself in the surgical-supply catalogues recently received. Instead of the shining equipment, he could see as he turned the pages only the elegant offices of his cousin Dr. Larouche. Nevertheless, because he refused to let himself confess that he had been avoiding her, and why, he said merely, "Yes, I have been busy."

"It is still not too late for you to escape."

The same idea had occurred to him once or twice in the last few days. He laughed halfheartedly. "What funny thoughts run through that head of yours. . . ."

"I once knew a little man in Brittany. He whittled for hours on end, and tended his little garden, and fished. People said he was simple, but on the contrary, he was very wise. He was an artist. Oh, not the things he carved. They were only soso. . . . No, he was an artist at living. Very few people are that kind of artist. It takes a very special talent—more talent than for anything else, perhaps. . . ."

"And how, may I ask, did your little Breton come by his wisdom?"

"I suppose he had a special sense of values. Most people have only the standard sense. They measure everything by the same rule—the group rule."

He sighed in spite of himself.

"And you shouldn't apply rules to your life, the way you do to mathematics!" she went on passionately. "It is sad to see people working life out like a multiplication table, all trying for the same answer. The answer is different for everybody! And everybody has to find his own!"

"There must be many who never find the answer. . . ." He looked past her.

"It is because, as I have said, they lock themselves in prisons of their own making, and never see out."

"Well"—he tried to break the spell—"the best a man can do is try to build himself a bright and beautiful prison, I suppose."

"No matter how hard he tried, it could never be as bright and beautiful as his heart's desire!"

Their eyes met. What she had been telling him he knew already, but it aroused again all the unrest and uncertainty in his spirit. He felt the wisdom behind the naïve metaphor and knew she was questioning the strength of his designs. The misery of doubt came over him like a cold sweat. He said, "After all, each must choose for himself," hating the triteness of it.

"That's just it!" Her face became beautiful when she was so earnest. "Each person has so many selves. You must be sure to choose for the *right* one!"

So many selves. . . . He was weary of the battle of selves within him. He needed her. . . . His fingers curved around her arms. For several moments he let his hunger feast on her face.

The truth came out of him against his will. "I have thought of you every day, Miriam."

He filled his arms with her, kissed her mouth, her eyes, her hair. He said her name against her lips, repeated, "I have thought of you . . . oh, how I have thought of you. . . ."

He knew he had fought in vain. All his determined efforts of the past week had come to nothing. The chains of restraint dropped from him, and he let the feel of her seep into his brain and blood with a grateful flow of relief.

Twenty-seven

Four days later he was called to "Belle Pointe."

He had not seen her in the interim. Since Wednesday morning, his thinking and feeling were in chaotic paradox. He resorted once more to the only remedy he knew—work. He was fighting again, fighting sickness in others to cure his own. At times he almost decided not to fight—to let happen what would, and blame it on destiny, fate, or even God. But that was lazy and cowardly—an insidious phase of this illness of spirit and mind that had overtaken him without his being aware of it, certainly without his wishing it.

They were at breakfast when Narcisse came. Zeph brought the message.

"You are assuredly not going?" Nanaine's question was more a command. Her attitude toward him had not improved when Madame de Gerbeau took Minerve to the city for confinement instead of leaving her in Victor's hands.

"It is my duty."

"Your duty! Nonsense!" She threw her napkin down. "Your duty is to yourself—to your dignity—or if you have none"—she alluded to his calling for Miriam's help in the matter of Hercule Moreau, the story having appeared in the *Trumpet*—"to the dignity of your family!"

"My duty is to my dignity as a human being, and to my conscience. But I'd rather not discuss it." He rose from the table.

Perhaps there was small point in the doctor's going to "Belle Pointe," after all, for when he asked Narcisse what the trouble was, Narcisse replied, "Mr. Néron Paviot is dead."

Mr. Paviot—to whom Nanaine always referred as "that godforsaken gambler Fauvette fished out of the lake"—was not dead. He was only, in the language of Leon and his friends, dead drunk. In yesterday's evening mail had come a letter from Caddo Parish advising that the oil well in which he was interested had been brought in as a gusher. No one knew exactly how many gallons an hour it was pouring out of the earth, and consequently how much gold it was pumping into the pockets of Mr. Paviot's faded and shrunken formals, but the figure in either case was fabulous. The postmaster Naquin could only say that enclosed with the letter was a money order which Mr. Paviot had promptly cashed and by so doing cleaned out the postal coffers.

At present, Mr. Paviot, having lain all night in Paul's Exchange, was stretched out on the piazza at "Belle Pointe," the toes of his tennis shoes straight up in the air, the skirt of his Prince Albert, bearing up bravely since the wharf disaster in

June, neatly composed about his lean frame. He was, to all appearances, dead, except for the ruddy glow of his nose, and an almost imperceptible twitch of his mustache acknowledging the efforts of a persistent fly. In a condition of complete alcoholic narcosis, he was unconscious of the comments going on about him.

"Bibi found him here," Palmyre explained, "when she came out to sweep. We missed him at breakfast. Narcisse has since been told that he spent the night drinking, but dragged himself home at daybreak." Her handsome face showed a mixture of worry and amusement.

"It were dose stair w'at stump him," Narcisse surmised. "He make it all right *dis* way"—he indicated a horizontal line with his thumb—"but he have difficult' wit *up*." And he jerked the thumb toward the gallery.

"Poor Mr. Paviot," said Miriam, who had brought a pillow to put under his head. "Though I suppose it is not quite accurate to call him poor now."

The doctor loosened Mr. Paviot's wing collar and string tie. Pulse and heart were normal, considering the patient's abnormal state.

"Look at Mamzelle Fauvette," Bibi exhorted, though all present continued to look at Mr. Paviot on the piazza floor. "She rotten rich as Miché Paviot, but she don't get drunk, her."

Ah. . . . He was glad for Fauvette, though indeed he had never thought it necessary to feel sorry for her.

"I do not have the time yet," Fauvette said. "I am very busy trying to find the pawn ticket to my great-uncle's scarfpin."

The doctor pushed up Mr. Paviot's coat sleeve and was a little amazed to find a bare arm. Evidently Mr. Paviot wore only a piece of a shirt. He gently insinuated the needle and injected a dose of apomorphia. With watch in hand, he waited for the emetic to take effect, requesting, meanwhile, that Bibi fetch a suitable receptacle. At the end of three minutes, he suggested that the ladies retire.

Five minutes later, Mr. Paviot stirred and emptied his celebration into a washbowl.

Upstairs on the gallery the ladies were awaiting the doctor's report.

"I will look in again tomorrow to see that everything is all right," he said. "Meantime, Mr. Paviot should be put to bed."

Fauvette and Palmyre left to supervise the carrying of Mr. Paviot to his room. The doctor was alone with Miriam.

"May I show you the finished painting of Masoom?" she asked shyly.

He followed her to the corner room on the west. French doors faced the front and side galleries. The doors were wide open, the green blinds thrown back. He had never been in such a room before. It was neither bedroom, sitting room, drawing room, nor studio, and yet it was all four. A broad couch covered with a Spanish shawl stood out obliquely from the farthest corner. A grand piano occupied the center, with a music bench instead of the usual black haircloth stool. On the cool matting before it, Dixie had been dozing until they entered. Now she was at his side, nuzzling his hand. Sketchbooks were strewn on a wicker table. From a peg beside a large secretary hung a mandolin.

She turned the easel that stood with its face to the wall, several canvases stacked beside it. An exclamation of pleasure escaped the doctor. Masoom lived and breathed, three dimensional, on the glowing cloth. The figure there was more than Masoom the flesh. A strange spiritual quality looked out from the dark eyes. He remarked on it.

"It is love," Miriam said simply. "She has never told me, but I know." She placed the easel back in its original position. "Oh, not the way Bibi loves Narcisse. Little Bibi is not big enough. It is something different."

He thought of Jolivet's pellagra files. Two weeks had passed since the thunderstorm had blocked his attempt to see Masoom's husband. He had not tried again, shunning the Chinchuba road, avoiding any place where he might find Miriam. He must go back—examine Choctaw Joe, talk to him. Perhaps the crucial point of his research depended on it.

"I have not seen Masoom in town for some time," he was reminded.

"Oh, she will be back. As soon as the money she earned for posing is spent. Besides, she's hurt her hand. She keeps it bandaged in moss all the time."

"A sure way to guard against sepsis," he said wryly. "How did she hurt herself?"

"I don't know. She's not very communicative."

"Well. . . ." He picked up his satchel from the music bench, anxious to be on his way.

"Before you go, I would like you to see a likeness of my father. Will you wait?"

He listened to her light step running to the other side of the house. He could see her, in his mind's eye, graceful as flame, warm and vibrant, and he was annoyed and ashamed at the faster beating of his heart. Pushing the vision aside, he turned over the leaves of some Debussy standing on the music rack of the piano. He straightened suddenly, startled by a sound like the crashing of a gigantic bass chord. It rumbled off into silence, and a moment later the echo answered from the woods.

Miriam returned, breathless, clasping against her bosom a small gold case.

"Did you hear that?" she asked. "Another piece of 'Belle Pointe' has just caved in and washed down into the lake. I saw it from my mother's window. Mr. Roussel wishes to furnish pilings free, but my mother will not accept his offer. She is investigating the cost of extending the breakwater at her own expense." She inserted her thumbnail between the leaves of the case and presented to him on open palms a miniature portrait in a velvet frame. "Look!" she said, her eyes glowing. "My father."

She resembled him. The face was open, straightforward, eyes set wide apart and intelligent. A well-shaped nose and chin gave character to an expression of gentleness. The head was covered with rippling hair a shade darker than her own.

"You have reason to be proud of him."

"My mother keeps this likeness on a table beside her bed. She

222

has a taper burning before it at night, so that she may look at it when she wakes. It is her most precious treasure. You see, she loved only my father, and forever. That is why I understand Masoom, because my mother loved like that. Oh, you should have seen them together. When they passed down the boulevards, people turned and stared after them. They recognized something special, something rare, they could not say what. It was almost funny. My mother and father would look at each other and smile. I have looked, I have studied the people I have met, but nowhere was there ever such a husband and wife!"

He handed back the case. Her face was flushed and happy. Apparently she had no idea. . . .

He left quickly, pleased with himself for not having touched her. But the buoyancy that had accompanied him on his return from "Belle Pointe" a few mornings previous was gone.

At the post office, he picked up a letter from his cousin Dr. Larouche. He turned it over with a feeling of distaste. He was in no hurry to open it, being able to guess what it said. "Your letter at last received, my dear boy. I stand ready to discuss with you at any time the concluding details. . . . When can you come?" He knew that Alcide's letter would not help the heaviness that had settled on him. Deciding to read it some other time, he put it in his inside coat pocket with his fountain pen and thermometer.

His office hours had already extended greatly overtime when the two daughters of Aurélie Coulon, now Jolivet, appeared with their five children. There they were, like a flock of blackbirds perched in the waiting room, all, down to the youngest, still in mourning. The children had the cough. To a concert of whooping and wailing, the doctor requested and received news of the Jolivets. Both were exceptionally well.

After they left, he sat at his desk, thinking of Jolivet. He must write to him; he had been promising himself to do so for some time. He had taken the liberty of mentioning the old practitioner's name in his paper on pellagra, careful to give credit for the remotest allusion to the older man's material. He drew out pen and paper and wrote a long letter.

He was late coming to the table. Dessert had already been served. His aunt heard his apologies with a hard face. She had by now doubtless received a full report of what had happened at "Belle Pointe," but she said, with a shrug, "I do not expect you to bring a man back from the dead in a moment." Papa inquired drowsily who was dead. "Nobody who is somebody!" Nanaine snapped. "And please try to keep your eyes open. Julien will be here in a little while to effect the changes in your will."

She looked at the doctor, expecting him to show surprise or ask questions. He disappointed her.

"Bazile," he said, "I won't trouble you to set the table again for me. Bring coffee and a tray to my room."

Twenty-eight

When he arrived at "Belle Pointe" the following morning, he was astounded to see the duRocher barouche drawn by Nanaine's two white horses standing before Palmyre Delamare's gate.

He made quick work of Mr. Paviot, whom he found on the back gallery with Fauvette. They were engaged in a game of poker, using silver dollars for chips. An ice bag was tied by a towel to the top of Mr. Paviot's head, Narcisse having bought a block from the *Camelia*. Mr. Paviot could now afford any luxury, including ice transported by boat from the city at great trouble and expense.

Bibi said Madame and Mamzelle were receiving their visitor in the drawing room. She led the doctor there at his request. Dismissing Bibi in the hall, he watched to see that she returned downstairs.

The ladies were standing. Palmyre was before the mantel, her fine head reflected in the pier glass hanging above it. Nanaine's back was to the door, but her face showed in the mirror behind

Palmyre. A parlor table was between the two women, and at one side of it stood Miriam. She alone noticed the door open and saw the doctor come into the long apartment.

"Since my brother's son is apparently not capable of deciding these matters of discrimination for himself," Nanaine was saying, "we must demand that you forbid your daughter to see him further."

"I am sorry, Madame," Palmyre replied. "Unlike you, I find my daughter thoroughly capable in matters of discrimination. I have never found it necessary to forbid her to see anyone. If you wish, you may *request* her not to see your nephew again." She raised her hand in Miriam's direction. "It is a subject to be discussed with her—not me."

"Are you"—Nanaine turned on the girl—"going to ruin his life? He has a splendid career before him. He is engaged to Mademoiselle Colette Roussel, a girl of excellent family—connected with his own, in fact. Are you"—she clasped her hands at her well-corseted waist, and drew up her bosom—"are you going to ruin all that for him?"

The doctor started across the room. His step went unheard on the thick matting.

"I do not wish to ruin his life, Madame," Miriam murmured. "I wish to enrich it."

"If you love him as you say, you will relinquish him—you will not see him again. You will prefer to sacrifice yourself rather than him!"

Anger blinded him. His aunt in the role of Alfredo's father. . . . The scene became unreal and ridiculous. He was back in the family box at the French Opera. *La Traviata, second act, a room in a country house near Paris.* . . . Suddenly he wished to laugh.

"You must promise!" his aunt demanded.

"I cannot promise you anything, Madame. Even if I wished to, I could not."

"Ah. . . ." She drew a deep breath and let it out again with a shudder of exasperation. "You are stubborn and self-willed, I see—like your mother. One should not, after all, expect you to take after your father—since you had none."

Whether it was anger or fear that leaped into Palmyre's face the doctor could not tell. They both looked toward the girl.

"Madame?" Miriam's eyes widened with a mild expression of inquiry.

"I see there are other things you don't know, Mamzelle, besides how to behave yourself. . . ."

"*Nanaine!*"

The doctor cut her sentence in two. In the mirror, she saw him advancing, his eyes narrowed, jaw set.

"If you are old enough to know and speak your mind so well, Mamzelle," she continued without flinching, "you are old enough to know that your mother and the man who bred you were not married. You are a—bastard." She used the ugly English word, maliciously, deliberately, for the first time in her life.

Palmyre showed the swift pain she felt. For a moment, she looked almost haggard, as if her beauty had suddenly fallen from her. Victor knew it was the moment of Nanaine's triumph. Justice had caught up with this evil woman at last and now she was suffering for her sin! He observed how Nanaine drew herself up, satisfied and self-righteous. She it was who had brought the sinner to bay. She had taken the work of a lazy God in hand and done it herself.

He felt crazily torn between riotous laughter, blinding anger at his aunt, and anguish for the mother and daughter. Nanaine's lines struck him as something contrived in a cheap and clumsy play. He was no longer at the opera but on a Mississippi River showboat. He was not surprised to hear his own voice, hoarse and badly managed, taking part in the performance. "We would all thank you to allow us to arrange our own lives."

Miriam alone remained what she really was. Chin up, breathing faster, but no shock—rather, a faint smile. No resentment, no horror.

"I know that, Madame."

"You *know* . . . !"

226

"Yes. My mother is much too honest to have kept it from me, or to have told me a lie. I am happy to be what you call me, since my parents were two people who sincerely loved each other. I love and admire them both!"

Victor's heart thundered inside him. She knew. Probably Palmyre had told her as soon as she was old enough to understand. And Miriam did understand—with a wisdom that would have been rare in a woman three times her age. He could have applauded. He wished to say "Bravo!" to her, but his throat had tightened and he could say nothing.

Nanaine's steel had turned against herself. It was she who was shocked, taken off guard, belittled and incredulous. When she could speak again, her words were thick and unsteady.

"*Admire* them! Like cowards, running off from her legitimate husband!"

"No, Madame, not cowardly. I think they were courageous."

Miriam smiled at her mother. The girl's coolness restored Palmyre's poise.

"What I did"—Palmyre spoke slowly—"whether you choose to call it cowardice or courage, was what I wanted to do. In my opinion, not doing anything at all would have been unforgivable."

It was true that she was proud rather than repentant of her sin. This was not confession—it was joyous reminiscence. No bowed head, no trite tears. The hurt look had vanished, and the doctor thought he had never seen her as handsome as she was at this moment.

Nanaine's lips came together in a tight line.

"The opinion of women without virtue," she declared, "does not interest me!"

"Come!" The doctor took his aunt's arm brusquely. "I will see you to your carriage."

His determined fingers sank into the flesh under her black bombazine. She felt his anger.

"If you please." She picked up the train of her skirt as if to keep it from contamination. "I have been here much too long."

He had three-o'clock dinner with the Roussels. Among those present was Harry Lockwood, his honest face incapable of hiding the fact that he would have preferred to be elsewhere. Harry now knew Leon too well to appreciate his company, but Julien exerted himself to patch up the strained relations between the two young men, and Harry was too good-natured to reject the older man's efforts. The truth was that the causeway project had taken on a slightly jaundiced air which Julien was intent on dissipating. The senior Lockwood had become gravely concerned with storms. He was now in Galveston studying the effects of the West Indian hurricane which had passed that way a few weeks previous.

There might have been an added reason for Harry's coming today—a purpose of his own—for before they sat down to table, he found a moment apart to say to the doctor, "I'd like to speak to you privately." Victor knew better than to invite him to "Clair de Lune," where he would be subject to Nanaine's arrogance. "Come to the office," he said, "any time you wish." But Harry was punctilious. "I don't like to take your time from your patients. It's a strictly personal matter." What could Harry want with him? All through dinner he wondered.

Colette, at the doctor's side, seemed distrait, saying little, eating little. He tried his best to bring her out of her moody silence, joking, tempting her to laugh, but she always slipped back again to her own thoughts. He guessed she was disturbed by Nanaine's visit to "Belle Pointe," by now the topic of the town. She was not alone in doubting the story Nanaine had so carefully spread, to the effect that she had gone to discuss with Fauvette a business matter involving Nanaine's gracious offer to sell back, now that Fauvette was in a favorable position to retrieve her treasures, a d'Eaubonne chandelier bought by the duRochers at auction years before. He could have told Colette the truth, but would it have improved her state of mind?

Féfé Larouche, on the other hand, who had maneuvered to sit at the doctor's right, ate like a hungry puppy and deluged him with prattle. "Oh, Cousin Vic, I would simply adore the Canal

Zone. Don't tell Mama, but in a novel I read, it said that white slavery is simply awful down there. You see, this girl was drugged and. . . ." A few minutes later she startled him by asking, "Cousin Vic, did you learn about free love from the people of Panama? It must be a simply fascinating place!"

At last the baba cake, drenched with claret, and the black coffee were served, and the long dinner came to a welcome end. The gentlemen retired to the coolness of the gallery upstairs to enjoy their brandy and cigars. Leon's customary elegance was today enhanced by the addition of a gold cigarette holder ringed with rubies and diamonds, which he waved about in a foppish and annoying manner.

With unconcealed urgency, Harry sought the doctor at the first opportunity and edged him into a secluded corner. His open face reflected the importance of his request.

"Doctor, I love Miss Miriam and wish to marry her." He said it all in a rush. "I am trying to get up courage to propose. If you could possibly—I know both she and her mother respect you very much—if you could put in a word—that is. . . ."

Victor was taken completely off guard. He was at a loss what to say. He heard himself stammering as badly as the young Northerner.

"I'll see—that is—I seldom go to 'Belle Pointe.' But of course— if the occasion. . . ."

"Thank you, thank you!" Harry grasped his hand and crushed it in his own. The doctor retreated to the company of the others, his mind in a turmoil. "Miriam, I wish to speak to you about. . . . Miriam, there's a young man. . . ." Bon Dieu!

He got away from "Beaux Arbres" as soon as he could. As he was leaving, Julien came up and said, "Nanaine is having the reading of the will at eight. I have it all in order. There were only one or two changes made." He hesitated. "Notably one. . . ."

Julien drew his chair closer to the table and turned up the lamp. He adjusted his pince-nez, and began. "Testament of

Michel Victor Pierre Jean-Marie duRocher, husband of the late Noélie Honorine Marie-Anne Labouisse. In the name of the Father, of the Son, and of the Holy Ghost. Amen."

Nanaine, sitting upright on the black haircloth sofa, fanned herself with a satisfied air. Papa slumped in the platform rocker, his long fingers interlaced over his piqué vest.

"All those who shall read this document, shall know, like myself, that I, legitimate son of the late Michel Victor Pierre Jean-Marie duRocher, grandson of . . . and great-grandson. . . ." The tiresome genealogy went on and on, like the Chapter of Generations in the Book of Genesis.

Papa was dozing before the long preamble came to a close.

"First, I declare that I have made an inventory and estimate of the value of my property. . . ."

Several pages followed, aggregating at a modest appraisal something above three hundred and fifty thousand dollars. Of this fortune Nanaine had been the administrator since the old doctor's retirement, handling it all with an expert hand. There followed the minor bequests to the servants, "memory money," as it was called, and the disposition of sentimental souvenirs. "I give to my son Victor my gold watch and chain, my gold spectacle case, and all my personal linen. I desire all table and bed linen and all remaining household furniture on the Royal Street premises to go to my sister. . . ." Nanaine nodded slowly.

Finally came the part of the will that mattered most, from a pecuniary point of view. Julien took off his glasses and wiped them with dramatic deliberation. He replaced them, seeming to find some difficulty in getting them to sit right. He took out his handkerchief and blew his nose. At last he bent his head again over the foolscap. Victor observed how his baldness glowed in the lamplight.

"To my sister, above mentioned, I leave as a brotherly token of affection five thousand dollars to be realized from the forelisted securities, this sum being thoroughly acceptable to her and one which I deem sufficient in consideration of the large personal fortune she possesses in her own right. . . ."

Julien had to wipe and adjust his glasses again. He seemed slightly embarrassed.

"All the rest of my fortune, both real and personal, I bequeath to my only son Michel Victor Pierre Jean-Marie duRocher"—Julien cleared his throat—"provided"—he continued, hesitatingly, "said Michel Victor Pierre Jean-Marie duRocher marries Colette Marie-Louise Josephine Roussel, legitimate daughter. . . ."

This was the *notable* change. No wonder Julien faltered in his reading.

Nanaine stopped fanning to study the doctor's expression. His eyes, revealing no feeling at all, met hers steadily. She began to fan again, gazing with a faint smile at Grand-père who, from his gold frame above the mantel, looked down on them all with his penetrating eyes. Papa's eyes were closed. He had slumped deeper in the rocker.

Julien finished quickly, slurring the phrases. "One thousand in cash to pay for my last expenses, physician, burial charges. Such are my last requests. This done of my own free will and signed. . . ."

Nanaine's influence was, to Victor, flagrantly present in Papa's own free will.

Julien dipped the pen in the inkwell. He looked to Papa to come and sign. Papa greeted him with a loud snore.

"Never mind. In the morning will do," he answered Nanaine's snort of impatience. "I shall come before leaving for the city."

He returned the pen to the holder. Smiling briskly, he applied himself to putting the pages of the will in order.

The doctor was getting ready for bed when he remembered Dr. Alcide Larouche's letter received yesterday. He might have forgotten altogether, except for odd allusions in the prattle of the doctor's daughter, Féfé Larouche, at the Roussels' dinner table. *Oh, Cousin Vic. Papa really wasn't as put out as he pretended—about your ideas being so different, I mean. It was Mama, you see. . . .* She was crestfallen and incredulous that he knew nothing at all about the simply fascinating subject of free love.

Anyway, Cousin Vic, I do admire you for calling a spade a spade. If it's smallpox—or something worse, you know?—she giggled—I think it would be simply silly to call it sunburn! That's why I adore the latest English novels. . . .

He got the letter and tore it open. The tone was sheepish, half apologetic and half reproving.

I am so sorry, my dear boy, so very sorry that you found it necessary to expose your views on the virtues of unconventional relations between the sexes.

What in the world was the man talking about?

It was especially poor form to do so before a group of ladies whom we hoped to reckon in the future, as in the past, as part of our esteemed clientele.

Ah. Olympe's Wednesday "at home," two weeks ago. The vicious furor about Palmyre Delamare. Mesdames Vigée and de Gerbeau leaving in the torrential rain, in a huff. He was amazed that his plea for tolerance had been so poorly interpreted.

Such ultramodern notions of love, dear boy, I seriously fear would make the husbands of our fair patients extremely nervous, to the extent, you understand. . . .

With a disgusted toss of the head he skipped to the next paragraph.

And while as a medical man I believe, of course, in sex. . . .

Victor smiled. His cousin could hardly help believing in something the existence of which was so universally evident.

I do not believe in mentioning the names of certain diseases in refined society, nor do I handle such cases—

So. The uproar caused by his treating the girl Coco had been heard all the way across the lake.

—unless the patient is a respectable member of our society. . . .

This phrasing made the doctor laugh outright.

. . . must equally deplore that you waste your practice on Negro deliveries, as ladies of distinction naturally. . . .

Thank you, Minerve de Gerbeau-Vignaud. . . .

And so in view of our wide divergence in ideas and in practice, I regret from my heart to inform you, dear boy, that I do not, on consideration, think such a partnership as was proposed would work out to our mutual advantage and. . . .

He did not finish. He crushed the letter in a furious fist, his lips drawn back whitely from clenched teeth. He was not enraged because Alcide had said no. Of that he was glad. But the reasons he gave—the rotten, cowardly reasons.

The shrimp were running again. He gave up the idea of going to bed. Down on the beach, in the red glare of the torches, he walked off his anger. The letter was in his trousers pocket, where he had thrust it in a lump. At the foot of the Cape Charles pier, Ovide Clouzat and his family had built a bonfire and were enjoying watermelons by its light. The goodhearted undertaker had called the dull-witted Hippolyte Naquin to join them in a slice. The doctor declined Ovide's invitation, but he walked up to the bonfire and cast Alcide's letter into it. It curled up quickly, black and tortured.

"M'sieur le docteur is stoking our bonfire!" laughed Madame Clouzat.

"I am burning a witch," the doctor said. "The last, I hope, left over from seventeenth-century superstition."

Though the Clouzats did not understand his joke, all of them, because they were catching plenty of shrimp and were on a picnic and were always happy anyhow, laughed hilariously.

"Very pretty!" Hippolyte added his mirth to the rest. "Fine!"

Twenty-nine

He had not gone back to "Belle Pointe." Five days had passed since he had last seen Miriam. He avoided every probability of a meeting. He had the peak season of malaria to help him. The mosquitoes swarmed on nights of windless calm. They were big and black—they made an unpleasant moist wad on the skin when slapped. "Me, I'd jus' as rather crack a cockroach on me," Glad said. Practically everyone already had the September chills. There was one thing comforting about the town's malaria: there would be less of it next year. On Wednesday night, the Council had met before an assembly of insistent citizens and voted a tax to close open ditches and install a system of underground drainage. M'sieur Morel, the banker, was pressed into agreeing to negotiate the loan to be repaid by the tax. The citizens had made it clear that refusal would result in a run on his bank.

At least that much was done. The next step was to see if Government aid could be enlisted in spraying the surrounding swamps. The doctor imagined men, as in Panama, going their rounds with queer machines strapped to their backs, spreading over stagnated pools the scum of crude oil that would suffocate anopheles larvae. . . . He checked his dreams. His thoughts were running on as if he intended to be here forever. . . .

As a matter of fact, a letter from the Rockefeller Institute in New York lay on his desk.

Madame Naquin was the last for the afternoon. Shivering in her shawl, she had come for quinine.

"Ha! It was lucky for Hercule Moreau that he did not die of his broken head!" Though Madame's teeth chattered, she managed to talk continuously while the doctor filled the capsules. "But it was luckier for Justin Dufour! Aristide Préjean has let him out of jail—but only because the jail was so filled with cockroaches and rats that there was no room for Justin! 'And you, M'sieu' Dufour,' I said to his father, 'you are luckiest of all that the doctor stopped you the day you wanted to destroy his instruments. Yes,' I said, 'for had you done so, Hercule might have died, and then there would have been *two* assassins of the name Dufour!' "

"Instructions are on the label," the doctor advised, handing her the box.

"Though of course he will have to pay damages," she clattered on. "The district attorney will see to that! Ah, it is another lucky thing that Madame de Gerbeau has a bachelor brother who takes snuff!"

The doctor found Madame hard to follow.

"For if she had not fancied Fauvette d'Eaubonne's great-grand-father's snuffbox as a gift for her brother, and bought it, where would the Dufours get the indemnity money?"

"Ah . . . ," said the doctor, remembering that Fauvette had paid her bread bill with the snuffbox.

"And that Fauvette!" exclaimed Madame. "Do you know what she said when asked if, now that she is rich, she would buy back her great-grandfather's snuffbox?"

"No." The doctor smiled. "What did she say?"

"She said, 'I do not give a sneeze for my great-grand-father's snuffbox!' Did you ever hear of such a want of senti-ment?"

"Perhaps she does not express her sentiment in sneezes," the doctor suggested.

He knew all about Fauvette's further fall from grace since she had become regally rich. The magic inherited from her mother, by which she had turned tables and chairs into capons and truffles, had converted the last of the d'Eaubonne assets into enough oil to recover even the vagaries of the Cotton Exchange and the ravages of the cane borer. *And what does she do?* de-manded the ladies over their coffee cups. Does she rush to the antique dealer to retrieve the d'Eaubonne bed in which Louis Philippe slept on his visit to New Orleans in 1798? No! She rushes to the music store and buys that modern mechanical horror, the pianola. The doctor, accidentally caught between cups, had tried in vain to divert the ladies' attention to things going on in the outside world. Did they see where the North Pole had been discovered? Brussels had received a telegram from Dr. Frederick Cook reporting his having reached the Pole in April of last year. But the ladies could not be bothered with trivialities. Cook. Who was he? Poles. What were they good for? Now, my dear, as to Fauvette. . . .

"She is leaving 'Belle Pointe' tomorrow," Madame Naquin was saying. "She has bought a house in *uptown* New Orleans, to live among *Americans!*"

"Did you say leaving tomorrow?"

"Yes. Tomorrow, and. . . ."

He would have to tell her good-by. He would miss her, one of the few free spirits in this root-bound society.

Someone knocked on the door. It was Colette. Doudouce was with her. Madame Naquin observed the proper presence of a chaperoning servant with disappointment.

The doctor was surprised to see Colette. She had gone to the city on *Le Cygne* with Julien early Monday morning, together with Madame Larouche and Féfé, at whose home she was to spend the week. She looked cool and fresh in a white summer suit and a white felt hat turned up on the side, a black plume curling around the brim. In his office, it was only as she raised her face to kiss him in greeting that he noticed the dark depressions under her eyes.

"Have you been unable to sleep again, Colette?" he inquired with concern. "Didn't you promise me you wouldn't worry about anything?"

She smiled wanly. "I have tried to keep my promise."

He looked at the calendar on the wall. "You are back early. We didn't expect you before tomorrow." When she sighed, he asked quickly, "Is anything wrong?"

"Oh, no. . . ." She took the chair he offered. He observed how nervous she was, lacing and unlacing her gloved fingers in her lap. "Papa would have gotten back this evening if he had had to swim. He received a letter from Palmyre Delamare, asking him to come see her. Leon saw it at the office. He told me."

"On business, I'm sure."

She looked down at her hands, bit her lip.

"He's having three drums of oil delivered by schooner at the sawmill. Leon and his friends used *Le Cygne* so much there was barely fuel enough to get to the city last Monday, so Papa is going to keep a supply on hand here. He hardly put his foot in the house before he was off to the bayou, to show them where to store the drums—so he said. But of course he was rushing to 'Belle Pointe.' "

"I know the drums were delivered, because one of the Negroes, in unloading them, crushed a hand. He was here a while ago to have it dressed."

"You needn't trouble to make alibis for Papa." She smiled ruefully. "He is expert at it himself."

"Let us give him the benefit of the doubt. At least we have my work on the Negro's hand as partial evidence."

"Vic, dear, that's what I came to talk to you about."

"Partial evidence?"

She was in too serious a mood to accept his pleasantry.

"No. Your work. Féfé Larouche told me—her father has reconsidered."

"Yes," he said briefly.

"Oh, Vic—what are you going to do?"

The subject of Dr. Larouche was distasteful to him. He shrugged off his annoyance.

"Stay here, I suppose."

"*Vic*—you *couldn't!*" Her horror was so genuine that he laughed.

"Then we'll go to New York." He stepped over to the desk and picked up the letter from the Institute. "The Surgeon General sent these people proof sheets of a report I've written for the *Medical Journal*. They offer me an arrangement under which I could devote my time exclusively to research."

"You mean you would be inoculating rabbits, and cutting up guinea pigs and keeping the pieces in jars and test tubes?"

He grinned at her concept of laboratory.

"Broadly speaking, yes."

"Oh, Vic—to bury yourself like that! To waste all your fine chances!"

"But it would be the opposite of burying myself and wasting my chances!"

She was too absorbed to notice the enthusiasm in his voice.

"That is no kind of work for you, Vic. Tell them no."

"But you would like New York!" He tried desperately to persuade her. He listed the museums, the opera, the theaters, the fashionable shops.

She shook her head. "Our place is with our own people, living our own kind of life."

His patience snapped. "Our place is where we make it—our people are *all* people!"

"But we can be happiest in Louisiana, Vic. . . ." She pleaded with her eyes. "I tried so hard to want to go to Panama with you —I used to lie awake at night and fight my feelings against it. Now I wish I could make myself want to go to New York! But to give up so much here—it would be throwing away our heritage, Vic, to say nothing of all your shining opportunities. . . ." Her voice trailed off, choked with tears.

"Then what would you suggest my doing?" He stood before her, arms folded.

She jumped up from the chair, gripped his shoulders. "Open an office of your own in New Orleans! You will be the finest physician in the city! You can! You will be so important, so prominent. You can be anything!"

"All I hope to be is a decent doctor."

He walked away from her and stood looking out of the window, fingering his watch chain. Perhaps it was selfish, even cruel, to expect her to leave all she loved for an uncertain and lonely life among people whom she might always look upon as strangers. He would have his work, but she would have nothing beyond his companionship, and even that at times would be curtailed. He criticized this dying regime because it could see only what lay on its own side of the fence. Perhaps, in the present instance, he was suffering the same nearsightedness. He did not wish to be unjust, unkind. Presently he turned and said with a sigh, "Then that is what you want?"

"Yes." She got up and went to him. "Because I love you so much that I want the best and most brilliant career for you. And it should be what you want, too, Vic. You were meant for it. Like your father and grandfather before you. Don't you see? It is your destiny."

"Our destiny is what—with God's help—we make it."

"Then make yours something we will all be proud of! Don't cheat us! Don't cheat yourself!"

He felt suddenly tired.

"All right. All right, Colette. I will do my best."

She moved closer to him and said softly, "You cannot change what you are, Vic, any more than you can change the marrow of your bones."

"I wonder. . . ."

She looked at him sharply, searching his face. Then of a sudden she was in his arms, whispering urgently against his neck. "Oh, Vic! Vic! I shall be so good to you. You'll see." She pressed herself against him hard, as if in promise. He was stunned by the closeness of her beauty, and deeply affected by her emotion. He bent his head and laid his cheek on hers, his mind a whirl of self-questioning and confusion.

Julien's trap was indeed at "Belle Pointe."

The doctor, as he walked toward the piazza, half reproached himself for being as able at alibis as his intended father-in-law. He recognized that his wish to say good-by to Fauvette was perhaps secondary to his hope of seeing Miriam. It was not like a farewell forever; Fauvette was going only as far as the city, where he could call on her whenever he wished.

He would have turned back if they had not spied him from the gallery. They were having coffee, Julien and Palmyre, Fauvette and Mr. Paviot. The latter was elegantly attired in a new

239

Prince Albert and striped formals. The tennis shoes had ceded to stylish four-button Oxfords.

"Yes, we are leaving," Fauvette confirmed. "With the schools opening, practically all the summer people will be returning. 'Go soon and avoid the rash,'" she said in English, quoting—she thought correctly—a bargain-day advertisement. It hardly mattered; Fauvette would no longer have to bother with bargains.

"We will stay until the pecans fall," Victor said, "so Zeph can thrash the trees."

"They had better fall on time. Nanaine will never miss the opening of the opera." Fauvette giggled. "I have engaged a box."

"We will be here neither for the pecans nor the opera," Palmyre said sadly. "I have just sold 'Belle Pointe.'"

Julien, who said nothing, was not as happy as he should have been under the circumstances. He had acquired the coveted property, but he was losing—if it could be said that he was losing something he never had—Palmyre Delamare. His chin was on his chest, and he slumped dejectedly in his chair.

The doctor also had received a jolt, but he covered it with a professional calm. He would have liked to ask when they were leaving and where they were going, but he checked himself. It should be of no possible concern to him beyond the bounds of normal curiosity.

It was Julien who put the pertinent questions.

"As soon as the act of sale is passed," Palmyre replied.

"That may take two weeks," Julien declared promptly.

She shrugged. "It is just as well. It will take all of that to pack and arrange our passage to New York. We will go by boat."

"Ah, New York." Julien brightened. "I go there at intervals on business."

"It is too bad," Palmyre smiled politely, "that we shall not have the pleasure of seeing you. We are going to live somewhere in France."

"But there is talk of war in Europe!" Julien objected. France was far, and he had no business there.

"Yes. But our friends advise it may not be for five years yet.

It is Germany they fear. But in five years anything can happen."

"Or in five minutes," said Fauvette, who knew.

"That is the way of the world," Mr. Paviot philosophized. "Changes are cooking all around us. It will take a war to bring them to a boil. And then—*presto!*—the whole world will be an entirely new dish! History shows that it happens as regularly as the stars keep their courses."

No one encouraged Mr. Paviot to expatiate. The doctor rose to go. Taking an inverted pleasure in pain, he was glad that Miriam was obviously out. He chided himself for wondering where.

They all went down to the gate. Palmyre evaded Julien by lagging behind to walk beside the doctor. "I decided it was best to sell 'Belle Pointe.'" She turned her full, handsome face up to him. "The caving in continues, and the cost of extending the breakwater out of my own pocket is too great. And then," she added with a touch of bitterness, "no one ever wanted us here."

"Perhaps you made a mistake"—he looked at the ground—"in coming back. Perhaps you made a mistake in bringing Miriam here."

"Who knows?" She smiled in an odd way. "At any rate, we are going now. I don't know exactly where." Victor glanced at her face and marveled at its serenity, she who seemed to have so little to be serene about.

On the banquette, Fauvette pinched both his cheeks and gave him a loud kiss on the mouth. "*You* are one I shall see in the city!" As he climbed into his buggy, he saw an automobile coming up the street. The senior Lockwood, returned from the Gulf Coast, sat in back, and Harry was at the wheel, with a lady in veil and duster at his side. The lady was Miriam.

Perhaps Harry had succeeded in his quest, without the doctor's help.

Thirty

The following Monday was Labor Day.

He left the office early. Without work he was like a ship without anchor. There was, of course, a great deal he could do on the pellagra files, and in the ill-equipped, stifling little laboratory; he tried, and got no further than a headache. He had an indefinable sense of discomfort that was like the onset of sickness; he felt nervous and tense and terribly tired. The thought struck him that he would like a drink.

Paul's Exchange was crowded. As he walked in through the swinging doors, he was greeted by affable comments. "Voilà Miché le docteur!" "Eh, là bas! Miché Vic!" Nearly all of them knew him now, and their liking showed frankly through their wine and beer. Only a few around Mayor Bidault sat silent and unsmiling. Dufour, the baker, was among them.

The doctor wedged in at the bar next to the fisherman, Alceste Moreau. Against the old man's protests, he ordered two cognacs.

"Tell Hercule I'll drop by tomorrow."

"His wife, she come today." Alceste teased himself with the bouquet of the brandy. "To stay at my house. At Hercule, it too much for her all alone. Up an' down dat high step—an' her any minute now."

"Yes," the doctor said. "You are right." To make conversation, he asked, "Where does Hercule live?"

"You know Roussel sawmill? But yas!" He knocked his knuckles against his head for asking a foolish question. "Jus' across d' road from dat. Firs' house behind 'Belle Pointe.' Nize high groun'. But he build on pillar jus' d' same. Hercule—he smart. He don't fool wit no high water—not him. You know wat he call his place? 'Beau Rêve.' Beautiful Dream. Dat pretty smart, heh?"

The old man went on and on, the doctor throwing in a question or comment now and then; but his attention focused on a loud discussion at the end of the bar near the entrance. Leon Roussel and the druggist, Guy Chauvin, were arguing the authenticity of Dr. Cook's claim to having discovered the North Pole. This morning's paper reported that while Dr. Cook dined with King Frederick in Copenhagen, Commander Peary of the United States Navy announced from St. Johns, in Newfoundland, that he had reached the Pole in April of the present year and saw nothing to indicate that Dr. Cook had been there a year before.

"Cook is a liar!" Leon shouted. "Our leading scientists say so!"

"I don't give a damn what *who* says!" In a drunken attempt to be natty, Guy had a boutonniere of deer's-tongue drooping from his lapel. "I say Cook got there first!"

"If Cook wanted to be believed, he should have dropped a couple of gumdrops by the Pole." Leon laughed loudly. "He took two barrelfuls with him. *Gumdrops!* A fine contribution to science!" He was as drunk as Guy.

Old Alceste insisted on returning the treat, and the doctor allowed him to order the bottle down again. "An' den my Hercule, he say, 'Papa,' he say. . . ."

The argument down the line was attracting the interest of others. They stopped to listen. It looked as if the admirers of the rival explorers were going to come to blows. Leon ordered more absinthe. Even Alceste became aware that there were other absorbing subjects besides Hercule. "Dat Pole very puzzlin' to me," he confessed. "You don' see it, you don' touch it—all d' same it been discover' *two time!*"

The doctor clapped the old man affectionately on the back and took his leave. He went up to Leon. The argument, which had at first amused him, seemed about to get out of hand.

"Leon, you've had enough. Why don't you go home?" He said it quietly, putting his hand on Leon's shoulder.

"I've had enough of *you*. Keep out of this!"

Guy, seeing his chance, shot out a fist at Leon. The doctor pushed Leon out of its path. For a moment, Guy was a grotesque clown, sprawling and pawing air. He caught his balance and lunged for the doctor. With a backward jump the doctor passed through the swinging doors behind him, and Guy in the same instant, his fists fighting the double doors as they swung inward again, fell through the entrance and onto the banquette on his face.

The tension inside the barroom was broken. As the doctor climbed into his buggy, he heard hilarious laughter. He looked back. Guy was all right. He was picking himself up, dusty and bewildered.

Weaving among the crowds on the beach, Masoom offered her wares. The doctor waved, and she raised a hand, Indian-fashion, wrapped to the wrist in moss. He drew up and called her.

"You have hurt your hand, Masoom."

"Not true." She thought he wished to buy something from her, else she would not have come.

"Take that moss off. Let me see it."

She put her hand quickly behind her back.

"Doesn't it pain you?"

"No. Not pain."

He sighed. It was impossible to break through her reserve.

"Well, if it gets worse, come see me. I can fix it."

"I come," she promised. She seemed relieved, as if she considered herself lucky to have gotten off so easily, and turned to go.

A sudden idea for putting the holiday to use came to him. For days he had been promising himself to get on with the pellagra research.

"Well, I'll ride out and see your husband. He's sick, isn't he?"

She whirled around, her great black eyes wide and wild.

"Not sick! *Not sick!*" she screamed. People looked.

"So much the better then. I'll pay him a friendly call."

She stared at him. Once while at medical school he had gone with some fellow students from north Louisiana to hunt venison, and had seen that look in the eyes of a cornered doe. He had never forgotten it, nor had he ever hunted deer again. She seemed transfixed to the spot. Then, as he gave Rougette the rein and the buggy wheels ground into the shell road, she turned and ran, her long hair flying, dropping little bunches of deer's-tongue and vetiver in her wake. The picnickers on the beach looked after her in amazement.

On the road behind the swamp, he met the boy Felix Fanchon and his father returning home after setting a kiln. Through the trees he could see the mud hill and the blue smoke rising from the crater, and he could smell smothering pine. The boy's smiling face was smudged with soot; the father, grinning, raised his arm to show that, despite the shriveled skin, it was back in working order. The people in the woods observed no holidays. For them, rest was regulated by the weather, not by the calendar.

Philo could tell him of no easy way to reach Masoom's house through the swamp.

"Masoom, she get out by d' bayou. She go down dere an' paddle her pirogue preddy smart an' no time she in d' lake. She go back and fort' from town like dat."

"There's a quicksand back of the house," Felix spoke up. "It mus' be good huntin' in dat swamp. But me, I never try it. They lose all their dog in dat quicksand."

"Well, that's one approach vetoed," the doctor said. "I guess I'll just get out and wade in from here."

"I bet I know what Miché le docteur do tomorrow," Philo laughed. "He buy new shoe."

At the first step, the slimy water oozed to the middle of his leg. He skinned his shins on the upturned roots of cypresses. Birds flew out in dismay and wasps threatened him, and he had to keep a hand constantly waving to ward off mosquitoes and blue-flies. Where the floor of the swamp curved above the water the crawfish built their muddy towers and toads sat blinking beady eyes. Sunlight seeped in slantwise through the thickness overhead, and in its warmth turtles basked on fallen logs. He kept his eyes alert for the deadly cottonmouth, his ears keen for the first warning of the rattler.

At times he was compelled to go around a tree that had crashed, or skirt a thicket of poison oak. He wondered why anyone should want to live in such a place; it was true that it possessed a weird and wonderful beauty, but the shallow water swarmed with reptiles, and where it moved at all, it crawled—the kind of sluggish paradise preferred by the cow alligator. It was certainly the most forbidding approach to a dwelling he had ever seen; it was as if the residents had chosen it deliberately to hold their privacy against all comers.

At length, the ground underfoot grew firmer, and finally he stood on dry land, his legs dripping slime. Philo was right: his shoes were finished. He stomped his feet and wiped them on the grass.

The house was hardly more than a broad hall, all doors thrown wide to the air, a rough ladder step ascending back and front. On the porch were oars and paddles, stood up in a corner, and fish nets and baskets. Bunches of bay leaf and sassafras, deer's-tongue and vetiver hung drying against the front boards.

Joe was sitting on a tree stump, the materials of Indian basketry spread around him—reeds, pine straw, ribbons of palmetto dyed red, blue, green, and purple. He was busily weaving, but the doctor paid no attention to his hands at first. He saw only the face. The forehead was high and broad and crested with black hair. The doctor could not see the eyes, lowered to work, but he imagined them deep and dark. The mouth was strong and full-lipped. It was at the base of the neck and on the chest, his denim jumper open to the navel, that the gray scabs and circular patches of white scales showed.

Joe, catching his half-finished basket between his knees, reached into his jumper pocket for tobacco pouch and paper to roll himself a cigarette. As the small cylinder formed between his fingers, the doctor noted the deformity of the digits. The joints were so shrunken as to appear missing, and the articulations at the ends of the stumps were peculiar white nodes. The backs of the hands were discolored with blackish areas, round and raised. From there the doctor's eyes went swiftly to the bare feet. The skin over the ankles was of the color and thickness of an elephant's, and cartilage absorption had proceeded so far that the toes seemed to have fallen off.

The finished cigarette between his lips, Joe was about to strike a match when his head inclined to the side and his whole body tensed. His narrowed eyes made a slow, careful circle from the direction of the swamp, fixing at last on the doctor who stood a few yards away. The doctor came forward. Joe jumped up, the cigarette falling from his mouth. He moved so quickly that Victor did not see him pick up the gun lying among the reeds at his side.

"Don't come," Joe said in English.

"I've come to help you." A sickly odor reached the doctor.

"I don't want help." He made a get-on gesture with the muzzle of the gun. "Go away."

"You *need* help," Victor insisted. "I know of a place that will give you treatment. Perhaps," he persuaded against his better judgment, "you can be cured."

The suggestion seemed to infuriate the man. He shouted at the top of his voice.

"Get out! Get away from here! I'll shoot! I'll kill you!"

His finger trembled on the trigger.

The sound of running came along the plank walk leading from the bayou. It was Masoom. She was a flash of fear, of fury, of anguish. She threw herself on Joe. She hung around his neck. She sobbed and clung to him. *"No! No! Not go!"* she screamed.

Of a sudden she stopped. She seized the gun from Joe and, quick as light, turned and faced the doctor.

"I kill!" Her eyes meant it.

"I'll go, Masoom. I don't want you to kill me. Not for myself. For you. They would send you to prison, and then you wouldn't see Joe any more. It would be worse than if you let us send Joe to the hospital."

She put down the gun, leaning on it.

"I don't go to prison. Joe don't go to hospital. We stay. Here. Our *home*."

Before starting back through the swamp, the doctor turned to look at them. Masoom was kissing her husband's face wildly.

Though he had not touched Joe or anything near him, the doctor considered it wise to destroy his clothes; they were hardly worth keeping anyway. He stopped at "Clair de Lune" to tell Zeph to bring a fresh outfit to him at the remote end of the beach where the Mamaloi had her cabin. There he stripped and washed in the lake from head to foot.

The Labor Day crowds were at the height of their merriment. The tub races had just ended and now the sailboat contests were beginning. As he drove homeward, he watched the tilted sails, big with wind and beautifully white against the blue sky, and heard the shouts of friends on shore following them with field glasses. Everybody was having a good time. He wondered how many had bought from Masoom this morning.

He remembered his first visit to Dr. Jolivet last May when Masoom entered the office. *Have you been selling that stuff in town again? You know what I'll have to do, don't you?* He must have threatened to send Joe away. *Why do you do it? Don't you hunt and raise enough to eat?* Tobacco, Masoom had said. Jolivet had turned to him with a crazy question: *Do you believe in love?* He had not been interested enough to think of it at the time, but he recognized now what was in the bottles Jolivet had given Masoom on several occasions. The amber-colored liquid was chaulmoogra oil.

He found Nanaine with Cumba, folding sheets that had been embroidered by the Sisters of the Sacred Heart and storing them on the shelves of the armoire. Nanaine was placing small sheaves of vetiver between the folds as he came in.

"Nanaine."

"Yes?"

"The vetiver must be burned at once."

"Nonsense! It's fresh! I just bought it from Masoom this morning!"

248

"The sheets that touched it must be burned, too."

"Our beautiful sheets! Have you gone mad?"

"Do as I say, Nanaine. We'll disinfect the armoire. And I'll send Zeph for carbolic. You and Cumba must cleanse your hands."

"What—what is it?" Nanaine stammered, her fingers to her cheek.

"Leprosy."

With a gasp, she drew her hand quickly away. Cumba screamed and fled. As soon as Victor uttered the word, he regretted it. Inwardly, he reproached himself for not having given some other reason.

Thirty-one

The next issue of the *Trumpet* carried a notice inserted by Dr. duRocher advising all who had bought from the Choctaw called Masoom to burn their purchases. He had considered the wording for some time, looking for an explanation that would prevent panic. *"To avoid contagion from disease. . . ."* It was as much and as little as he dared say.

His reporting the case to the State Board of Health required less time, but involved, in a way, more effort. He disliked intensely the necessity for driving Joe and Masoom from their unenviable Eden. He debated the possibility of allowing them to remain until the new and permanent physician arrived—whoever and whenever that might be—and decided against it. His duty permitted no half-measures. He could understand Jolivet's slipshod handling, prompted, as the old doctor admitted, by an excess of sentiment, but he could condone such an attitude neither in Jolivet nor in himself. Any effort to evade an act of cruelty against these two would constitute a criminal offense against the whole town.

At any rate, the situation in the last weeks had changed completely, and the only reason that could possibly justify an unethical decision had been eliminated. Now Masoom herself was infected. There was no mystery to the hand carefully concealed in moss. From an emotional standpoint, it was perhaps a good thing that Joe's affliction had spread to Masoom. Now there need be no separation. She could go with Joe. What she dreaded apparently more than the disease itself—being parted from him—was no longer a threat.

There was a place in Iberville Parish—the old Indian Camp Plantation, about eighty miles up the river from New Orleans. Not good, but not altogether bad. Better, at all odds, than behind the bars of the Isolation Hospital in the hot and crowded city. There might have been a happier home for these people if ignorance and fear had not destroyed it nine years before. A suitable site had been purchased and a decent refuge erected with funds appropriated by the State legislature; on the eve of transferring the patients, objecting residents of the locality burned every last building to the ground. This was the most deplorable and perhaps the most dangerous feature of the disease: the prejudice and panic that attended it. It had to be fought as actively as the disease itself. It was, in fact, another plague. Here, the doctor thought grimly, was one more battle for some hardy medical son of Louisiana who could face a good fight.

He finished his application to have Joe and Masoom entered at the old Plantation. There they would at least receive all the attention presently available. The State had drawn up a contract with the Sisters of Charity whereby they assumed gratuitous domestic charge and nursing care of the patients. The place was well staffed with volunteer nuns who had established residence in the abandoned colonial home, while the patients were assigned to the former slave cabins. The doctor would have preferred sending Joe and Masoom to a neat cottage instead of a slave shack. . . . His mind slipped off to a vision of small white houses, lawns and gardens, administration buildings, recreation centers. . . . He checked himself. Such projects were for politicians to ponder.

Despite his precautions, panic rose. The ghastly gift of the

West Indies was too well known in the hot lands along the Gulf not to stir suspicion, and Cumba no doubt had initiated a chain of confirmation that had linked its way through the entire town. Echoes of the local furor reached the other side of the lake. A small but sensational item appeared in the city papers, quoting the notice in the *Trumpet* for the benefit of Masoom's Labor Day customers.

A frenzy of wash boiling and disinfecting seized the community. In practically every back yard a furnace was going; frightened servants poked simmering linens with broomsticks for hours. Inside, the ladies were busy dissolving corrosive sublimate in gallons of boiling water; in some homes, even the walls and furniture were washed down.

In the handsome houses along the beach, at the sound of the word "lèpre," sensitive women fainted. As usual, Madame Vigée was hardest hit. She stumbled over a pan of formaldehyde left in a dark corner and sprained her ankle. Coucou mistook a bowl of sublimate solution for his drinking water and almost died. And to add terror to tragedy, there was no doctor a decent woman could call. Madame Vigée had as great a grudge against Victor as God had against her.

By dusk of Wednesday, the fear reached its peak.

Going to the post office for his evening mail, Victor found an unusual crowd gathered at the bank corner, all men. The doctor opened his box and extracted the State permits for consigning Joe and Masoom to the Plantation.

When he came out into the street again, the crowd had swelled by the addition of the mayor and the town marshal, Aristide Préjean. Bidault was mounted, and Aristide's horse was surrounded by a pack of nervous hounds from the jailhouse kennel. There were now more than a hundred men in the restless group, including leading citizens and tradespeople, as well as the riffraff of the town, surly half-blacks and voodooists.

"What's going on?" he asked the barber, Alex Gravois.

"They are going out after Choctaw Joe. You didn't see the

notice in front of Town Hall? Colin Menard posted it." Alex took out a big lead watch and looked at the time. "In half an hour they'll start. There will be some dirty doing."

"What do they want with Joe?" the doctor asked angrily. He looked around and noted for the first time the bowie knives in belts, the rifles and grass-blades. Some carried clubs, and one man had a rope over his shoulder. A wave of fear swept over him.

"They want to get rid of him," Alex said. "After your piece in the paper, Colin Menard went up the bayou nosing for news, and he hid, and saw him. Colin says he stank and had neither fingers nor toes."

The doctor cut through to the core of the crowd, muscling men out of his way. Sullen mumbling and rowdy swearing closed in after him. In the center, he found Colin Menard, a rifle under his arm, standing on a butter tub. Even this platform failed to raise Colin's short stature above the heads of the others. The doctor picked him up by the waist and set him on the ground. The swift transition took the breath out of Colin and left him speechless. There was some laughter among those who were the doctor's friends. Colin's face reddened with rage. The doctor jumped up on the tub, his heart pounding in his ears. This crowd was *his* doing. Now he must stop them.

"Listen—all of you!"

The mumbling subsided. They turned to look at him curiously. He took out the letter he had just received, and waved it above his head.

"A State officer is coming to take Joe and Masoom away! They'll be cleared out in the next twenty-four hours! There's no need of violence!"

He looked down at the faces. They registered every degree of reaction from credulity to contempt. He pulled the permits out of the long envelope and prepared to read them in proof of his statement.

The mayor's voice cracked the calm.

"It's up to you, my friends! Can you risk your women and children rotting alive—for twenty-four hours longer?"

"Now!" screamed Colin Menard, the abject terror of the lepro-phobiac crawling over his face. "We want him out of the way *now!*"

His hysteria spread through the mob. The stillness broke. There was a stirring, then shouts, yells, curses.

"Time to start!"

All the faces melted into one huge ugly mask. It came surging toward the doctor. He felt the tub dashed from under him and he fell backward against a solid wall of moving men. He caught his balance, snatching desperately for the sheets of paper that had been knocked from his hand. Boots and heavy shoes stamped over his fingers, grinding the flesh. When at last he picked up the permits, they were mangled shreds, clotted with street mud and smeared with his own blood.

The mob was already on the march. Aristide Préjean on his horse, followed by his yelping hounds, drew up the rear. The doctor threw himself after the constable.

"Stop them!"

Aristide looked down at him and shrugged. He was an old and seasoned Ku Klux Klansman. It wasn't that he approved of vio-lence. It was simply that sometimes he knew better than to try to stop it. He understood the mind of the mob. Besides, harsh measures among these men might lose him votes in the next elec-tion. He was there to do his best, not to attempt the impos-sible.

The disorderly column headed toward the woods. It had all happened so quickly that for a few moments the doctor stood there bewildered. Then he jumped into his buggy. At a fast clip, he could take a back street and still come out on the main road ahead of them. He had to get Joe and Masoom out of the way before the men arrived. It was he who had started this mob. If anything happened, it would be his fault—his fault. . . .

A lamp was lit in the house on piles. The pair were at their evening meal. Masoom, speaking rapidly in a high voice, with many motions of her hands, was probably mimicking some customer who lived in a fine house on the beach, and Joe was laughing so heartily that he failed to hear anyone come up the ladder steps. He became aware of a third presence only when the doctor, disheveled and dripping as on the previous occasion, stood facing him in the open doorway.

The laughter froze. Joe reached for the gun lying beside him, at the same time rising and pushing back his chair. Masoom jumped up in alarm, upsetting an earthen dish. Baked yams went rolling over the floor.

"Angry men are coming to hurt you." The doctor was out of breath. "Take your wife and go down to the lake in your pirogue. Come back tomorrow."

Joe seemed dazed. The doctor repeated his warning. Masoom had not understood. She looked from one to the other of them, wide-eyed. They heard the first shouts of the mob entering the swamp.

"Hurry!"

It was already too late. The mayor and the marshal, on their horses, had cut in at the bridge and come along the bayou's edge. The doctor recognized the crack of Bidault's merciless crop on his horse's flanks, heard the loud whinnying protests as the animal struggled through the marsh. The hoarse baying of the dogs was coming closer. Presently the clatter of hoofs sounded on the plank walk that led from the bayou's brink, and the shadows of the mounted men flashed through the trees.

Joe poised his gun as Bidault broke through into the yard. The doctor thrust him against the wall. "No!" he shouted. "No!" Masoom, frantic, was slamming doors shut, fastening wooden bolts. The fury merging in from the swamp grew louder. Bidault and the marshal galloped once around the house, then forward into the forest, apparently to meet the others. The dogs clambered up the ladders front and back, bellowing. Masoom had still to fasten the back door. A great hound lunged for Joe's throat. He caught it neatly with a shot between the eyes. The others fell back at the flash, Joe thrashing out at them with his maimed feet. He kicked the ladder down and the dogs went crashing with it to the ground. Aristide must have heard the shot and the frenzied baying that followed. He whistled and the hounds went racing into the woods. Joe and the doctor pushed the table against the front door, wedging chairs under the wooden bolts of the side openings.

Through cracks they could see the red flare of burning pine knots coming toward the house out of the woods. It was getting dark quickly, with that onrush of night over the lowlands once the sun has set. All at once, the men, in ragged and maniac disarray, burst through the trees into the clearing. They seemed to merge magnetically again, marching swiftly forward in a solid mass.

"Let me out. I'll talk to them." The doctor had no idea what he would say. He had failed before. There was nothing in his mind but desperation.

Masoom opened a door and the doctor slipped through to the porch and shinned down a piling to the ground. He went to meet the men and they recognized him in the light of their brands. Their voices rose from an uneven roar to a crackling confusion of questions, demands, threats.

"Where is he?"

"We want Joe!"

"The woman, too!"

Victor shouted back at them. His words rang out over the swamp and came back again from the woods.

"They can't hurt you as long as you don't hurt them! Can't you understand that? Let them alone and they can't hurt you! Lay your hands on them and they're likely to kill you, too—only not as fast!"

It was Guy Chauvin who shouted, *"We can get rid of them without laying a hand on them!"*

The din of voices became deafening. The doctor could distinguish nothing coherent, but the intention of the men was obvious and it froze him in his tracks. They were going to set fire to the house. Aristide Préjean rose in his saddle and shouted into the hubbub, but his mouth seemed to move without sound.

255

One of the Mamaloi's most devout supporters moved forward, his brand blazing. Inside the house, Joe must have realized. A shot came through a diamond-shaped aperture high in the door. It went through the palm of the man's hand. The fire flew up into the air, fell to the ground in a nest of pine needles, and began to creep. A rain of shot was directed toward the diamond, while the wounded fellow's yell drove the mob into a frenzy. As one man they rushed forward, brandishing their flares. Some threw the burning brands on the porches, front and side and back. Others crept up under the piles and let the flames lick through the boards into the dry palmetto that covered the floor. Soon smoke instead of shot was pouring through the diamond opening. It seeped through the boarding, and from under the eaves.

The doctor stood apart, numb, feeling the horror of utter helplessness. As the blaze shot through the roof he saw Joe, snaking on his stomach to the edge of the back porch, slide down a piling to the ground. The burst of flame from the roof distracted the mob, and the Indian might have gotten away unnoticed. But a few yards from the house he did a strange thing. He turned, raised both hands above his head, and gave out a yell that sounded back from the depths of the swamp.

The furious pack went after him. Despite his mutilated feet, Joe was as swift as a stag, and he knew every tree and thicket for miles around. Ordinarily, it would have been a simple matter for him to elude pursuit, but the odds were against him. The whole terrain was lit up by the burning house, which by now was a torch raised aloft on its flaming piles; the trees around had caught, and the fire ate greedily into the resinous pines, creating more giant flares to illumine the swamp. The reflection brightened it to the glow of sunrise. For a while, Joe was a black shadow, darting between cypress columns. Shots rang after him. Then, of a sudden, he was gone. They did not find him where, if hit by their bullets, he would have fallen. Cursing, clutching their flaming pine knots, they splashed through the ooze searching for him. Once the mayor's horse fell, tangled in cypress knees, and the mayor thrashed him to his feet again. Aristide gave the whistle that loosed the hounds.

The men diverged in a circle, spreading a human net. Victor ran with them, pleading, shouting, trying in every way to distract them, but to no avail. For almost an hour they beat the palmetto bush. Then in the distance, they heard the triumphant bellow of the hounds.

As the posse closed in, Victor caught a glimpse of the Indian treed like a cat in the bare branches of a cypress. The rotten trunk stood at the edge of a smooth gray bog where nothing grew. Limned there against a naked background, Choctaw Joe was an easy target. It was Colin Menard who fired. Joe toppled from his perch into the bog. He picked himself up, bleeding from the arm. For a moment, he seemed about to rush back into the midst of the bellowing dogs, to plunge into the thick of the converging men. Oddly, no one else fired. As they bore down upon him from three sides, he turned and pressed desperately forward, but the dogs did not follow. They began to behave strangely, running along the brink of the bog, whimpering, whining, sniffing nervously. Joe was making slow progress. He waded up to the ankles as if in glue. The men stopped. For a full minute, no one moved.

Joe pushed beyond the center of the bog, now in up to the calves of his legs. The watching mob came to life.

"The sonofabitch might get through that quicksand!"

Colin Menard shot again. Guy Chauvin aimed but missed. Others fired, and two more shots told.

The Indian stood rooted there to the middle of his legs. His arms went writhing above his head in the struggle to pull his wounded body out of its prison. To the thighs now. The crowd of men watched, horrified yet fascinated. To the chest. The neck. No further shots were needed. Now the head was under. The last were the clutching hands, with their wasted bits of fingers.

The sand closed in with a sucking noise. Only an irregular stain on the surface showed where Joe had been. It was the color of wine in the glare.

The doctor had hoped to the last that Joe would get away or that something would happen to swerve the men from their purpose. Now it was over, and his futility in the face of their passion ground into him. He recorded the satisfied look of the illiterate, the stupid horror of the men, habitually humane, whose hot heads now were cooling, the indifference of Aristide Préjean, Bidault's sarcastic leer; and he felt the blood rush to his brain. His rage smashed savagely at them.

"You damned fools! You idiots! Are you satisfied? Are you cleaner than the leper now, with a murder on your bastard hands?"

"How about yourself?" The mayor's face twitched. He half rose in his saddle. "Letting lepers run around loose among us— you don't call that murder, heh?"

"File an affidavit against him!" Guy Chauvin shook his fist above his head. "Take his license away, by God!"

There were murmurs of dissent among those who felt friendly toward the doctor. But others, devotees of voodoo, recalled how he had offended their Grand Zombie.

"Only half the menace is removed!" the mayor shouted, suddenly remembering. "The woman probably got away!"

"It's your fault!" Colin Menard pointed a shaking finger at the doctor. "You warned them!"

"He's their friend." Bidault laughed. "But he's certainly no friend of your wives and children!"

The mayor's incitation showed signs of success. The ignorant muttered ugly oaths. In loud voices they debated whether Masoom was burned to death in the house or left alive to appear again in the town. The thought of a leper loose in their community terrified them all over again, and they vented their phobia in anger against the doctor. Exhausted by his final outburst of rage and numbed by the night's events for which he held himself responsible, Victor could only stand his ground, looking on like a man paralyzed. Gradually, out of the jostling crowd, a protective group formed about him—the barber, Alex Gravois, big Télémaque Moreau, eldest son of Alceste the fisherman, and others. The angry ones muttered threats but hesitated to attack, perhaps drained of their desire for violence by all that had already happened. Out of the circle of his friends, Victor stared blankly, seeing nothing but a blur, waiting—he hardly knew for what.

Few noticed that the swamp had grown brighter, hotter. Sweat rolled down the faces of some. At first they paid little heed to the smell of smoke. Aristide Préjean began to shout, excitedly. When they realized the swamp was on fire, the marching wall of flame was only yards away.

Every man chose for himself. The death bog lay before them, and the country toward the bayou side where the fire had started was a roaring furnace. The hunt had drawn them deep into the swamp, confusing their sense of direction, but they took no time to stop and reason north and south. They fled wherever the fire was not closing in, running and stumbling and leaping over roots and logs.

The doctor surmised the Chinchuba road ran straight ahead, but it was too far off to reach in time. The wind was carrying the fire forward, spreading it in a crescent which would cut off the road before he could get to it. If his guess was correct, the house of Philo Fanchon stood somewhere back of the bog, and the wagon path that cut in from the Chinchuba road should be in the direction where the baying of the escaping hounds could still be heard.

He sloshed through the ooze for an hour or longer without a sign of the higher land that bordered the wagon path. The fire crept after him. It caught in moss, making fantastic filigrees of flame, and sucked up the marsh gases, and hissed and steamed at the watery base of blazing cypresses. Birds shrieked and bewildered rats and 'coons got in his path, and the whole crackling swamp was alive with sound and motion. Once he thought he heard a human scream.

He pressed on, not daring to rest a moment. In some places the colonnades of cypress grew so close that he had to wedge between them. Wherever he found dry footing, snakes scurried to hide. A moccasin, coiled around the limb of a tree, dropped its head in his path. In a dim recess to his right, he heard the splashing of an alligator that had her nest there. Owls and bats, glowworms and moths confused the air. He swept his face free of cobwebs, brushed spiders and centipedes from his shoulders and hair. And always he fought the maddening mosquitoes, wiping them from his neck and cheeks in wet smears.

He came to a lagoon. The fire behind him was gaining ground. He took off his sodden shoes and torn coat and threw them into a clump of cattails. The coat gave him a degree of protection against mosquitoes, but it would hamper his swimming. He plunged into the lagoon, eyes alert for reptiles.

A scallop of sand sloped down from the opposite shore. He waded in and sat down to catch his breath. He had no idea how long he had been in the swamp—five or six hours perhaps. With a grim smile, he remembered his watch. In the glare he made out that the water-soaked mechanism had stopped working a little after midnight. The fire would not cross the lagoon. He could rest.

By the first streak of day, he figured out that he had been going north, instead of west as he wished. He started out again. His bones ached, his face and feet and hands burned. His whole body was tortured with the bites of gnats and sand flies. Behind him, blue vapors rose where the fire was wearing itself out. He could see higher land ahead. Presently he made out a cabin in the western woods. It was the shack belonging to the boy Felix Fanchon.

He went in and threw himself on the mud floor. His legs shook with strain and fatigue. Vaguely he wondered if Felix would be hunting and might pass the shack before long. He would send him to "Clair de Lune" to fetch clean clothes. He must be careful to touch nothing in the shack. After a while he could get down to the bayou back of Fanchon's and take a bath. And how thirsty he was.

He listened for a shot to tell him Felix was around. For a

time, he heard nothing but the sough of the wind and the steady hammering of a woodpecker. He laid his head on his arm and fell into a dead sleep.

The baying of a hound woke him with a start. Before he could gather his senses, the dog was in on him, bounding, yelping, crazy with success, throwing her clumsy weight against him as he stumbled to his feet.

"*Felix!*"

He shouted for the boy to call his dog off.

In the half-daze of abrupt waking, he had not recognized Dixie. Miriam, not Felix, ordered her down.

The scarf he had given her was knotted loosely around her shoulders. Her costume was bizarre. She wore riding boots and men's trousers and a white smock tucked in under a cummerbund sash. The boots were thick with swamp ooze.

In an instant, her arms were about his neck. Her lips pressed wildly against his rough face—cheeks, chin, mouth—in a delirium of joy. She drew her fingers through his disordered hair, crushed her cheek against his again and again.

"Miriam!" He gripped her arms, held her off from himself.

She looked at him from head to foot.

"I don't care. I've been in the swamp, too. I'm just as filthy."

"No. Not that. I was in the house with Joe and Masoom. They. . . ."

"I know. I know all about it. It's all over town since early morning. I don't care. All I care about is that you're safe!" She clung to him. "Oh, they said you were lost—all sorts of rumors—that you were hurt. . . ."

"No. No, I'm all right."

"They said you might have been trapped in the fire and burned alive. Like Colin Menard. They found him at the edge of the Chinchuba road where he dragged himself to die." She twisted her fingers around his arms. "Hold me. Hold me hard. I don't care."

It was so long since he had seen her. A faint perfume came from her hair and he buried his hot face in it gratefully. His physical hunger and thirst dropped away, and he felt the surge of a new need. He covered her with his arms and fiercely crowded her against himself until he heard the breath leave her in a little glad gasp. He kissed first her lips, long and tenderly, then her eyes with their strange look of wonder and warmth.

She shivered and laughed. She laid her head briefly on his shoulder with a satisfied sigh, then looked up as if she had remembered something.

"Narcisse is with me. I brought you some food. Do you know what time it is?"

"My watch stopped when I swam the lagoon."

"I know. About the lagoon, I mean. That's where Dixie lost the scent. She kept going down to the water and running back. But she found your coat and shoes in the reeds. Then I was sure." She caressed the scarf around her shoulders. "I gave her the cue with this. You said it smelled of arnica and carbolic—you'd carried it around in your pocket for so long. You remember?"

"I remember you'd never wear it."

"I want to save it—to keep it forever."

"You should not have gone into the swamp, Miriam. It was dangerous. Was Narcisse along?"

"No. He was scared of alligators. Dixie and I started over again from the Chinchuba road, on the other side of the lagoon. The swamp is still smoking, but the fire is out everywhere except over toward Fanchon's place. They're fighting it—digging trenches to stop the spread."

"I was hoping Felix would come by. I wanted to send him for my clothes."

"I should have kept Mr. Paviot's pants for you. Don't you recognize them?" She stood back so that he could get a full view of the familiar gray-striped formals.

He smiled. "Mr. Paviot never looked so ravishing in them."

"It must be noon. Narcisse can go for your clothes. First I'll call him to bring the basket of food. The carriage couldn't get all the way in here."

"You think of everything."

"No. I think only of you."

He found it hard to part with her even for a few minutes. He caught her against himself again. She gave him her mouth eagerly.

Thirty-two

The death notice went up on the lampposts.

Colin Menard, bachelor, aged forty-six years,
a native of Louisiana and son of the late. . . .

The *Trumpet,* after twenty years, was silent. "Ah," said Ovide Clouzat, "at last, so much news, and now—no newspaper. . . ."

Colin was missing still another sensational item. Mayor Bidault filed an affidavit against Dr. duRocher for failing to register a quarantine disease and allowing an infected person—Masoom— to leave the premises and compromise the public health. The doctor had no way of proving to the State Board his prompt discharge of duty, though he had reported the case within twenty-four hours of its coming to his attention. Alex Gravois drew up a petition to protest against the doctor's suspension, but many who were mortgaged to the mayor, or otherwise obligated, like Aristide Préjean whose constabulary was a political sinecure, were afraid to sign.

The doctor had no time to worry about Bidault and his petty attempts at vengeance. He was presently more concerned with private than with professional matters.

Colette was ill. She had been waiting at the gate when Narcisse, having previously fetched his clothes, had driven him in from the woods. Though she had known for some hours that he had been found, when she saw him alight from the carriage, whole and sound, the reaction from anxiety was so great that she had gone limp against the pickets. He had carried her to her room, followed by Doudouce, sobbing and wringing her hands. "She walk d' floor all night," Doudouce told him. "She eat nothing since she hear Miché Vic in trouble—she on'y cry and pray."

Nanaine's attitude toward him, as soon as she realized he was safe, was one of cold reserve. She allowed herself a single acid comment: "Who empties slops must expect to get splashed." The doctor guessed that greater than the disgrace incident to his involvement with shopkeepers and rabble was the noisome fact that Narcisse, servant of Palmyre Delamare, had driven him home in the "Belle Pointe" carriage. Moreover, the story of how the doctor had been found was on every lip, for as long as Narcisse lived, no one would miss the *Trumpet*. Even the contents of the lunch basket were known from the bakery to the beach, and while some thought Miriam brave, most called her brazen.

Friday night, after a strained silence through supper, his aunt announced, "We shall return to the city as soon as we can get ready. We shall not wait for the pecans." Already Grand-père was down from his summer space above the mantel, waiting to be wrapped in canvas and crated.

Victor went directly from the table to see Colette, as he had done morning and noon. She was sitting up against her pillows, and Doudouce was braiding her heavy hair. Her face, outlined by the dark plaits, was startlingly pale. He drew a chair up to her bedside.

"Did you eat your supper—like a good girl?" He took her hand, and finding it hot and dry, felt her forehead.

"She nibble—she not eat," Doudouce said, busy tying back the window curtains for air.

"You must do better than that," he reproved Colette gently.

"I'll try." Her voice was toneless.

"Did you sleep this afternoon?"

"Yes. A little. But I dreamed again of the levee cracking—and the river rushing in—and I woke up afraid—and oh, so tired!"

"You are making yourself sick, darling. Try not to think of frightening things."

"Help me"—her eyes, turned to his, were dark with distress—"to hold things together, Vic. . . ."

264

He wondered if Narcisse's reports had anything to do with stirring up her morbid fears. It would have been natural for her to offer some comment, even criticism, but she evinced no emotion beyond relief that he was home and unharmed. If she felt again the jealousy that had once flared up, fed by Leon's stories, she did not show it. Her attitude revealed only the agony she suffered during the uncertain hours when he had been in danger. He was deeply moved by the evidences of her concern for him.

He had a sudden idea. "Colette, why can't we be married sooner? There is nothing to stop us. It could be at Christmas, darling. . . ."

"All right," she said dully. "Christmas. . . ."

Her apathy disturbed him. He sat there stroking her forehead for a few moments, then rose to give Doudouce instructions for the night.

"Now, I want you to sleep," he said, coming back to Colette. "Do you understand? No worrying, no foolish dreams."

She closed her eyes, and like one who makes any answer at all to stop the questioning, she murmured, "It is the situation between Mama and Papa—and Leon's conduct. . . ."

He stood looking down at her quiet face as Doudouce drew the mosquito bar. What thoughts were turning behind that smooth forehead? Perhaps he should have said something to her about what had happened in the woods, something to reassure her. But what could he tell her, with honesty? It was true that his attraction to Miriam still existed, despite his most vigorous efforts to break it. Standing there at Colette's bedside, he resolved again to apply a rigid discipline, shutting the girl out of his mind and his life.

As he closed the door of the room behind him, he thought, I am glad of my aunt's decision to return to the city as soon as possible.

The following Sunday morning, Cumba fell sick. She was suffering from an emotional disturbance. She swam in sweat, she vomited, her heart palpitated. The difficulty was in getting her to take medicine. Glad had to slip the doctor's dosage into a vile brew of Cumba's own concoction to be sure it found its way into Cumba and not into her mattress.

The doctor understood Cumba's trouble. He had caught her red-handed in an attempt to place a wanga under his pillow when she brought the customary black coffee to his bedside. Hearing her come cautiously into the room, he pretended to be still asleep. She put the tray down on the table. He saw her hand go to the knot of her fichu, hesitate while she made sure of his regular breathing. Then her fingers plunged into her flabby old bosom and brought out a small red flannel bag that he afterward found to contain gunpowder and red pepper. He grasped her wrist. She dropped the charm with a gasp of fear and surprise. That the ridiculous combination was a wanga to break up a love affair was all he could get out of her. She trembled and wailed and wrung her hands and chanted her habitual appeal for mercy. "Ah, Miché! for the love of God! Have pity on a poor old woman!" He said to her, "If my aunt has instructed you to do that, I shall have to forgive you." But she would not be caught. "No, no! Grand Zombie tell me do it. Dat's who tell me!"

He went to see her on his return from church. Doudouce was kneeling at her bedside. An ominous electrical storm was brewing; the room was dark and noisy with thunder, and neither of the women saw or heard the doctor enter.

"I see she pour black water roun' your well. Dat fo' dead an' drownin'," Doudouce warned. Her voice rose, quavering. "So you do what Grand Zombie tell you, or dat Noonoon over at Miché Ulysse house, she get you sure enough!"

Cumba groaned and shuddered. She raised herself on her elbow and screamed.

The doctor's hand fell on Doudouce's shoulder. He jerked her to her feet.

"Get out of here! Get out of here with your filth!"

Doudouce cringed. Her teeth chattered. "I only tell her fo' her own good. I only say what I see. . . ."

"Get out!"

266

In his anger he all but hurled her to the door. Then he saw Colette, her face still pale from her recent illness, her eyes big with surprise and alarm. She had thrown a cravenette over her Sunday silks as insurance against the menacing sky, and held something in the crook of the voluminous sleeve.

"I heard Cumba was sick. I brought her some wine."

"She's sick because she's a fool! And your devoted Doudouce is helping her immensely!"

"Oh, Vic," Colette pleaded, "don't be cross with them."

"I'm tired of this nonsense!" His anger filled the room. "Voodoo is more than just useless, it's dangerous! Can't you see?"

Doudouce huddled close to Colette, shaking before the doctor's wrath. Colette came to her defense.

"How do we know, Vic?" The words were small and choked. "How can we be sure it's useless?" An hysterical note crept into her voice. "How can we be sure of anything!"

He turned on her harshly. "If you want to encourage them, it's your privilege! But I have no time for humbug!"

Her hand tightened around the flacon she held. She leaned against the doorframe, stunned and trembling. She put out her hand, but he strode past her without seeing it.

The storm fell, drenching him to the skin before he reached the house.

All day he was annoyed with himself for having allowed the servants with their juvenile folly to upset him. He needed to relax. His Sunday clinic over, he went down to the boat landing for *Bonne Chance*, the skiff Alceste Moreau had presented to him in appreciation of his having saved Hercule. He headed out and rowed off in the direction of "Belle Pointe," telling himself that he wanted to see the damage to Madame Vigée's bathhouse which—Bazile had reported at dinner—had been struck by lightning and demolished. But after viewing the shambles briefly, he passed on to the point. He rowed close to shore, wryly amused that his heart, at the prospect of glimpsing Miriam somewhere on the beach with her sketchbook on her knee, beat as if he had just finished a race. But instead of Miriam, he saw Julien's trap before the gate.

He turned the skiff away, feeling once more the confusing mixture of disappointment and triumph because he had not seen her. He noted, where the Bayou Castain emptied into the lake, that the current had carried another few feet of ground with it. The water swirled almost directly under Palmyre's bedroom window.

As he headed *Bonne Chance* for home, a forlorn pirogue trapped in a tangle of water hyacinth drew his eye. He rowed up to it and read on the slim prow: IALESKE. It was the Choctaw word for "Adieu." The paddle rested on the bottom of the boat.

For two days Aristide Préjean had led a posse in search of Masoom without crossing a trace of her, but the doctor still clung to his hope that she had not burned to death in the flaming house. He had seen Joe stop and shout as he fled; it had been an obvious scheme to attract attention to himself while Masoom escaped to the pirogue lying at the end of the plank walk. Now the doctor knew he had been right. Masoom had paddled her way out to the lake and must be hiding in the uninhabited woods on the other side of the Bayou Castain. The pirogue had probably slipped adrift in the morning squall. Somewhere back of the farther shore Masoom was waiting for Joe.

He rowed in and pulled his skiff up on the sand. The land was low and bristling with palmetto. It would be hard even for an Indian to live in this mosquito-infested waste. Of a sudden he stopped, struck by the remembrance of a child that had been washed up here after the wharf disaster in June. He went swiftly to the spot where the beach hooked into the lake, catching the passing drift.

Masoom lay in a small clear pool, face downward. He took a handful of her long black hair and turned her over. She had been dead for some days. The body was beginning to bloat and the gars had claimed part of an arm, yet even decay could not make her ugly. Her features held a striking serenity.

She must have heard in some way that Joe was gone, or perhaps, when he failed to join her, she had guessed. There was even a possibility that she had followed, Indian-wise, through the swamp and had seen him trapped in the quicksand.

The doctor brought his skiff up. He spread the floor with palmetto. He lifted Masoom and laid her in the stern.

Probably no one would ever know exactly how she had died, but what evidence there was indicated that she had taken her own life. There were no signs of accident. The pirogue was not capsized. The paddle was not missing—it had been laid down with deliberation. However it was, the doctor was responsible, he knew that. Old Jolivet would have taken a different course, and there would have been no mob, no fire, no deaths—no deaths, at least, until leprosy laid a hand on the town. Who was to say which way was right?

The ceremony at the edge of the bog was brief and simple. Haltingly, Victor said a short prayer for the repose of Masoom's soul as Ovide Clouzat let the corpse in its canvas casing slide into the sand. In a few minutes it was gone. The place of Masoom's burial was some distance from the spot where Joe had disappeared, but nothing could part them now. The two men washed their hands in the alcohol the doctor had brought along.

Homère was lighting his lamps when they got back to town.

"I need a drink," the doctor said, sitting beside Ovide on the wide seat of the coffin cart.

"Only one?" Ovide whistled softly. "When I bury a woman such as Masoom, I need a bottle, me."

"Drive by Paul's Exchange."

The presence of the undertaker at the bar created a stir of morbid merriment. Jokes flew swiftly. Ovide was an undertaker with many friends.

"Don't tell us you have come to drink to our health?" Alex Gravois said.

"But certainly!" Ovide winked. "The devil's orders. Yes, Papa LàBas prefers fine, fat kindling. It burns better."

"Dat Papa LàBas sure busy dis morning," said Télémaque Moreau, at the doctor's side. "Mother of God, w'at lightning! I was out on dat lake feeding my fish carts. I hear one big noise. I look, and *zut!* a waterspout. The fines' funnel I ever see. Christ, dat t'ing move fast!"

The bartender put another glass of beer before him. Télémaque, having already had several, was very talkative.

"Dat show dis morning tell us we got dat damn equinox. Yas, my friend. My ol' man"—he meant Alceste—"say we get dose bad storm wit'in ten day one side or d'other dat equinox. Yas, dat sun gettin' himse'f ready to slide across dat line again. Better look out!" He blew the foam from his beer and took a long draught. "Dat t'understorm mean somet'ing, my friend. Dat Gulf, she been stirrin' a mess since beginnin' Augus'. Now dat equinox jus' nine day off, my ol' man say look out—hold onto yo' skin, boys, he say. . . ."

". . . *Peary a goddamned liar!*"

A fist crashed on a rear table, and the drinkers at the bar turned and looked. Guy Chauvin, standing, was swaying drunkenly toward Leon Roussel's face. They were arguing again as to which of the two, Dr. Cook or Commander Peary, had discovered the North Pole. The controversy had been raging in the newspapers for days; in the city, it was reported, it was the sole subject of discussion on the streets. Clubs and organizations had taken up the feud, fiercely defending their favorite. Cook's admirers pointed out that King Frederick of Denmark was going to bestow gold medals on their hero. Peary's supporters said Dr. Cook had made a fool of his royal patron. *"Peary says the honor is his,"* the headlines screamed. Cook called Peary a faker. Peary called Cook an impostor.

"Eskimo testimony is in favor of Peary!" Leon shouted. This evening his gold cigarette holder held a small Havana cigar. Harry Lockwood and Marcel Lavalle were with him. Harry, fingering his glass absently, had the unhappy look of a man trapped by circumstance, but as the doctor raised a hand in greeting, the young man's face lit up.

"It's in favor of Cook!" Chauvin banged his fist on the table again.

Leon got up unsteadily from his chair.

"Come on, Leon." Harry tried to pull him down again. "You can settle this tomorrow."

"Let me alone." Leon shook himself free. Harry looked at him with ill-concealed dislike.

Justin Dufour went up to join in the squabble. The North Pole was probably the least of his concerns, but never missing a chance to quarrel with Leon, he promptly became a supporter of Cook. The argument grew louder and angrier.

"Let's go," the doctor said to Ovide Clouzat. There was nothing anybody could do with Leon, and he hated to see his cousin make a fool of himself.

"Doctor!"

Harry Lockwood rushed out after him. They talked on the banquette.

"I know you're a busy man and I may not have another chance to tell you good-by."

"Your work here is finished?"

"Or just begun. We don't know yet. My father has to know more about these hurricanes. If they're as bad as the one that hit Texas, he wouldn't recommend the causeway."

"I hope you'll be back, both of you," the doctor said sincerely. He had found Harry an entirely likable young fellow.

"Doctor. . . ." The young man hesitated. He plunged on. "Miss Miriam admires you greatly. We all know that. . . ." His thought was obvious: It can mean nothing to you. You are going to marry Colette. If you were to persuade Miriam in my behalf. . . . "Did you have a chance to put in a word for me?"

"Not yet." An odd, sinking sensation mingled with some embarrassment. "But I will, Harry. I'll keep my promise. You may depend on it."

"Thank you. But it will have to be soon."

They shook hands.

Thirty-three

He had slept badly. All through the night his mind was a mist of people, places, voices. He reached out of the mosquito bar, and turning up the lamp on the bedside table, looked at the clock. It was after four. In a little while it would be light. He got up and dressed. His eyes burned, and he poured the pitcher empty and dashed handfuls of cold water on his face from the washbowl.

He went out on the front gallery. Already Alceste Moreau and his sons were setting out for the catch. Far down the beach their lanterns moved eerily in the darkness.

A sudden distaste for the coming day, for all the coming days, descended on him. He shrank with a feeling almost like dread from the approaching fall and his imminent debut as a fashionable practitioner in New Orleans. Never before had the idea overwhelmed him with such definite revulsion. It was not what he wanted to do with his life. It was what he wanted *not* to do with it.

He no longer wanted to recapture, even for a short interval, that careless freedom of boyhood he had dreamed of when he came in May. He now wanted the freedom, rather, to assume care. He wanted to continue his studies in pellagra, not with guinea pigs but with people. God knew there were enough unfortunate victims back there in the woods. He wanted to fight the crafty Mamaloi and the mayor and the whole sinister business of voodoo. He wanted to eradicate the fear and intolerance that had killed Choctaw Joe and Masoom. He wanted to track the anopheles down until a malarial chill was a rarity instead of the rule. Nanaine and Colette spoke of the great opportunities awaiting him in New Orleans. The real opportunities were right here!

On his return, he had hoped to find all things the same. Now he chafed under the deliberate apathy of a society that declined to adjust itself to a changing world. His struggle took concrete shape in his constant clashes with his aunt. He felt surrounded and suffocated by the past. For her, it was a citadel to hold against all attack; for him, it was a trap from which to escape. He respected old families and faiths, but he as readily accepted the problems of the present and the challenge of the future. He had no patience with submissive adherence to a system. It was a man's privilege to follow his own vision, even to make his own mistakes.

At the same time, he recognized the advantages of this way of life into which he no longer fitted. In its stubborn stability lay the essence of its strength, as well as its weakness. Old customs, tried traditions offered a handy rule for determining the dimensions of daily life. Relieved of the burden of decision, existence took on a comfortable dignity, a serenity and grace not to be disparaged; in human relationships, precedent established a simple scheme of harmony. Every man had his place. Each knew and acknowledged his obligations. There was little of the striving and struggling found in less rigid societies. The accepted patterns of behavior often served as a convenient excuse for failure; a man could always shrug and say, "What else was I to do?" A pleasant, if artificial, peace prevailed.

Waiting there for the dawn, reaching uncertainly for the future, he became sure of one thing: for him there must be more than the artificial peace. This special world of privilege, created for him by generations of his ancestors, was not enough. In it, a man was constrained to do what an abstract *they* expected of him, instead of what he expected of himself.

Perhaps I am not ambitious, he thought. And again, with a wry smile for the personal world he wished to build, perhaps I am *too* ambitious. Friends and family wanted a man to be ambitious on their terms. If he followed his own bent, he would be called a failure by some. But would you call Alceste Moreau a failure—when he was happy, content? Was to be content to have failed? Down on the lake the lights of the fishermen's lanterns moved out to the graying horizon and hard work, but work they loved. He thought of Alceste Moreau's neat white cottage; and he wondered at the real peace that was a part of so many small lives.

But *Colette*. . . . It was to the life he wished to shed that Colette inflexibly belonged. He could understand why she was unwilling to leave it. It stood for certainty and safety. In her attitude there was none of Nanaine's morbid pride and relentless isolation, but rather an understandable clinging to what was known. It was a security dependent upon the absence of change, and therefore a pathetic illusion. Yet, was it fair to ask her to relinquish her privileges? He could certainly not promise her the distinction and prestige of the present. Perhaps she was right, wiser than he. High places already attained should not be lightly forsaken. Perhaps with her beauty and goodness she could make the old order beautiful and good for him—or at least tolerable.

He passed a hand over his forehead. He hardly recognized himself lately. One minute he was fleeing to a luminous land of unlimited freedom, the next he was drawn back, like a wayward child subtly persuaded, to a dusk where Colette was the one splendid light.

He turned abruptly at the sound of horses. The carriage gate at "Beaux Arbres" creaked open, and he saw Leon and Marcel Lavalle ride out and disappear up the beach road. It was unlike Leon, who often slept till noon, to be abroad so early.

Alex Gravois returned the shaving mug to its proud place in the center of the shelf. He turned it so that the doctor's name in gold letters, and the motif of skull and crossbones that Alex had copied from an iodine bottle, glittered to the best advantage.

"There you are!" He whipped the sheet from around his patron's neck with a flourish. Alex was, for the doctor's taste, always a little too generous with the bay rum and Florida Water.

As he got out of the chair, Felix Fanchon rushed into the barbershop. "Quick!" he panted. "A man's been shot!"

The boy had run all the way. He was out of breath, and his bare feet were covered with red dust. The doctor took a moment to make sure that his emergency kit was in order. He spoke softly to Rougette, and the buggy hurried out of town and up the Chinchuba road, Felix giving the direction.

Under an oak at some distance from the bayou's edge, the druggist, Guy Chauvin, lay groaning in blood. Justin Dufour knelt beside him mumbling encouragement. A few yards away stood Leon and Marcel, the latter looking pale and distressed. He kept knotting and unknotting his fists.

"How did it happen?" The doctor opened and drew back the sodden shirt. There was hardly need to ask. The setting was obvious. A strong feeling of disgust welled up within him at such stupid, useless bloodshed.

"Young Roussel shot him!" Justin spat out a string of curses against Leon.

"It was fairly done!" Felix protested. "One of the two has to get it in a duel. It is not like creeping up behin' a man's back!"

"You don't think so, heh?" Justin snarled. "That sonofabitch Roussel knows damn well Guy Chauvin can't hold a glass of water steady, much less a gun! It's like killing a cripple!"

"What did your friend accept the challenge for, then?" Felix persisted.

"He was drunk. He didn't know what he was doing."

"Then he should 'ave call it off when he was sober."

Lately, Guy Chauvin was never sober. Even now he reeked of drink. The doctor finished his examination. The wound was in the upper part of the chest. He gave a hypodermic to ease the pain. The immediate necessity was to get the man back to town.

"I see you have your delivery out there," the doctor said to Justin. "We'll get him home in that."

They carried him to the road and laid him in the bakery wagon, among the baskets of bread and the sugary pans of brioches. Dufour's customers would be served very tardily today. The doctor turned his back on Leon and walked to his buggy. He felt that there was nothing he could say to his young cousin. Felix, dazzled by the adventure of a duel under his very nose, climbed up on the seat beside him.

"You know w'at the quarrel was about?" Felix talked on excitedly. "About the Nort' Pole! Me, w'en I fight wit pistols, it will be about somet'ing closer to me dan dat, by God!"

The sun was well up when they reached town, and the September heat beat relentlessly on streets and rooftops. As Guy lived in a stifling room behind the drugstore, Justin wished to take him to the Dufour house adjoining the bakery. The drivers were surprised, as the buggy and delivery wagon turned the corner, to find a knot of people before the shop. Inside, Madame Dufour was screaming wildly.

Their story had preceded them. Alex Gravois, who had been present the night before when the argument over Cook and Peary culminated in the rendezvous, at once put two and two together and arrived at a rather inadequate four. He could not say who it was that had received the bullet, and Madame Dufour, whose acquaintance with the Codo Duello did not draw a clear distinction between principals and seconds, was sure—since nothing at all was sure—that the victim was her beloved son Justin. The details of her hysterics left the bakery with every loaf of bread. Madame Naquin, coming to fetch her French flute, had all she could do to keep her friend from committing some violence. Now, when the mother saw her son jump down from the wagon, whole and healthy, she began to scream more loudly than ever.

The gaping crowd parted, allowing Justin and the doctor to carry the wounded man to one of the bedrooms behind the shop. He was bleeding badly. Since Madame Dufour was helpless, it was Madame Naquin who turned back the spread and replaced the bolster with pillows. Dufour, the baker, brought hot water. The doctor had to ask Madame Naquin several times before she finally left the room.

At sight of his blood spilling on the white sheet, Guy became terror-stricken. While the doctor was selecting his instruments, the druggist struggled to a half-rising position, and either from fright or pain, fell back in a faint. Victor welcomed his unconsciousness; with a sense of relief, he dismissed Dufour, whose clumsy hands would not now be needed to help with the chloroform. He probed for the bullet and dislodged it. He saw that the man had a chance if he could manage to suture a

276

severed artery. Guy stirred; he began again to groan and mumble.

"I am dying!" the druggist gasped. He was asking to see someone. The doctor lowered his head to catch the name. "Père Guichard. . . ." With a remarkable return of strength, Guy repeated in a firm voice, "I wish to see Père Guichard!" Though not a practicing Catholic, he wanted to be confessed. Protesting hysterically, he would not allow the doctor to continue, fearful of dying before he could talk to the priest.

Justin hurried off, and in a few minutes was back. Madame Naquin, doing the honors of the house, ushered Father Guichard to Guy's bedside.

"Have the goodness to leave us alone," the priest requested.

Madame lingered, fluffing a pillow, drawing a curtain.

"If anything is needed, I shall call," the priest said with severity.

He held the door for Madame. She settled her shawl around her shoulders and passed through with great dignity, and some indignation.

Victor hurried out to see what he could do, meanwhile, for Madame Dufour. When she understood that the druggist was going to die in her house, in her bed, she had gone into convulsions.

As he entered the confusion in the shop, a familiar voice was ordering Madame's solicitous friends and neighbors to get out. He could hardly believe his eyes when, as the women reluctantly retreated, he saw Dr. Jolivet.

It was almost noon before the two doctors left the baker's house together. Victor drove toward the office leisurely, so that he and Dr. Jolivet could talk on the way.

"Well," he said, "we did all we could for Guy Chauvin. If you hadn't happened along to give me a hand. . . ."

"I certainly didn't come to help *him*," Dr. Jolivet objected. "I was looking for *you*."

Victor turned to look at the man sitting there beside him on the buggy seat, and, for the first time this morning, had a chance to take in details. The old doctor's hair was freshly marcelled, the tips of his gray mustache waxed to points. In a youthful sack suit that flattered his lean figure, he looked altogether debonair. A boutonniere bloomed in the buttonhole of his coat, and a silk handkerchief spilled out of the breast pocket. It was obvious that Aurélie was good for him. Suddenly remembering his manners, Victor asked about her.

"Aurélie is fine"—Jolivet beamed—"we are both fine! It is a scientific fact, my boy, that spooning improves the health! A physician with the London hospital has just published a paper on the subject."

"I take your firsthand testimony rather than the London man's word." Victor laughed. "I have not had much time to prove it for myself."

"No." Jolivet grew serious. "You have really made amazing progress with the pellagra puzzle."

"In such business as that, one can make amazing progress in the wrong direction." He sighed. "I was offered a research fellowship at the Rockefeller Institute. I turned it down."

"At your age, for such a chance I would have given"—Jolivet ran the edge of his left hand knife-wise around the wrist of his right—"that. But of course you are tied to the hospital at Ancon."

"No longer. I resigned."

"Ah. Do I begin to see a pretty face?"

Victor changed the subject.

"There is one pretty face we will never see around here again, Doctor. Masoom's."

"I heard. My son-in-law, Ovide Clouzat, wrote me the whole story." Jolivet hesitated. "Don't worry, my boy, you did the right thing—what you thought you had to. And you won't lose your license."

"I hadn't come to that worry yet. I had others on the list ahead of it." His mind switched back to Jolivet's previous statement. "Did I understand you to say a minute ago that you were looking for *me?*"

"Yes. That's why I'm here—to see you, and also to see the

mayor. If he does not withdraw his affidavit, I think I can make him. Besides, I have written the State Board the truth about the case myself. I am the one who should be debarred."

"It would be a poor reward for fifty years of faithful service."

"On the contrary, it would be a very fine reward. Fools who won't take a vacation ought to have it thrust on them. But to me it matters neither way, for I have already suspended myself."

"I'm glad you feel philosophical about it, because I doubt if you can persuade the mayor."

"He'll be persuaded. I shall remind him of a little argument he and I have never settled."

The younger man raised his brows.

"I was never satisfied with the way Madame Bidault died," Jolivet said. "I had been treating her for diabetes. It looked like diabetic coma. But it could have been a lethal narcosis similar to coma—like that produced by chloral hydrate."

"You said nothing at the time?"

"I intimated my suspicions to Bidault. He threatened not only me, but my daughter, Madame Clouzat, and her family."

"So you didn't act?"

Jolivet raised his shoulders, palms turned upward and thumbs outstretched. "What was the use? Madame Bidault had no one. No children. No relatives. She was gone. Nothing could change that. And if I were wrong, the mayor was here to make it miserable for all of us. My daughter has had a hard enough time raising a family for Ovide, I can tell you, without further interference from Bidault."

"Still. . . ."

"Oh, I know what you are thinking. But listen, my boy. There are two kinds of people in the world: the *conformers* and the *reformers*. The conformer does the easy and obvious thing. He adapts himself to environment and circumstance, as water finds its level—then stays there to stagnate. The reformer does the opposite, clashes with circumstance. He makes his own environment. Perhaps in these two kinds of people you have the difference between right and wrong, good and bad, freedom and slavery. Anyway, I was born a conformer. I have never loved the world exactly as it is, but I was too lazy to do anything about it. Believe me, to discover a world is nothing. At most it is accident. But to change a world—that is wizard's work!"

"At any rate, you are not too lazy to try to change the mayor's mind."

"That was Ovide's idea. Ovide said, 'If I don't have a doctor around here to kill off the sick, my business will get even worse.' You know Ovide."

As they turned into the street before the office, they found it unusually lively for that time of day. At the bank corner, before the post office and the drugstore—closed now—men and women had gathered, talking excitedly. Horses waited forgotten, and wagons and buggies choked the roadway. Children stood around with eyes and ears wide open.

"Let's see what's going on here." Dr. Jolivet made for the crowded banquette.

Felix Fanchon ran up to Victor. "Miché le docteur! The mayor has disappeared!"

"Excellent!" Jolivet said with enthusiasm. "One plague less."

"They want to tar an' feather him! But he get away on his horse!"

Ovide Clouzat joined them.

"That Guy Chauvin—he believes in traveling light, heh? He gets Madame Bidault quick off his soul before it starts for the other world!"

"It was him who make dat dose!" Felix threw in. "Madame, she jus' sleep away!"

"Ah!" Jolivet threw his hands out wide, then brought them together with a loud clap. His eyes met Victor's.

"It will be very embarrassing for Guy when he meets Madame," Ovide said. "But if I know him at all, he will have the nerve to complain to her that he was never paid off."

"The mayor did not keep his promise!" Alex Gravois informed them. "Five thousand to supply a poison that would induce a natural-looking death. But he kept all of Madame's money for himself. And of course Guy could not complain—he dared not open his mouth."

"Except to pour liquor into it," said Ovide.

The confusion mounted when Télémaque Moreau announced that the marshal, in bed with malaria, was unable to head a posse, and refused to let the hounds out except under his lead. The marshal was loudly accused of lying about his illness, in fear of the mayor. The excitement climbed.

"How did all this come out?" Victor asked.

"Madame Naquin tell it!" Felix would never forget this day of sensational events. "She listen at the keyhole while Guy confess to the priest!"

"Madame Naquin," Ovide commented, "will be a great help to the Recording Angel when *she* gets to heaven. Nothing escapes her but her own tongue."

A hound bounded past and disappeared into the post office. It was Dixie. A tremor ran through Victor. With every nerve straining toward the spot where the dog had vanished, he struggled to get possession of himself, to hold himself in check. He failed completely.

"I'll be back." He touched Jolivet on the arm. "I'm going to get my mail."

The post office was deserted. Even Mr. Naquin was in the street, beset with questions he was expected to answer by virtue of being Madame's husband. In the corridor where the boxes were it was quiet and dim. At the sound of his step, Miriam turned and smiled.

"I peeked in your box. It is empty."

His mail was in the buggy, but he said, so that she would not know he had come after her, "My friends have forgotten me."

"Not I." There was that look of the wise child about her and, as always, it held him rooted. "We have been busy packing, but I've had time to notice that you have changed your schedule."

"Yes," he admitted.

"Your pretty prison—is it nearly completed?"

He had on order some basic equipment, but he had done nothing yet toward leasing an office in New Orleans.

"No."

He was contributing very little to the conversation, irked by her flippant reference to his "prison." It made little difference that his plans no longer included society's favorite physician, Dr. Larouche, a fact he saw no reason to explain to her; for he knew that by his intention to set up a competing practice, he had changed nothing for himself, and she would be quick to see it. At the same time that he was annoyed by her question, his heart beat insanely, and he had an overwhelming desire to kiss her.

"When your prison is all finished, you will perhaps deserve it, Doctor."

"For what crime?" He smiled, but he was disturbed.

"For treason. Against yourself."

"Perhaps."

"The other day I was packing our books, and when I came across the Scriptures, I happened to open it at the Psalms. I read about the grass upon the rooftops, that withers before it grows up. . . . That is like having a splendid vision which you do not follow, isn't it? Or a special gift, which you do not use."

"At least I don't have to worry about splendid visions and special gifts."

"You say that to me, who have seen your courage with Madame Gaspard, your cleverness with Hercule Moreau!" She shook her head.

There was something he had to know—something suddenly more important than himself and his uncertainties.

"When are you leaving?"

"Sunday."

Somewhere deep inside himself he winced. He knew he would feel this twinge of parting every time she came up in his memory.

Out of the heavy silence, she said, "I loved you from the moment I saw you—on the boat. I offered you the binoculars. Do you remember?"

282

"Yes."

"That I love you—are you glad?"

He was careful not to commit himself, keeping all expression out of his face. "I'm not sorry."

"I'm glad," she said earnestly. "No matter what happens, I'll always be glad."

She had never been so lovely. The blue of her eyes was almost black. It was months, it was years since he had kissed her. . . .

A great shouting rose in the street and they heard running steps. Going to the door, Victor saw that a horse was the center of attention, a horse he recognized as the mayor's, the wild one they called "Pluton." But the mayor was not in the saddle.

Thirty-four

On Sunday, the trunks stood ready to be drayed to the *Camelia* next morning. Grand-père, in canvas and crate, waited against the wall. Nanaine had put away the bronze Argands from the mantel and all the ornaments, and with Cumba's help had shrouded the mirrors in cheesecloth. The gallery was bare of rockers, the hammocks were stored away. The skiffs, *Bonne Chance* and *Sans Souci*, keels up, rested high and dry on blocks in the basement. Already the summer house had an air of loneliness and desertion.

The doctor felt none of the melancholy on leaving "Clair de Lune" he had experienced in his younger years. A strange elation filled every hour of his busy day. Something had gone out of him, and something else had come to take its place. The lake, the most familiar trees, and commonplace corners of the town seemed new and different to him. He had shed all concern, and he was almost gay. Not even the dim prospect of finding a man to relieve Jolivet in two weeks—the limit of the old doctor's reluctant promise—depressed his high spirits.

Since his meeting with Miriam in the post office last Monday, he had let the days pass without naming them. He no longer fought himself, or her. He gave himself up to a kind of luxurious madness, refusing to think beyond the immediate moment. He took her voice, the memory of her candid eyes and generous, impulsive nature wherever he went. Even to the bedside of Olympe Roussel. Now that Leon had shot a man, at last Olympe had a legitimate reason to faint, and she was making the most of it, fainting daily. Even to his talks with Colette. Last night, sitting with her on the gallery at "Beaux Arbres," trying to comfort her though he knew in his heart Guy Chauvin might be dead when he said it—*I did all I could for him. . . . No, there's no use getting a surgeon from the city. . . . I'm leaving him with Dr. Jolivet. . . . His long experience. . . .* His voice sounded far off in his own ears, while he heard Miriam at his side: *That I love you—are you glad . . . ? I'll always be glad. . . .*

Reverting to his old schedule, he had seen Miriam every day at the post office. And there was Thursday in the woods. . . . The girl Coco had not been in the previous week for treatment; when he talked to her mother, she said Coco was down with malaria, and he had gone to make sure the woman was telling the truth. On his way back to town, he saw Miriam, idle, in her old place under the oak. "I came to tell our tree good-by," she said. "It is my last chance. We are dismissing Narcisse after today." They spoke of inconsequential things. Bibi was going to work for the butcher's family. Narcisse? He had no place and was looking for none. A man who was too lazy to worry was certainly not going to worry about being lazy. . . . Then she smiled. "Before we leave—there is something you have never once said to me." He knew what she wanted; but he could not bring himself to say, "I love you, Miriam." He was careful not to encourage her, or to encourage himself. He remained silent.

His promise to Harry Lockwood was heavy on his conscience, and several times Harry's name was on the tip of his tongue. But each occasion passed without presenting a favorable opening, and somehow the doctor could not force it. Now it was Sunday, the last day. And he had said to himself all night and all morning what he would not say to her on Thursday: *"I love you . . . I love you, Miriam. . . ."*

He saw Colette to her carriage after church, then climbed into his buggy and drove toward Chinchuba, knowing that Miriam would not be there. He had to have it out with himself.

At the bridge, he got out and walked along the bayou. He threw himself down in the shade of the oak Miriam called "our tree." Everywhere he looked he saw her—in the branches overhead, in the bright sky beyond. He closed his eyes and saw her still.

He recognized that he was in love—deeply and desperately in love—for the first time in his life. He wanted Miriam with every cell of his blood. Yet it was the whole woman he wanted—the rich mind and the gentle heart and that intriguing quality of childish innocence underlying the amazing wisdom. Possessing her would be far more than mere satisfaction of his passion. It would be an infinite adventure of the spirit. It would have the completeness and perfection of a circle.

For some time now he had known how it was going to be with Colette. She was beautiful, warm, tender; she was intelligent and accomplished—all that was desirable—designed to stir dreams in men and draw affection and admiration with the magic of a magnet. He had seen the effect of her entrance at any gathering. The young men proud and grateful if she so much as smiled or looked at them—the clamoring for places on her dance program—the wistful brooding among the bachelors as she waltzed by in the doctor's arms. He admired her, was excited by her, but it was not the same thing that held him to Miriam. He could not have said why. Their life together, his and Colette's, would be tranquil, serene, distinguished no doubt by mutual devotion, certainly envied, and even perhaps quietly happy. But the joy, the laughter, the abandon, the adventure and wonder of life he could never give her, for they would belong to the memory of Miriam.

The droning song of locusts. . . . Lying there with his hands laced under his head, he closed his eyes and a dream crept up on him: Miriam waiting for his daily home-coming, here in Mandeville, in a little white cottage like Alceste Moreau's. . . . Now I am getting sentimental. He raged at himself. He hated sentiment because he feared it. There was no place for it in a profession that required a man to be cold, calculating, meticulously logical. Compassion, yes; but never sentiment. He would not allow an idyl to blur the present issue. He brushed the dream aside.

He forced himself into a professional attitude. Love was a race habit. It was the business of novelists and song writers to disguise it in moonlight and roses. Men were only receptacles of seed, a woman's body a device for the production of other bodies. What the layman called "love" was merely chemistry, glands and nerves, the timeless urge to breed. It was a function, like sleeping and eating. Someday, perhaps doctors would find a way of making the heart give up an unfeasible fixation, as now the apomorphic needle could make the stomach give up its poisons.

He drifted to practical considerations. There was his father's will and the money. He disposed of that at once. Let it go—he did not want it. Money was a mirage. He had seen too many lives passed unlived in its accumulation, too many deprived of so much because by having money they were deprived of nothing. The relentless tyranny of "family" he could not dismiss so readily. What would Miriam have to suffer as his wife? The pettiness, the snubs. Anger boiled up in him at the mere thought of it. And could she under such conditions remain happy with him? Would it not be best for her, really, to marry Harry Lockwood and go North? In the North, where nobody would know. Security, peace of mind—on all counts, Harry was the sensible choice for her. A good character, a fine future. And he's nearer her age. I'm twelve years older. How do I know that her feeling for me is not a young girl in love with love?

He lay there until the sun was overhead, twisting his mind this way and that. For the hundredth time he reminded himself he must not allow emotion to sway him—he must hew to the line of reason. And the line of reason led to Colette. She was the symbol of all that was good and gracious and worthy in the society for which their lives had carefully prepared them. That Colette could not relinquish that world, that she was capable of so strong a loyalty, made her so much the more admirable. Their kind of love, if less spectacular, would prove more enduring. He could name a dozen marriages, made merely for the sake of clan and convenience, that had long outlived the most flaming love matches. Quite aside from all these considerations, the arrangement between him and Colette carried the obligation of a contract. Not that she would hold him to it—not that he would allow an autocratic social code to bind him. But he held himself to it—an easy point of honor (he smiled) when so beautiful a bride awaited a man. Though the engagement had not yet been officially announced, the nuns in the city were already busy with their fine needles on her trousseau, the embroidered nightgowns and negligees, the dozens of this and the sets of that. . . .

He must put Miriam out of his mind, once and for all.

He came out of the woods, his decision made. He congratulated himself on having forced the analytic to overrule the emotional, on having solved his problem with professional detachment—for the good of all concerned. That he experienced none of the elation of triumph need not bother him. The most important decisions in life bore their fruit over the years and not all in a rush.

Driving by the bank, he passed Ovide Clouzat in the coffin cart, and seated beside him a boy who looked like the moss picker's son, Numa Gaspard, though Ovide was going at such a fast pace that the doctor could not be sure. Ovide raised a black crepe of the kind used to hang on the front door of a deceased person's dwelling, and waving it over his head, shouted something the doctor failed to make out. Guy Chauvin must be dead.

He turned back toward the bakery, and there found the expected crowd of curious and meddlesome women. What he had not expected was the large smile Madame Dufour gave him, and her gay, if peculiar greeting. "Thanks to Miché le docteur, I do

287

not burn my bed!" He made his way to the bedroom alone, and was about to knock, when the silence within reminded him that there was no need. Pushing open the door, he stepped into the darkened room and saw Guy Chauvin stretched out, white and still, between fresh sheets. Victor looked toward Dr. Jolivet, standing quietly before the drawn window shade.

"Well," Victor considered, "perhaps it is better for him this way."

"I'm not sure," Jolivet answered softly.

"I mean—he would have had to answer to the law. . . ."

"That's what I mean. A few days ago, he was worrying about saving his soul. Now he'll have to worry about saving his neck."

"What?" Victor frowned, unable to believe. Then he walked over to the bedside and saw the sleeping man's gentle respiration. He reached down, felt his pulse. "By God!" he said under his breath.

"Yes." Jolivet shook his head affirmatively. "He's going to live. Good work, my boy."

Victor's first thought was to tell Colette. She is one who will be glad, he said to himself. And there are others who ought to be— Leon himself, Olympe, Julien.

"I'll go along with you." Dr. Jolivet followed him out. "I've fixed the patient to sleep an hour or more."

Their passage through the shop was blocked by the women who had flocked around Madame Naquin, newly arrived and out of breath. Everybody was speaking at once, and it was impossible to make any sense out of the loud babble, but surely some juicy bit of news had just been delivered. When Madame saw Dr. Jolivet, her eyes seemed to bulge out of her face, and she could only point to him and stammer, half-choked with excitement over what she wished to say.

"Ovide Clouzat"—she gulped—"Town Hall. . . ."

"Good God." Dr. Jolivet wiped his forehead with his silk handkerchief. "Now what!"

288

Victor did not wait for Madame Naquin to recover her fluency. He was already in the buggy, Dr. Jolivet beside him.

The Town Hall was open, and men were moving about inside. Ovide's black crepe had been tacked up on one leaf of the doors, thrown wide, and as the two men alighted on the banquette, Ovide, himself, came out with his hammer, and a placard which he proceeded to affix to the bulletin board. The doctor was relieved to see him whole and even more hearty than usual.

"Eh, là bas, you two!" Ovide called over his shoulder. "Come help us dust off the ballot box!"

The mayor had been found. It was Alphonse Gaspard who discovered him lying dead below a giant oak some way back from the Chinchuba road. The Gaspards had been out gathering moss, and Alphonse, attracted by the fighting cries of birds and noticing a black cloud of buzzards reeling against the sky, went to see what was causing the commotion. The swarming vultures had torn even the clothes from the big festered body, and Alphonse hardly recognized the gruesome mess that had been the mayor. The boy Numa had gone to town to fetch Ovide Clouzat.

What had happened, Ovide explained to Victor, was quite obvious. It was Bidault's intention, with the furious town at his heels, to hide at his turpentine distillery until he could arrange his escape, but his horse, Pluton, that once had belonged to Ovide, intended otherwise. Ovide could imagine Bidault beating Pluton with his crop until the blood came, and he could imagine Pluton thinking, He wants me to go fast, eh? Very good. I will show him. So Pluton became a runaway horse, carrying the cursing mayor beyond the distillery, and with malice aforethought, plunged into the oak forest where the branches were low. The mayor's neck could not have been better broken. Ovide finished his recital: "I have often heard people say, 'He breaks his neck in his hurry to get home.' But this is one smart fellow, this Pluton. He saves his own neck and breaks the mayor's in *his* hurry to get home." Pluton was back in his old stall behind the undertaking shop.

Victor stood without speaking, wondering about this sudden turn of events. He recalled one of his first meetings with the mayor early in the summer. It was at the stable. Bidault had been beating the horse unmercifully. At that moment he had begun to hate the man. And now he was dead, a victim of his own cruelty.

"It jus' go to show you w'at funny thing these dying is." Old Alceste Moreau wagged his white head. "A man who never been sick one day his whole life. . . ."

"Yes," said Dr. Jolivet, thinking of Guy Chauvin's doubtfully happy return to life. "Death has certainly been cutting some odd capers around here lately." He joined the men inside, saying he would ride home with Ovide.

As Victor was getting back into the buggy, the Lockwoods drew up in their automobile. Harry saw him and hurried over to speak. The senior Lockwood waved a greeting and continued on into the hall, leaving Harry to the urgent business he had with the doctor.

"I've had no luck so far." An anxious look came into his good young face. "I wonder if you. . . ."

"I'm going there now," Victor decided on the spur of the moment.

It was his last chance to make good his promise.

Julien sat with Palmyre in the piazza. A strong wind was blowing from the lake, and Palmyre wore a Paisley shawl.

"The morning paper says a severe storm is sweeping up from the Gulf," Julien said by way of alibi, "and I have come to suggest to these ladies that they postpone leaving on the evening boat."

"All the servants have gone. Our trunks are packed." Palmyre motioned to the baggage at the foot of the stairs.

"Since your servants are dismissed, may I have the honor," Julien begged, "of sending a carriage for you?"

I shall have a fine case of hysterics on my hands if you are fool enough to send your own, the doctor thought.

"Thank you. The Lockwood gentlemen are calling for us. They are leaving on the same boat."

Victor said, "I have something to say to Mamzelle, concerning Harry."

Palmyre smiled. Perhaps she understood. "Miriam is in the west room."

Kneeling, she was laying volumes of bound music in a shipping box. The grand piano was closed, the couch was bare, and the mandolin gone from its peg. A collar for Dixie and a leather leash lay on the piano bench.

She stared at him as if she could hardly believe her eyes. Then, rising slowly, she said with a quiet smile, "Our last day here marks the first time you come to 'Belle Pointe'—without a reason. . . ."

He wished to blurt out his business and get it over with, but broaching the subject without preamble seemed too abrupt, brutal. Awkwardly, he offered another excuse. "I've come to say good-by."

"Yes. . . . 'Good-by'—horrid word—like 'never.'"

"I'll say 'God bless you,' then."

He had noticed when he came in that the scarf he had given her was about her shoulders. Now—of a sudden—the sight of it galled him. It somehow had a mocking quality, like the sound of "never". . . . It affronted him with recollections of the day he gave it to her, of the morning after the night in the swamp. . . . Only a few hours ago at the bayou he had put all this definitively behind him; and now the absurd bit of silk was bringing it back, stamping it on his mind with the imprint of everlasting memory. The silly stuff seemed to sneer at him, and he felt an odd anger creep up to his brain, anger at anything, at everything, at her, at himself.

"Your scarf"—her fingers went over it softly—"I have kept it out until last." That transparent honesty, through which one seemed to see into her very soul, shone in her face.

"You are making a foolish fetish of that thing!"

"No. . . ." She looked at him in surprise. "Nothing is foolish that makes one happy."

He walked around the box to her. "Throw it away, Miriam. You shouldn't feel like that!"

"Why?" Her eyes widened.

"Because it's not good for you!"

He whipped the scarf from around her shoulders, crushed it into a ball in his fist. It happened so quickly that he had crossed the room to the side gallery before she realized what he was doing. She ran after him, crying *"No! No!"* but it was too late. He had already cast the scarf over the treetops. It caught on a branch, flapped frenziedly for a few moments, then the growing wind snatched at it again, and carried it off.

She leaned against the door frame, her hands behind her, staring at him as if he were a stranger.

"Why did you do that?"

He said more truthfully than she could guess, "I don't know. . . ."

"Is it"—she was still staring at him—"that you don't want me to have any part of you—is it because you want to discourage me?"

He hesitated. "Perhaps."

"Then why did you kiss me—why did you take me in your arms?"

"Because you are a lovely woman."

"Don't men ever kiss women *not* because they are women, but because they are—themselves?"

"I don't know," he said again. He felt oddly weak.

"Then you are one of those men who believe love is all physical." Her lip trembled. "You think of the heart merely as a machine."

He said bitterly, "That is my business."

"But coming to say good-by—isn't that sentiment—isn't that *feeling?*"

"I came"—he found himself groping for words—"I came actually to talk to you about Harry Lockwood, Miriam."

292

"Oh!" She drew in a sharp breath. He knew he had been clumsy. Presently, she smoothed out the shock with a rueful smile. "Then you do have a reason for coming to 'Belle Pointe,' after all."

"He is a fine young fellow, Miriam. He. . . ." Groping again. . . .

"I know. He wishes to marry me."

"Do you like him?"

"Yes," she said dully. "But I don't love him."

"Perhaps that will come."

"Are you telling me to marry him?"

"I don't think you would be making a mistake."

She walked over and sat down on the piano bench.

"I've always said I would do anything for you—anything you wanted. And now—you want me to marry Harry Lockwood." She continued in a wooden voice, "Perhaps you are right. . . ."

He checked an impulse to go to her, to reach out his hand.

"Someday you may thank me." He had to leave—before he made a fool of himself.

She straightened. "I thank you now! For your kindness, for your consideration! For your altruistic interest in me!" She turned and buried her face in her arms, folded over the closed keyboard. "I hate you!" She sobbed desperately, like a little girl, and kept saying, "I hate you!" as if by repeating it over and over she could convince herself.

As he drove away from "Belle Pointe," he felt nothing at all—like a dead man feels nothing, he thought.

Thirty-five

The small black cloud on the southeastern rim of the lake grew larger. Thunderheads massed along the horizon, and the sky was burnished with lightning. The tide rose with the rising wind, and by four o'clock the rain began, gusty and cold.

An hour later, from the gallery at "Beaux Arbres," he watched the *Camelia* leave the Cape Charles wharf. Somewhere beyond her wet decks, probably in the shelter of her parlors, were Harry and Miriam. Through the hum of rain he heard the boat's signal bell jangling. He followed her white wake far across the gray water. She became a speck, then only a smoky stain. Then she was gone. . . .

Twilight came quickly. Homère had difficulty lighting the lamp at the corner. The wind struck in hard puffs, driving the rain this way and that. In the gathering darkness, the whitecaps on the lake shone like streaks of light, crashing endlessly against the breakwater. No one was on the street. An occasional buggy passed, its driver unseen behind the celluloid window in the oil-cloth, its curtains flapping crazily.

One such buggy stopped at "Clair de Lune," and a woman, wrapped head and shoulders in a shawl and wearing the guinea-blue full skirt favored by Negresses, got out and ran into the basement. She reappeared almost at once. He failed to make out, in the teeming rain, who she was. But it mattered little. The gathering storm, black and wild, matched his mood exactly.

As the night wore on, the wind increased. The sky was thundering excitement, split through with blinding flashes of green and blue. The rain hammered against the house, and the waves, now over the breakwater, banged against the beach and receded, broken, with a dull roar. Toward two o'clock Monday morning, a fury of gale and deluge broke loose, continuing for half an hour, quieting, then repeating itself at closer intervals, each time with more volume. There was no sunrise—only a slow change from utter blackness to a weird, grayish dawn.

Glad came with the black coffee, reporting that Cumba was sick again. "She up all night, out in the woodshed making her stinkin' stew and seeing all the awful thing what going to happen. Then she eat that stew to stop grigri and be surprised when she get sick at her stomach. Me, I be surprised she *don't* get sick." On leaving the room, she added, "Zeph say won't be no boat a morning like this. Your aunt sure upset we can't leave today."

He dressed and went out on the gallery. The drive of rain sent him back for his oilskin. The lake had come up over the beach; water stood in the street. The storm exhilarated him oddly, taking his mind off himself. The horizon was completely lost in a whirl of spray, but the lightning almost constantly lit the sky, and the thunder crashed, deafening, peal on peal. Sometimes a purple bolt traced a dazzling pattern across the water, streaking it with flame. Far down the beach, as behind a curtain, he could see Alceste Moreau and his sons frantically working to get their fleet of skiffs into the shelter of the ravine.

There were some odds and ends of things he had yet to do so that the two weeks Dr. Jolivet promised to stay on would be as easy as possible for the retired practitioner, but Victor made no attempt to go to the office. He doubted if anybody was out on a morning like this. By ten o'clock, the gale was uprooting trees, sending huge limbs flying through the air. The blasts came from several directions at once, tearing the solid sheet of rain to ragged drifts. Tufts of moss and swirling clouds of sodden leaves rode the air currents. The lawn was soon covered with debris. Between the peals of thunder, the plop of branches into water and the shotlike crack of pecans falling on the roof punctured the steady roar of wind and rain.

He went down to the servants' quarters to see how Cumba was. Colette was there, helping Nanaine renew the heated flatirons, which they wrapped in flannel and placed against Cumba's icy feet. The old servant lay still, muttering to herself and moaning.

"Colette, you shouldn't have come," he said with concern. "It's dangerous for you to be out in this weather."

"It is only a matter of crossing the lawn." This morning her face was brighter than it had been for weeks, her smile radiant. "Papa and Leon are out. They have gone to the Bayou Castain, to secure *Le Cygne* to the sawmill dock."

"It's a good thing they didn't try to get to the city this morning."

"Oh, Leon wanted to." She laughed, almost joyously. "He invited himself to a wedding."

"Did he?" Leon's brass was intolerable, the doctor thought, but in truth, one of his lesser faults.

"Yes. Leon told me yesterday—Harry Lockwood—he said he intended to marry"—Colette stammered—"right away, before they went back to Chicago. . . ." She broke off, coloring.

Nanaine had been replacing cooled irons on the furnace, but she had taken in every word.

"It is true!" She straightened up and faced them. "They have gone, thank God! All of them! Good riddance!"

"Here, Colette." The doctor picked up her wet cravenette from the back of the chair, where it hung beside Nanaine's. "You had better go home before the weather gets worse. A tree could fall on you."

He enveloped her in the loose coat so that it covered her hair and fell down over her shoulders. He went with her to the other side of the hedge and saw that she reached the house safely. When he returned, Glad was emerging from the adjoining room where she had been polishing lamp chimneys ᴠ .th dry salt.

"Zeph say it gonna be mighty awful dark tonight." She shook her head.

The lake advanced. By noon, it was coming in at the gate. A river flowed up the shelled walk, and then the lawn became lake. The carriage bridge floated away. While they were at table, the water came up between the boards of the basement, and began to move in slow trickles across the floor. The day was an endless dusk, and lanterns had to be lit. During dessert, a blast of wind tore out one of the lattices, sucked it up, and carried it off beyond the treetops. Dinner was never finished.

The doctor, barefoot, his trousers rolled to the knees, went down to fasten the carriage gate, which had blown open and was banging itself to pieces. In the open, the hum of wind and water deafened him. The rain stung his face and hands and beat on his oilskin. Birds were blown about as if they were leaves. The

296

mounting pulse of the storm filled him again with a strange excitement, partially blotting out his bitter feeling of loss.

The water was knee deep as he waded back. The basement now was a large pool where chairs and tables bobbed and bumped. The skiffs had slipped their blocks to float, bottom side up, amidst the furniture. He went for Zeph, who brought rope, and they fastened the boats to the brick pillars of "Clair de Lune." "Better tie them high," Zeph said. They stood in the skiffs and knotted the ropes just under the gallery. He brought the oars upstairs and set them in a corner of his room, thankful for something to do, grateful to be too busy to think. . . .

The lake had become a mass of waves topped with foam. The mountains of water ran against each other, violently, filling the air with spray. For a few minutes, Zeph and the doctor stood in water to their thighs, watching, fascinated by the violence. The bathhouses were going. The force of the water washed them overboard, or else the wind, twisting them off their pilings, tossed them upward like playthings, to let them fall bursting half a mile off. The two men saw a wave erase "Clair de Lune's" bathhouse in one huge surge, and a second afterward the long pier before "Beaux Arbres" was wrenched away, to spatter far and wide like a handful of matches. They looked down the beach for the Cape Charles wharf and could find no trace of it.

The roof of the carriage house went. The panic of the horses reached them faintly through the storm. The doctor went next door to "Shiloh" for Rougette. Uncle Ulysse refused to send his own horse to safety. "She will die in the thick of the charge," he said stubbornly, "as a brave mare should." His fanaticism sometimes touched the borders of insanity. . . . The horses from the stables at "Beaux Arbres" were brought, and together with Nanaine's two nervous Arabians, were taken by Zeph and the Roussels' stable boy to the higher ground of the Catholic school compound. When Zeph came back, the water in the front yard was up to his waist.

The doctor, through the glass panes of the salon doors, marked the rise. Behind him, Nanaine sat at the marble-topped table playing solitaire, confident that the storm would not dare to disrupt the dignity of the duRochers. Now and then she paused to cross herself at a flash of lightning or the crack of a falling tree. Papa slept in the platform rocker, his short pointed beard on his chest.

White-crested waves raced in the street. Then on the banquette. In the yard now. Dashed against the third, the fourth, the fifth step. . . . Pilings from the breakwater and wharves, beams from the shattered bathhouses, even whole trees, pushed against the picket fence; it shook and swayed, and the doctor wondered how long it would hold. If the fences fell and let in loose piles to ram again and again into the foundation pillars, the beach houses would all be cast into the flood.

Half an hour later, the last white points of the pickets vanished, and the tide poured into the yard, carrying with it a churning mass of timber and rubbish.

"When the fences go," Victor said, "we must go, too."

Nanaine laid the deck down and looked at him sharply.

"What do you say?"

"We must get out. We can go to the bank building."

"Leave 'Clair de Lune'? You are crazy! I will not go." She resumed her game, slapping the cards down on the table one by one.

With Zeph, he got the Roussels to Julien's office above the bank. Leon was no help at all. He had jammed a hand in closing windows at the sawmill, and was even more furious because, in the ardor of unaccustomed toil, he had put his jewel-studded cigarette holder down somewhere in the warehouse and left it there. In stylish ulster and matching cap, he rode sullenly in the skiff with his father and the servants, pushed by Zeph, since by now the water would have reached the ears of the stable boy. The doctor, in the lead, shoving debris aside as he went, pulled the skiff carrying the Roussel ladies. Doudouce refused to be separated from Colette, holding her darling close, trying to shield her from the biting rain. The force of the gale made umbrellas impossible, and the ladies had to depend entirely on shawls and their cravenettes for protection. Among the precious things Olympe wished to save was a package of cigarettes for Leon. Since her own pockets bulged with jewels, she handed it to Colette.

At the bank building, the doctor lifted Colette out of the skiff and carried her to a dry level on the staircase. She clung to him with an odd intensity; her arms remained locked around his neck even after he had put her down, and when he looked into her face, he was surprised to find there something he had not seen when they started out—something more than natural anxiety or fear of the storm. Her eyes were wide and a little wild.

"Vic"—she pressed her face against his and put her mouth close to his ear—"I. . . ."

He waited. She only clutched him more tightly and began to cry.

"What is it, Colette?"

"Oh, Vic! I'm afraid! *I'm so afraid!*" She crushed her cheek against his chest, sobbing.

He stroked her shoulder. She was shaking from head to foot. "Everything will be all right, dear. Don't be frightened."

Suddenly raising both hands, she drew his head down, kissed him hard on the mouth. Still sobbing, she lifted her skirts and ran up the stairs.

The doctor and Zeph returned to the beach again and again, removing residents from their endangered homes. Madame Vigée was more than ever hurt with God: purposely to plague her, he had sent the storm just when she had a sprained ankle. Her daughter, Madame Larouche, had been enduring the polluted air of the town since Friday, when, despite the presence of *that woman,* she had returned to help her mother through her latest affliction, and Féfé, of course, was with her. From the de Gerbeau place came Madame in her black toque, Celeste in her futile scarves, and Minerve and the wet nurse carrying the baby. The wind whipped away the shawl Madame de Gerbeau had draped over her head and shoulders, exposing her correct attire to the mercy of the rain. Minerve bit her fingernails, worrying about her husband who had returned to his seat on the Cotton Exchange on the morning train.

For once, no one paid any special attention to the wealthy beach families, now refugees being pushed through the flooded streets in skiffs like so many cows being rustled to the pound. People were busy with their own affairs. Flatboats, pirogues, and improvised rafts hurried in all directions. Boxes, hen coops, house furnishings waltzed solemnly on the current; cordwood, shingles, doorsteps floated everywhere in mad confusion. And down upon it all poured the whistling rain.

When at last they returned to "Clair de Lune," the water was up to their chests. There was no telling now where the lake left off and the shore began; the waves, breaking against the oaks on the beach, were atomized by the wind, creating a thick mist. The air was so filled with a flying compound of sand and rain that it was difficult to face it, and nothing was visible beyond the trees.

Still Nanaine declined to budge. " 'Clair de Lune' has been through hurricanes before," she insisted. "The house will stand. It is like ourselves. . . ."

The servants, their quarters flooded, were gathered in the hall —Glad and her three children, and Bazile, who would have no table to serve tonight. Cumba was not there. "She went back to her ol' monkey business in the woodshed," Glad said. "Couldn' stop her. And she never come back."

Zeph and the doctor found a China-ball tree lying athwart the spot where the woodshed had been. Cumba's plaid tignon was caught in its prostrate branches. They probed under the tree for her body, but felt only a swift rush of current. There was nothing they could do. They came back to the house.

"You'd better take *Sans Souci* and get your people to the bank," the doctor told Zeph. "You can spend the night in my office. The key is under the mat."

Zeph shook his head. "We stay here. Maybe you need two boat—carry doze t'ing Miss Nanaine want save."

"I gave you *Sans Souci*. It is *your* boat."

"Maybe we got to save—"

"You've got to save your baby," Victor cut him off hotly. "You want him to be a doctor for your people, don't you?"

"Miché Vic people come firs'." Zeph shook his head stubbornly.

"Nobody comes first, or last either. Get a pair of oars out of my room. And get out of here!"

It was the first time he had ever given Zeph an order. He had always asked. Zeph, on his part, had never refused. On Zeph's face there spread a slow smile.

The doctor changed to dry clothes and returned to the salon. The lightning and thunder had subsided during the course of the evening, while the wind steadily increased. At six o'clock, he guessed its velocity to be around seventy-five miles an hour. All sound had merged into a vast, even roar. Shifting bars and shafts of rain made the course of the air currents opaque and visible. Huge waves raced toward the house, breaking against it into conical peaks. Presently the staircase went, crumbling easily. Now *Bonne Chance*, knocking against the pillar to which it was tied, was in danger of being dashed to pieces, and he went to pull it up on the gallery. He crawled to it, unable to stand in the gale. Circling one arm around a column to pin himself in place, he wrestled with the wind to get the skiff up.

It was no longer safe to leave the skiff in the open. The wind could snap the rope, pick the boat up, and carry it off. He fought to keep the door open while he dragged the skiff into the salon. A glass pane caved, hurled in jagged pieces against the rear wall. A whirling veil of spray blew in, spindrift of the sea outside. Nanaine's cards scattered like disturbed flies. The lamp went out, and Papa stirred, whimpering, "Where are we?"

Night closed in, dense and black. Now they felt, rather than heard, the pounding of the waves, the thunderous banging and booming of piles and uprooted trees against "Clair de Lune's" foundations. The beams of the house shuddered under the strain. At intervals the whole structure swayed, and Nanaine saw her Pleyel piano and its haircloth stool march with fantastic precision toward the center of the room. She got up swiftly and blew out the lamps under their hurricane screens on the mantel, realizing they might topple over and explode. The doctor put the storm lantern on the floor. Bats, driven by fear from the attic, circled and swooped around the light, casting their fluttering shadows on the high ceiling.

All the house was tightly closed, the battens fastened with iron hooks, and a suffocating, moldy smell hung in the air. They caught the leaks from the roof in pitchers and washbasins. In the beginning, there was only a dripping, but now the water came through in thin, steady streams, splashing out of the full vessels onto the floor. The doctor spoke to Nanaine, and found that he could not hear his own voice. The roar of the storm had become so dense as to be equivalent to a profound silence which swallowed up all customary sound. Their lips moved, windows rattled, and battens strained at their hooks, but they only saw these sounds.

As they sat there, a small wave poured through the crack under the doors. Nanaine fetched a bath towel and the doctor stuffed it into the opening. At that moment, "Clair de Lune" shivered like a ship under the impact of powerful seas, but they heard nothing except the steady, solid roar.

Nanaine indicated with a motion of the hand that she wished to go to bed. The doctor could not help admiring her calm. He took the storm lantern to light her to her east-wing bedroom. As they entered the hall, they were met by a wet draught that for a minute knocked the breath out of their bodies. Holding the lantern aloft, he saw that the trunk of a pecan tree lay aslant Nanaine's bed. The treasured old tester by Dufau was smashed. Water poured in through the gashed ceiling.

"The black bag!" Nanaine had to scream to be heard.

He entered the wrecked room and got the bag of heirlooms—jewelry that had been in the family for decades—from the bottom of the armoire. It took all his strength to close the bedroom door behind him and shut the wind out of the adjoining hall.

Nanaine was at last willing to leave "Clair de Lune." She was astounded that the house built by Grand-père should cede to the elements, indignant that God had allowed the hurricane to damage the duRochers. It was ungrateful of God, after so many years of prayerful devotion on her part. She and Victor gathered the silver in a pillow slip. They wrapped Papa in shawls and an overcoat.

But it was too late to leave. An hour earlier, to assess the velocity of the wind, Victor had unhooked one of the battens and thrust his hand out. He had drawn it back tingling at the finger tips as if it had been pricked by needles. He had judged that the wind was blowing at around a hundred miles an hour. It had nearly torn the batten from his hands, while the gale leaped into the room like a wild beast, spitting spray. Now he wished to test the wind again, but the battens jammed. He pushed with all his might, but was unable to budge them. The increased wind had sealed the doors shut. He tore his fingernails at them, bruised his shoulders. Those inside could not get out, even if it had been other than folly to attempt to manage a skiff in the tumultuous flood. They were prisoners.

"We'll have to wait for the lull!" Only by shouting close to his aunt's ear could he make himself heard.

Another wave rolled in under the door, pushing the towel before it. Another and another came. They watched the water rising, minute by minute, higher and higher.

Nanaine took out her rosary and instructed God to send the lull.

Thirty-six

It was, Victor knew, the center of a hurricane that brought the lull. The center, or eye, was an area of dead calm. Before it approaches, the wind is blowing with maniacal fury in one direction; after it crosses, the wind is blowing with the same or greater force in the opposite direction. The giant wheel of the wind whirls, but the great hub of its motion is lifeless.

He knew that any place in the path of the true center would be given a respite. They must be ready for it. He had taken off his shoes. They looked ridiculous on the mantelpiece; but now the whole salon was a caricature: Papa stretched out on the sofa, Nanaine sitting on the table, the skiff, roped to a doorknob, afloat in more than a foot of water. He went for the oars. The center must be near. He was alert for the first unsteadying of the uniform roar.

An hour passed. The lull should have come by now. It was overdue.

He doubted if "Clair de Lune" could withstand another half hour's buffeting. Nanaine took up the lantern, leaving them in darkness, and waded to the next room. She returned with a piece of Blessed Palm, and setting a match to it, watched it shrivel up on a card tray. She sprinkled the ashes on the water.

Waiting. . . .

It was nearly ten o'clock when the behavior of the wind changed. It grew fitful, eccentric, coming in colossal puffs, as if enormous shells were bursting close by. Once more they could hear the loose piling hitting, like the boom of cannon far off, and the groaning of sills. Then they could hear each other speak. He opened the door, pushing on a leaf of the battens.

The pressure of the wind had relaxed. The batten moved.

The release was only partial. He waited a quarter of an hour for the wind to settle, but the dying down did not come. Then he realized that the center was passing elsewhere, that the violent gusts, undetermined in direction, indicated only the chaotic fringe of the center. This was all the respite they could expect. In a short time, the lull would pass, and the wind, from the opposite direction, would begin again.

"We must be quick."

He pulled the skiff out on the gallery. Turning the lantern

toward "Shiloh," he saw to his astonishment that the whole side wall of Uncle Ulysse's library was gone, and half the house hung down into the water. A faint light showed beyond the wreckage.

He took the skiff and crossed the lawn, which now was lake, to see if the old man was still alive. He found him huddled in his four-poster, clutching a torn map, Bragg, the parrot, screaming on his shoulder. Water foamed around the legs of furniture, sucked at curtains, lapped against the papered walls. For once, the aged captain, possessor of one of the proudest records in the Confederate Army, was afraid. He met the doctor with a pale, luminous stare. "I call Noonoon but she does not come," he said childishly. The doctor threw the blanket from the bed over him and helped him through the disordered room.

Nanaine, enveloped in a cravenette, waited with Papa on the flooded gallery at "Clair de Lune." When she recognized Uncle Ulysse through the rain, she declared she would rather die than ride in the same boat with him. Time was passing—precious seconds. Victor seized his aunt and lifted her bodily into the skiff, setting her down beside her brother. He deposited the bundle of silver in her lap.

"The black bag!"

He had almost forgotten it. As he handed it to her, Uncle Ulysse, arranging a shelter for Bragg under the blanket, accidentally knocked her arm. The bag splashed into the water and sank. She turned on Ulysse, enraged.

"*Imbécile!*" she screamed.

"Call yourself a fool, you clumsy female!"

In the struggling light of the lantern, they looked at each other, aghast. They had spoken, after forty years.

At Julien's offices in the bank building, no one thought of sleep. The second half of the storm was beginning. They were out of the fringe, and chaos mounted with every minute. Each gust could be heard coming by its distant howling, which rose in a fearful crescendo till it hit the building like a gigantic fist.

The refugees sat on the available chairs and on the floor along with their servants, a disheveled mingling of whites and blacks. Some of the ladies looked hardly human with fright. Madame de Gerbeau still wore her sodden toque, but she appeared as dirty and disarrayed as the Roussels' kitchen girl, who had slipped into the water when stepping from skiff to stairway. Madame Vigée clutched a flask of holy water, with which she sprinkled herself and Coucou every time the building swayed, and Madame Morel, prostrate with panic, had the gasping appearance of a half-dead fish lying on a wharf. Olympe hugged herself in a damp afghan, uttering weak bleats. She was beyond fainting.

Perhaps Julien was the most pathetic. In the hall outside, he paced up and down, up and down, wiping his sweating hands on a handkerchief already wet, mopping incessantly at his jowls and forehead. There was irony in the fact that the pretentious offices of the Causeway Corporation sheltered victims of the storm, almost a prescient malice in the way the wind had punched out the windowpanes with their arrogant gilt lettering. Much of the property Julien had bought up so greedily had not yet been insured—"Belle Pointe," Jolivet's, even the sawmill. The hurricane was sweeping a fortune out of Julien's hands, as well as his dreams of grandeur.

Even Colette was like a beautiful bird that had been caught in a cloudburst, her hair wind-blown and the hem of her skirt dripping. She looked shrunken and miserable, huddled in the long, loose folds of the drenched cravenette. She was shivering. The doctor went over to the corner where she sat on Julien's henceforth useless safe.

"Take off that wet wrap, Colette. You'll catch cold. Here. Let me help you." She acted like a person who has received a blow. "What is the matter?" he asked quickly. "Are you all right?"

She shook her head as if to wake herself. "It's just— Papa. . . ." Julien was passing the door for the hundredth time. "His dearest dream— Oh, Vic, Vic! This is the end of everything!"

Leon leaned against the wall smoking his last dry cigarette. He gave a low laugh.

"You're in the right row but the wrong seat, little sister. It's not *that* dream he's sweating about." He took a long draw and blew the smoke ceilingward, smiling wisely.

Victor crossed the hall to see how Zeph and his people were faring. They were sitting in the waiting room. A candle Glad had brought from home burned in a glass on the floor.

He went into the office. He was lighting Jolivet's battered old storm lantern when Colette entered.

"Vic!" There was a note of panic in her voice.

"I'm coming, Colette."

"Harry Lockwood is not going to marry that girl!"

The flame of the lantern leaped. He adjusted it.

"I want to tell you how I know!"

He turned. Her appearance shocked him. She was as white as chalk. He went over to her, observing that though she still shivered, moisture stood out on her forehead.

"Yesterday when you sent me away from Cumba, you gave me Nanaine's cravenette instead of my own from the back of the chair. There was a letter—I found it only on our way here, when I put Leon's cigarettes in the pocket. It was addressed to you. I couldn't wait—I read it, there in the skiff—in all the storm. Doudouce sheltered me. . . ."

She paused for breath, lips parted. He continued to look at her without speaking.

"It was open already—but that's no excuse. I had a feeling. . . ." She swallowed hard. "It was from Harry Lockwood."

She held out her hand, clenched around a wet and crumpled note. He smoothed out the page and held it to the light. Harry was thanking him. "But she would not have me, after all. I suppose this rejection is final." There was an attempt at gaiety in closing. "We understand a hurricane is predicted. We'll witness it from the other side of the lake, where the hospital is handy. . . ." The doctor recalled a Negress stopping at "Clair

307

de Lune" in the rain late Sunday afternoon. Now, in memory, he recognized the tall figure of Zabette. She had been delivering the letter.

In a gesture of disgust, he tossed the note on the desk.

"My aunt deliberately withheld this message."

"I kept it from you, too, Vic! There on the stairs today—I tried to make myself give it to you! But like Nanaine, I wanted you to think she had accepted him." Her hands gripped his shoulders convulsively. "I wanted it to be ended, between you and her! Because I love you, Vic! I've always loved you! Ever since I was a child! Ever since I can remember!"

She was beside herself. A comb fell to the floor, and the heavy mass of her damp hair rolled loose down her back.

"From the beginning, between you and that girl. . . . From that very first day on the boat, I knew—I *felt*. . . ." She pressed her cheek furiously against his, speaking fast and brokenly into his ear. "Oh, I don't know how I knew! But I did, I did!"

There was nothing he could say. His silence frightened her. She broke away and saw his face.

"Vic! Don't look like that!"

"My aunt—" he said hoarsely. "For all her pride—playing a cheap trick like withholding a letter—resorting to trash like grigri. . . ."

Her eyes half closed. "The charms—no, Vic—not Nanaine. It was I."

"You mean to say. . . ." His frown deepened. He shook his head.

"I didn't want the girl here, near you! I wanted her to go away! And I wanted to keep you from her! I listened to Doudouce—I let her frighten Cumba into placing grigri in your room. And Doudouce bribed the servants at 'Belle Pointe.' I was willing to try anything, everything! On St. John's Eve, I even went with Doudouce—I gave Cumba money to buy the Mamaloi's help—I would have done anything to hold you!"

"*Colette.* . . ."

She winced at the pity in his voice.

"And it was all so futile! Because nobody was taking you away from me! You were already gone when you came from Panama. With every day that passed, I could see you going farther and farther. Do you think all my worrying was over my parents and Leon? It was on account of you that so often I couldn't sleep! You no longer belonged to me, or to us, or even to yourself! You belong to this thing that terrifies me—this outside world that you say is coming in upon us! I lost you—oh, Vic—I had lost you completely before I ever had you!" She began to sob, digging frantically into his arms.

"Come. Come now." He put his hands over hers, prying her fingers loose. "Try to rest a little. Come sit here."

She let him help her into Jolivet's old swivel chair.

"Leave me—I want to be alone for a few minutes, Vic." Her face was twisted with a curious kind of pain, as if she were having a struggle inside herself that equaled the violence of the wind and water outside.

He went to Jolivet's laboratory and set some fragile equipment on the floor for safety. All this was like some insane dream, and he stood for what seemed a long time with his hand over his eyes, trying to adjust himself, to get his racing mind in order. When he returned, she was on her feet again.

"I'm going to tell you." She was trembling so cruelly that she had to lean against the desk. "You need never know that I knew it. But *I* would know for the rest of my life."

"Never mind now. Tell me another time." He took her hands. They were stiff and cold.

"I said I would do anything, *anything* to keep you. But that isn't true. I don't love you as much as Nanaine does. I don't love you enough to hate myself!"

She was close to hysteria.

"Whatever it is, you can tell me tomorrow."

"No. I have to tell you now." She wet her lips. "She's here. On account of the weather—they didn't leave Sunday!"

He dropped her hands. His heart started to bang against his ribs so furiously he thought he could hear it.

"Leon just told me. Papa and Leon went to look after 'Belle Pointe' this morning and found them there."

He stared at her.

Then it was not alone the shattering of his visions of money and power that sent Julien pacing up and down the corridor. He was frantic about Palmyre, left at the most dangerous and un-protected spot on the lake.

Palmyre and Miriam. . . .

"Vic!" Colette's voice rose in a scream. "No—no, Vic! Send Zeph!"

She ran after him, imploring. He had a vague impression of Zeph asking a bewildered question, of pushing Zeph out of his way. He collided with Julien in the dark hall. Nanaine saw him through the open doorway.

"Where are you going?"

The attention of the refugees focused on him as he paused on the threshold, barefoot, his wet trousers rolled up, the old storm lantern in his hand. He had a sudden feeling that he stood there facing all the past, for the last time.

"I'm going to get Palmyre Delamare and her daughter! And bring them here!"

Olympe made the customary gesture of reaching for her smell-ing salts, but her Irish crochet bag had been lost in the flood. His aunt's eyes narrowed, drove into him. They said, If you go, you need never come back! The eyes of all of them said the same thing: You can never come back to us. . . .

Only Colette had looked at him differently.

"Vic!"

He threw the light of the lantern up the staircase well and saw her on the landing. She ran down the steps.

"Send Zeph! Please, *please,* Vic. . . ." She threw her arms around his neck.

It was yesterday that the white man used the black man's life to ease and enrich his own. And I have bidden a definite fare-well to yesterday. He tried to free himself, but she clung to him.

"Please don't go! You'll be killed!"

If anything happens to Miriam, he thought, I shall have no wish to go on living.

"Go back, Colette!"

She was unaware of the water, high up the stairs, swirling around her skirts to the knees. He raised his free hand, unclenching her fingers from behind his neck, and turned toward the street door.

"If you go, I'll go with you!"

"Go back!"

She shook her head. Her eyes were enormous in her white face. He had no time to persuade her. He pulled the door open and the wind pinned it back. Water poured in and broke like surf on the stairs. He fought to keep his grip on the lantern. Its light pierced the rain only an arm's length.

"Vic! Don't go! Vic! Vic!"

Her voice came to him as a faint echo. He cast the light around and saw that she had come farther down, in water to her waist. He made a sign for her to return. She continued to stand there. He cupped his hand to his lips, and shouted with all his might, "Go back!"

Her face was a mask of suffering, of struggle. *I love you. . . . I want to go with you. . . .* She poised on the edge of the stair as if to plunge. He tried to shout again, but an odd hypnosis froze his throat. He waited, every nerve taut, to see what she would do. She stared into the wild current, the darkness. . . .

Slowly she turned and went back up the stairs.

Sometimes he gained a foot, only to be blown back two by a vicious wind blast. He knew there would be less current in the back streets. It was in the roadways leading from the lake that the flood swept irresistibly.

He passed the post office and the drugstore, and now there was almost no counterforce, only the slap of waves crested with dirty foam. But his way was choked with wreckage, and the wind drove timber and pilings against him. In shoving aside what looked like a raft, he tore his hand on nails. He touched something soft and hairy—a dead dog. The rain stung like buckshot; his shirt was in shreds. A bed came floating to meet him, a ridiculous ghost, and a few steps farther on he collided with a sodden mattress.

At each intersection he had to battle the current again. His idea was to cross the town through the back streets and turn beachward to "Belle Pointe" when he reached "Beau Rêve," the house of Hercule Moreau. At one point, he lost his bearings. Bidault's livery stable should have been on his right, before him, and there was nothing at all—only churning water lashed by rain and glutted with rubbish. For a few seconds he felt lost, sickening with the idea that he had somehow confused his direction. He stood there terrified, thinking he would never get to "Belle Pointe." Holding the lantern high, he saw a mass of carriages, wheels, surrey tops, struggling horses and mules whose screams were lost in the noise of the storm. He realized with horror that the livery stable had been swept away.

As he started forward again, he saw that the sky toward "Belle Pointe" was stained a yellowish pink—the reflection of fire! He pushed ahead crazily, bruising and tearing himself. I'm frightened, he thought. My God, how frightened I am!

His panic made him incautious. Abruptly the ground went from under him and he found only water under his feet. He foundered, and the lantern flew up out of his hand to splash a little distance off and disappear. He must have fallen off the edge of the road into an open ditch. It was like stepping off the rim of the earth into infinity. He struggled until he felt something solid underfoot again. But in the darkness he was suddenly blind. For a while he was unable to move except as the wind and water moved him.

He groped along, guided by the spreading glow in the western sky, maddened by the urgency that he must hurry. He reached open country, and here the tempest was a boiling fury, over which the wind sped with a whistling noise that made the ears ache. A wave caught him, rolled him off his feet, flung him yards off to crash against a floating tree. He crawled out of the wave, crushed and stupid and weak. The flood was over his head now, and he had to swim. The next wave that broke might carry him away with it, and he clung to the tree trunk, half-naked, his body raw from the whipping rain. Spray drove into his eyes, choking him when he opened his mouth for breath.

A rumble as of thunder broke through the fury. All at once, the sky behind him was solid flame. It was the sawmill that was on fire—not "Belle Pointe." What before had struck him cold with dread now warmed him with gratitude. He had light. In the sudden flaring up, he saw Hercule Moreau's deserted house a stone's throw away.

Another report came from the burning sawmill. It was a second drum of oil exploding. Leon—his beautiful cigarette holder, a lighted cigarette left in the warehouse. . . . The fire must have been smoldering in the rain all day, until it reached the gasoline.

The tide washed in from bayou and lake at once, smashing against "Belle Pointe" with a force that sent spume leaping high above the torn roof. The gallery rail was gone. He clung to a column, bracing himself against the suction of whirlpools. When he had caught his breath, he hoisted himself up and crawled along the gallery, all one with the flood. If he had tried to stand, the wind would have tossed him back into the water.

She was in the corner room on the west—her room. Panes had been blasted out, the door blinds hung broken on their hinges. Glow from the burning sawmill filled the apartment. She was sitting on top of the piano, barefoot, in Mr. Néron Paviot's striped trousers and a smock. A wild, crazy joy surged through him when he saw that she was alive. Dixie crouched beside her, wet and shivering. The dog felt his presence first. She stirred and stood up, and he saw that she barked.

Miriam had the look of one dazed. He waded across the room to her. Great pieces of plaster had fallen in, the wallpaper flapped in strips, and splintered laths hung down from the ceiling. He took her limp hands in his own, scratched and bleeding and shriveled from so long in the water. He put his mouth close to her ear and said loudly, "Palmyre!"

She closed her eyes, jerking her head in the direction of the east wing. He splashed through the rooms until he came to a great hole in the wall where the double doors to Palmyre's bedroom had been. A wave rolled in through the hole. Beyond, the red light from the fire shone only on tossing water.

He came back to Miriam. When she saw him alone, she put her hands up over her face.

He knew they could never reach the bank building. Then he thought of Hercule Moreau's house. If they could get there, if the house was still standing. . . .

"Belle Pointe" rocked, settling back into position with a shudder. The glow from the fire was dimming. There was no time to debate the best chance. He lifted her down from the piano. He took off Dixie's collar and leash, buckling the collar around his own leather belt and knotting the leash securely around Miriam's waist, tying her to him.

Her lips moved painfully. *Dixie.* They would have to leave the dog behind. There was no help for it.

The tide now was with them, and the wind was at their backs. The greatest danger was from the pounding wreckage. Once in the water, Miriam seemed to recover her senses. They swam furiously to avoid being crushed between the bobbing trunks of two floating oaks. They clung to clumps of debris until their hands were raw. His arm about her waist, he reached for the branch of a tree for a brief anchorage while they caught their breath, and found a hissing snake coiled around it. After that, they noticed that the tops of trees often furnished refuge for snakes, and avoided grabbing onto branches. Great piles of weed and water hyacinth went by, crawling with reptiles. These were the worse obstacles; they swam around them desperately.

Another rumbling report came from the sawmill. A great mass flew up into the rain and came down in a blazing shower of boards and splinters. *Le Cygne.* . . . The fire had spread to the boat.

Logs from the mill swarmed before Hercule's house. The velocity of the wind had thrown planks up on the gallery and driven them into the roof, where they stuck like thorns in flesh.

He lifted her through a side window where the batten had blown away. Their faces and bodies were covered with bruises and cuts, such clothes as the wind had not ripped from their backs were torn to rags. He found a candle in a cupboard and lit it. It was less dangerous than a lamp. Numb and exhausted, they laid themselves down on the dry floor of the kitchen. The other rooms, two steps below the kitchen, were flooded.

He had no idea what time it was. The hurricane was at its height. All the aerial currents in creation seemed loosed to meet in one spot. Anything might happen. Hercule's house, built by himself, who knew hurricanes, was holding against the force of water and the hammering of debris, but earlier in the day the doctor had seen an entire cottage lifted from its foundations, hurled through the air for half a block to strike the flooded ground and burst into a mass of wreckage. Or the fire from the sawmill could blow this way, and the new pine lying on gallery and roof would act as ready kindling, regardless of the rain.

They lay there listening to the vast uproar, not knowing what was in store for them from one moment to the next. They could not hear each other speak, but he could see her fright. She shuddered. He took her in his arms and held her close.

Their battered bodies grew warm against each other. They did not need to speak; in the unsteady candlelight their eyes spoke for them. *If in the next hour we are dead, we shall at least have had this much of life.* . . . It was something that both of them knew had always been meant to be between them, something glad and generous and simple and splendid, without shame or self-consciousness or guilt.

Toward morning the wind showed signs of subsiding.

Thirty-seven

They walked through the silent rooms of the house that Hercule Moreau had named "Beau Rêve." A gray layer of sand covered the floors, ribbed like the bottom of the lake. Dead fish and frogs lay embedded in it. Where the front door had blown in, the bedroom was a shambles. They went out on the gallery. The sky, instead of a stormy black, was now an even, luminous gray. The doctor still had no idea of time. It might have been eight or nine o'clock. The wind was no more than a good sailing gale. It stirred a thin mist of tired smoke, all that was left of Julien's sawmill.

They were thirsty. They went down to the mired yard, but the well had been filled in with mud and debris.

She wished to go to "Belle Pointe," clinging to the hope that by some miracle Palmyre was alive. They walked, careful of nails and splinters, picking their way between wreckage and dead things deposited by the withdrawing tide. Deep pools pitted the road; in one of them lay the body of a Negro boy. Birds were stuck against every surface like flies on flypaper. In the top of an oak there was suspended the carcass of a drowned calf. The cabins of the sawmill workers had vanished, and all that remained standing on the point was the skeleton of "Belle Pointe" itself.

The water had sucked deep into the sand, undermining the house so that it listed. Most of the columns were gone and the galleries sagged. There was no trace at all of the east wing. There the last and most awful caving in of the point was accomplished, and the meeting of lake and bayou, widened by yards, flowed triumphantly through "Belle Pointe's" eastern piazza.

The ladies who would not sign for the continuation of the breakwater could congratulate themselves. Sitting high and dry in the bank building, they would be quite satisfied with God. They would forgive Him for a negligence better late than never corrected. At long last His accounts balanced.

"She went to her bedroom to get my father's miniature," Miriam said. "It was the only thing she wished to save."

She began to sob convulsively, her whole body shaking with her sorrow. He put his arms around her.

They walked westward along the beach in silence, her hand in his. He was almost unable to believe all that had happened. He looked at the wreckage about them, unaware that they themselves were a part of it. His trousers were in ribbons from ankles to knees, his bruised body bare from the waist up; and she, in Mr. Paviot's formals belted with the leather leash, her tattered smock tucked in, looked like a boy, her short hair still damp. Superimposed on the horror and tragedy of the previous night was the wonder of what had happened at Hercule Moreau's house, "Beau Rêve"—"Beautiful Dream." . . . And nothing, not even they themselves, seemed real or credible.

In the side streets, people were already busily about. Many had returned to the scene of their former homes to pick up the remains of their household possessions. Cottages were turned around, furniture and wearing apparel scattered far and wide. Buggies and wagons had gone adrift to settle fantastically in unlikely places. And haggard men and women searched the debris of collapsed buildings for the bodies of relatives.

The doctor and Miriam came to Fauvette's "Joli Bois." The whole front wall was ripped out, and the last sticks of furniture removed as thoroughly as if Madame d'Eaubonne, mother of Fauvette, had returned from the dead and auctioned it all off to subsidize one more princely dinner party. The last vestiges of d'Eaubonne elegance were gone.

Next door, Madame Vigée's "Tranquilité" had lost its belvedere, its turrets and gables, its galleries and wings. Madame would bitterly bewail God's special wickedness toward her; for He had perversely left her the nude statuary brought by her husband from Europe. On the lawn, the armless figure of a Diana lay near a dead mullet, and nude nymphs reclined about in what Madame would interpret as obscene positions, their blouses and breechcloths blown to oblivion.

The damage to the de Gerbeau place was lighter, though

equally malicious. Madame de Gerbeau would doubtless have preferred that her whole house be destroyed rather than have her commode deposited in the middle of the banquette. Nothing could have been more incorrect.

"Beaux Arbres" had lost dormers, stairs, doors, and roof. The garçonniere, where Leon was accustomed to house his friends, was a pile of brick. The carriage house was down and his fine automobile crumpled and deposited on its side in the Cherokee hedge. The chaise longue where Olympe spent so much of her time recovering from fainting spells was hanging freakishly between broken rails of the buckled gallery. The wind had emptied Colette's wardrobe. Paris gowns dragged in the mud and draped the branches of ravaged trees.

All about "Shiloh"—in the twisted shrubs, the bedraggled hedges—were strewn volumes of Uncle Ulysse's library on the War Between the States. Pieces of maps, mangled notebooks, pages of manuscript on which he had spent twenty years of his life—the paraphernalia of his fanatic unforgiveness was scattered abroad in ruin. Somewhere in the collapsed part of the house Noonoon was caught, crushed.

But it was "Clair de Lune" that brought a choking tightness to his throat. The brick pillars had been washed away from under one side and half the house had crashed to the ground. The other half, badly listing, was like a face bruised and beaten beyond recognition. Windows and doors had blown in, the tree that had fallen athwart Nanaine's room had carried a good part of the roof with it. There was a gaping gash in the wall, revealing hanging rafters. The house was past repair, beyond redemption.

Caught in a tangle of seaweed and broken lattice was a familiar fragment of canvas that caught the doctor's eye. He walked up to it and turned it over. It was what remained of the portrait of Grand-père. The piercing dark eyes that he as a child had associated with God's had been gouged out on a sharp piece of wood, part of the crating that had been put around the portrait to protect it.

318

Miriam touched his arm. He hardly dared look at her for fear she would vanish, as so much had vanished, and with her all the sweet significance of the hours at "Beau Rêve." But she was whole and alive and very real.

"We must find Father Guichard," he said.

They turned their backs on the desolation of "Clair de Lune."

A few moments before, looking at the old house, he had had a brief feeling that all was lost. Now, looking at her, he knew in a rush of warmth that this was not so. Walking beside her, having her near, he was aware of a kind of singing content. It was as if some question had been answered, something in his life had been settled, some yawning sealed. He was no longer tired or bewildered or numb. On the contrary, he experienced an extraordinary surge of freshness, fulfillment, and strength. The world about him, for all its wretchedness, seemed new and exciting and full of promise.

She guessed what was going through his mind.

"Maybe it had to be like this. Maybe we had to lose so we could gain. Maybe. . . ." Her voice blurred. *Palmyre*. . . . She didn't finish her sentence.

"We'll have a great deal of work to do," he said gently. There would not be time to grieve.

The victims of the hurricane would require care for months. The poverty and misery and disease in the woods would be worse than ever. "A man's place," she had told him once, "is where he is *needed*."

"Our greatest problem will be fresh drinking water," he thought aloud. "Even springs that are not choked will run polluted water. We'll have to see that people boil every drop."

"I'll help you," she said, "in everything."

He put his arm around her shoulder. As they turned into the street that led to the priest's house, the sky behind "Belle Pointe" brightened. They stopped and watched the sun break through the clouds.